Invisible Strings

A

Novel

By

Sonja Marcus

Dedication

This is book is dedicated to all of the strong, badass women in my life. You know who you are. May you all find joy reading this, thank you for being so inspirational.

Playlist

"Ruin the Friendship" — **Taylor Swift**

"Holy Ground" — **Taylor Swift**

"Gypsy" — **Fleetwood Mac**

"Better Off Alone" — **Alice Deejay**

"There Is a Light That Never Goes Out" — **The Smiths**

"London Boy" — **Taylor Swift**

"'Tis the Damn Season" — **Taylor Swift**

"New Slang" — **The Shins**

"Welcome to New York" — **Taylor Swift**

"High Infidelity" — **Taylor Swift**

"The Middle" — **Jimmy Eat World**

"100 Years" — **Five for Fighting**

"Guilty as Sin?" — **Taylor Swift**

"Tolerate It" — **Taylor Swift**

"Invisible String" — **Taylor Swift**

Table of Contents

Chapter 1

January 2002, North Carolina

"Remind me why we're driving all the way to Duke just for a frat party?" Taylor asks, half-laughing, half-annoyed, as she blends concealer under her eyes while her friends take shots of cheap vodka around their dorm room.

"Because, Taylor, the basketball team will be there," Katie shouts over the blaring stereo.

"Aren't they supposed to be, I don't know, practicing? Isn't it literally basketball season right now?" Taylor moans, exhausted by her friend's Duke obsession.

"Shut it, T," Lindsay chirps, tossing her hair. "We're going. And you can thank me later after you've hooked up with one of these guys. Now finish getting ready; I'm dying for a real drink." As designated driver, she's abstaining from the nauseating vodka until they reach campus and her driving duties end for the night.

The three of them; Taylor, Katie, and Lindsay met in their dorm on the first day of freshman year at UNC Chapel Hill. Three smart, beautiful girls, each wilder than the last, they rarely reject an invitation to a party. Which is why, on this icy January night, they're heading to a Sigma Chi party at Duke.

Despite their shared interests, partying, studying hard, and causing just enough trouble; the trio is an unlikely one. Taylor is from Wisconsin, Katie from Los Angeles, Lindsay from Boston; their backgrounds are as different as their accents. Katie grew up with a single mother and earned a full academic scholarship. Taylor turned down a free ride to the University of Wisconsin in her hometown, knowing that if she didn't leave Madison, she never would. She's had wanderlust baked into her for years. Lindsay comes from a wealthy Boston family; when her parents visited in November, they took the three girls out for a swanky dinner and bought them more champagne than they could drink. Lindsay's older cousin is a Duke professor with an apartment near campus, though he's practically living with his girlfriend now, so he lets Lindsay and her friends crash there whenever they need it; as long as they give him notice.

With music blaring; Nelly, Ja Rule, Mary J. Blige, Usher, all the anthems of 2001, they make the twenty-five-minute drive from Chapel Hill to Durham, screaming lyrics out the windows like they're the stars of their own music video. They park outside Lindsay's cousin's place.

"Do you guys have your fakes?" Taylor asks as they climb out.

All three of them use fake IDs regularly.

"We're going to a frat party, Taylor," Katie snaps. "It's not like they're checking IDs at the door."

"T's right," Lindsay agrees. "If the party sucks, we can hit the bars. They might come in handy. Gum? Cigarettes?"

"Check, check, and check. And I swear I won't 'get lost' this time," Taylor promises.

Her friends exchange a look. Fiercely independent, Taylor has a habit of disappearing when they go out. Sometimes with a guy she's met, sometimes simply to smoke in peace. Whatever the reason, it terrifies her friends. The first time it happened, back in October, they ambushed her the next morning.

"You can't just vanish," Katie scolded. "We thought you were in a gutter or kidnapped by some serial killer."

Lindsay had nodded vigorously.

So Taylor told them the truth about her upbringing and why she tends to roam.

"My parents are hippies," she explained, shrugging while her friends stared in disbelief. "They seem normal, but they let me and my brothers run wild. Total hands-off parenting." Lindsay and Katie gaped, unable to imagine that much freedom.

"My brothers are twenty-one and twenty-four. I grew up around them and whatever substances they were into. I got drunk at thirteen. My parents always had pot around. What I'm telling you is: I can handle myself. I didn't mean to freak you out, but I'm not stupid. Just... don't go nuts if it happens again, because it probably will. But I'll try to warn you next time."

Katie and Lindsay rolled their eyes at that. Lindsay slipped her arm around Taylor, baffled by the idea of hippie parents. She'd had to hide every bad decision she'd ever made from her strict family.

"Fine," Lindsay said. "But at least tell us before you wander off so we're not panicking."

And so they made an informal pact: Taylor could wander, but she had to notify them first.

Their concern wasn't unfounded. At five foot ten, usually in heels, with long blonde hair, piercing blue eyes, and a body that drew attention even when she wasn't trying, Taylor turned heads everywhere they went. Shortly after the three girls became inseparable, Katie had admitted, "At first, I wanted to hate you. I was so jealous, your looks, your confidence, the way every guy stares at you. But you're so goddamned nice and smart, it took about two days for me to love you." Lindsay had agreed. When the three of them went anywhere, the attention from the opposite sex was inevitable.

"Where is this frat? Do we call a cab or walk?" Katie asks now.

Lindsay and Taylor glance down at their shoes and say in unison, "Cab." They burst into hysterical laughter. Fashion over function, always. And fashion often meant shoes designed by people who clearly hated women.

"Yes," Lindsay adds, "and while we wait, we can take another shot!"

Moments later, a taxi drops them in front of the frat house. It's a few minutes past ten, and people are already spilling across the expansive lawn.

They head through the open door, weaving through bodies and music, scanning for the kitchen, or wherever drinks are being poured. Within minutes, each of them has a cup of Jungle Juice: Kool-Aid, Everclear, and whatever liquor someone had lying around. They've learned to drink it slowly; more than two cups and your night ends with the room spinning or your head in a toilet.

"Let's mingle!" Lindsay shouts over the beat. "I still don't remember how I even heard about this party," she mumbles.

Taylor and Katie exchange a knowing glance, suppressing laughter. Lindsay could make friends with a brick wall. People flock to her warmth, her loud laugh, her endless charm. She's always being invited to parties by people she met five minutes earlier. It's one of the many things they adore about her.

Taylor scans the room. At well over six feet in her heels, she has a perfect vantage point, but she still doesn't see any basketball players. Instead, she mostly feels like the tallest person in the building. It's early; maybe the athletes will show up later. The girls drift through the house and eventually stumble into a massive formal room that was probably a library once but has now been sacrificed to serve as a dance floor. Floor-to-ceiling windows overlook the cup-littered lawn, probably beautiful in daylight, now just a depressing landfill of red solo cups. Giant speakers blast music so loud the floor vibrates beneath their feet.

Drinks in hand, their free arms thrown in the air or tangled in their hair, they dance and laugh, fully aware of the male gazes following them. J. Lo and Ja Rule's latest single thunders out of the speakers, and as soon as "I'm Real" starts, the girls launch into the ridiculous choreographed routine they invented during a very drunk night in their dorm. It draws immediate attention, guys staring, some smiling, a few looking desperate to cut in. When the song ends, they retreat, exchanging looks and silently agreeing to hit the bathroom and refill their drinks.

Of course, the fraternity bathrooms are a disaster. No vomit yet; it's still too early, but the stench alone is enough to make anyone question their life choices. "Ugh, why are guys so gross?" Taylor moans, rinsing her hands and wiping them on her black pants because paper towels apparently don't exist here.

"We're not all gross," a vaguely familiar male voice says from somewhere outside the doorway.

Taylor pokes her head out and nearly faints.

"Daniel Collins? What the hell are you doing here?" she blurts, stunned.

"Taylor Evans?" he laughs. "I go to school here. What the hell are *you* doing here?" He pulls her into a warm, tight hug, and for a moment, she forgets how to breathe.

"Oh my god, this is so random!" Taylor shouts. "Katie, Lindsay, come meet Daniel. We've literally known each other forever. Born on the same day, our moms met in the hospital nursery." Katie and Lindsay greet him, and he kisses each of them on the cheek, charming without trying.

Taylor takes him in. Really takes him in. She hasn't seen him in seven months, but honestly, she hasn't *really* seen him in years. They went to elementary, middle, and high school together. Their moms are best friends. But aside from obligatory family hangouts, and the painfully awkward seventh-grade spin-the-bottle kiss neither of them has ever mentioned, they drifted apart. In a graduating class of over 700, it was easy to dodge the boy you grew up with, especially the one tied to a humiliating adolescent memory. Their mothers never got over the disappointment.

Daniel was always the nice guy. The one who made sure kids with special needs were included. The one who taught ice hockey to children with Down syndrome. The guy everyone liked, surrounded by a pack of loyal friends. He was such a relentless do-gooder that

Taylor never thought of him as boyfriend material. And, of course, their moms forced them to share a homemade angel-food cake for their joint birthday every damn year until they finally rebelled at fifteen.

But now? God. Now he looks unbelievable.

At least six-foot-three, solid but not bulky, the awkward lanky boy she remembered has vanished. In his place stands a man. With a Black mom and white dad, his skin is the kind of warm caramel shade that seems unfairly perfect. His jawline? Not safe. His smile? Fatal. Amazing what a few months can do.

Taylor feels heat crawl up her neck. She hates how obvious it must be.

As she's looking at him, an old memory resurfaces; her favorite story from childhood. The day she was born. The day her mom, Alyssa, met Daniel's mom, Tanya.

The very beginning of their intertwined lives.

* * *

The story begins like this. It is February 1983 in Madison, Wisconsin. Tanya Collins has just delivered a healthy baby boy, named Daniel after her late husband; the man she lost tragically during her seventh month of pregnancy. Down the hall, Alyssa Evans has delivered her third child, a beautiful baby girl named Taylor, who will join her two sons, Eric, age five, and Alex, age two.

Tanya and Alyssa meet while checking on their babies in the maternity ward nursery. Tanya, exhausted and raw, stands before the glass with silent tears streaking down her cheeks. Postpartum hormones, grief, fear, it all sits heavy on her shoulders. Her pregnancy had been brutal, plagued with all-day morning sickness, and now she faced motherhood alone.

Meanwhile, Alyssa, a seasoned pro compared to Tanya, is beaming at her daughter. She spots Tanya's tears instantly and gravitates toward her.

Both women look like they've gone twelve rounds with childbirth. Alyssa wears a smile anyway, understanding that the agony will fade, the baby will eventually latch without pain, and sleep will someday return. Tanya has no such reassurance and begins to cry harder, ashamed of the breakdown. She tries to blame hormones, but the truth is brutal: her husband isn't here to meet their son.

"Hey, are you okay?" Alyssa asks gently. "I'm Alyssa. I don't mean to pry, I just wanted to check on you. You look like you could use a friend."

"Thank you," Tanya sniffles, straightening her posture as if that alone might hold her together. "Bit emotional today, I suppose." She lets out a weak laugh. "Honestly, I'm a mess. First child, terrified out of my mind, and my husband died two months ago. I don't know how to do any of this. Sorry... sorry, I'm fine. Just tired."

Alyssa lets out a soft, awkward laugh and steps closer. As a distraction, she points to the baby wearing the pink cap with perfect tiny features. "That's my daughter. She's my third, but trust me, I remember all the fear you're feeling. My first terrified me too. But my husband was there, so I won't pretend I understand your exact stress..." She winces. "That came out wrong. I just mean you have every right to feel overwhelmed. It's normal. Honestly, I'm still scared every day. I think fear is just part of the motherhood contract."

Tanya lets out a breath she didn't realize she'd been holding. "Thank you. That really helps. I'm Tanya. And that little guy in there" she points at Daniel, red-cheeked under a pale blue cap "That's my son."

"He's gorgeous," Alyssa says warmly. "How big was he? What were his stats?"

"His... stats?" Tanya repeats, confused.

"Yeah; weight, length, all that." Alyssa nods proudly toward her daughter. "Taylor was seven pounds fourteen ounces and twenty inches."

"Ah. Well..." Tanya smiles shyly. "Daniel was nine pounds even and twenty-one inches."

"Jesus Christ," Alyssa blurts. "Nine pounds? You poor thing and you're tiny!"

Tanya laughs, the first genuine one since Daniel was born. "I *was* tiny. I gained forty pounds. I looked in the mirror this morning and barely recognized myself." She grabs her still-round stomach with a sigh.

Alyssa waves her off. "Please. It'll disappear. Breastfeeding helps with the weight, did wonders with my first two. Speaking of, I need to grab Taylor for a feeding." She hesitates, then says, "Hey... are you sure you'll be alright? I've got my hands full with my boys already, but I'd love to meet up sometime if you want. Let Taylor and Daniel grow up together. It's so important to have mom friends. Here, I'll grab a pen from the nurse's station and give you my number. What room are you in?"

"Room 311," Tanya says, relief softening her features. "And I would love that. Truly. I can't promise we'll have our bearings anytime soon, right now I feel like that's years away." She laughs, lighter this time.

"You'll be just fine," Alyssa says with a wink. She touches Tanya's arm with a reassuring squeeze. "Call me soon, okay? You're not alone."

Within weeks of leaving the hospital, they were inseparable and the friendship that began in that nursery became one that would shape their children's lives forever.

* * *

Back to reality. As if reading her mind, Daniel says, "Our moms are going to flip out," laughing with that gorgeous, easy smile. "I knew you were at UNC, but I never thought we'd just... bump into each other like this." Then he notices the four empty hands. "Come on downstairs. Let's get drinks."

As they head back down, Katie and Lindsay latch onto Taylor's arms, giggling like idiots. "My God, Taylor," Lindsay whispers, "does this mysterious lover boy Daniel have any friends?" All three laugh, and Daniel glances back with a smile, leading them straight to the Jungle Juice station. He hands cups to each of them and grabs a beer for himself.

"Such a gentleman," Katie whisper-hisses in Taylor's ear.

Taylor elbows her sharply, praying she won't embarrass her. The four slide into a quieter corner and start talking.

"So, Daniel," Lindsay says. "Give us some dirt. You've known Taylor forever. Was she always cool or did she only become cool because of us?"

Daniel grins. "Taylor? Honestly, I barely recognized her without her bifocals and braces." Taylor punches him lightly, and he laughs. "Kidding. She was always cool. Her parents didn't give a damn about anything, and her older brothers were handing her booze half the time. She was smart, pretty; I mean, of course she was cool. I was jealous of her family, actually. As the only child of a single mom, I had rules. So many rules. Not the Evans household."

Taylor silently thanks the darkness for hiding her blushing face.

Gwen Stefani starts playing, and Katie suddenly grabs Lindsay. "You two catch up, we're going to dance. Be right back!" They vanish into the chaos, leaving Taylor alone with Daniel.

"So..." Daniel starts. "Tell me about UNC. What's your major? Are you seeing anyone?" he asks in a single breath.

"Wow," Taylor laughs. "One thing at a time, pal. I haven't officially declared, but I'm leaning toward Anthropology with a Creative Writing minor. Did the usual Bio-Chem-Calc nightmare last semester, thank God that's over. Now it's upper-level classes. What about you?"

"You skipped a question," Daniel says with a wink. "But we'll come back to it. I'm majoring in Econ. Hoping to move to Manhattan after graduation, work in Investment Banking, save some money, maybe go to Business school. Who knows. And, although you didn't ask" his voice dips, "I recently broke up with my girlfriend."

He doesn't mention the trust fund. He never does. It always feels strange coming out of his mouth.

"I'm sorry about the breakup," Taylor says. "What was her name? And no, I'm not seeing anyone. A few casual things last semester, nothing serious."

"Ah, got it. Sarah. She told me we were too young to 'get serious.' We met the first week of school; things were great. She even met my mom at Parent's Weekend. Then she ended it before Christmas. Unfinished business with her high school boyfriend, I think."

"Yikes. I'm sorry, Daniel." Taylor jumps on the chance to shift the topic. "How's your mom? How's Tanya?"

Daniel nods gratefully. "She's good. Still teaching Spanish at the high school. How's your family?"

"Same circus as always," Taylor laughs. "My parents are still at UW. Eric and Alex are both in Manhattan, Alex at NYU, Eric at Bear Stearns. So if you ever want to talk finance or need a reference, I've got connections. I'm planning to visit them soon, maybe over spring break."

"That's awesome. I might take you up on that," Daniel says. Then, tilting his head: "Need a refill?"

Taylor knows she shouldn't. But she takes a swig, nods, and follows him back to the drinks table.

As they wait, a group of about six extremely tall Black guys walk in, and Taylor instantly recognizes a few, Duke basketball players have officially arrived. She should be excited, but instead she finds herself hoping Daniel keeps talking. Still, she knows she must alert her friends. She grabs Daniel's hand and pulls him toward the dancing area, spotting that Lindsay and Katie already see the players and are semi-stalking them toward the kitchen.

Katie makes eye contact with Taylor, flashing an exaggerated "OK" sign. Lindsay drags her toward the players, who naturally attract a crowd. At Duke, the basketball players might as well be royalty, everyone wants to be near them.

"Off they go," Taylor sighs.

"Where?" Daniel asks, genuinely confused.

"My friends. They came to meet the basketball players. Now they're stalking them."

Daniel laughs. "Don't let me cramp your style. If you want to go with them, go ahead. I should probably find my buddies anyway." He scans the room casually.

Taylor's stomach drops. Just a little. "No, no, I'm having a great time. If you need to find your friends, I get it. But I'm not here for basketball players. Just a random night out with the girls."

Daniel turns back to her. Really looks at her. Then he leans in.

The kiss lands out of nowhere and exactly where it should. Taylor melts into him instantly, one arm wrapping around his neck, the other threading through his hair. She has no idea if they kiss for thirty seconds or ten minutes. When they finally pull apart, breathless, she knows exactly where this night is headed.

"Jesus Christ," Daniel mutters. "Where'd you learn to kiss like that?"

"I could ask you the same," Taylor smirks. "So... what now? Want to dance?"

"Sure. You lead," Daniel says, grinning as she pulls him toward the dance floor, giddy and electrified.

Lindsay and Katie are already dancing, sweaty and drunk, when Taylor and Daniel weave toward them.

"Taylor! Come here!" Lindsay yells. "Dance with us!"

The four of them dance, orbiting around each other under the pulsing lights, occasionally breaking away to refill their drinks or slip outside for a cigarette. At one point, Daniel leaves the dance floor and disappears into a cluster of the friends he arrived with, who are apparently heading to another party and trying to rope him in. He declines with an easy smile, and when he returns to Taylor and her friends, he's almost disbelieving at how much fun he's having watching them, impressed by their energy, their loud, off-key singing, and the way they seem to know the lyrics and dance moves to every single song that blasts through the speakers.

Somehow, it is already one a.m. The frat house feels packed to the gills, humid with sweat and spilled beer, and Katie starts complaining about her feet hurting and needing to eat something.

"Can we please go, and order pizza? I can't possibly stand up any longer" Katie moans dramatically.

"I'll go back with her," Lindsay quickly tells Taylor, leaning in so she can be heard over the music. "After all, I've danced with and kissed a Duke Basketball player. My night is complete. You and Daniel should stay. You have the code to get into my cousin's place, right, you know, just in case?" she asks with a wink.

"I have it, but I feel bad leaving you guys" Taylor tells her friends, a pang of guilt slipping in even as anticipation buzzes beneath her skin.

"Please, this was obviously meant to happen," Katie whispers, earnest now. "I mean, what are the odds of you two just bumping into each other? These things happen for a reason," Katie says with conviction. "You have to stay with him and see what happens."

With that, Katie and Lindsay give Taylor tight, lingering hugs and exchange "nice to meet yous" and "take good care of our girl here" with Daniel, sizing him up one last time, and then they head outside to get a cab, disappearing into the cool night.

Taylor and Daniel look at each other and Taylor suddenly feels self-conscious, like the floor has shifted beneath her. "So!" she says too loudly, "should we stay here? Go to a bar? I have a fake so we can go wherever if you want." She's talking too fast; her usual ease and cool persona having vanished shortly after kissing Daniel, leaving her exposed and buzzing.

He smiles at her, slow and warm, which makes her feel a bit more comfortable. God, she thinks to herself, when did he get so insanely gorgeous? The boy she grew up with has been replaced by this confident, impossibly handsome man, and it takes her breath away.

Daniel says, "Let's go back to my dorm and chill out. My roommate is out for the night."

Relieved that Daniel made the decision to go back to his dorm, Taylor links her arm in his, liking the way it feels to be connected to him, and they walk out the front door together. The lawn is filled with people, and the red solo cups scattered about appear to have increased exponentially since they arrived, like drunken confetti. Fleetingly, Taylor thinks of how appalling this scene would be in daylight, and she tries to block it out and focus on the positive. Like the tall boy, no, the man, at her side.

The walk back to Daniel's dorm takes about ten minutes, the air cool against her flushed skin. Taylor has to go into the girls' hall to use the bathroom, and he waits for her in the hallway, leaning casually against the wall like he has all the time in the world. His dorm room is bigger than hers and has that distinctly male smell of unwashed laundry covered up with too much cologne and deodorant. It's not entirely unpleasant; it feels lived-in, real. There are papers and books scattered all over the place, and he and his roommate have arranged the room such that the beds are bunk beds, with a futon under one bed, and a TV facing the futon under the other. It's a clever use of the space, but Taylor is beginning to question the logistics of sharing a twin-size bunk bed, be it for sleeping or anything else, her pulse quickening at the thought.

Daniel walks over to the mini fridge next to the TV and asks Taylor if she wants anything to drink.

"What have you got in there?"

"Beer, beer, rum, and coke. Or beer." Daniel laughs, the sound easy and familiar.

"I'll take a rum and coke, easy on the rum, please."

Daniel pours Taylor's drink with surprising focus, grabs a can of Coors light for himself, and sits next to her on the futon. Their shoulders brush, and the contact sends a small thrill through her. They each take a sip of their drinks and quickly they're kissing again, as if it's the most natural next step in the world. Daniel sets their drinks on the coffee table and gently lowers Taylor onto her back and gets on top of her. They are tangled up there for a while, the world narrowing down to warmth and breath and the press of his body against hers, both growing more excited by the second. In an attempt to prolong whatever this is turning into, Daniel comes up for air and a sip of beer. Taylor does the same, taking a long swig of her drink, trying to steady herself.

"When did you get so beautiful?" Daniel asks. "I mean, that came out wrong, I've always thought you were gorgeous. Remember when we kissed playing spin the bottle at Sam's house in seventh grade?"

"Yes, how could I forget that?" Taylor laughs, taking his hand in hers, their fingers intertwining easily. "Who'd have thought, just six years later and here we are. Though it feels like a lifetime ago, if I'm being honest."

"I know, I know, hopefully I'm better now than I was then?" Daniel asks, half teasing, half serious.

Taylor laughs and nods reassuringly. Daniel gets up to lock the door. "Just in case Mike comes home unexpectedly, but he should be out for the night. But you never know here, people get shitfaced and walk into the wrong room, or want to drink or smoke and just barge in. Want to go up?" Daniel asks, nodding toward the bed.

"Um, sure," Taylor replies, "after you."

Daniel climbs up the ladder to the bed. Taylor follows Daniel up the ladder, feeling almost ridiculously uncoordinated as she climbs, hyper-aware of every tiny movement, every brush of her knee against the metal rungs, every breath she takes. When she reaches the narrow mattress, they settle on their sides facing one another, the closeness dizzying. Daniel reaches out and slowly threads his fingers through her hair. The touch is gentle, reverent. Taylor inhales and catches the faint scent of her Herbal Essences shampoo, suddenly grateful she showered; grateful he might notice; grateful that *he* is noticing her at all like this.

They start kissing again, soft at first, exploratory, their hands brushing over familiar places that suddenly feel brand-new. What begins tentative grows in intensity, their touches becoming warmer, bolder, as if each kiss pulls them deeper into something they hadn't quite prepared for. Clothes come off in quiet, breathless increments, the air between them thickening with anticipation. Taylor quickly gathers her long hair into a ponytail, her hands trembling slightly, her pulse thundering in her ears.

Daniel slips down the ladder to grab a condom, and the brief separation feels like a held breath, like time stretching itself out just to torture her. She can hear him moving below, quick, purposeful, and by the time he climbs back up, she's practically vibrating with a mix of nerves and want. The second he appears, she grabs him by the front of his shirt and pulls him toward her, kissing him with a fierceness she didn't know she possessed, surrendering completely to the gravity drawing them together.

"Oh my God, Daniel, I want you so bad," she breathes against his mouth, unable to hold the words in.

He's breathing hard too, his hands shaking slightly with the same urgency she feels. He moves with practiced ease, but the look on his face, hungry, disbelieving, overwhelmed, makes her feel like this moment is different for him too.

What happens next is fast, consuming, and impossibly intense. It's messy in places, perfect in others, a collision of old familiarity and a brand-new heat that takes them both by surprise. The room seems to tilt and narrow around them, the sounds of the party outside fading until all Taylor can register is the rhythm of them, the warmth of him, the way being with him feels electric, like touching something she wasn't supposed to but can't pull away from.

When it's over, they collapse together, bodies still tangled, breaths syncing without effort. She can feel his heartbeat under her palm, strong and steady, and he keeps his arm draped around her as if letting go would break the spell.

It is, Taylor realizes, the most intimate she's ever felt with someone, more so than boys she dated for months. This connection feels older somehow, threaded with years of shared memories and something unspoken she can't quite name. Maybe it's nostalgia. Maybe it's the alcohol. Maybe it's something deeper, something that's been quietly waiting for its moment.

Whatever it is, she decides not to pick it apart. For once, she lets herself simply be in it.

"Wow," Daniel mumbles. "That was amazing. You are amazing."

"Ummmmm yeah, that was, like, insanely good," Taylor murmurs breathlessly, a small disbelieving laugh escaping her.

They lie there in companionable silence for a few minutes, the room humming with the afterglow, then Daniel props himself up on his elbow and looks down at her.

"So Taylor, since I have you here, tell me everything," Daniel says as he goes back down the ladder. "I'm just grabbing our drinks, be right back."

"Like what?" Taylor asks as she pulls the sheet over her naked body, suddenly self-conscious now that the frenzy has quieted. "I'm not all that interesting."

"I highly doubt that. Let's start with, I don't know, what do you want to be when you grow up?" Daniel asks, his voice drifting up from below.

"Oh Jesus. I just want to travel. It's hard to think about the future. I'm living in the moment now, trying to do well in school while having fun, you know? I do know I am going to spend a semester, maybe a year if I can swing it, studying abroad." Taylor tells him, knowing full well that she's rambling and talking way too fast. Nevertheless, she continues, "beyond that, like, after graduation? Write and travel. Hopefully make enough money writing that I can see the world a bit. You know? What about you? Do you think you'll ever go back to Madison, like, permanently?"

"Dunno," Daniel responds with a heavy sigh. "Sometimes I feel like I have to, to take care of my mom. But do I want to? Not really. Maybe when I'm old and ready to start a family but definitely not anytime soon. Wait, did you say you're considering doing study abroad for a full year? That's intense, yeah?"

"Yeah, that's my plan. Maybe a little intense." Taylor giggles, the sound soft in the dim room. "But between us, I've been dreaming of the independence that I imagine comes with being alone in a totally new place. I guess I had a taste of it just by coming to a school where I didn't know anyone, but it's still the U.S. I went from one college town to another."

Daniel nods, replying, "I hear that. Although Durham isn't quite the college town that Madison or Chapel Hill are."

"Not to say that I don't love UNC, I really do. The girls you met tonight, they're truly the most amazing friends. I feel so lucky we found each other, basically day one of school! Sorry, I'm rambling. What about you? How's Duke? Do you love it? Are you planning on going abroad at all?"

Daniel laughs. "Lots of questions in there, Taylor."

Hearing him say her name, Taylor feels her pulse increase a bit. There's no denying her attraction to him. The way he looks at her, it is clear that he is truly listening to her and considering every word that comes out of her mouth. Very different than most guys, who are interested only in what's under her clothing.

"I love Duke," Daniel continues. "Great people, although very different than Madison. There's a lot of money kids here. Which is weird. I'm friends with some, actually. Sometimes I wonder if I'm the only minority they've ever met who isn't on their family's payroll. They're good people, but it's like they don't even have to think about spending. Never worked a day in their lives. They've got daddy's credit card and there really aren't any limits."

"Oh my God, I know," Taylor agrees. "There's plenty of money kids at UNC too. Not bad being friends with them though . . . maybe you'll get an invite to someone's vacation house. I spent a long weekend last semester at Lindsay's family's place down in Florida. Her parents weren't even there but told Lindsay to charge every expense to their card. It was crazy. And then there's us Wisco kids . . . I remember you working at Dairy Queen. I'd come in sometimes, after lifeguarding in the summer. Do you remember that?"

"Of course! You and all of your friends, straight from the pool," Daniel says with a raised eyebrow. He could never forget Taylor coming in, hair still wet, the outline of her swimsuit underneath her tank top. He could barely focus on making Blizzards whenever she walked in there.

Taylor laughs. "Sorry I wasn't friendlier. I should have talked to you more, but you guys were always so busy and looking like you were having so much fun." To be honest, she always felt self-conscious around Daniel, despite having known him literally forever. That was the real reason she wasn't chattier with him back in the day.

"For a high school job, it had its perks. Cute girls coming from the pool, free ice cream."

"So, back to going abroad? Are you going to do it?" Taylor asks, genuinely curious now about how brave he'll let himself be.

"Honestly, I'm not sure. I know Duke has a great Econ program in London that I could do. But I guess I'm on the fence. I'm really happy here. Not sure I want to leave and risk that, you know what I mean?"

"I hear you. You'll have lots of time to explore later, I'm sure, but why not do it now while you're young and free?"

Avoiding the question, Daniel responds, "Speaking of exploring," and slips his hand between her thighs and kisses her again, long and deep and a few minutes later is going down from the bunk to get another condom. By this point it's 4 a.m., but Taylor's feeling a strange energy pulsing through her, a mix of exhaustion and adrenaline and something that feels dangerously like hope.

After their second go, they collapse in a sweaty heap, gasping for breath once again. Taylor concludes that the first time wasn't just a fluke. Daniel is officially really fucking good in bed, and the realization makes her both giddy and slightly nervous about how much she already cares.

"Hey, can I get you some water or anything?" Daniel asks.

"Actually yeah, water would be great, thanks. I'm also going to run to the bathroom super quick."

"I can walk you there. Here, you can put this on," Daniel says, handing her a t-shirt and a pair of gym shorts from his dresser.

"Thanks, how do they look with my shoes?" Taylor jokes, putting her heels on along with the 'dude going to the gym' ensemble Daniel gave her, amused at the ridiculousness of her reflection.

"Honestly, you could wear anything and look stunning." Daniel tells her, and the sincerity in his voice makes her blush.

She finds herself blushing yet again, and they head out into the hallway to the bathrooms. Daniel is waiting for her outside of the girl's bathroom, holding a big pitcher of water like some sweet, slightly rumpled knight.

"Where'd that come from?" she asks.

"The communal kitchen down the hall. Where everybody keeps their leftovers and where we have the annoying mandatory dorm meetings."

Taylor grabs the water from him and takes a huge swig directly from the pitcher. She is officially parched. "Aaaahhhh thank you. I didn't realize how desperately I needed that."

"Of course," Daniel responds, and follows suit, guzzling straight from the pitcher.

They head back to his room, and Taylor is suddenly overcome with exhaustion, the night finally catching up to her. As they make their way back up to his bed, Daniel expresses the same sentiment.

Taylor lies down under the blankets, facing away from Daniel, and he wraps himself around her, his arm a solid, comforting weight around her waist. They both drift off almost instantly, no words spoken. As Taylor falls asleep, she feels a comfort and sense of safety she doesn't recall ever having before. Bliss, she thinks. This is bliss.

Bliss is too quickly replaced with a hangover. Taylor wakes with a start as she hears her crappy cell phone buzzing. "Ugh, fuckin A," she mutters to herself. Daniel doesn't stir, for which she is grateful. Time to get herself together or at least put some gum in her mouth and see who's calling her.

Taylor stealthily climbs down the ladder and grabs her phone, seeing a missed call from Katie. She checks the time and sees that it's 10:42 a.m. She and her friends had planned on heading back to campus by 11 a.m. "Fuck," she exclaims to herself while slipping on a pair of Daniel's sneakers and a sweatshirt, and sneaking outside with her purse, being sure to leave the door ajar so she can get back inside.

She quickly finds the balcony and steps into the chilly morning air. She lights a cigarette and calls Katie back.

"Where are you?" Katie asks when she picks up.

Taylor takes a long drag on her cigarette and responds, "At Daniel's dorm, sorry I slept so late, but you won't believe what happened."

"I can guess what happened! Did you sleep with him? Tell me you did, Taylor, he's so hot."

"Yes, twice. I can't believe it. I'm in a bit of shock combined with a hangover to be honest with you. Was this a terrible mistake?"

Katie tells Taylor, "We can pick you up at his dorm, what's it called? Be ready in fifteen minutes and we can head back to campus. I have to be at the library all day if I want to go out tonight."

Taylor tells Katie the name of the dorm and its general location on Duke's campus, takes a final drag on her cigarette and heads inside to the bathroom. The lights feel cruelly bright and draw attention to the mascara smudges under her eyes.

"Jesus Christ," she mutters while doing her best to get rid of the makeup under her eyes and pinch some color into her cheeks. Her blonde hair, which she managed to get into a 'messy bun' at some point last night, now more closely resembles a bird's nest. She does her best to fix her hair, uses the bathroom and heads back to Daniel's room, unsure of what she's going to say, or if he'll even be awake.

She quietly opens the door and looks up. He's still asleep and she feels a sense of relief, along with a little guilt. The sparks from last night have faded in the harsh reality that the daylight so cruelly brings, and the passion she felt last night has been replaced with mild embarrassment at her uninhibitedness. She quietly changes back into her own clothes, knowing full well she'll have the "walk of shame" look in her "going out" clothes and high heels.

She folds the clothes borrowed from Daniel and leaves them on his desk chair and starts digging around his desk for a pen and piece of paper. Once she finds them in Daniel's mess of economics papers and books, she writes a quick note.

Daniel,
Have to run now, my friends need to get back to campus. It was really
fun seeing you and catching up. Thanks for a great night. If you want
to hang out again my number is 608-555-3239.

XO,
Taylor

She writes the note as quickly as possible, before she can change
her mind about whether to leave her phone number for him. She
realizes that by doing so she's setting herself up for a game of "will
he/won't he call" that may drive her mad. But she prefers that to the
brutal embarrassment that would ensue for both of them if Daniel
had to have his mom get Taylor's number from her mom. They'd
never hear the end of it. After one last look at Daniel, she feels a
potent mix of bliss, panic, and vulnerability. Some internal voice
telling her, This wasn't just about the great sex. Taylor sighs quietly,
leaves the note on top of his laptop, grabs her purse, and slips out the
door.

Taylor waits in the cool late morning air, still processing what
happened last night, and starts giggling a bit. The sunlight and fresh
air shock her back to reality, breaking the spell of the passionate night
with Daniel. By the time her friends pull up to the dorm she's
laughing harder, and when she plops down in the backseat, she's
practically hysterical.

"What the fuck, Taylor?" Lindsay asks. "What's wrong with
you? Why are you laughing so hard?"

"Ohmygod you guys, I can't stop laughing. It just hit me, and I
can't stop." Taylor takes a few deep breaths to calm herself down,
while Katie and Lindsay are clearly annoyed and concerned at the
same time. "Okay, I'm getting it together. Did you guys have fun last
night? Did you go out after the party, or just back to the apartment?"

"We went back and ordered pizza, which seemed like a great idea at like 2 a.m. Ugh" moans Lindsay, clutching her stomach. "More importantly, tell us about your night, Miss Taylor! Clearly, something happened based on your current psychotic state."

Taylor, having finally recovered from her fit of giggling, smiles and gives them the highlights. She keeps it light and refrains from the connection she felt with Daniel, sticking to the juicy bits she knows they'll be interested in. They ask her where it will go from here, are they going to see each other again; to which Taylor shrugs and tries to change the subject, switching over to the day that lies ahead. She doesn't want them to know she left her number with him, or that she has no idea what, if anything, will come of this crazy encounter.

The three girls move on to the day's plans, studying and group project meetings will take up the bulk of the afternoon for all of them, and they have yet to finalize their Saturday night plans. As they walk into their dorm, they agree to meet up later for dinner, and will decide what to do tonight at that point.

Taylor walks into her room, exhausted, and changes into sweats, brushes her teeth, and falls into bed. She wakes at 3:15 in the afternoon and is slightly panicked that she slept half the day away. She packs up her schoolwork and heads to the library, stopping at the snack bar for sustenance on the way over, her mind drifting back, again and again, to Daniel's sleeping face and the note she left behind.

And Taylor's life carries on, filled with coursework, a teaching assistant position she lands early in her sophomore year, and plenty of parties. Katie and Lindsay remain her closest friends, and they will stay that way for many years, long after their college days are behind them. Even when they have no idea where Taylor is or what continent she's on while she chases the adventures she's always dreamed of.

As for Daniel, he does call her a few weeks after their night together. He's polite but direct. He's gotten back together with his girlfriend, Sarah. He tells Taylor he had such a great time with her and wanted to see her again, but they both acknowledge it's a bad idea given his renewed relationship. During that call, he says something that lodges itself in Taylor's mind for years, resurfacing at the worst moments: "I'm not sure I could handle the intensity of being with you, Taylor." She's left speechless, unsure what exactly he's afraid of. She's far more disappointed than she lets on, but she tells him she understands and wishes him luck with Sarah, her voice catching as she speaks.

After the call, she goes outside, smokes a cigarette, and cries a little. Taylor rarely cries, she's a beacon of strength, her enthusiastic, up-for-anything attitude usually snuffing out any melancholy before it can settle. But today she lets the tears fall, hoping to drain the sadness from her system before pulling herself back together. And this one rejection from Daniel, possibly the kindest person she will ever know, leaves a small, lingering scar, an unplanned tattoo she sometimes forgets about, but most days feels haunted by, full of *what-ifs.*

In the moment, though, she leans into her inner strength and tells herself it's time to move on, time to pull it together.

So she throws herself back into her studies, her friends, and the rest of college life, practically forbidding herself from thinking about Daniel. But despite her resolve, in the months that follow she finds herself ruminating on him almost obsessively; something about the way they connected that night, mixed with their shared history, makes it impossible to get him out of her mind.

Chapter 2

2002 – 2003

Throughout her sophomore year, Taylor doesn't just thrive academically, she thrives at everything. She juggles a reporter job at the school newspaper (the tiny stipend immediately earmarked for her study-abroad fund), her TA position, a full course load, and a social calendar packed to the brim. It's chaotic, but she feeds on the momentum, vibrating with purpose.

While her friends are consumed by parties and exam schedules, Taylor is quietly orchestrating her biggest dream yet: a full year abroad. Not one semester, the full year. And somehow she convinces the University to approve it. She even talks her way into becoming the paper's travel writer, promising dispatches from every city she explores and a set of features on Barcelona itself. The pay is tiny, but it's something. She sends samples to up-and-coming travel magazines too, hoping someone will take a chance on a young, hungry voice with a cheap Eurail pass and a knack for finding beauty in budget travel.

Her parents are worried, of course.

"Won't you be lonely? Homesick?" they ask.

Taylor can only stare at them. Loneliness has never been part of her emotional vocabulary. She likes her own company; people like her; Barcelona will like her. And half her acquaintances are also Europe-bound, whether for a semester or a full year. She'll have no shortage of couches to crash on or friends to meet.

She plans to get the Eurail pass that will let her hop across borders on long weekends, and she's heard whispers from students who went before: arrange your classes right and you can carve out three-day weekends, or four, if you're strategic. Her Spanish is solid. Her confidence even more so.

The summer before she leaves, she stays in Chapel Hill working, a TA gig, articles for the paper, and finally heads home to Madison for two short weeks before her flight. The days blur into high-school-friend catch-ups, last-minute European shopping, and long afternoons with her parents. She finds herself savoring her mother's cooking in a way she never did growing up.

Then, on one of her final nights there, while they're finishing dinner on the back porch, her mother casually detonates a bomb:

"Oh! By the way, Daniel's going abroad too. London. First semester."

Taylor's fork freezes mid-air. She tries to look casual, failing miserably.

"Really? Do you know when he leaves? Is he traveling around too?"

Her mother keeps talking, August departure, probably some travel, trust fund flexibility, and Taylor is halfway between panic and fascination. Daniel with his old-money New England grandparents, the awkward tension with Tanya, the complicated family legacy he was born into... and the one night she still can't fully forget.

Then her mother adds, "Tanya sent them some of your writing samples. They loved them. If you want an internship with their firm someday, just reach out."

Taylor nearly chokes. Working for Daniel's family sounds like a fever dream she's not ready to interpret. But it's an opportunity she can't afford to dismiss.

She thanks her mom, grateful and stunned.

Then her mother shifts topics, Christmas travel, the cities Taylor wants to visit, and the conversation slides back into familiar territory.

In a rare soft moment, her dad tells her how proud he is of her. Then, in classic dad-fashion, ruins the tenderness with, "Just be careful, okay? You wandering around Europe looking so... blatantly American makes me nervous."

She laughs, hugs him, and teases back, only to learn he means her blonde hair, her height, her sunny disposition, all of it.

Later that night, Taylor stands in front of the mirror of her childhood bedroom. She studies herself. Could she pass for French? Dutch maybe? Scandinavian definitely. But Spanish? No chance.

Still, Spain has been calling her since freshman-year Spanish II, when she first learned the country's history. Something about Barcelona lodged itself in her chest and never let go.

On Tuesday, August 5th, 2003, her parents drop her at the Dane County airport. Her passport is tucked safely into her purse. She hugs them goodbye, ignoring the quiver in her mother's eyes, and walks into the terminal.

Years later, Taylor will cackle at how *American* she looks in the memory: loose white sweatpants with black side stripes, a bright red tank top and matching sweatshirt, black platform sandals showing off red polished toes. A messy blonde bun. She looks like an Abercrombie bag come to life.

The Madison to Chicago hop is quick, and after triumphantly locating the international terminal at O'Hare (a rite of passage), she settles into her seat for the long flight. The plane feels enormous. She almost has enough legroom.

When the flight attendant hands her a free glass of wine without even asking for ID, Taylor feels like she's already halfway to adulthood. She sips, flips through her guidebook, orders another glass, and eventually drifts to sleep somewhere over the Atlantic, dreaming of new streets, new languages, and the next version of herself waiting across the ocean.

Chapter 3

August 2003, Barcelona

Taylor wakes to the sound of the pilot announcing that they are on track for an on-time arrival at Barcelona–El Prat Airport and the plane should be landing in approximately one hour. Bleary-eyed but giddy with excitement, she gets up to use the restroom and brushes her teeth, returns to her seat, and checks her map for the hundredth time to make sure she tells the cab driver the correct instructions.

Taylor was able to secure over three weeks of housing in the university dorms before school starts, which will provide her with a safe home base until she gets her bearings. However, once those weeks are up, she will need to locate her own housing, most likely in an off-campus apartment. This terrifies her mom, of course, who was unaware of this setup until a week before Taylor left, but Taylor managed to convince her that it would all work out and promised that she would begin the housing search immediately upon her arrival.

The Barcelona airport is a case study in international glamour. Glittery stores and world travelers surround her, and Taylor suddenly feels very young and naïve. She follows the other passengers through customs, then on to baggage claim, where she spots her two giant suitcases quickly. She hoists them off the conveyor belt and struggles to pull them behind her while also carrying her overstuffed backpack and purse. She feels instantly ridiculous in her casual, oh-so-American attire compared to the effortlessly glamorous travelers all around her, so she hurries out to the taxi area. Fortunately, there is a long line of taxis waiting and a short line of people, so within just a few minutes she is watching the driver load her massive bags into the trunk and then settling into the backseat.

After giving him the address, Taylor begins speaking to him in Spanish, hoping he won't be one of the Barcelonans who refuse to speak Spanish and stick to Catalán, with which she is unfamiliar. Fortunately, he speaks Spanish with her, and he gives her a few suggestions of places to visit and some off-the-beaten-path restaurants that are only known by locals and that she won't find in any of her guidebooks. Twenty-five minutes later, he drops her off at the university housing, located in the Pedralbes section of the city. She thanks him, pays the fare in euros, and collects all of her bags.

Pedralbes is one of the quieter sections of the city, especially during the month of August, when city dwellers escape on their summer holidays. She gives the building and the surrounding area a once-over, pleased with the green, quiet streets and the appearance of the dormitory.

Taylor wheels her bags into the small lobby of the four-story building that will be her home for the next three weeks. Minimally decorated, it is indistinguishable from any other building apart from its obvious newness. The smell of fresh paint is in the air, and while Taylor is taking it all in, a young male voice says loudly, "Hola, señorita, ¿qué pasa?"

She greets him and gives him her name, explaining that today is her check-in date, and confirms her three-week stay. He hands her the key and directs her up to the second floor, to room 221. She takes the elevator up, remembering something she read in one of her many guidebooks: in much of Europe, the first floor is considered floor zero. So she's technically on the third floor by American standards.

The elevator opens to an outdoor hallway, like what one would find at a motel in the U.S. The view is pretty; the sky is clear blue, not a cloud to be found, and she can see gardens and university buildings nearby. There are ashtrays scattered about, which will be most convenient for her mischievous smoking habit.

Taylor opens the door to her room and is pleasantly surprised. After hearing a few horror stories about accommodations in European cities (and having never left the continental United States), she wasn't sure what to expect. There's a bed, a desk and chair, and a private bathroom (thank God). The window at the back of the room looks out onto a beautiful little courtyard filled with bougainvillea and a small pond, with a handful of benches scattered around it.

Fortunately, Taylor had heeded her mother's advice and packed her summer and early fall clothes in one suitcase, along with her cosmetics, toiletries, and shoes. The other suitcase, with the winter clothes and jacket, can remain unopened until she is settled into her permanent apartment.

She uses the bathroom, pleased to see it is stocked with soap, toothpaste, and towels. Then she gets down to the business of unpacking, emptying one suitcase and her backpack. The fatigue is catching up with her, but her adrenaline is pumping hard. She's really here, in Barcelona. After all these months (or really, years) of dreaming of this, it is finally her reality.

She removes her passport and a wad of euros her parents had bestowed upon her before she left and stashes them in her desk drawer. Barcelona has a reputation for gypsies pickpocketing tourists, and the last thing she wants to deal with on her first day here is having her passport stolen.

Feeling accomplished and organized, she goes out to the outdoor hallway and lights a cigarette. There are a few passersby on the street below, but the dorm itself is fairly empty. Taylor knows she should feel tired and jet-lagged, but the excitement of being here is giving her a second wind.

She has a few things to check off her to-do list before she can focus on finding an apartment. First on the list: get a cell phone. Second: find a grocery store nearby where she can get some food to keep at the dorm. Third, and at this moment the most exciting, given that she isn't even of legal drinking age back home, is to find a nearby liquor store. She knows she'll want to keep some cheap wine in her room.

Taylor puts her cigarette out in one of the ashtrays and goes back into her room. She gets her computer set up, the internet working (a miracle!), and sends off a quick email to her parents to let them know she has arrived safely. Next, she emails Katie and Lindsay to tell them the same and that she can't wait to meet up with them once they get to Europe.

Both girls are doing their study abroad during the first semester, Lindsay in Rome and Katie in Paris. They have grand plans to get together as much as possible, all vowing to try to keep their Fridays free of classes in order to guarantee long weekends that allow for travel.

After sending the emails, Taylor takes a shower in the tiny bathroom. Europe has a lot of things going for it, Taylor thinks, but the bathrooms aren't one of them. The shower is miniature, the toilet barely flushes, but at least she has her own bathroom, a luxury she's never had, having grown up with two older brothers.

She towel-dries her hair, puts on a little makeup, and gets dressed. Unsure of what to wear on her first day here, she settles on a short denim skirt, a low-cut black tank top, and a black sweater in case she gets cold later.

By this point it's already 4:00 p.m. (or 16:00 European time, which Taylor needs to get used to using). She puts her map and guidebook in her purse and sets off in search of a phone. She heads back to the lobby with the intention of asking the young man working there where she should go to get a cell phone.

He greets her kindly and suggests she go to El Corte Inglés, a large department store with a location nearby, only a ten-minute walk from the dorm. He tells her it's near the María Cristina metro station, and she immediately knows where to go, thanks to a month of dedicated map studying.

She thanks him after learning that he's a grad student named Pedro, originally from Madrid, but that he has been in Barcelona for six years and has no intention of ever leaving. He declares the city to be the best on earth, and his enthusiasm for the city is contagious.

Taylor isn't sure what she was expecting El Corte Inglés to be, but it definitely wasn't this. The place is huge. They sell electronics, makeup, clothes, groceries, toiletries, you name it, they have it. Like a really upscale Wal-Mart. Taylor does her best to stay focused and locate the electronics section so she can get herself a cell phone and get the hell out of there before spending any unnecessary money.

She follows the signs to electronics and gets a mini lesson in European cell phones from the clerk. He shows her how to make calls, send text messages, and save contacts. She'll need to charge the phone for around twelve hours before it will work properly, and should she run into any problems, he encourages her to return and says he'd be happy to help. She thanks him gratefully for his tutorial and pays. He winks at her, and blushing, she goes on her way.

To-do number one now complete, Taylor walks out of the massive store quickly and starts heading back in the direction of the dorm. There are men in suits and women in dresses leaving their offices. Some are rushing toward the María Cristina metro station, presumably to get home to their families. Others, mainly younger men, linger, some chatting on corners, others heading to tapas bars in the neighborhood. Taylor can't help but notice (and enjoy) seeing so many handsome men, most of whom have their ties loosened and top buttons undone, seemingly a signal that the workday is done and the fun is beginning.

Taylor gets a burst of energy after seeing all these young professionals out and about and starts thinking about what to do tonight. She's bookmarked a million places to go, many historic: museums (the Picasso Museum, the Dalí Museum in Figueres), buildings (Sagrada Família, the Gaudí houses, to name a few), parks (Park Güell, Parc de la Ciutadella, Parc del Laberint d'Horta); others with the sole intention of fun: bars, clubs, shopping centers.

She stops at the grocery store, which is about one-tenth the size of your average American grocery store. Momentarily baffled by the tiny spot, Taylor grabs a basket and puts in some fruit, digestive biscuits, cereal, and two bottles of red wine. She wanders the aisles for a few minutes before going to pay.

Next up is the tobacco store, where she gets two packs of Marlboro Lights for an astonishingly low price, far less than half of what she pays back home. Mission accomplished, she thinks to herself, lugging her haul up the hill back to the dorm. She decides to take a break and sits on a bench on the outskirts of the Jardins de Vil·la Amèlia, smoking a cigarette while taking in the breathtaking scenery.

By this point it's close to 7 p.m., and Taylor realizes she's famished. She knows enough about Spain to know that dinnertime can be as late as 11 p.m., but there's no way she can hold out for much longer. She continues the walk back to the dorm and unloads her bags as soon as she arrives, quickly charging her phone in the hopes of being able to use it tomorrow.

Taylor has been hyper-focused on her study of the city's geography for the past month. She has practically memorized the metro map and neighborhoods of Barcelona and is familiar with the different metro lines, which stations allow connections to other lines, and the stations she thinks she'll use the most. Nevertheless, she's not planning on going anywhere without her little metro map, and probably not without her massive guidebook as well.

Rather than check out any of the dance clubs or bars she's highlighted, Taylor makes the executive decision to make tonight a chill night and go for a tapas dinner instead. She's not particularly tired; if anything, she feels elated by the sense of independence and freedom she has at this very moment.

She resolves, for her first night in Barcelona, to head to the city center, Passeig de Gràcia. Her destination is Tapa Tapa Bar de Tapas, which she realizes is totally cliché, but she needs to get a sense of Spanish food, the one thing she is woefully unprepared for on this journey. What better place to do so than a tapas joint that presumably, based on the name, caters to tourists while still serving traditional Spanish tapas?

Taylor refreshes her makeup, adding an extra layer of eyeliner and mascara, sweeping bronzer along her cheekbones, and applying lip gloss. Her skin is still a bit dewy from her walk earlier, but in a good way. She assesses her outfit, deeming it acceptable for a chill night by herself. She grabs her guidebook and tosses it into her bag. She's more interested in people-watching tonight but feels like having a book with her will be a good backup, a crutch against feeling too awkward.

She pours a half glass of the red wine she bought earlier and brings it outside to the "balcony" area, where she sips it and slowly smokes a cigarette. It's heavenly.

Don't forget this moment, you're alone, and free, and your life is just beginning.

Years later, she will look back fondly on this day, who she was in that moment, her optimism, and the overarching (albeit naïve) sense that she could conquer the world...or, at the very least, Barcelona.

She puts out her cigarette and goes back inside, washes her cup out, uses the restroom, and grabs her bag. Locking the door on her way out, Taylor looks at her room number and takes a mental picture, lest she forget it later.

She exits onto the street and walks back down toward the metro station. She descends the stairs into the underground and walks to one of the ticket kiosks. After speaking only Spanish all day, she's secretly relieved that the machine has an English option. She picks it, grateful for the brief mental break. She opts for a ten-ride ticket, figuring she'll reevaluate after a few days in the city and maybe go for the monthly pass.

Taylor checks the map to make sure she's heading in the right direction to arrive at the Passeig de Gràcia station and proceeds down another flight of stairs. The metro station is well lit and not nearly as dingy as she expected. Her only knowledge of underground transportation comes from the stories her brothers have told her about the New York subways. This doesn't seem nearly as bad. She hasn't seen any rats yet, which is a good starting point, she reasons.

There are even timetables informing passengers when the next train will arrive. After a mere three-minute wait, Taylor's train pulls in. She's surprised by how packed it is, but quickly remembers that Barcelona is a late-night city, and all these people are either just now coming home from work or starting their nights out.

A quick word on Passeig de Gràcia. It is one of the major avenues in Barcelona and a hub for shopping and business, along with restaurants and bars. Taylor read in one of her guidebooks that it is Barcelona's version of the Champs-Élysées in Paris. It is located in the center of the Eixample (pronounced "uh-SHAM-pluh," Taylor learns quickly) neighborhood and stretches from Plaça Catalunya to Carrer Gran de Gràcia.

In addition to being a major center for shopping, it is also home to some of Gaudí's most famous architectural masterpieces: Casa Milà and Casa Batlló. And last, but not least, in Taylor's mind, there's a Starbucks located on one of the smaller side streets just off the main drag. In short, Taylor plans on spending a lot of time here.

In fact, her grand plan is to try to find an apartment in this area. It's about a thirty-minute trip from most of Eixample's metro stations back up to her school. She thinks of this as she emerges from the underground into the hustle and bustle of the city. This neighborhood has a markedly different feel than the leafy, garden-heavy neighborhood of Pedralbes, where she is living for now and where her school is located. And while she appreciates the quiet and calm of Pedralbes, her priorities in being here are certainly not centered on calm. She wants noisy restaurants and bars filled with young people, and this neighborhood fits the bill.

Taylor wanders past some news kiosks selling magazines, candy, and tobacco. She's furtively relieved to see some tourists wandering about, which she'd never admit, of course, but it makes her feel less "American" looking. Normally she'd wander around and pop into some shops. Tonight, though, she's focused on food. She's not sure how many hours it's been since her last meal but knows it's been far too many. So when she arrives at Tapa Tapa, there's a feeling of relief:

first that she's managed to find the place, second that there are some empty tables.

The host sees her and immediately asks her in English, "How many?"

She responds in Spanish, "Solo yo, y prefiero una mesa afuera, por favor."

The host smiles, grabs a menu, and seats her at one of the outdoor tables that allows for watching people mill about Passeig de Gràcia. It's perfect. Now to conquer the menu, which at first glance appears to read like War and Peace, it's that lengthy. She easily orders a carafe of the house red wine, thrilled once again at not being carded. The idea that she can legally drink here is totally exhilarating, and she can't help but smile as the waiter leaves to get her wine.

Okay, Taylor, she tells herself, focus on Spanish IV class, where you learned all the different foods. The thought immediately sends her down the "Daniel rabbit hole," as she thinks of it. Daniel's mom is a Spanish teacher and would occasionally give Taylor some pointers when she was younger. She hasn't thought about him since her mom mentioned his study abroad plans in London the other night, which now feels like a lifetime ago.

She can't stop herself from wondering whether, if she decides to visit London, she'll contact him beforehand to meet up. And since everyone who studies abroad in Europe inevitably ends up in Barcelona for a weekend at minimum, will he reach out to her?

Ugh, stop it, Taylor tells herself. She needs her friends around to distract her and stop this downward spiral into the "why didn't he want me" abyss. After all, being rejected by guys isn't something Taylor is used to; she's usually the one calling things off. She suddenly misses Katie and Lindsay terribly. She decides she'll email them again tomorrow and get a weekend on the books where they can all meet up.

Now, back to this goddamn menu. Calamari is an easy choice. But these are tapas, you're supposed to order a few. Patatas bravas, ensalada rusa, pulpo (octopus, no thanks!), bomba, boquerones, croquetas. Christ, Taylor thinks, what the hell am I going to order without having to ask the waiter what all this means?

The waiter approaches with her wine, and she takes a chance on what seems safe: patatas bravas, calamari, and ensalada rusa. She knows ensalada means salad and saw a mention of atún in the description, so that should be relatively benign.

Feeling relieved to have ordered something resembling a meal, Taylor forbids her brain from thinking about Daniel and all the what-ifs that come to mind. Instead, she sips her wine and looks at her guidebook. At this point in the day, starving and jet-lagged, she doesn't give a damn if she looks like a tourist.

She starts making a vague itinerary for the week: sights to see in Barcelona, along with nearby places like Sitges, a beach town she can get to by train. Maybe even the botanical gardens just an hour outside the city. She's planning on saving the bigger in-country trips, to Salamanca and Madrid, for later in the fall, when she'll have other UNC friends to visit. Classes don't start until mid-September, so she basically has a month to herself.

Taylor's been toying with the idea of spending some of this time exploring the Greek islands, but the thought of being a tourist among tourists, which will surely be the case for most of August, isn't appealing. She could try to escape to one of the more remote islands, but then the concern becomes less about tourists and more about the fact that she doesn't speak a word of Greek, other than ouzo. Perhaps Greece is best saved for next summer, before she heads back to the States.

But before she can travel too far, she needs a place to come back to, which means starting the apartment search tomorrow.

As she idly flips through her guidebook, Taylor notices a group of drunk guys walking along Passeig de Gràcia. They're speaking English, but with British accents. They're red-faced, loud, and the epitome of why she imagines people dislike tourists. She notices one of them pointing at her, and the next thing she knows, the four young men are approaching her.

"S'matter, love, why are you by yourself?" one of them asks.

They're not bad-looking, but they're obnoxious and stumbling around, and Taylor is not in the mood to deal with a bunch of drunk guys. So instead of speaking to them in English, she responds in Spanish with a quick, "Lo siento, no hablo inglés."

They laugh and ask her again, in English, if she wants any company. Before she can politely decline, the waiter appears with a plate of potatoes smothered in red and white sauces.

"Patatas bravas," he exclaims enthusiastically.

She thanks him loudly, for the food, and mentally for interrupting the interaction. He gives the guys a look that says, get the fuck out of here unless you're going to order something. The guys roll their eyes and walk away, but not before wishing Taylor "Bon appétit," complete with a bow.

Taylor rolls her eyes and digs into her food. She'd forgotten that with tapas, dishes come out as they're ready rather than all at once. These are the best potatoes she's ever eaten. Hands down. She's unsure if they're actually that good or if she's so famished that anything would taste incredible right now.

As she's about halfway through her potatoes, the waiter returns with her other two dishes. She thanks him again, and he refills her wine glass.

The ensalada rusa looks a little scary, but she gives it a try. It's delicious, if a bit too heavy on the mayo, but she'd definitely order it again. The calamari is sublime, perfectly crispy and far superior to the rubbery stuff she's used to back home.

Taylor has heard stories of people going abroad and gaining twenty-five pounds, so she knows she'll have to watch what she eats. She's tall and thin but works hard to stay that way. Regular gym visits and calorie counting are the norm for her, as they seem to be for nearly every young woman of her generation. Years later, a friend of Taylor's will remark that nearly every woman who lived through the 1990s developed some form of disordered eating, and Taylor will agree wholeheartedly, a devastating but true observation, if there ever was one.

Back in the here and now, Taylor decides she'll have to assess gym options, but if she can't afford to join one, all the walking she'll be doing will surely count as exercise.

Now completely stuffed from her first official meal in Barcelona, Taylor pushes the plates away from her and continues to sip her wine as she watches the passersby meandering down the street. Young couples walk hand in hand, loads of tourists check out the sights, and native Barcelonans are just now heading out for the night. She lights a cigarette (ashtrays on every table here!), smokes it leisurely, and when she sees the waiter, asks for the check.

After paying and finishing her wine, she reluctantly stands up; the fatigue suddenly hits her like a Mack truck. She walks back to the metro station, double-checks the signs to make sure she's going the right way, and heads underground. The ride is quick, and she feels hazy from the huge meal after so many hours without food, and sleepy from the wine. While Taylor prides herself on her ability to function on little sleep, tonight she can't wait to crawl into bed.

Once she emerges from the metro station, she walks briskly back to the dorm, the neighborhood far less lively than Passeig de Gràcia but still busy, given the hour. She manages the walk from the station to the dorm in thirteen minutes and heads straight to her room. After washing her face and using the bathroom, Taylor collapses into bed, finally succumbing to her jet lag.

The next morning, rays of sun peek through the blinds, hinting at another glorious summer day in Barcelona. It takes Taylor a moment to remember where she is, the surprise of waking up somewhere new taking hold. She stretches and checks the time. She's stunned to realize she slept eleven hours straight through. This is a personal best, she thinks to herself. After washing up, she checks her new cell phone and is thrilled to see that it's fully charged. She wants to call home, but it's around 2 a.m. there, and she doubts her parents want a call at this hour.

Taylor checks her email instead and sees one from her mom. Alyssa thanks her for letting them know she arrived safely and wishes her tons of fun. She also asks her to pick a weekend when she and Taylor's dad can come for a visit. She reminds Taylor that they did the same when her brothers were abroad, and neither of them were "totally mortified by our presence." Taylor laughs at this, remembering stories her brothers shared about those weekends, the drugs they were secretly on, the amounts of alcohol consumed. Speaking of brothers, she's happy to see an email from her eldest brother, Eric. The subject line is "Stuff," and the email contains his "rules of studying abroad in Europe" and basically nothing else. She laughs, remembering him telling her most of this over the phone a few months ago. She reads through the email:

1. Do NOT shroom in Amsterdam. If you do (but really, don't), be with someone you trust and stay in your hostel or wherever. Don't roam around, TRUST ME. Stick to pot there.

2. Mixed drinks in Spain contain 100 times more hard liquor than anywhere else on Earth. Drink with caution.

3. Do NOT leave your drink unattended.

4. Attending class is optional; travel is more important. Find a classmate to swap days with and share notes so you have more time to visit other cities.

5. Barcelona's beaches are topless. But you, as my sister, need to leave your top on.

6. In Paris, pre-game, pre-game, pre-game. Drinks are expensive as hell.

7. Spend time in Athens and then ferry around the islands for
    as long as you can afford. You will never regret Greece.

8. Barcelona, Barca de Salamanca for seafood. The BEST.
    They'll bring out a bottle of liqueur at the end of the meal;
    you can just stay and drink as long as you want.

9. Dudes in Rome have no shame. Proceed with caution and
    stick with friends.

10. I'll send you more advice if I remember any, unlikely but
    possible! Be safe, have fun. I'm so fucking jealous you are
    there. Also, I'm seeing someone; it's getting serious. Be
    prepared to have a sister-in-law in the next few years.

Jesus Christ. Leave it to Eric to drop a bombshell like that in the
last line of an email. Taylor wonders if their parents know about Eric's
newest flame. They certainly haven't mentioned anything to her. As
soon as the hour is acceptable, she plans on calling Eric to see what
the hell is going on. They're pretty close, given the five-year age
difference, and she's stunned that he hasn't mentioned this to her yet.
Now she's wondering what else he's got going on, and if Alex has any
crazy life updates he hasn't shared.

Her relationship with her brother Alex is more complex than her
easygoing camaraderie with Eric. She and Alex are closer in age, so
they often overlapped in school, an awkwardness she and Eric never
had to deal with. Alex also suffers from bipolar disorder, so his mood,
medication, and well-being are a consistent source of anxiety for
everyone in the family. With a few exceptions during high school,
including a bout of mania when he didn't eat or sleep for three days
straight, both his depressive and manic episodes have stabilized. But
Taylor often feels as though she's walking on eggshells around him,
never wanting to do or say anything that might trigger an unwanted
emotion, or worse, an episode. And, while far less serious, Alex has
major "middle-child syndrome"; he enjoys reminding everyone in the

family how much less attention he gets than the golden eldest son or the beautiful baby daughter.

Taylor sighs and feels a sudden appreciation for her parents and how they've raised three kids, one of whom suffers from mental illness, with such a sense of ease. It can't have been easy, and yet they've managed it so well. Good friends helped; she knows that Tanya (Daniel's mom) was the rock that Alyssa needed in some of the most difficult times, and vice versa. She hopes that when, or if, she has kids, she can be the type of mom to her children that her mother has been to her.

All of this sentimentality feels rather heavy for so early in the morning, so Taylor makes a mental note to show her parents some gratitude the next time they speak, then proceeds to eat a few snacks, considering it breakfast (it's nearly lunchtime, after all), pack up her bag, and head over to the University. She's heard through the grapevine that one of the best ways to find apartments is to check the bulletin board postings on campus.

She locks her door and pauses on the balcony for a cigarette. There are a few more people milling about today, but overall, the dorm remains relatively quiet. God, I'd kill for a coffee, Taylor thinks, realizing she's going to need to locate a coffee shop more local than the Starbucks that's a metro ride away. Fortunately, she needn't look too far; there's a snack-bar-type place in the main University building that sells sandwiches, snacks, candy, and coffee.

Taylor orders a café con leche and is surprised by how small it is. But it packs a nice punch, just the jolt of caffeine she needs. She walks around a bit, checking out the study areas and a map of the building. The upper floors are classrooms; the main floor she's currently on consists of lounge-type spaces and a computer lab. There seem to be flyers all over the place, so she starts checking out the various bulletin boards and postings.

Taylor knows exactly what she wants (an apartment in the heart of Eixample, with her own room and her own bathroom, preferably in a building with an elevator). She knows the private bathroom is a stretch, but she's going to try. She's on a budget of 300 euros per month, and that's the maximum. She's aiming for cheaper so she can use her hard-earned money for travel and going out. And although her parents would cover any deficit she may incur, she doesn't dare ask them. While Taylor's family is comfortable financially, they aren't rich by most standards. She's grown up knowing the value of a dollar, with an implicit understanding that her parents would splurge on education, but that was it. If she and her brothers wanted anything fancy, they had to work for it.

With frugality in mind, Taylor tries to keep an open mind as she peruses the available apartments for rent. The first few listings are in the areas surrounding the University, Pedralbes, Poble-sec, Sarrià. All great locations, but not where she wants to be. After extensive searching, she leaves with three different options: one on Carrer de Rosselló in the heart of the Eixample neighborhood; one on Carrer de València, also in Eixample; and another on Carrer dels Còdols, in the Gothic Quarter. The third one is not in her ideal location, but Taylor has done enough research to know that this area could be really cool to live in, despite some impracticalities with transportation to and from school.

After writing down the contact names and numbers for the three apartments, Taylor stops into the snack bar area for a sandwich. For two euros, she's enjoying a tomato and mozzarella on a baguette the size of a Subway foot-long. It's so cheap, and so good, perfect amounts of olive oil to complement the cheese and fresh tomato. And this, from the school's tiny little snack bar. She's beginning to understand how people pack on the pounds while studying abroad in Europe. She eats on one of the benches outside the school. There are a few students socializing and smoking, but all in all it's the type of quiet you'd expect at a college in early August.

Taylor finishes her lunch and starts the quick walk back to the dorm. She's planning on checking the locations of the three apartments on the map and, assuming they're where she thinks they are, calling the numbers and setting up times to see them. First, though, she needs to figure out how to use her new phone. Once she's ensconced back in her dorm room, she settles onto her bed with the phone and instruction manual. Apparently, everyone here uses text messaging to talk with friends and family within Europe. This is a new concept; it sounds to Taylor like sending a short email, but via phone rather than computer.

She's unsure which method, text messaging or calling, to use when reaching out to the contacts listed on the flyers for the apartments. Erring on the old-school side, Taylor opts for phone calls. She starts with the Gothic Quarter apartment, and after some negotiation, the woman who answers agrees to speak Spanish rather than Catalan. It turns out she has already rented out the room to someone, and they're moving in next week. Strike one. Maybe this is for the best, she thinks, knowing she wasn't totally sold on that neighborhood anyway.

Next, she calls the Carrer de Rosselló apartment and gets a voicemail. It's a young-sounding woman who speaks Spanish, and Taylor leaves a message explaining her interest in the room. She sends a follow-up text with her contact information, then proceeds to call the apartment on Carrer de València. Another voicemail, this one belonging to a stern-sounding older man. Again, she leaves a message and follows up with a text message.

She loves this text messaging but realizes quickly that she needs to limit the number she sends out each month. Checking the time, Taylor decides it's late enough in New York to call Eric and get the scoop on his mystery girlfriend. She calls his mobile, unsure whether he'll be at home or work at this early hour.

"Hello?" Eric answers wearily, momentarily confused by the international phone number that's popped up on his caller ID.

"Eric! It's Taylor. I got your email. Oh my God, I cannot believe you are seriously seeing someone," Taylor blurts out.

Laughing, he responds, "I am, and I'll tell you all about her. I'm glad you got my email. That's all extremely sound advice, by the way. Don't forget any of it, okay? So! Tell me about Barcelona."

Taylor gives a brief synopsis of her first twenty-four hours in the city and explains that she needs to find a place to live before she can feel settled and relaxed enough to properly explore and enjoy the city. After which she continues, "Okay, enough about me . . . so you're seeing someone and it's serious enough that you're thinking about marriage?! How long has this been going on? What's her name? Do Mom and Dad know? Because they didn't mention a word to me about this."

Taylor can practically hear Eric smile through the phone and across the Atlantic. "Her name is Lauren, and she's incredible. We met at a happy hour at some Mexican place with the best margaritas. I'll take you there whenever you come to visit. Anyways, it's been like six months and we're talking about moving in together. Mom and Dad don't know yet, so don't spill the beans. I don't need them meddling, you know."

"They won't meddle. Do you really think they give a shit what any of us are doing, as long as we're safe and not asking them for money? You have to tell them, six months is a long time, especially for you. Does Alex know?" Taylor asks.

"Good point on the 'rents. But still. Alex knows; he's come out with us a few times and they hit it off really well. Surprisingly," Eric adds, which makes Taylor laugh; she was thinking the exact same thing before Eric said it. Alex is a tough one to impress. He continues, "Lauren's an only child, so she was really happy to meet Alex and really wants to meet you, too. I can't wait for you to meet her, Taylor. She's so fun. I've told her all about you."

"I can't wait to meet her, and you sound super happy. Wow, this is a lot to take in. How is Alex? I need to call him and check in."

"He's great, from what I can tell. Taking his meds, seeing his psychiatrist, doing what he needs to do to stay on track. First-year law school is a bitch, so hopefully he can keep his shit together. But New York fits him like a glove. He's been everywhere, has a lot of good friends, and we all know he graduated with stellar grades," Eric says with a hint of sarcasm.

"Oh, I know all about his grades." Taylor laughs; Alex's GPA from undergrad being the constant source of pride for Taylor's parents over the past three months. "Eric, my phone just buzzed, which I think means I got a text message, which hopefully means one of the apartment rentals I called is responding, so I should go. But thanks for your helpful tips, and I can't wait to meet Lauren."

"Same here, and promise me you won't shroom in Amsterdam! From firsthand experience, I can tell you it's a bad idea. Be safe, and call me anytime if you need anything, okay? Love you, little T."

"I promise," Taylor laughs. "Love you. Bye!"

Wow . . . Eric in love. He's always been the guy with the short attention span when it comes to dating. He's tall and handsome and successful, so he attracts women but tends to lose interest quickly. A bit of a player, actually, if Taylor is being honest with herself. But he's got a heart of gold and would literally take a bullet for any member of his family, so to hear him so happy makes Taylor smile. "That bitch had better not break his heart," she mutters to herself.

She checks the face of her phone and sees that she does, in fact, have a new text message. It's from Carla, the woman renting out the room in the apartment on Carrer de Roselló. Taylor can come by tonight at 6 p.m. to see the place. Yes! This is a start. She responds to Carla and immediately starts researching the area. It's near the Hospital Clínic metro station, which is a relatively easy commute to school. It's a stone's throw from her beloved Passeig de Gràcia, so shopping, restaurants, and bars would all be at her fingertips.

After a good chunk of time studying her map, Taylor starts feeling antsy. She takes a shower, a long hot one, shaving her legs for the first time in at least four days. It feels heavenly. She lets her hair air-dry, applies lotion to her freshly shaved legs, and starts putting on makeup. She decides that after last night's long and peaceful sleep, she's going out tonight. She reasons she can see the apartment at 6 p.m., do some window shopping in the surrounding neighborhood, grab dinner somewhere, and then head to a dance club. There are few things in life that Taylor loves more than dancing her ass off to great music. She realizes that, without a wing-woman, she'll need to be careful. She's certainly not against hooking up with a guy if she meets someone, but she knows enough to use some discretion before heading home with some random guy.

Before venturing out to see the apartment, Taylor calls home and catches her parents before they head off to work. She fills them in on everything (with the exception of Eric's love life and her actual plans for the evening) and thanks them for allowing her this opportunity to be here. Alyssa and John are thrilled to hear from their only daughter and repeatedly remind her to be careful and have fun. After lots of head-nodding and eye-rolling to herself, they finally end the call. Why is it that speaking to parents, whether over the phone or in person, inevitably ends up with the child rolling their eyes and feeling perpetually annoyed? Is this universal? Taylor actually really likes her parents, and yet they still manage to drive her batshit crazy.

Already a little after 5 p.m., Taylor decides to head out. She's dressed on par for a night out, wearing a cute and very short sundress, high wedge heels, and a sweater draped over her arm in case it gets chilly later. Her blonde hair cascades over her shoulders, and she has extra mascara on to highlight her shockingly blue eyes. She stuffs a pair of comfortable flip-flops in her bag in case the heels prove to be more than her feet can handle. She walks to the metro station, enjoying the late-day sunshine on her face, soaking in the heat. Taylor has a fleeting moment of appreciation for her independent nature; most of her friends would balk at the thought of going out alone, but she is excited by the unlimited opportunities that await her in this fabulous new city.

Upon emerging from the underground at the Hospital Clínic station, Taylor is turned around a bit, unsure of which direction she's facing. She resists the urge to pull out her map and instead just starts walking, looking at the street signs and trying to figure it out. She's still got thirty minutes before seeing the apartment and, since she's in the neighborhood, decides to walk past the apartment on Carrer de Valencia to pass the time.

After walking a handful of blocks from the metro station, she lands upon Carrer de Valencia, but now has to figure out the cross streets. Map time, Taylor decides, feeling like the ultimate nerd and tourist. She checks the name of the cross street on the map and realizes she is only one block off. She continues walking, passing mom-and-pop tapas bars, a pharmacy, and some small, trendy-looking stores. Lots of potential on this cute street.

She's feeling optimistic until she arrives at the number from the listing. The only dumpy building she's seen thus far! It's not awful but definitely lacks the splendor she'd been imagining. The building looks to have about ten floors, and the façade is in rough shape. Overall, the street and the neighborhood are a nine out of ten, but the building itself, maybe a three?

Trying not to feel defeated, Taylor checks the time and realizes she's due to see the Roselló apartment in ten minutes. She picks up her pace and arrives there with two minutes to spare. This street is similar to Carrer de Valencia, although with fewer shops and more residential in feel. There is an internet café a block from the apartment building, which is a huge selling point. By not living on campus, Taylor knows she'll be sacrificing internet access in whatever apartment she lands in.

This building is fine, she decides. Brick, with six stories, a decent façade, and, from what she can tell, a clean lobby and mailbox area. Taylor texts Carla to let her know she's here, and almost immediately a beautiful woman, maybe thirty-five, appears and opens the door. As Carla lets Taylor into the lobby, she makes a mental note of the layout: mailboxes on one side, and a mosaic wall on the other.

Carla begins speaking extremely fast, almost manic Spanish, to Taylor. Carla explains that she and her boyfriend own this apartment but live elsewhere, so they rent it out to exchange students or young professionals. The apartment has three bedrooms and one bathroom (so much for her own bathroom). As of now, there is only one bedroom occupied, a young gay British man named Nicholas, who is rarely home, usually either out on the town or spending long hours pursuing his doctoral degree. She doesn't specify in what, and Taylor doesn't press for details.

Carla points out the elevator (check!), but since the apartment is only on the second floor, they take the stairs. Apparently, Nicholas is on holiday in the Canary Islands with his family and won't be back until later in August. Carla opens the door to a large living space, encompassing the living and dining rooms, and Taylor spots a little balcony at the end of the room. To her right is a tiny bedroom, tiny to the point that she's unsure if her suitcases would even fit within its four walls. Carla shows her a small kitchen, complete with a washing machine (but no dryer!), the remaining two bedrooms, and the bathroom.

It is clean, there are ashtrays scattered about indicating that smoking inside is allowed, books line the built-in bookcases on the walls, and the rent is only 200 euros per month, a fraction of what she'd be paying to stay in the dorms (or likely anywhere else for that matter). Taylor asks Carla whether moving in in early September is an option, and if she could stay until the end of next May, possibly even into June. Carla thinks for a moment and nods in the affirmative. To reserve the space, she'd collect September's rent up front. She would then provide Taylor with a key, and they'd be in touch as needed. Taylor agrees immediately. Something about the apartment just feels right. And to have a gay roommate who she wouldn't need to worry about hitting on her, and British to boot? Carla and Taylor agree to meet up tomorrow, as Taylor doesn't have enough cash on her, and Carla needs to make a copy of the key.

On her way out of the building, Taylor feels giddy with excitement. She snaps a picture of the exterior of the building, knowing that she'll want to keep this memory with her for years to come. She has managed to find an apartment in a foreign city all by herself, and in record time. Despite her innate independence, this feels momentous, and she decides to hit up a local tapas bar for a celebratory drink.

It's just shy of seven p.m. at this point, and people seem to be enjoying the gorgeous weather and making the most of happy hour this Thursday evening. Taylor finds a cute little spot on a corner not far from her future apartment and slides onto a barstool. The crowd is young, but the bartender appears to be about a hundred years old. He points to an easel above the bar, on which she sees a list of drinks and tapas, the prices so low she does a double take. She orders a rum and coke from the old man and watches him fill a tall glass nearly halfway with rum, then fill the rest with a splash of coke and some ice. Jesus, Taylor thinks, her brother wasn't kidding about the drinks here. She sips slowly at her cocktail and people-watches a bit, smoking a cigarette just for something to occupy her while she peers around.

As much as Taylor enjoys her alone time, she's not actually used to having so much of it and suddenly feels mildly awkward as she eyes groups of friends engaged in loud, boisterous chatter. It's the opposite of how she felt just an hour ago, when she was basking in the freedom of solo exploration. She suddenly wishes her friends were sitting next to her, gossiping and laughing.

Rather than feel sorry for herself, Taylor pulls out her guidebook again and decides she's going to hit up Maremagnum later tonight; it's a fun, albeit touristy, spot near Port Vell with shops, bars, and clubs. Is it the most authentic place to go? Definitely not. But from what she's read, it's a guaranteed good time, with fun music and an eclectic crowd from all over the world.

After deciding on her destination for the night, Taylor gets pulled into her guidebook, learning about the coolest architecture in the city and already planning tomorrow's sightseeing. A few minutes later, she looks to her right, a few barstools away from her, and sees a young (mid-twenties?) man sitting there, khakis on, collar of his shirt unbuttoned, looking as though he'd just left a long day at the office. His hair is dark, almost black, and his olive skin had clearly enjoyed a healthy dose of Mediterranean sun over the summer. Taylor realizes she is basically staring right at him. He must sense that she's looking at him, as he turns his gaze toward her and smiles.

About two minutes later, the bartender hands Taylor another rum and coke and informs her that it is compliments of the young man seated "allí." Already flushed from the stiff first drink, Taylor finds herself blushing the color of ripe tomato and beginning to perspire. She looks over at him and smiles, thanking him by mouthing, "gracias." Before losing her nerve, Taylor walks over to him, extends her hand, and says, "Mucho gusto, me llamo Taylor."

Clearly taken aback by her quick and easy Spanish, he replies, "My pleasure, bella, my name is Manuel." His English, while heavily accented, is quite good, but Taylor continues speaking in Spanish.

After an hour of flirty and surprisingly intimate conversation (she's already told him all about her family and childhood, for Christ's sake!), Taylor and Manuel decide to stay where they are and order tapas and more drinks. Talking about their pasts while simultaneously seeing a potential future in the other, Taylor is feeling sparks for sure. Manuel orders a ton of tapas for them to share, without any input from Taylor, which would usually annoy the hell out of her, but she finds herself accepting it with him. She assumes it's a cultural rather than misogynistic thing.

Manuel is twenty-six years old; he works in finance and grew up here in Barcelona. He spent a semester in London during university and has been taking English classes since primary school. He is, like Taylor, also the youngest of three siblings, and once Manuel left for university, his parents moved south and are spending their golden years in Málaga. He lives here in the neighborhood and has already dropped subtle hints about showing Taylor what his apartment looks like.

He's also devastatingly handsome, and Taylor feels young and immature around him, these feelings enhanced by the six-year age difference. But he is kind, smart, funny, and she finds herself able to talk to him with ease. They eat, drink, and chat without interruption, and before Taylor realizes it, it is already 10:30 p.m., and she's got to pee. She leaves Manuel and heads to the restroom, where she checks her hair and makeup, adds a bit of lip gloss, and walks back to her barstool. Manuel watches her cross the room, and they lock eyes and smile. He puts his hand on her back and guides her into her seat, a fresh cocktail waiting for her.

They drink for a while longer and eventually pay the bill, which Manuel insists on paying, despite Taylor's objections. She asks him if he'd like to join her at Maremagnum, and he laughs a bit before telling her, "If you want to go dance, sweetheart, I will take you somewhere far better to dance."

Before Taylor can fully process what's going on, they're in a taxi, heading to some trendy dance club that is off the grid and, apparently, so exclusive that it is "invite-only." They sit hip to hip in the taxi, and Manuel begins to feel her thighs, his hand moving dangerously close to her underwear. She laughs nervously and hopes the driver doesn't notice, although this must happen all the time. Taylor briefly studies his profile: dark, almost black hair; dark brown eyes; tanned skin; strong jawline. "And on my second night here," she thinks to herself. Not bad.

Just a few minutes later, they arrive at an industrial-looking building in the nearby neighborhood of El Raval. There's a queue outside with cool-looking Spaniards smoking and chatting while they wait. Manuel pays the taxi fare, pulls Taylor's hand, and helps her out of the car with an ease suggesting they have known one another for years rather than just a few hours. He places his hand on the small of her back, and they line up at the end of the line. After where his hands were during the ride, Taylor wonders what else may happen. They both light cigarettes and resume chatting, standing extremely close together, his hands occasionally grazing various parts of her body, but so lightly that it gives her chills and makes her want more. He's about the same height as Taylor with her heels on, so probably around six feet, one or two inches. She's always relieved when a guy she likes is taller than her; given her propensity for wearing high heels, it makes it easier if she isn't towering over her love interest.

The queue moves quickly, and they soon enter a dark subterranean lounge area with music blasting. The current song is some bizarre remix of Madonna's "Like a Prayer," and Taylor quickly feels at home. Manuel leads her to the bar, where he pushes through the throngs of people and orders them drinks. He waves to another guy across the bar, presumably one of his friends, who calls them over. Manuel gives him the "one minute" signal, and then swiftly takes Taylor by the arm and out to the dance floor. The rest of the night is a messy, sweaty blur, complete with what feels like hours of dancing among hundreds of other messy, sweaty clubbers, and a lot of making out with Manuel.

Finally, at around 4 a.m., Taylor hits a wall and declares herself ready to go. If she isn't in her bed in the next fifteen minutes, she's worried she'll fall asleep in the club, or on the street corner, for that matter. She's been drinking all night and tells Manuel she needs to leave. He is in no rush to leave the club, and rather than try to go home with her, as Taylor expected, he suggests they exchange numbers. Relieved (but, if she's being honest, mildly disappointed that he didn't even try to take her home), Taylor gives him her number and vice versa. He walks her to the street, kisses her one final time, running his hands through her sweaty hair as he does so. Once they pull apart, he smiles at her and tells her he will call her soon. He helps her into a cab, and she is zoomed back to the calm of her dorm, where, after clumsily paying her taxi fare and walking up to her room, she falls into bed.

The next morning, or rather early afternoon, is a painful one. Taylor guzzles water and takes Advil, uses the bathroom, and crawls back into bed. She's been hit by jet lag, a hangover, and exhaustion all at once. So much for her architectural sightseeing plans for the day. She soothes her pain by thinking about last night and drifts back to sleep with sexy Manuel on her mind. She wakes up again a while later, and one of her favorite Counting Crows lyrics comes to mind: "Well, I woke up in mid-afternoon 'cause that's when it all hurts the most." So apropos. In that moment, it feels as though that line was written by Adam Duritz for her current state.

After bumming around and trying to feel human again, Taylor forces herself to eat, continues drinking water, and drags herself into the shower. She panics and remembers she's supposed to meet Carla again this evening, pay her first month's rent, and get the key to the apartment. Frantically, Taylor checks her phone and sees that Carla has asked her to come by at 7 p.m., fortunately still a few hours away.

There is also a text message from Manuel, which makes her smile. He asks if he can take her for dinner tonight. An early dinner, he says, "Is 9:30 p.m. ok?"

Taylor laughs at his idea of early and responds that yes, that would be lovely. She's happy to have something to do after wasting the day away, hungover and exhausted.

After Taylor finally gets herself dressed and applies some makeup, she checks her email and sends hellos to her family and some friends she's planned to meet up with in various cities across Europe in the upcoming month, inquiring about their plans and schedules so she can begin to solidify her travel itineraries. At 6:30 p.m., she departs for the metro station and, after emerging above ground, ducks into an ATM to obtain the money for Carla, plus some extra to pay for dinner tonight. Manuel told her to meet him at Barca de Salamanca, a seafood restaurant by the beach; ironically enough, it's the same place her brother Eric told her to be sure to eat at. She can't wait to tell him that his favorite restaurant in Barcelona is also popular among the locals.

At 7 p.m. sharp, Taylor meets Carla in the lobby once again, and they go upstairs to what will be her new home in just a few weeks. She can move in on September 1st. Carla gives Taylor Nicholas's mobile number and tells her that she gave Taylor's number to him as well. The exchange is brief but polite, and Carla gives Taylor a hug on her way out, encouraging her to reach out anytime. Taylor thanks her new landlord, tucks the key into a secure pocket in her purse, and heads out, relieved not only to have a place to live but also to have an older woman she can reach out to should the need arise.

To kill time before meeting up with Manuel, Taylor pops into a few stores in the neighborhood, already sensing that her Ralph Lauren junior's department sundresses and denim skirts with cute tank tops are not helping her blend in, per se. She's been observing the women here, who all appear almost impossibly thin and petite, usually clad in tight jeans and tight tops despite the heat. And the shoes! Not a flip-flop in sight, much to her dismay. She buys a few tops and a new pair of sunglasses from Zara, which she's never heard of but which has some great options. After paying for her goodies, it's nearly 8:45 p.m., so she decides to head down to the beach and find the restaurant.

It's a quicker metro ride than she anticipated, so Taylor still has thirty minutes to spare. She walks toward the restaurant and stops into a little beach bar along the way. *A rum and coke will calm my nerves and cure the traces of the hangover from last night's excess,* she thinks. She sits at the bar nursing her cocktail, despite having sworn to herself earlier in the day that she'd never even look at alcohol again. She lights a cigarette and chats with the bartender, who is from Scotland, of all places. It feels reassuring to speak in English for a few minutes, and she gets the scoop on the beachside bars from her new Scottish pal, whose name is Finn. He explains that this particular bar is pretty quiet until 11 p.m., when people begin to finish up with dinner; from then on, it's packed.

Finn also gives her some intel on being an obvious foreigner in the city, with his red hair and beard, he sticks out like a sore thumb, and they exchange numbers before Taylor departs to meet Manuel. She promises Finn that she'll be sure to come back to his bar soon, which is true; she likes the casual vibe here, and they part ways.

She's feeling more relaxed after the drink but still a bit apprehensive. What if the conversation doesn't flow like it did last night? She felt a major spark, did Manuel feel the same? He definitely seemed to, but maybe he was wasted. Would the age difference be an issue? Taylor takes a deep breath to calm her mind and uses the restaurant's bathroom quickly, reapplying her lipstick before meeting Manuel. When she emerges back into the evening air, she looks around for her date with the intense and rather uncomfortable sensation of being watched. There is a line at the hostess stand, with loud, gregarious waiters darting effortlessly between people delivering food and drinks to the tables.

After about a minute of standing and waiting, Taylor feels strong male arms around her waist. She startles, then turns around to face Manuel. Even better looking than she remembered! He kisses her on both cheeks, takes her hand, and leads her to an outdoor table. He's already ordered drinks, a beer for himself and a rum and coke for Taylor. As they settle in and talk, Taylor resists the urge to pinch herself. Here she is, barely forty-eight hours into her journey, having dinner with an insanely handsome, older, kind Spanish man. She actually has to hold back a giggle and refrain from asking their waiter to snap a picture of them.

Food comes and goes at a rapid pace, each dish better than the last. Drinks are drunk, cigarettes smoked between courses. Their conversation is easy and flirty, and Manuel is not at all shy about using his hands to display his affection for Taylor. She is happy to reciprocate and is more than pleased when he, with an unexpected air of shyness, asks her to come back to his apartment for the night. He's quick to add that it's fine if she doesn't want to, but he enjoys her company and would love for her to come see where he lives.

Now that the future of the evening has been settled upon, Taylor and Manuel wrap up their meal, and Taylor is delighted when the jovial waiter brings them an unidentified bottle of what tastes like Schnapps and a plate of pastries, on the house. Just like her brother told her! They enjoy some of both and head out, stopping for a last drink at what Taylor now calls "Finn's bar," after her new favorite bartender, and for the fact that she has no idea what the place is actually called.

Taylor feels people staring at them as they leave the restaurant and walk along the beach. Manuel is the epitome of tall, dark, and handsome, and Taylor's light skin, light hair, towering height, and clearly non-European wardrobe make them quite the (beautiful, if oddly matched) sight. Taylor feels a sense of security walking with Manuel; he knows the city, he belongs here, and at this moment, she has the wonderful sensation that they have this big, beautiful Barcelona all to themselves.

"Back so soon?" Finn bellows enthusiastically as Taylor and Manuel break through the masses of people at the bar. He was right, this place has really picked up over the past several hours and is now officially packed. "Who's your friend, then?" Finn asks with a wink.

Taylor introduces the two men, and Finn delivers their drinks, apologizing for not having more time to chat; he's swamped with drink orders. Finn disappears to the other end of the bar to serve his thirsty customers, and Taylor and Manuel toast "Salud" to one another. After a few minutes of talking, listening to the bumping music (a Michael Jackson remix at the moment, Taylor wonders if they only play remixes here), and watching the crowd, Manuel puts his hands on Taylor's shoulders and pulls her close, asking if she wants to head back to his apartment. She nods affirmatively, and they finish what's left of their drinks. Finn, while busy tending bar, runs over as he sees them preparing to leave, and Taylor bids him adieu. She promises to come back soon, and her new friend blows her a kiss goodbye.

The rest of the evening (by now, early morning) unfolds in a nearly picture-perfect way. Taylor and Manuel spend the night together, and she is pleased to find out that he is very much a gentleman in bed. After arriving at his apartment, he tidies up the bedroom before bringing Taylor in. She is impressed by how clean the place is; this is a legit apartment, a far cry from the messy dorm rooms and filthy frat houses she is used to visiting. Suffice it to say, she falls asleep blissfully satisfied and content.

When Taylor wakes up, the other side of the bed is empty. A glass of water is perched on the nightstand, and she takes a giant sip, then proceeds to the bathroom. The apartment is empty, and she starts to panic. She checks her phone and doesn't see any alerts. Just as she starts fumbling with her phone, preparing to call Manuel, she hears keys unlocking the door, and he enters carrying two coffee cups and a bag of pastries, with a big smile on his face.

"Bella, el desayuno!" he says kindly and gives her a big hug and kiss.

Taylor is beginning to wonder why he isn't heading to work before realizing that it's Saturday.

They sit at his kitchen table and enjoy their coffee and breakfast, talking about the day and what to do. Manuel asks if he can take her to the beach later, and she's more than happy to oblige. For now, though, all she wants to do is go back to the dorm and take a shower (and brush her teeth). As they finish their coffee, Manuel looks at her seriously, his dark, soulful brown eyes taking her all in. Taylor is familiar with this look. This usually means "we need to talk" and either ends with "this isn't going anywhere" or, more likely for Taylor, "I want to be exclusive; will you be my girlfriend?", to which the answer has historically been no. She likes to keep her options open, and in the rare instances of having a boyfriend for more than a month, she's felt tied down and as though her freedom was being infringed upon. Daniel was the one guy she actually wanted to date but couldn't, but their shared history and their one-night stand certainly complicated her feelings about him.

Fortunately, Manuel just lets her know that he is going to visit his parents in Málaga in a few days and stay for much of August. No discussions on exclusivity, no ending things before they have had time to begin. He appears concerned that she may be upset without him around, and she reassures him that she is actually planning on doing some travel herself, and by no means should he feel bad or worry about her. Manuel's face relaxes into a smile upon hearing this, and Taylor is touched by his concern, not used to a guy really caring about her well-being after only a few days. She's not sure whether it's the age difference or the fact that he's Spanish and better mannered than his American counterparts, but whatever the reason, she's happy about it. Taylor agrees to meet him that afternoon to spend some time at the beach.

She hurries back to the dorm, taking the metro despite really wanting to just fall into a taxi. She's grateful that she stuffed her flip-flops into her bag again last night; not only do they provide much-needed solace to her feet, but they also minimize the "walk of shame" look she's got going on. Four-inch heels in broad daylight are suspect no matter where on earth one may be. Taylor arrives back at the dorm, showers, and collapses onto her bed, still in a towel. After responding to a few emails from friends, she starts searching her drawers for her bikinis. She's cognizant of the fact that many women on the beach go topless here, but already knows she'd be humiliated doing so. Nevertheless, she sorts through a handful of swimsuits, chooses her most flattering bikini, throws a sundress over it, and lays back down on her bed.

She's sore and exhausted, but in the most delightful way. Taylor's first few days in Barcelona have been a literal whirlwind, and she spends a few quiet moments just reflecting on the time she's spent with Manuel. His personality is warm and genuine; he's truly a stunning man, and he knows the city inside and out. Her mind starts to wander again. Does she want a boyfriend while she's here? Will that interfere with her plans and making friends at school? Will dating Manuel be a distraction and alleviate the feelings she still has for Daniel? She realizes she's getting ahead of herself; she's only known Manuel for two days, but gets the sense that he is really into her, beyond just hooking up.

With a weary sigh, she's up again and packing her bag for the beach. Taylor and Manuel meet at Barceloneta Beach and spend a beautiful late afternoon soaking up the sun and dipping their toes in the Mediterranean, the cool blue water the perfect antidote to the burning sand on their feet. She finally breaks out her camera, with hesitation, not wanting to embarrass herself or Manuel, and they ask a guy sitting on a towel nearby to take a picture. He snaps a few photos, and Taylor is already looking forward to showing Manuel off to her friends once she's back in the States. And despite Manuel's suggestion to remove the top of her bikini, she's managed to keep it on and avoid the embarrassment she knows would haunt her if she were to take it off and join the dozens of other women who are brazenly topless.

At some point, Taylor dozes off while lying on her towel in the sand; she wakes up to see Manuel looking at her adoringly. She hates that word, the cheesiness of it, but that's the only way to describe the way he's gazing at her.

"Ugh, I must look awful!" she laughs, covering her face with her hands.

He hands her a cold bottle of water and kisses her, telling her, "No, bella, not awful, perfecta."

Manuel pulls Taylor into him, so they are facing each other with their arms and legs entangled. Taylor closes her eyes again and revels in this moment; she can't recall a time when she's ever felt this content. On a beach in the Barcelona sun, with a gorgeous, kind man literally wrapped around her... what could surpass this? Only one other moment comes to mind, and that was in Daniel's dorm room last year. Taylor quickly pushes the thought out of her mind. They remain like this for a bit before Manuel asks her what she's doing later, and if she would like to accompany him and some of his friends for dinner. He reminds her that he's leaving tomorrow to visit his parents and isn't quite ready to say goodbye to her.

Taylor considers the offer, and despite wanting nothing more than to stay with him the rest of the night, she has a few concerns. First of all, the logistics: she's in a bikini and sundress with flip-flops and no change of clothes. Second, is she ready to meet his friends? Is this too much, too soon? Before she can overthink it and get lost in her own head, she asks Manuel both of these questions. The logistics turn out to be easy, they are meeting at a restaurant that's a fifteen-minute walk from Taylor's dorm, on Avenida Diagonal. So she will have time to run back and change into a look more appropriate for a Saturday night dinner in one of the chicest cities on the planet.

To the second question, Manuel gives an easy answer: he would love his friends to meet her, as he expects to be seeing a lot of Taylor once he returns from Málaga. It would be great, he reasons, that she meets his pals now. Perfect, Taylor thinks, and gives him a hug. She explains that she needs to go home (home! She can't get over the fact that she is actually here, living in Barcelona) and change clothes. She asks if he wants to meet her at her dorm before dinner for a cocktail. They agree that he will meet her at her place at 8:30 p.m., giving them some time before their 10 p.m. dinner.

Taylor rushes back to the dorm, popping into some local stores to replenish her alcohol and tobacco stash. She reapplies deodorant and makeup, changes her outfit and shoes, and anxiously awaits

Manuel's arrival. At 8:40, he texts her that he's downstairs. She practically skips down to the lobby to meet him, grabs his hand, and brings him back upstairs. He's amused by being in a dorm again, understandable at age twenty-six, but appreciative when Taylor pours him a rum and coke, complete with the ice she just got from the ice machine. It's like a hotel, she thinks to herself upon making this wonderful discovery. Flashbacks to the basketball tournaments of her younger days, when she and her teammates found such joy in staying in shitty chain hotels in random Wisconsin towns. The ice machine brought her right back, and for a split second, she feels a slight twinge of homesickness. But the feeling passes as quickly as it arrived, and she is back in the moment with her sexy Spanish... what? Surely not boyfriend yet. Is lover too cliché? Perhaps, she thinks, but it feels appropriate.

Manuel looks around her minimalist abode, and she's quick to remind him that this is a very temporary home, once she moves into the apartment on Carrer de Roselló, she will add pictures of her friends and family, which are still carefully wrapped and packed in her unopened suitcase. He's far less concerned with Taylor's dorm room than with Taylor herself. Within a few minutes, their clothes are on the floor, and they're going at it, this time by far better than last night, because they are both sober, more or less.

Afterwards, they lay in bed together, breathing heavily, and Taylor mumbles, "Wow," and rolls onto her side, facing Manuel. He wraps his arms around her, and she feels herself nodding off, realizing she'd be perfectly satisfied to fall asleep with him right now and skip another night out. But she rallies, knowing that Manuel is leaving tomorrow and that he wants her to meet his friends. She fixes her makeup (again), gets dressed (again), and they drain their drinks. It's nearly 10 p.m. now, so they begin the walk to dinner, hand in hand.

The restaurant is packed when they arrive, filled with a combination of families finishing up their meals and young, attractive people in their twenties and early thirties just starting their nights. Manuel spots his friends: four men and one woman, who is so insanely chic and perfect, Taylor feels as lanky and awkward as a newborn fawn. Introductions are made; it turns out the other woman at the table is the girlfriend of Manuel's best friend from their university days. They've all known one another for years, so Taylor does her best to listen to their stories and observe, fully cognizant of the seemingly universal dislike of Americans that is so prevalent around the globe at this moment in history. She tries not to be too loud and is sure to mention her dislike of the current Bush administration, which immediately pleases the group, allowing her fears to dissipate a bit.

They drink, eat, and have discussions about politics in Europe that are far above Taylor's head, so when she is finally asked about her upbringing and life in America, she is relieved to have a topic she can discuss with ease. She briefly tells them about growing up in Wisconsin (all the snow!), her brothers and parents, and her two years thus far at UNC. She tries to speak quickly, not wanting to bore them. She's so relieved that Manuel's friends are pleasant and kind; she hadn't realized until they arrived at the restaurant how nervous she actually was to meet them.

Throughout dinner, Manuel casually slides his hand up and down her thigh, and she can't help but wonder... is he insatiable? It's only been a few hours since they had sex, and he already seems ready for more. Suffice it to say, he is the most mature sexual partner that Taylor has ever had, so much so that she feels herself getting excited every time his hand caresses her thigh, her mind heading directly back to her bed and what they did earlier in the evening.

By midnight, everyone is done with dinner and preparing to head out to a bar. Taylor is feeling the exhaustion of the past few days creeping up on her and regretfully tells Manuel she's going to head back to the dorm; she doesn't have the energy to be fun and doesn't want to be a burden on the group. He tells her he will accompany her to the dorm and go out from there. Taylor is grateful for this, as she doesn't want to say goodbye to him just yet, especially with his friends as their audience. Before getting up from the table, Taylor tells the group what a fun time she had tonight and thanks them for welcoming her to their meal and being patient while she spoke her American version of Spanish (she may be fluent, but she will never speak with the speed or clarity of the natives). They toast to her with what little remains in their drinks and tell her they look forward to seeing her again. While Manuel pays their portion of the bill and tells his friends he will meet them later, Taylor smokes a cigarette and finishes her sangría.

A brief taxi ride later, they are back at the dorm, and back in Taylor's bed almost immediately. Manuel tells Taylor he could barely keep his hands off her at dinner; Taylor is appreciative that he is feeling the same sparks that she is. After a quick but extremely satisfying round in bed, Manuel kisses her and asks if she wants him to stay longer. Already drifting off, Taylor hugs him and tells him to go out and have fun with his friends. He dresses and promises her that he will be in touch while he's away.

Taylor gets herself ready for bed and falls into a deep sleep, remarkable in its absence of dreams. She wakes up to another sunny Barcelona morning and is happy to be free of a hangover, and to have an entire day to herself to do some sightseeing. And go to Starbucks! She decided at one point the previous day that she would literally travel to the ends of the earth for a mocha Frappuccino. Being that it's a Sunday in August, she's unsure as to what, if anything, will be open today. She's doubtful that any of the museums or Gaudí houses will be open, so she decides on a visit to Park Güell after she's been properly caffeinated.

A quick metro ride lands her on a serene, shady street just off Passeig de Gràcia. She sees the familiar Starbucks sign, and it feels like coming home. And with an outdoor area where everyone is smoking, it's like a dream come true.

She orders, after mentally translating mocha Frappuccino into Spanish, and enjoys her drink outdoors, smoking and idly perusing her guidebook while eavesdropping on her fellow customers' conversations.

An hour later, she's ready to explore and sets off. She's wearing what may be the most glaringly American outfit possible, straight down to the sneakers and yoga capri pants, but she's dressed for a lot of walking, as this appears to be her best antidote to all the food she's been consuming.

After a longer metro ride, Taylor is let off in the Gràcia neighborhood, and aside from the Asian and Northern European tourists, the area is quiet and calm. She has done a great deal of research on the park and will be submitting a piece on it, which she has already entitled "An Oasis of Calm in the World's Most Cosmopolitan City – Park Güell." She will send this, and as many other articles as she can drum up, to the school paper back at UNC. She has also, through Daniel's family connections (nepotism! much to Taylor's dismay and utter disapproval, but Daniel's mother insisted, and her own mother insisted), somehow gotten an "internship" and will also be submitting all of her school paper pieces to a very hip new travel website owned by Daniel's grandparents' conglomerate. The internship is paid (and high paying, relatively speaking), and aside from an editor, she doesn't officially report to anyone; she just submits her writing and gets paid by the word. The goal, of course, is to do such a killer job that she gets hired as a full-time staff member after college graduation, but that seems so far away that Taylor can barely even think about it.

It turns out that Daniel's super-rich grandparents own a publishing company that they're desperately trying to bring into the 21st century by gaining a better web presence for their historically print-only magazines. Although neither Tanya nor Daniel have much of a relationship with his late father's parents, Tanya insisted on reaching out to them when she learned of Taylor's interest in writing. And sure enough, they pulled through. Taylor's mother made some snide remark along the lines of how they show up financially but never emotionally; still bitter that they basically estranged themselves from their own son (Daniel's father), and never made much of an effort to get to know Daniel, her dear friend's son.

In any case, Taylor is certainly benefitting from this connection and has already sent Daniel's grandparents a thank-you note on her fanciest stationery, at Alyssa's insistence.

"It's all about the connections," her mother always says, sure to elicit eye rolls from Taylor and her brothers. They all know she is right, of course, but would rather die than admit it.

Taylor arrives at Park Güell, pays her entrance fee, and starts exploring the park, happy that she chose her comfy sneakers over a more stylish option. After an hour of wandering about, checking out and snapping pictures of the main focal points, such as the Dragon Staircase and the Porch of the Laundry, she pulls a towel from her bag and settles down on the grass in the "Gardens of Austria" section of the park. She removes her notebook and pen from her bag and starts writing about the unique areas of the park and the history underlying each of them. She's not sure how long she's writing for, but suddenly she's four pages into her rough draft, enough that she can start typing it up, and with a few edits and fact-checking, it will be ready to send off for submission.

Once Taylor returns to reality and looks up, she realizes the crowd has thinned out considerably; the tourists are likely heading back to their hotels for a siesta before dinner. Taylor stuffs her notebook and pen into her bag, pulls out her water bottle and some snacks that she brought along, and enjoys the gorgeous view. She decides to call home and check in with her parents, assuming they'll be awake by now. As is so often the case when young adult children speak with their mom and dad, the call on Taylor's end is filled with eye rolls and the obligatory promises of being careful, getting enough sleep, not drinking too much, etc. None of which, Taylor realizes, she's actually been doing. But her parents are happy to hear from her and happy that she is already writing and sightseeing. She omits the budding relationship (if that is, in fact, what it is) with Manuel, not ready for a lecture or additional questions.

After hanging up, she feels guilty at the reprieve she feels by saying goodbye to her parents and ending the call. They mean well, Taylor knows this rationally, but she's always had a tough time with being treated as an incompetent kid, even when she was one (and, in some ways, continues to be). Her independent, can-do attitude makes it hard for her to deal when people baby her. Her closest friends understand this and have learned to behave accordingly, respectful of her independent nature. But by virtue of being the youngest (and only female) child of the family, her parents and brothers are always a little too worried about her.

She starts packing up her things, shaking the grass off her towel and folding it back into her bag. The whole night is open in front of her. Begrudgingly, she feels a pang of missing Manuel. Too soon to get attached, she reminds herself... he lives here, and she is, despite already beginning to feel like a true resident, merely a visitor to this glorious city. With a sigh, she finds her way back to the metro station, and right before heading down the steps, feels her phone vibrate with a new text message.

M: Hola bella, qué tal? Ya estoy en Málaga, espero que estés bien. Te echo de menos. Un beso, Manuel

Taylor feels that rush of joy that accompanies such interactions in a new relationship, and she's delighted to know that Manuel is thinking of her. She decides to wait until she's back at the dorm to respond, letting him sweat a little, she thinks, laughing to herself. After the metro ride and walk back to the dorm, she sits down on her desk chair, exhausted from all the sun she got today, and starts mentally composing her response to Manuel's text message. She responds, plugs her phone into the charger, and takes a quick shower.

Before her thoughts on Park Güell get lost, she sits down at her computer and types out her writing from today, adding in a little history and editing as needed. An hour and a half later, she's pleased with the piece. She saves it, sends it to the school paper, sends it to the travel website editor, and takes a deep breath. First piece done, and within her first week. Not bad. She checks her inbox and sees some emails from Katie and Lindsay, both of whom are packing and preparing to come over to their respective European cities. She smiles and responds, giving them packing advice, providing a glossy overview of the time she's spent with Manuel, and finally asking them where she should go before school starts.

They respond almost simultaneously, both with the same answer... Ibiza! Taylor laughs; of course, they both recommend the world's most notorious party island. What did she expect? She thinks about it for a few minutes and realizes they have a good point. If she's going to visit an island, it's best to go when it's so hot that walking around the ruins of a dusty old city would be painful. Better to save the historical and educational city visits for the fall, right? Plus, she knows she can get cheap airfare from Barcelona to Ibiza.

On a whim, Taylor suddenly decides that she will pay Finn a visit at the beachside bar tonight. She reasons she can grab dinner at the bar and run her Ibiza plan by him, knowing that he has likely been there himself, or, at the very least, have some advice or insider info for her.

Taylor dresses quickly and puts on light makeup, misting herself with Clinique Happy perfume as she finishes up in the bathroom. As usual, she throws her guidebook and flip-flops into her bag; the guidebook is a handy diversion for the metro ride or while dining alone, the flip-flops necessary if her heels become insufferable. Just as she's heading out, she feels her phone vibrating and sees an actual call coming in from the U.S. She answers quickly and is happy (and a bit surprised) to hear her brother Alex's voice on the other end. Alex has completed his first year at NYU Law and has been slammed all summer doing an internship, so her contact with him has been limited at best recently.

In actuality, Taylor has a far more complicated relationship with Alex than she does with Eric, despite the fact that she and Alex are closer in age. Given his bipolar disorder, Taylor is far more reserved with Alex than she is with the rest of her family. She is terrified of saying the wrong thing and upsetting him. She recalls some of his "episodes" growing up, and they weren't pretty. His mental illness is always lurking in the back of Taylor's mind, a persistent cause of guilt and concern that she can never shake. She worries about him constantly, so hearing his upbeat voice on the other end of the phone is a huge relief.

"What's up, sis? How's BCN treating you?"

"Alex, hi! How are you? I love it here," Taylor says with a giggle. He tells her about his internship and how relieved he is that it's ending soon, and that he will be able to go to Madison for a week before starting his second year of law school. She fills him in on her adventures (minus the Manuel part) thus far and asks him for his thoughts on Ibiza.

Taylor listens patiently to Alex's concerns about her safety in Ibiza. He ultimately tells her to go, but not until giving her a lecture on the precautions that solo female travelers need to take. Taylor can't help rolling her eyes, but she appreciates his concern and advice. She stifles the urge to tell him, *No shit, dumbass, I'm not completely brain-dead.*

After the Ibiza discussion, Alex asks, "So, have you heard about Eric's golden girl, Lauren?"

"He just told me. He said you guys have met and hit it off. Is that true? Do you actually like her, or is she a total bitch like all of his previous girlfriends? What does she do?" Taylor asks.

Alex laughs his hearty laugh and tells Taylor, "I barely know her. She seems fine, but she definitely has the potential to be a total bitch, given her snooty roots. But she's hot and, from what I can tell, treats Eric really well. She's more fun than his usual girlfriends; she goes out a lot and drinks, and doesn't constantly make snide remarks about everyone else. So that's an improvement from his usual type. They seem to be getting serious, but he told me not to talk to Mom and Dad about it just yet. She works in fashion merchandising, or something. Sounds like a fake job. I mean, who actually works in fashion?"

"Yeah, he told me the same thing about not telling Mom and Dad. What do you mean by her snooty upbringing?" Taylor asks.

"She's from Greenwich, Connecticut. Need I say more? You know Mom's friend Tanya, that's where her husband was from. And his parents basically disowned him or whatever for not going to an Ivy League school."

Taylor flinches at the mention of Daniel's family and switches the subject as soon as possible.

"Ugh, can you even imagine some Greenwich snob coming to Madison and meeting Mom and Dad? And us?"

Taylor and Alex both burst out laughing.

"So, do you think they'll get married? Live happily ever after?" Taylor asks with a heavy dose of sarcasm.

"Honestly, too soon to tell, but I will keep you in the loop, I promise. In the meantime, take care of yourself and please be careful. I don't always say it, but I love you and worry about you. So, for Christ's sake, don't get blackout drunk, always go out with friends, never ride the subways alone, and don't do anything dangerous or stupid, okay?"

Moved by his concern, Taylor makes the same promise to Alex that she made to Eric just a few days earlier. "I love you too, Alex. Thanks for calling me. It was really good to hear your voice and catch up."

They hang up, reiterating promises to be in touch regularly, and Taylor treks down to the metro station, off to see Finn. But after the conversation with Alex, she now has Daniel on her mind... again. The guy she's known literally her entire life has been consuming an unhealthy amount of her thoughts ever since that fateful night last January, over a year and a half ago. She tells herself to get a grip and shakes away the thoughts, instead focusing on her new apartment, Barcelona, and the upcoming school year. The thrill of anticipation from what lies ahead for Taylor is overwhelming, and despite her best efforts, a grin forms on her face. *I can't believe I am really here,* she thinks, not for the first time this week. She takes in the warm Barcelona evening air and once again feels the need to pinch herself to distinguish her current reality from a dream come true.

Snapping out of her reverie, Taylor takes the metro down to the beach area and sidles up to the bar, spotting Finn right away. It's quiet tonight; it's still relatively early, coupled with the fact that it's a Sunday in August. Finn finishes up with the only other customer at the bar and comes over to her.

"You're back!" he exclaims loudly.

"I am. And tonight, I come with questions. Ibiza... have you been? Should I go before school starts? Is there anywhere else you'd recommend I go over Ibiza?" Taylor asks excitedly, pressing her palms down on the bar as she speaks.

"Wow, that's a lot of questions. Let's start properly with a drink. Rum and coke?"

Taylor smiles and nods, and Finn brings her the cocktail and a food menu.

"I have been to Ibiza; it is absolutely amazing. I'd go back in a heartbeat. You should totally go. I'll look back at my travel journal and give you places to stay, eat, and go out."

"Oh my God, that would be great. I would so appreciate that. I want to go somewhere alone before all my friends start showing up in Europe, and I thought Ibiza would be a good choice. It will be a great opportunity to get some writing in. Cheap flights from here, too, and all that. By the way, here's my mobile number," Taylor says, jotting down her number on a scrap of paper from her purse.

Finn takes it and texts her from his phone. "There, now you have mine. I'll send you my recommendations tomorrow, gotta remember where I stashed that old travel journal. It's got everything in there, so whenever you're traveling, hit me up for advice. France, Germany, Italy, Greece, you name it. And everywhere I go, I go on a budget, so you don't have to worry about breaking the bank, as you Americans say."

Taylor fights the urge to jump over the bar and hug him, instead expressing her gratitude verbally with great enthusiasm and placing a food order. Within fifteen minutes, Taylor is staring down a plate of grilled calamari (Finn convinced her to try it over the fried version she's accustomed to) with lemon aioli, and an order of patatas bravas. Both are delicious, and she does her best to eat slowly, but realizes she's barely eaten all day, aside from the Frappuccino and some snacks. Finn refills her drink, and they chat when he isn't busy with customers. After her second rum and coke, she's tired and the place is getting more crowded. She smokes one last cigarette, pays the bill, thanks Finn for his advice, and heads home, excited to plan her Ibiza adventure first thing tomorrow morning.

Upon returning to the dorm, Taylor gets a second wind and is suddenly wide awake. She decides to call Lindsay, who is due to arrive in Rome in just over a week to begin her semester abroad. The two friends have already discussed the possibility of a long weekend somewhere before classes begin, and Taylor is anxious to chat with a friend, email lacking the ability to really get into the nitty-gritty details she has grown accustomed to sharing with her girlfriends.

Lindsay answers on the second ring, sounding perplexed. "Hello?" she asks with caution and a bit of dread.

Taylor laughs. "What's up, biatch? It's Taylor, calling from the world's greatest city!"

"Oh my God, Taylor!" Lindsay shrieks. "Hold on, let me go somewhere else. I'm at the country club with my parents for cocktail hour," Lindsay says with such annoyance that Taylor can practically hear her rolling her eyes across the Atlantic, making her giggle and miss her friend even more. A moment later, the noise on the other side of the phone line subsides, and Lindsay continues, "Ok, I'm outside now. Jesus Christ, it's a fucking sauna here! How's Barcelona? What are you doing calling now? Isn't it the middle of the night? Are you with that guy? What's his name?"

"Easy, tiger," Taylor responds. "I'm alone right now. That guy is Manuel, and no, he's in southern Spain visiting his parents. Tonight, I was visiting a new friend who tends bar at a cute place on the beach. I was, incidentally, asking him about what to do in Ibiza, where I'm heading later this week."

"Ugh, I'm so jealous. Listen to you, you have a friend who 'tends bar.' What are you, suddenly a goddamned expat? And does your new boyfriend know you're running off to Ibiza, the sex capital of the universe? God, I'm stuck in this hellhole for another week; I cannot WAIT to get out of here!"

"You can hold out, Linds, it's just another week. And he's not technically my boyfriend, by the way. It's been like three days. Although I wouldn't be against it, my God, he is insanely gorgeous and kind and smart. Did I mention he's twenty-six? Like, a proper adult," Taylor tells Lindsay.

"You're such a bitch," Lindsay says jokingly. "A few days over there and look at you. You're already coupled up."

"Anyways," Taylor responds, eager to change the subject, "I want to see you as soon as possible. You still up for that trip we talked about? Where should we go? I won't be in my official apartment for a few weeks, otherwise I'd insist that you come here. But we're not allowed to have guests in the dorm, and I doubt you'd want to spend a long weekend sharing my twin bed anyway."

"So, about that. My parents overheard my plan to meet up with you before school starts, and they insisted on treating us to a long weekend in the south of France. It's kind of a midpoint between Barcelona and Rome. So, Nice? Cannes? Saint-Tropez? We can pick anywhere, but they are footing the bill, within reason."

"Lindsay, are you serious? I can't accept that," Taylor says, stunned by this insane gesture of generosity.

"I'm serious, and you'd damn well better, otherwise I'll be all alone in a foreign land," Lindsay says, slurring her words a bit. "And you wouldn't do that to me, Taylor."

"Wow, of course, my dear, I could never leave you to your own devices with a bunch of gazillionaire yacht owners. Jesus, I'm floored. Well, please let your parents know how appreciative I am, okay? I still can't believe this. We're going to have the best time. I wish Katie could come. And, hon, I know it's cocktail hour, but how drunk are you? You sound like you've been drinking for hours."

"I'm on number two, but I haven't eaten today; things were crazy at work, and I had to come here right after I clocked out. Some fancy-pants friend of my parents is receiving a philanthropy award tonight. Like, I should hope he's a philanthropist, for fuck's sake," Lindsay says with a laugh, "the guy is worth like a billion dollars. Speaking of, I've gotta go back inside before they see I've gone missing. But this week we shall plan our romantic weekend on the French Riviera!"

"Lindsay, I can't wait, and please remember to thank your parents! I love you, be safe, and go eat something before you fall down."

Taylor says "ciao" to Lindsay and they hang up, both enthused to see each other. And for their reunion to be taking place in the south of France... this is like a dream come true. Taylor can hardly believe this is happening. Once it sinks in and she's back to reality, Taylor does her nightly routine: washing her face and moisturizing, changing into comfy shorts and a giant T-shirt, and falling into bed with her notebook, jotting down what her first few days in Barcelona have entailed before drifting off to sleep, pen still in hand.

The next several days unfold rather uneventfully. Taylor does lots of walking, sightseeing, and writing about the local spots she's been checking out, including the Gaudí houses and the Sagrada Familia, along with some of the off-the-beaten-path neighborhoods she's visited. She submits her writing work well ahead of her self-imposed schedule.

Using Finn's experience and advice, she manages to secure a four-night stay at a relatively cheap (but supposedly nice-ish) hotel in Santa Eulalia del Río, right near the beach of S'Argamassa on Ibiza. Finn assured her that this is a hotel where the sangria is only a few euros per glass but made with a special variety of citrus that grows exclusively along the Balearic Sea. Plus, he promised that the views are otherworldly, the blues and greens of the sea visible from nearly every spot in the hotel.

On Thursday, August 14th, just eight days after her arrival, Taylor finds herself back at the Barcelona airport, en route to Ibiza. She will soon learn that on this very date a massive blackout has struck the Eastern Seaboard of the United States, leaving her brothers, along with tens of millions of other Americans, literally in the dark. But for now, her mind is blissfully free of worry, and her only concern is finding the gate for her flight.

Chapter 4

August 2003, Ibiza

Taylor and Manuel have been texting up a storm, their messages to each other ranging from the mundane (*Spending the day with my parents on the beach* from Manuel, *Wandering the alleys of the Gothic Quarter, such incredible architecture!* from Taylor) to the risqué (*I can't wait to get my hands on you again, I can't stop thinking about your body* from Manuel, *I just got out of the shower, wish you'd been in there with me* from Taylor).

Every time her phone pings, Taylor feels a rush of adrenaline, hoping it will be a message from Manuel. Despite their physical attraction and chemistry, Taylor is wondering if diving into this headfirst is a wise idea, for myriad reasons. Does he want to be exclusive? And if so, does she? She's only twenty years old, for God's sake. Will he mind her traveling all over the continent on weekends? Will he be jealous, or annoyed that he can only see her when her schedule permits? And what happens when her time here is up?

Taylor shakes her head and pushes her doubts away, focusing instead on finding a good magazine at the airport news kiosk. Grabbing a *Cosmo Español* and a large bottle of water, she makes her way to the gate for the quick flight to Ibiza. As the plane ascends into the perfectly blue sky, Taylor flips through the magazine but ends up dozing off for a few minutes; when she wakes, they are already arriving at Ibiza's airport.

As the small plane taxis to the gate, Taylor packs her things into her purse, grabs her carry-on bag once the seatbelt sign goes off, and practically skips off the plane, along with hordes of other young, beautiful people heading to Ibiza to party it up for the weekend. After a twenty-five-minute cab ride, she's at the hotel. Although it's nothing fancy, it's just right, as Finn promised. She sends him a text message letting him know that she's arrived, that the place is spot-on, and thanks him profusely for the suggestion.

The small, modest room makes up for what it lacks in size with a large balcony overlooking the hotel's garden, which is bursting with colorful bougainvillea, hibiscus, and oleander. *If I could bottle the scent of this garden, I would make millions,* Taylor thinks to herself while inhaling the delightful smells. The beach isn't far, and Taylor can smell the salty air of the sea and hear the waves. She throws on her bathing suit and cover-up, grabs her camera, and heads toward the beach, which is beginning to clear out as the afternoon morphs into early evening.

S'Argamassa Beach is relatively secluded, aside from a handful of young people kayaking and hanging around at no-nonsense beach bars. Taylor spends the next hour walking with her feet in the water, checking out the aqueduct from centuries past, and snapping pictures. She's already looking forward to writing about her days here in Ibiza. Once she's satisfied with the pictures she's taken, Taylor plops herself down at one of the beachside bars and orders a mojito.

While sipping her drink, Taylor checks her phone, wondering if Manuel has texted. There's nothing from him, but she sees a missed call from her parents. She dials them back, and her mom answers on the second ring.

"Taylor! Hi honey, thanks for calling back. How are you, sweetheart?"

"Hi, Mom, all good here. I got to Ibiza today. How are you? Everything okay?"

"Oh, that's wonderful. Take as many pictures as you can so you can remember this time in your life forever. And so I can live vicariously through you, of course. We're fine here; I was actually calling because Tanya and I are planning a ladies' trip this fall. She'll be visiting Daniel, of course, and I'll come to you. And Tanya and I may do some traveling together as well; we're thinking of going to Paris for a few days either before or after we visit you guys. What do you think of that?"

At the mention of Daniel, Taylor has a brief moment of panic and nearly spits out the sip of mojito she's just taken. He won't be coming along with Tanya and Alyssa, right? The idea is moderately terrifying. Try as she might, Taylor just can't fully shake her feelings for Daniel. There are so many "what-ifs," and in addition to their history and family connections, the mere mention of him sends her into a tailspin. She quickly regains her composure, and at that moment the bartender brings over her food. She takes a quick bite of the patatas bravas and responds,

"Mom, that's so fun! I would love for you to visit. I already have some places in Barcelona that I'd love to show you. When are you guys thinking?"

"Well, that depends entirely on your and Daniel's schedules. We'll obviously do our best to visit when it's most convenient for the two of you. Don't want to cramp your style."

Taylor cringes at her mother's use of what she considers hip language and laughs a bit.

"Ok, Mom, thanks. What about Dad? Will he care that you're ditching him to go jet-setting with Tanya?"

"Oh please, your father is a grown man. I may ship him off to New York to check in on those brothers of yours while I'm gone. Lord knows they don't call home nearly enough. I try not to bother them, but for Christ's sake, would it kill them to call us once a week?"

Taylor is taken aback by her mom's sudden outburst; she never complains about this type of stuff, in stark contrast to so many of the parents of Taylor's friends, who seem to expect daily check-ins and are overly involved in their grown children's lives.

Before Taylor can respond, her mom quickly apologizes.

"Sorry, hon, I didn't mean that to sound so harsh. It's just tough having an empty nest. I miss the hustle and bustle of a full house. I'm not sure I'll ever get used to having you three out on your own."

Before they hang up, Taylor and her mom toss around some potential dates for the trip, and Taylor finds herself astonishingly excited to see her mom and show her around Barcelona. She also feels a pang of sympathy, surprised by how much her mom misses having all her kids around. After saying goodbye, Taylor checks the time; it's nearly 7 p.m. already. She eats her food, finishes her mojito, and pays the bill.

Back at her hotel, Taylor lies down in bed for a power nap to energize her for the night to come. She immediately falls asleep, apparently tired from the traveling and the sun, and when she wakes, it's already 10:15 p.m.

"Fuck," she yells to the empty room. She hops out of bed straight into the shower, and afterward starts doing her makeup, rummaging through her clothes to find the right outfit. She decides on a tight, strapless little black dress, akin to the women in Robert Palmer's *Addicted to Love* music video, minus the sleeves.

She does her hair, which is still damp from the shower, and throws on a pair of heels. By 11 p.m., Taylor is satisfied with how she looks. An extra swipe of red lipstick, and she's off. By sheer luck, a couple is getting dropped off in front of the hotel just as she walks out the lobby door, so she grabs a taxi and heads to Amnesia, the be-all and end-all of Ibiza nightlife.

The specifics of the night are, more or less, lost to alcohol: hours of dancing, some casual flirting with a handful of guys, none of whose names she could hear over the bass of the music. In short, Amnesia lived up to its expectations, and Taylor is happy to have experienced it. No hooking up with anyone, which is a relief, alleviating any potential guilt she may feel with Manuel. She leaves the club as the sun rises, drenched with sweat and with throbbing pain in her feet. The insane part, she thinks while walking out into the early morning, is that the club is still hopping. Hundreds of people are still going strong, dancing, drinking, and doing one of many combinations of illicit drugs. Taylor is relieved that, at worst, she'll be dealing with a mild hangover.

She finds a taxi and slumps into the backseat after informing the driver of her destination. As the taxi makes its way to her hotel, Taylor realizes she hasn't checked her phone since the night before. There are a few texts from Manuel, ranging from the "I miss you" variety, morphing into, "Hey, why the hell haven't you responded? Are you okay?"

Taylor responds right away, explaining that she was at a club all night and didn't hear her phone, which is, in fact, the truth.

She clicks send as soon as she's ensconced back in her hotel room, brushes her teeth, guzzles down some water, and climbs into bed wearing just a t-shirt. Hours later, she's woken by the sound of birds in the garden outside her room. It's past noon, and she feels surprisingly well-rested. There's a missed call and two text messages from Manuel; he sounds annoyed in the texts, she thinks, a bit possessive in fact, and Taylor feels herself going on the defensive.

She calls him back, and after what feels like an interrogation, once he's satisfied that nothing untoward occurred the night before, he's back to himself. Taylor feels uneasy. They hadn't established any boundaries prior to his leaving for Málaga, and she doesn't like the obvious anger in his voice when he heard about what she's been up to. On jealousy, Taylor recalls a quote by Lope de Vega: "There is no greater glory than love, nor any greater punishment than jealousy." Touché, she thinks to herself.

Some of her friends, she knows, would be flattered by Manuel's contrived concern; Taylor, however, sees it for what it is: distrust and possessiveness, both of which, she's realizing by the second, are major turnoffs. Rather than dwell on her current predicament, Taylor decides to spend the day visiting some of the more important historical sites on Ibiza, intending to distract herself and take notes so she can write about them once she's back in Barcelona.

Notebook and camera in hand, Taylor has what can only be described as an enlightening day exploring Ibiza. After trekking up a seemingly never-ending hill to reach the Cathedral, the interior is so stunning that it leaves Taylor feeling serene, peaceful, and happy, despite the fact that she is sweating profusely from the climb. She spends a few quiet moments sitting in a pew, taking it all in, enjoying the solitude and quiet. Today's explorations have proven to be the perfect remedy to the unease she was feeling earlier.

By the time Taylor returns to her hotel, it's nearly seven p.m., and she is famished, exhausted, and feeling vaguely hungover from last night. She's learned the best cure for a hangover, aside from more alcohol, is dunking herself into cold water. She throws on her bikini, grabs a cover-up and a towel, and literally runs to the beach. She tosses her towel and bag on an empty beach lounge, and sprints into the sea. Once the water is deep enough, she dives in headfirst, momentarily shocked by the sensation. As her body adjusts to the temperature, she swims for a few minutes, allowing the cobwebs currently occupying her brain to clear. Ten minutes later, the remnants of her hangover have disappeared.

She slowly exits the water, dries off, and throws her cover-up over her suit. Craving a good meal and a cigarette, she heads back to the beach bar where she went just a day earlier. Taylor is relieved to see an older, more local crew tonight, none of whom pay her much attention, despite the fact that her hair is dripping wet and she appears, she imagines, moderately unhinged. The bartender recognizes her from yesterday and asks if she wants another mojito.

"Vino blanco hoy, por favor," she tells the bartender. No way she's doing hard alcohol tonight, the mere thought of it makes her nauseous; best to go with white wine. The bartender nods and brings her the wine, along with an ashtray for the cigarette she's already lit. Taylor decides against ordering food here; she knows another all-nighter of clubbing is a no-go, so instead she will have dinner at Tijuana Tex-Mex, giving her a popular restaurant to include in her Ibiza write-up. The restaurant is located in the hip and lively San

Antonio section of the island, which is on her itinerary anyway, so she figures she can kill two birds with one stone.

Taylor drains her drink and is lightheaded due to lack of food and sleep, so she quickly pays the bill and heads back to the hotel, where she changes into going-out attire, does her makeup, and regroups. She grabs a taxi and is in San Antonio before 10 p.m. She walks around the neighborhood for a few minutes, sees the beach and a few resorts, before realizing that if she doesn't eat soon, there's a chance she may faint. A glass of wine and a ton of Mexican food later, she's feeling great. She brought along her guidebook, which has become her go-to when dining alone, and has even managed to take a few pictures of the restaurant.

She's sent some flirty texts to Manuel, more as a test rather than authentic emotion. He's responding as though the awkwardness surrounding Taylor's activities last night never happened. She decides, with her usual conviction, to give him the benefit of the doubt. He's spending multiple weeks with his family, for Christ's sake, who knows what kind of drama and stress that may be causing.

By the time Taylor has finished her meal and enjoyed some great people-watching, it's after 1 a.m., and people are starting to head out to the clubs. The buzzed part of Taylor's brain tells her to go out clubbing again; fortunately, the good-judgment part wins over, and she's back at the hotel and in bed by 2 a.m., which is, apparently, early by Ibiza standards.

Taylor's next few days in Ibiza unfold seamlessly. She hits up the best beaches, beach clubs, and restaurants (amazing, the perks you get when you promise a positive write-up!), along with a few more historical spots. When she returns to Barcelona, she has a plethora of Ibiza recommendations and musings which, when neatly wrapped into an article, offer the perfect four-day itinerary to Europe's best (she can only assume) party island.

Chapter 5

August 2003, Barcelona

On Monday, Taylor is back in Barcelona after a wild, wonderful few days in Ibiza. She returns to the dorm by late afternoon and decides to spend a quiet (finally!) evening in, doing laundry and dealing with class selections, which have become available online for the fall semester. Once the laundry is in the wash, Taylor spends the next hour perusing the course catalog, focusing as much on the timing of the classes (Friday classes are an automatic no; ones that meet only once or twice per week are a win) as she does on the course material.

She winds up selecting three classes conducted exclusively in Spanish, all of which will count toward her major, and one class in English (Math, Taylor doesn't think she has the bandwidth to learn math in a foreign language; she can barely do it in English). None of them meet on Mondays or Fridays, so not only did Taylor get the best classes in terms of material and credits, but she also has the optimal schedule to allow for long weekends, whether that means traveling around Europe or partying here in Barcelona, which she has already adopted as "her" city. Once the class selections are confirmed in the University's system, she returns downstairs to the laundry room to collect her things. The dorm, which had been eerily quiet in the two weeks prior, has begun to pick up and has a livelier atmosphere, with many international students starting to trickle in.

Once her clothes are hung to dry in her closet (finding a dryer in this city appears to be a lost cause), Taylor grabs her massive European guidebook and purse and walks a few blocks to a small local restaurant near the Monestir de Pedralbes, which she's passed a few times while exploring the neighborhood. Settling into an outdoor table, she orders a glass of red wine (just one for tonight; she needs to give her body a bit of a break from alcohol, but not having at least a glass of wine with dinner in Spain just seems wrong) from the bored waiter, a teenager who seems irritated that he's spending his summer evenings waiting tables at his family's restaurant. Taylor orders paella with shrimp and gets lost reading her European guidebook, focusing on the south of France, where she will be meeting Lindsay on Friday.

Although she misses Manuel, and their texts have been filled with sexual innuendo, Taylor is still a bit off-put by his reaction to her night out in Ibiza. A guy being possessive is a huge turnoff in her mind, and Manuel certainly seems to have that jealousy trait. *Tread carefully,* she continues telling herself. A few days alone in Barcelona, followed by what she expects to be a raucous weekend with one of her best friends, ought to be the ideal distraction from her worries. Lindsay, being an experienced traveler, has thrown out a few suggestions for their trip, but she has designated Taylor as the ultimate decision-maker. And what a decision to make! As a kid, Taylor's travel consisted of sporting events in nearby states, with a rare trip to Gulf Shores down south, and once to Disney World. She might as well be traveling to outer space, what with all this glamorous jet-setting.

Lindsay, while giving Taylor decision-making authority, has been hinting heavily at St. Tropez. After doing some research on the internet and in her European guidebook, Taylor sees no reason to deny Lindsay this wish, despite her hesitation at what the price tag is going to look like. Although Lindsay specifically said her parents are of the "spare no expense" type, Taylor still feels a bit guilty at the thought of taking a free ride. She's already mentally drafting her thank-you note (and gift) to Lindsay's parents.

Taylor finishes her meal, which was surprisingly delicious for a hole-in-the-wall local restaurant, pays the bill, and heads back to the dorm. She calls Lindsay on her walk back, letting her know that, after extensive research, she thinks St. Tropez would be the best spot, if Lindsay is okay with that. Lindsay squeals with delight and yells,

"Mommy, T wants to go to St. Tropez too!" Taylor laughs, and Lindsay gets back on and says, "Sorry about that, I was just reeeeaaalllly hoping you'd say that. We can go yacht-spotting and look for celebrities. My parents will help me book a hotel, a car, and make restaurant reservations, so all you need to worry about is getting yourself there, and we'll have a place to stay. I can't wait!"

"Linds, again, this is beyond generous. I am so grateful to your parents for hooking us up like this. I'm at least buying you lots of meals and drinks, ok?"

"Whatever, babe, thanks, and seriously don't worry about it. They love you and are happy to do it, so not another thought, okay? Now, I'm in final packing mode, so I've gotta run. But I can say, you've made a great choice, and I can't wait to see you in just a few days."

The two friends say their goodbyes, and Taylor hangs up feeling ecstatic about seeing Lindsay, in St. Tropez, no less.

Raised comfortably middle-class, Taylor is still mildly shocked by just how rich Lindsay's family is. Despite being raised like a princess, Lindsay manages to be normal and down-to-earth, with only the faintest hint of snobbery that comes out from time to time. But her periodic slips are made up for by her unending generosity, which is one of the things Taylor loves the most about her.

Taylor falls asleep that night mentally packing her best clothes for St. Tropez while simultaneously planning her to-do list for the remainder of the week. She rises early the next morning, planning on heading to Barcelona-Sants, the city's main railway station, to buy a Eurail pass. After some quick research, however, she realizes that the train isn't a particularly viable option between the two places, nor is the bus, which is basically a twelve-hour ride. After a mild panic attack, she finds surprisingly cheap airfare from Barcelona to Nice, France. Lindsay was planning on flying into Nice as well, so Taylor figures they can coordinate times and share a car to St. Tropez. *Phew,* she thinks, crisis averted. She emails Lindsay to coordinate times, and by the end of the day they have arranged for flights that land within an hour of each other.

Taylor spends her week hanging around the city, doing tons of writing, avoiding alcohol and meals out (both for her finances and her body's sake), and on Thursday she has a long visit to the nearby monastery, El Monestir de Pedralbes, which dates back to the 14th century. The monastery is one of the finest examples of Catalan Gothic architecture, and its beauty is astounding. A proud atheist, Taylor is surprised by how intrigued she is to spend nearly a full day wandering around the former living space of nuns, but the history of the place is overwhelming.

After spending the day surrounded by religion, Taylor decides a visit to her pal Finn and a few drinks are in order. She returns to her dorm in the early evening, finishes her packing for tomorrow's trip to St. Tropez, and heads to Finn's bar on the beach. By the time she arrives, it's around 8:30 p.m., the earliest acceptable time for dinner (for tourists, at least, the locals wouldn't be caught dead eating before 10 p.m.). She'd already texted Finn to confirm that he was working tonight, and as soon as he sees her enter the bar, he smiles and starts mixing her a rum and coke.

Taylor takes a seat at the bar, and she and Finn catch up, Taylor telling him all about Ibiza and her upcoming trip to the south of France. Finn lets out a low whistle. "St. Tropez, eh? That's some fancy shit. Lads like me, that's not our scene."

"Yeah," Taylor agrees, "it's not my scene either, but I have a very rich and very generous friend, and she grew up 'summering in France,' so to speak. More money than I can imagine, so that's the only reason I'm able to go."

"Well, hey, cheers to that," Finn says, pouring a shot of rum for each of them. They clink glasses and pound back the rum, doing their best to ignore the burning in their throats. Before the crowd gets bigger, Taylor orders food, chats a bit more with Finn, and makes it an early night.

Despite wanting to stay as the crowd grows and the music ramps up, tonight a mash-up of Michael Jackson and Madonna (she's sensing a theme in the musical selections here), Taylor forces herself to head home, saving her energy for her weekend with Lindsay. She promises Finn she'll be back next week, feeling comfort in having found an English-speaking friend and a watering hole where she feels safe and welcome.

Chapter 6

August 2003, St. Tropez

Taylor lands at the Nice, France, airport around 5 p.m. on Friday afternoon, after an uneventful and brief flight. After wandering around the airport for a few minutes, she finds Lindsay's gate, and they greet one another with a giant hug and squeals of excitement that draw stares from passersby. They make their way to the chauffeured car that Lindsay's parents arranged (Taylor can hardly believe this is her actual life) and settle in for the drive to St. Tropez.

The chauffeur pulls up to Hotel Le Mouillage, which happens to be a two-minute walk from La Bouillabaisse beach. It is charming and perfectly French, chic but not intimidatingly so. The boutique hotel overlooks the bay and has the most glorious garden, filled with exotic flowers and plants. The terraces of the rooms are tastefully decorated, all offering spectacular views of either the garden or the Golfe de Saint-Tropez.

After they check in at reception, Taylor and Lindsay make themselves at home in their adorable room, which has a surprisingly large terrace with a view of the sea.

By the time they unpack and do themselves up for the night, it's already past 9 p.m.

They enjoy a glass of wine from the complimentary bottle that was in their room and smoke a cigarette on the terrace before heading out for dinner.

Taylor and Lindsay decide their first night will be an early one: no going out partying, just dinner at a nearby restaurant and then bed.

The forecast for tomorrow is perfect, and they both want to enjoy the beach all day, which will be far more pleasant sans a raging hangover. They are in bed by midnight, both exhausted from traveling and drinking too much French wine.

By 10 a.m. the next day, they're on the beach. It's already packed with beautiful people, many of whom are topless. Lindsay raises her eyebrows and says, "When in Rome!" while removing her bikini top. Taylor laughs and feels a stab of envy at her friend's audacity (and her perfect boobs).

"Be my guest, but mine is staying on."

"You're such a prude Midwesterner," Lindsay laughs with an eye roll. "Your body is perfect; you should show it off."

"Ha, ha. Far from perfect, but thanks. And if I'm a prude Midwesterner, I don't even want to know what a slutty Midwesterner would look like!"

Their day on the beach proceeds rather uneventfully, magazine reading interspersed with dips in the sea and a nap. Along with some ogling of their fellow beachgoers, mainly the middle-aged men, they conclude, are far too confident in their nudity. By midafternoon, they pack up and grab sandwiches from a tiny shop on the corner next to the hotel. They have their lunch on the terrace, shower, get dressed for the night, and head for the port to check out the yachts.

Tomorrow they will hit up Nikki Beach, considered the hippest of the St. Tropez beach clubs. Apparently, Naomi Campbell celebrated her birthday there last year, the thought of which terrifies the hell out of Taylor but animates Lindsay to no end. When Taylor expresses her unease at the idea, Lindsay calms her with, "You'll fit right in, T. Your legs are long enough, for Christ's sake. Besides, we're two girls, and not bad looking if I may say so myself! Don't worry, this place isn't some decadent, old-money scene. Will we see models and famous people? Yes. Will you fit in? Also, yes. So, calm down. We'll go, we'll drink, and who knows, maybe meet some cute guys."

Taylor is excited about writing about Nikki Beach; her write-ups thus far have gotten rave reviews. Daniel's grandmother actually emailed her, saying that her youthful and entertaining perspective is exactly what they're aiming for. Her editor had similar feedback, basically telling her to keep up the good work, and her pieces will continue to be published and well-compensated. Given the nice cash flow she's got going, Taylor is more determined than ever to keep pumping out work, and she can treat Lindsay to dinner and drinks tonight, which is long overdue.

For now, though, the famous (infamous?) yachts await them. They head to the Port de Saint-Tropez, once a modest harbor for small fishing vessels, today a modern spot for VIPs to drop anchor. Cameras in hand, they discreetly snap pictures of the biggest yachts, some of which look bigger than the house Taylor grew up in. Taylor knows Lindsay is rich, but this is next level even for her. Jaws dropped, they stroll the port, then check out the Place des Lices, a little oasis with benches and a fountain. They take a seat and rest their feet, clad in four-inch wedge sandals, for a few minutes. Lindsay gushes about the yachts, and they speculate which famous people they may spot out and about tonight: supermodels, actors, artists, this place is truly a playground for the jet set.

Once their feet have recovered, they continue walking and find themselves at Hotel Le Byblos for cocktails. Byblos is an uber-posh hotel; it's been on the map since Mick Jagger married model Bianca Perez and stayed at one of the hotel's suites in 1971. Ever since, it's been catering to the "who's who" of the international VIP crowd. After a bit of digging, Taylor realizes they can make this their one-stop shop for the whole night: sip cocktails by the pool, order dinner from the Bar Lounge, and finally, head to the notorious nightclub, Les Caves du Roy.

Somehow, it's past 7 p.m. already, so cocktail hour is officially swinging.

"Pace yourself," Lindsay tells Taylor as they sip their pinot grigio. "It's going to be a long night, so we have to start slow."

"I know, I know," Taylor says with an eye roll. She lights a cigarette and uses her lighter to light Lindsay's as well. "I know it's bad, but don't you love how everyone here in Europe smokes? Back home, there's such guilt associated with it, and so much judgment. Here, nobody gives a shit."

"I've been thinking the same thing," Lindsay responds. "But we have to quit after college, remember that. Enjoy it now, before long we'll be old boring married people with babies... like my sister!"

Taylor laughs. Lindsay is perpetually bitching about her older sister and how she's basically morphed from a wild party girl to a responsible adult with a husband and small child. "C'mon, you complain, but I know you love being the fun aunt."

"I know, it's just she's a totally different person than when we were growing up. And being the fun aunt is the best, but still. They have a baby named Chad. Who looks at an infant and thinks, 'Yes, let me name this tiny child Chad?' Chad is a date-rapist lacrosse player name, right?"

At this, Taylor nearly chokes with laughter on her wine.

"Speaking of which," Lindsay continues, "What's going on with your brothers?"

"You're associating date-rapist lacrosse players with my brothers now? That's the segue you choose in order to ask about my brothers?" Taylor asks with a laugh.

"No! Of course not. But if we're being honest, they do have that look about them. Don't tell me you don't know exactly what I'm talking about."

Taylor rolls her eyes but can't help but agree, just a little bit. Her brothers do have that cool, aloof, jock look about them. "So, juicy tidbit," Taylor says, eager to move on, "Eric, my older brother, has a serious girlfriend. Alex has met her and everything. And Alex seems to actually like her way more than the usual girls Eric dates, so this could be the one."

"Oooh, do we hear wedding bells? Have your parents met her?"

"That's the funny thing. Eric is being super cagey about telling our parents. But apparently this woman, Lauren, is from some swanky town in Connecticut and comes from money. Alex and I have therefore decided she's not a gold digger, so that's a good start."

"Which town in Connecticut?" Lindsay asks.

"Greenwich," Taylor responds. After speaking the word, her mind goes directly to Daniel for a split second before she forces herself to remain in the present.

"Of course it's Greenwich," Lindsay says with an eyeroll and a hint of exasperation in her voice. "I had a friend from camp who lives there, Erica Collins. They have an estate! With, like, actual horses. Like a twenty-million-dollar house or something insane. Her parents threw these wild parties the week I stayed there; it was like out of a movie. Truly insane."

"Back up. What did you say her last name was?"

"Collins. Why? Don't tell me you know her... she was a total cokehead by senior year of high school. She's at Princeton, but only because her family is so well-connected."

"Oh my God, Lindsay," Taylor shrieks while grabbing Lindsay's arm. "Collins is Daniel's last name. Remember, hot Daniel who I hooked up with at Duke our freshman year?"

"Um, yeah, of course I remember hot Daniel. Could they be related? Isn't your mom, like, best friends with his mom or something incestuous like that?"

Taylor laughs vigorously, her head arching back. "Christ, I've got to figure this out. I suppose it is a common enough last name. So, Daniel's dad died before he was even born. I know his dad had an older brother, who I think went to Princeton. His grandparents, who I'm working for, by the way, live in Greenwich. Wait, what were the parents' names?"

"Claire and Robert. Are you telling me that Erica could be Daniel's cousin? That would be beyond. Ask your mom. Call her now," Lindsay insists.

"Ok, I will. I mean, this is not normal. Did you know Daniel and I were born on the same day? That's how our moms met, at the hospital," Taylor tells Lindsay while dialing her parents' home number.

"Wow, Taylor," Lindsay says with mock enthusiasm, "It's like you guys were literally born for each other."

"Fuck off," Taylor says with a laugh, just as her mom answers the phone. "Hi Mom! How are you? I'm here with Lindsay; we have a pressing question."

"Taylor! Hi, love. How are you? Isn't it Saturday night? And aren't you in St. Tropez? Is everything okay?"

"Yes, Mom, everything is fine. Great, actually." Lindsay lights two cigarettes and hands one to Taylor, which she accepts and shoots Lindsay a look of gratitude. "Mom, did Daniel's dad have a brother? Named Robert?"

"Yes, I believe that was his name. I think he has a daughter your age, in fact. She's Daniel's cousin, obviously. Why on earth would you need to know that?"

"So, kind of a long story, but Lindsay's friend from camp might be Robert's daughter. Erica Collins."

"Wow! Let me check with Tanya later; I don't recall the girl's name. What a coincidence that would be. It really is a small world."

"Okay, thanks, Mom. No rush at all, but let me know whenever you find out."

Taylor finishes the call as quickly as she can, sends her love to her mom and dad, and hangs up the phone.

"Well, fuck me. I think your camp pal is, in fact, Daniel's cousin. She's double-checking, but it all adds up. What are the odds?"

"The rich East Coast is smaller than you think, my friend," Lindsay tells Taylor with a wink. "And, like I said, something about this doesn't surprise me. I have a feeling about you and Daniel. You're born on the same day, you grew up together, you randomly find each other, and sleep together, at Duke. And now this," Lindsay says with raised eyebrows.

"Ugh, I've sooo been trying to keep myself from thinking about him. You know how I obsessed about him for weeks after we hooked up last year. If anything was meant to happen, beyond what did happen, it would've happened by now, right? I feel like Daniel is untouchable for so many reasons. He is basically perfect, smart, great-looking, and literally the nicest human I've ever met, not to mention the fact that our moms are best friends. Besides, I've got Manuel. Who happens to be twenty-six, gorgeous, Spanish, and really good in bed."

"Fair enough. But wasn't Manuel super possessive and weird about you going to Ibiza alone? I know that's a red flag for you, Miss Independence."

"Yeah," Taylor sighs. "It was definitely a red flag. But we have so much fun together, and he's like an actual adult. We'll see what happens. We packed a lot of 'getting to know you' stuff into just a few days. I think once I'm settled in my apartment and he's back from his family time, I'll have better insight into the whole dynamic of our relationship. Anyways, what about you? Can we find a hottie for you tonight?"

Lindsay has a long-term boyfriend back at UNC named Walter, but they've agreed to an open relationship while she's studying abroad.

"Maybe. I hate thinking about Walter back at school and whatever bullshit he's probably doing. At the same time, the thought of hooking up with anyone else feels so foreign and weird." Lindsay looks up at the sky, which has become dark at some point in the past few minutes. She takes a deep breath and replies, "But yes. I need to get my groove on. So, you're my wingman tonight, yeah? Assuming you're not looking around also, that is."

"No, tonight is all about you. I actually really like Manuel; wouldn't want to fuck that up. At least not yet," Taylor giggles. "Although, who knows what he's been doing in Málaga the past few weeks. That's what I'm wondering. Will I get back to find out he's been sleeping with every girl he sees?" Taylor shakes the thought out of her head and regroups. "So yes, darlin, I'm your wingman tonight. But Lindsay, I really like Manuel. Did I happen to mention how gorgeous he is?"

Lindsay laughs while Taylor lights another cigarette; their glasses of pinot grigio have been magically refilled. A food menu is in front of them, and Taylor checks the time. It's 9 o'clock already.

"Linds, we need to eat!" She thrusts a menu towards Lindsay, who looks at it disinterestedly. Lindsay has always been someone who Taylor and her friends need to watch on the eating front, or lack thereof. She is super thin, not in the fit way that Taylor is, but in a moderately unhealthy way that requires a lot of check-ins from her family and reminders from her friends. She claims she's not anorexic, but Taylor is well-versed in the therapy that Lindsay had to have throughout high school.

They eventually order a variety of appetizers to share, tapas-style, which Taylor is quick to order on behalf of them both. After a little more wine and a few more cigarettes, the girls share their food, Taylor keeping a close eye on Lindsay to be sure she eats a reasonable amount. She does, thank God, sparing Taylor the lecture.

The sad reality is that neither Taylor nor any of her friends has what could be considered a healthy relationship with food. They grew up with the heroin-chic look shoved down their throats via Calvin Klein ads in every magazine they read, Kate Moss, Jaime King, along with myriad other nearly invisible women, embodying what they and their male counterparts expected women to look like. What the 1990s managed to do to the self-worth of young women is criminal, Taylor thinks to herself on a regular basis. It's fucking exhausting, even for Taylor, who prides herself on keeping a relatively 'normal' view toward food and her weight. But she can't help but get so angry whenever she sees one of her friends succumb to an eating disorder; it seems almost inevitable these days. They either start starving themselves or start eating massive quantities and then vanish to the bathroom for twenty minutes after every meal.

Taylor sighs, tired of thinking about weight, food, and appearance.

"What's the matter, love?" Lindsay asks, noticing Taylor's exasperated sigh.

"Oh, nothing. I was just thinking how unfair it is that guys can eat whatever they want, and nobody gives a shit about what they look like or if they have an extra ten pounds on them. Not the same for us. That's all. We're supposed to be tiny, tiny, tiny, and barely take up any space at all."

"You know I agree with you, but now is not the time to be thinking about that. We're in Europe, you have to enjoy it, and part of that is the food. And the drinks," Lindsay tells Taylor while taking a swig of her wine. "At least, that's what my therapist told me." Taylor laughs and gives Lindsay's hand a squeeze.

By 10:30 p.m., they've eaten enough to soak up the alcohol, had enough wine to loosen up for the club, and Taylor manages to pay the bill while Lindsay slips off to the bathroom. Mission accomplished, she thinks to herself. Lindsay returns from the bathroom, cheeks flushed, clearly excited about something.

"So, wingman, I just met THE hottest guy. And he's heading to Les Caves du Roy in a minute. He's French but speaks perfect English. So, whenever you're ready, let's hit it and go there. I'll get the check."

"Done, mademoiselle. I already paid."

"You bitch! I can't believe you did that. Taylor, please let me pay you back."

"Not a chance. This is the least I can do. So, accept it, bitch." Lindsay throws her napkin playfully at Taylor and sits down. They finish their wine, head to the ladies' room, and maneuver their way to Les Caves du Roy. From her guidebook, Taylor has learned that Les Caves du Roy is probably the most famous nightclub in France; quite possibly one of the most famous in the world. Even Cameron Diaz, Nelly, and Eminem have been here, along with basically anyone else she's ever heard of. And a lot of rich people she's never heard of, but who are apparently famous in the land of the super elite.

The bouncers look like a strange combination of Navy Seal/bodybuilder/Secret Service guys all rolled into one entity. Fortunately, Taylor and Lindsay are appropriately dressed for a VIP club. Their makeup and hair are impeccable, more from sheer luck and good genetics than actual effort, but they slide into the club without any issues, joining hundreds of other beautiful people dancing, mingling, and drinking. Lindsay grabs Taylor's hand and leads the way, strutting to the bar.

The bar is crowded, and they have to wait a few minutes for their drinks. Lindsay insisted earlier on paying for their drinks at the club, which is lucky for Taylor because the drinks are exorbitantly expensive. Taylor expected St. Tropez to be a major splurge, but these prices are well beyond her expectations. They drink, dance, and mingle the night away; at some point, Taylor checks the time and it's 2:30 a.m. Despite the hour, the crowd is growing, and the drinks are steadily flowing. At one point on the dance floor, Taylor loses sight of Lindsay, only to turn around and see her dancing with an extremely attractive man who happens to be wearing a wedding ring.

"Oh my fucking God," Taylor exclaims to herself.

Lindsay is grinding with him, and his hands are on her ass. Taylor makes her way toward them, hoping to intervene before anything even more inappropriate happens.

"Linds!" Taylor yells over the bumping house music. "I'm going to the bathroom, come with me, will ya?"

"Ok, hold on," Lindsay yells back. She turns and kisses her dancing partner, then trots off to the bathroom with Taylor.

Taylor suddenly feels very sober and realizes that Lindsay is officially hammered. She's slurring her words and appears unsteady on her feet. And she's got the hiccups, which Taylor has learned from experience is a good predictor that she's going to puke later on tonight.

"Okay, Linds, let's use the bathroom and then go drink some water. No more alcohol for a bit."

Lindsay gives Taylor puppy-dog eyes and whines, "But I want more champagne. What's his name has a table. He invited us to hang with them!"

This is like dealing with a toddler who is refusing to leave the playground, Taylor thinks to herself.

"Fine, but you're drinking water. And don't think for a second I'm letting you go home with him; he's wearing a wedding ring for Christ's sake." Taylor slips in this detail in an attempt to engage Lindsay's moral compass. She knows Lindsay wouldn't hook up with someone else's husband, despite how hot they may be, or how wasted she is.

So, they eventually find themselves at a table, with champagne being consistently replenished. They've both guzzled the water provided, and Lindsay is looking less green and has toned down the flirting. At 3:45 a.m., Taylor has officially had enough of this place and is ready to go. She still can't get over the connection between Lindsay's friend Erica and Daniel... what are the odds that this girl is Daniel's cousin? It makes the Daniel obsession begin anew, which is the last thing she wants to be thinking about right now.

She gives Lindsay a little kick under the table and mouths, "Let's go," as discreetly as possible. Lindsay pouts her lips and gives Taylor her sad, puppy-dog look once again, pouring another glass of champagne while simultaneously grabbing her camera out of her purse.

"Pictures," Lindsay yells enthusiastically. She grabs Taylor, and they pose, clinking their glasses with the jam-packed dance floor behind them. "We need documentation of this. You'll thank me later!"

And Lindsay was right. Despite her annoyance in the moment, when Taylor looks back at this time in her life through photos, she feels herself being transported back to this carefree, youthful time. Whoever said that youth is wasted on the young was spot on.

But at this actual moment, she's tired and cranky, just wanting to collapse into bed. Lindsay finally gets the hint and stands up briskly, declaring that it's time they called it a night.

"Thank God," Taylor mutters.

They manage to extract themselves without doing any damage, aside from Lindsay's kiss with the guy she was dancing with. The walk back to their hotel passes in the blink of an eye, and by 5 a.m., they've both stumbled into bed, makeup still on.

"Thanks for getting us back here, Linds. I was totally turned around and would still be wandering the streets if you hadn't guided us," Taylor mumbles into her pillow.

"Don't thank me, thank God," Lindsay says with a laugh before passing out. Taylor can't help but laugh so hard she almost pees and has to drag herself to the bathroom. That phrase will be a joke between them for years to come; of all the memories they make on this long weekend in St. Tropez, that one will ultimately provide the most laughs.

The following morning is rough, to put it mildly. They rise at 11 a.m. to the sounds outside their hotel room. Sunday. Today they're going to Nikki Beach for the day, hungover as all hell and on barely six hours of sleep.

"Taylor, days like this are when it's a good thing to be twenty years old. When my sister drinks now, which is practically never, she's in bed for like two days. It's ridiculous, but she says every year the hangovers get worse. So, get your ass up and let's get ready for a day at the beach club," Lindsay instructs, bossily.

"Are you always this bossy? Jesus Christ. You're the one who kept us out all night." Taylor buries her head under a pillow and moans. Lindsay tosses a bottle of water from the minibar onto her bed; Taylor drinks it in one sip, then registers that she probably just drank a water bottle that will set her back at least $7. She peeked at the minibar prices when Lindsay was showering yesterday, and her jaw almost hit the floor.

"Fine, fine, I just need a few minutes." Taylor goes out to the balcony with her phone and a pack of cigarettes and sees a few text messages from Manuel that she'd missed last night. He misses her, he said, and he would be back in Barcelona on Thursday; could she have dinner with him that night? She responds that yes, she would love to have dinner, and that she misses him too. As she reaches the end of her cigarette, Taylor feels herself starting to feel human again... it must be the water kicking in. Or the nicotine. Either way, she and Lindsay get ready for the beach.

Taylor had let her editor know that she'd do a writeup specifically on Nikki Beach, as it is the "youngest" of St. Tropez's beach clubs. Her editor was thrilled and said she couldn't wait to hear about the "champagne-soaked debauchery" that went on there. Taylor loved that line and wanted to incorporate it into her piece. The other two notorious beach clubs, Club 55 and La Voile Rouge, couldn't be more different from one another. Club 55 is notorious for old money; the vibe is ultra-luxe but not rowdy. La Voile Rouge, on the other hand, is the wild one. It's where you go to get shitfaced, naked, or both. Nikki Beach is a lower-key version, with a young, hip clientele.

Taylor shoves her notebook into her purse; she'll need to take notes throughout the day... what is there to eat? What famous people show up? How much is bottle service? The goal is that she and Lindsay will get a bit of VIP treatment, as Taylor is going to chat with whoever is in charge there about giving them a glowing write-up... hopefully in return for some free food and drinks. She will come to realize the naïveté of this idea later on, but at the time it seems perfectly reasonable to her sheltered Midwestern brain.

But no matter what, they still need to look the part, so she and Lindsay primp and prep, bikinis under sarongs and barely-there tank tops. By the time they finish their hair and makeup, it's almost 12:30 p.m., their hangovers have vanished, and they're starving for lunch.

Once they arrive, the place is already packed with gorgeous people. It's even more ridiculous than the club last night. Taylor immediately realizes she'll never have the chance to chat with anyone in charge; her plan for comped drinks and food quickly disappears. They'll be lucky to get a place to sit within the next 30 minutes! Fortunately, the people ahead of them in line are larger groups, and, given that they are a party of two, they're seated almost immediately upon arrival.

Everything here is white... the tablecloths, the pool chairs, most of the clientele's apparel. Most of the clientele, for that matter. Diverse, it is not. Everywhere you look, bottles of champagne are being popped and poured into flutes, then kept in shimmering, sweating ice buckets. Lindsay and Taylor stare at each other upon being seated, and Taylor bursts out laughing.

"Lindsay," she says quietly, "what the fuck are we doing here?"

"I have no idea. I didn't know what to expect... but this is absurd. Look at everyone. Thank God we wore heels and did our hair."

Taylor discreetly takes her camera out of her bag and snaps some pictures; she knows right away she can't take out her clunky writing notebook and take notes here. She'll have to document the day via photographs and hope the pictures (and her memories) don't come out blurry.

They order champagne first, which seems to be the unwritten law here. Once their flutes are full, they order food. Lindsay already laid down her Amex black card, her way of telling Taylor, "This is my treat, don't even bother arguing." Taylor thanks her and keeps her mouth shut.

After eating their lunch (delicious) and drinking more champagne than either of them intended to in the middle of the day, they find a single lounge chair for their belongings, strip off their sarongs and tank tops, and jump into the pool. Along with what feels like hundreds of other people, ranging in age from older teens to possibly seventy-year-olds, and ranging in intoxication level from moderately buzzed to rip-roaring drunk. Taylor can't help but wonder how many people have peed or puked (or both) in this pool, despite its appearance of shimmery aqua perfection.

She puts the thought out of her mind and instead focuses on the beauty surrounding her, both the people and the scenery. After spending some time chatting with Taylor in the pool, Lindsay cocks her head toward a group of young men not far from them. Taylor follows Lindsay's gaze, which lands upon a cluster of tan, fit, and unjustly handsome guys. Taylor looks at Lindsay and lowers her sunglasses, á la Brandon Walsh from the iconic show of their adolescence, *Beverly Hills, 90210*, and Lindsay bursts out laughing.

"Taylor, for fuck's sake, don't be so obvious. Now they know we were looking at them."

"Who cares? Is that surprising? I mean, look at them. They're ogling all the girls here; I'm just giving them a taste of their own medicine."

After hearing Lindsay laugh, the group of guys turns their heads and looks back at them. Taylor, feeling uninhibited from the champagne and just from the novelty of being in St. Tropez, gives a flirty wave before turning her back to them and facing Lindsay.

"Taylor, you slut, they're coming over here now," Lindsay whispers far louder than she intends to.

There are four of them; they are twenty-three and twenty-four, and they're here "on holiday." Taylor has quickly learned that Europeans don't "take vacations," they "go on holiday." She's unclear as to what the distinction is, but she's quickly adapted her vocabulary to be culturally appropriate. They're from Rome, as it so happens, and they quickly take to Lindsay, giving her suggestions in broken

English of the best local places she must go to once she has settled into the city, clubs, bars, restaurants, the best spots to watch a soccer match. They have a running list, and their enthusiasm grows with each place they mention.

"Hold on!" Lindsay laughs. "I'm going to need to write all of this down." They tell her not to worry, they will all give her their mobile numbers, and she can reach them anytime. For better or worse (likely the former), they are flying back to Rome tonight and have to leave for the airport soon. But not without sharing their numbers... the six of them get out of the pool; pictures are taken, a bottle of champagne seems to appear out of thin air and is split amongst them, and mobile phone numbers are exchanged. Taylor is grateful for her camera and the fact that she and Lindsay will have photographic evidence of these beautiful Roman men. Their friends from UNC would never believe this without proof.

When it's time for the guys to head out, it's clear they are desperate to stay and see where this encounter may lead. Kisses are exchanged, some friendlier than others, and Taylor and Lindsay say goodbye and giggle their way back to their lone beach chair.

"Lindsay, that was perfect. Now you have friends in Rome." Taylor laughs.

"Friends with benefits, I hope... I can't even decide which one was the cutest. I also have no idea who was who, if I text any of them, it'll be Russian Roulette to see who actually shows up," Lindsay says with a wicked laugh.

They stay at Nikki Beach for a bit, people-watching and chatting while soaking up some sun, before Lindsay pats Taylor on the knee and says, "Alright, darling, time for a disco nap. Let's go back to the hotel and rest so we can have our last night here be a good one."

"Fine," Taylor mock-whines, secretly relieved that she can get a nap in. Day drinking has never been her strong suit, usually making her tired, irritable, and bloated. A nap will do the trick.

Lindsay closes out the tab; Taylor asks to chip in but is immediately rejected. Taylor doesn't actually want to know what Lindsay is paying for their modest lunch and some champagne, but she knows it's high in the triple digits. She thanks Lindsay with a hug and a kiss on the cheek.

Back at the hotel, their disco nap turns into a full-blown sleep, and by the time they wake up, it's after 9 p.m. Taylor's mouth feels gritty from all of the champagne; she checks the mirror and sees her hair is askew and her eye makeup is smudged all over the place. She looks, she thinks, frighteningly like a drug addict. Lindsay doesn't look much better.

"Linds, I have to be honest," Taylor starts saying.

"Wait, let me guess? You don't have it in you to go out again tonight?" Lindsay responds.

"Yeah, exactly. But I can rally if you want," Taylor replies with forced enthusiasm.

"Thank God, same here. I'm exhausted. I hate day drinking. This is what always happens. I have an idea. Let's clean ourselves up and just have dinner here at the hotel. The restaurant is cute and relatively quiet. Is that good?" Lindsay asks.

"Perfect. That's perfect." Taylor is relieved she and Lindsay are on the same page, and they go about the business of getting ready.

By 10 o'clock, they're seated at the hotel restaurant, which is deceptively glamorous given its no-frills appearance from the exterior. They are seated on the patio with a stunning view of the sea. The lights of St. Tropez appear to shimmer and dance on the water, and Taylor idly wonders why anyone who has the means would choose to live anywhere but here. It's crowded but not uncomfortably so, and they order cocktails and smoke cigarettes while talking more about the Roman guys, then Manuel, and eventually Daniel.

Lindsay brings up the topic cautiously, asking Taylor if she's planning on going to London while she's here in Europe.

"Maybe... it's not at the top of my list, to be honest. Cold and rainy. I'm from Wisconsin; I've dealt with cold my entire life. I'm here for the Mediterranean lifestyle. But maybe, why do you ask?" she replies, already knowing the answer.

"Well, I know Daniel is in London. It seems to me he may be a fun person to visit, that's all," Lindsay tells her while raising her eyebrows.

Taylor rolls her eyes at Lindsay and laughs. "Yes, Daniel would be fun to visit, if I didn't have a hot Spanish novio waiting for me back in Barcelona. Besides, it's weird enough that we hooked up last year, don't you think? I'm not planning on making a habit of it." Taylor responds a bit defensively, knowing she's putting her guard up; years later she will recognize this move as a self-defense mechanism trying to prevent Daniel from breaking her heart.

"I understand, but when I saw the two of you at that frat party, it was... like, electric. And the next day, when Katie and I picked you up from the dorm? You were so happy. Just something to think about, T. That's all," says Lindsay.

"Don't you think it's weird that our moms are basically best friends? And that he had a chance to see me again, and didn't take it? That was harsh. Honestly, I'm not sure I'm even over it yet." Taylor sighs, knowing full well that she definitely isn't over it. Not by any means.

"Fair enough. Anyways, sorry to bring up a sore subject... I hope I didn't upset you." Lindsay places her hand over Taylor's.

"No, it's fine, I hear you. It's just I've spent a lot of time thinking about Daniel, and I think it would be better, at least for now, for me to focus on me. And maybe Manuel too, actually. Sooooo, let's talk about something else. Give me some gossip from your fancy town from the summer."

Lindsay indulges Taylor with some ridiculous tales from her swanky country club and the antics she witnessed over the summer, bringing them both to tears with laughter. They eat, drink in moderation (compared to the previous nights, that is), and by 1 a.m. are blissfully asleep in their hotel room.

The following day they wake early enough to get in some time at the beach before having to pack and head back to the airport. The day of departure, Taylor thinks, is usually one of melancholy. But not today, not when she's heading back to Barcelona. She has that feeling again, of such gratitude and good fortune that she thinks she should pinch herself. She basically just had a free weekend in St. Tropez, and her actual semester abroad hasn't even started yet.

The ride to the airport (again in a chauffeured car, although this time Taylor is less enthralled as the novelty of this extravagance has worn off a bit) is filled with plans being made: which cities to meet up in, who is studying where, and which weekends will be best for travel. When they say goodbye in the airport terminal, they hug with vigor and promise to see each other soon. With Lindsay, as with all of her closest friends, Taylor knows this is a promise that will be kept.

Chapter 7

August – September 2003, Barcelona

Taylor arrives back at the Barcelona airport in the early evening and hops on the train to the city. While she enjoyed the glitz and glamour of chauffeured cars, champagne at all hours of the day, and St. Tropez in general, riding the train to the metro and then walking back to her dorm is more her speed. Taylor has already decided that tonight is a laundry and writing night, if she can stay awake. The indulgences of the weekend have caught up with her, and she's made a pact to take it easy the next few days, get shit done, and give her body a break from partying. She's moving into her apartment next week and will want to hang out with Manuel once he's back, so the next few days are for hunkering down and being productive.

Taylor keeps her promise and manages to do a "showstopper" (per her editor, though Taylor was quite impressed with it herself) writeup on her visit to St. Tropez, catches up on email, does laundry, and buys school supplies. The thrill of fresh new folders and binders, she thinks to herself while browsing the store, will never get old. By Wednesday evening she's feeling antsy, so she texts Finn. He's not working tonight but doesn't have plans, so they decide to meet up for dinner at a tiny mom-and-pop tapas bar near Plaza España. He's a regular there, he assures her, as they walk from the metro station to the restaurant.

The conversation flows easily between them (a benefit of having zero attraction to someone of the opposite sex, at least in Taylor's case), and the owners bring out complimentary wine as soon as they sit down at their table. Finn was right, they are treating him like a long-lost son, and he soaks it up. The whole atmosphere is cozy and welcoming, and Taylor is again grateful she managed to form this unlikely friendship with Finn. They talk, drink, and feast on tapas for hours, eventually realizing that it's far later than either of them intended to stay out. After splitting the bill (which was shockingly low, given everything they consumed), they meander the back streets and head to the metro station, where they part ways.

Taylor hadn't considered who would be riding the metro or hanging out at the stations at this hour; if she had, she would have taken a cab or gone home earlier. Suffice it to say, she's lucky she makes it back to her dorm. As she arrives at the Maria Cristina metro station and is walking up the stairs, a group of young men behind her start yelling crass phrases, much of which she doesn't fully understand (sexist insults not being something they teach in high school or college Spanish). She ignores them and walks faster; just as the exit to above ground becomes visible, one of the guys grabs her calf, and she falls forward.

Taylor can't recall how she got up and out of the metro, but she knows it involved a kick to a guy's face and running faster than she'd ever run in her life (in heels, no less). She sprints all the way back to the dorm, locks the door behind her, and collapses on the floor.

"Fuck me," Taylor says aloud, breathless, still stunned and terrified. She's relieved to have her purse and phone; at least they didn't mug her. Suddenly she wants Manuel. Hands shaking, she digs into her purse and finds her phone. It's 2:15 a.m., far too late to text him, and she doesn't want to worry him. She leans her head back on the door and can practically hear her parents' and brother's voices in her ear: "Be careful, Taylor. Don't be out alone late at night. Don't do anything stupid." Thank God I'm not totally drunk, she thinks. Another glass of wine at dinner, and she may not have been able to get away so easily.

Slowly, Taylor gets off the floor and starts getting ready for bed. Her sleep is jumbled and unsettled; she has dreams but can't recall them, only that they are unpleasant, and several times cause her to bolt upright in bed, covered in sweat. The incident at the metro station has really made its way into her brain; she can't seem to shake it even by the following day. On Thursday morning she rises earlier than she would have liked, having given up on getting any decent sleep. She goes for a run to try and clear her head, which helps a little, but she still finds herself literally shaking off the discomfort she feels.

So, despite having several days before moving into the apartment, she begins packing the few personal items she had displayed, including some pictures and knickknacks to remind her of home. This mundane task helps keep her mind off what happened last night. After looking at a picture frame featuring a photo of herself and her parents from high school graduation, Taylor starts missing her parents, her mom in particular. After thinking of her mom, she decides to call home.

"Hello?" her mother answers expectantly.

"Hi mom, it's your favorite daughter calling," she says with forced enthusiasm.

"Taylor, I was just talking about you! Your ears must be ringing! How was the rest of your weekend in St. Tropez with Lindsay? When do you move to your apartment?" Her mother bombards her.

"Well, let's start with who you were talking to about me?"

"Oh, just Tanya," she laughs. "Daniel just left for London and she's freaking out a bit, you know, so I was telling her how quickly you've adapted to a new city."

"Oh-kay. Well, I'm sure he'll be fine. I mean, it's not like he needs to speak another language or anything," Taylor says spitefully, surprised to hear the note of bitterness in her own voice. "Anyways, St. Tropez was amazing, obviously. We had the best time. I'll send you the article I wrote; my editor loves it."

"Oh, that's wonderful, I'm so proud of you. Working hard while in school, way to go. And please send me all of your articles; you know how I like to send them around to my friends."

Taylor rolls her eyes and heads out to the balcony for a smoke. She wonders why every time she speaks to her parents, she finds herself desperate for a cigarette, but it's a consistent reaction, just like the eye roll. "Sure, I'll send them to you. By the way, there will be some checks arriving soon in the mail. Can you please deposit those into my checking account?"

"Of course, I'll do it as soon as they arrive. Now, when do you move into your apartment?"

"Monday. Actually, I was just starting to pack up, and I wanted to thank you for your suitcase advice. Very helpful. So, what else is going on? Have you and Tanya figured out your timing for your ladies' trip?"

"Well, we're thinking the week before Thanksgiving, so November 15th through the 22nd. How would that be for you? I can send dad to New York to spend time with Eric and Alex, and Tanya and I can gallivant around Europe! What do you think?"

"Sounds good to me," Taylor says, and it truly does. She's surprised at how much she misses her mom at this moment. Some of that is a function of what happened last night as she was leaving the metro station; she just wants a proper hug. "I really can't wait to show you around Barcelona! You'll love it here, ma. So, are you and Tanya going to London together and then here together? Or are you splitting up and visiting your kids separately?"

"Well, we haven't fully thought it through. But the plan is that we'll spend three days in London to see Daniel, and then three days in Barcelona to visit you. So, Tanya will probably be with me, sharing a hotel, but we've agreed to allow each other some alone time with our kids, of course. Apparently, Daniel has some days off that week, so we will start in London on Sunday, and come to you on Tuesday or Wednesday, so as not to interfere with too many of your classes."

"Perfect. Once you're figuring out your hotel arrangements, let me know. I can give you the address of my new apartment, I move in on Monday, like I said, and you guys can try to stay around there. Although this city is so easy to navigate. Riding the metro is so much less mysterious than I expected." As Taylor says this, she has a flashback to last night and finds her body shuddering again at the memory.

"Sounds great, thanks, honey. I can't wait. Hey, did you know that Eric has a girlfriend? I just found out, and it sounds like I'm the last one to know," her mother huffs.

"Well," Taylor says slowly, choosing her words carefully, "I just found out too, if it makes you feel any better. Sounds like she's quite the catch, from the way Eric describes her. Even Alex likes her, and he's not an easy one to impress."

"I just wish he'd have told me sooner," her mom says petulantly. "They're moving in together, for Christ's sake! And I just heard about her. Why wouldn't he have told me sooner?"

"I don't know, mom. Maybe he was just waiting to see if it was serious. Maybe he didn't want to get your hopes up? You know boys. When are you going to meet her?"

"They're coming here for Labor Day weekend. So, tomorrow night," her mother wails, sounding alarmed.

"Wow, that is quite a shock. Well, I'm sure she will love you guys, so don't worry about it. But I'm dying to know how this goes and what she's like, so let me know, will ya?" Taylor asks.

"Of course. Ok, on that note I need to get cracking on work. I'm taking tomorrow off so I can get the house ready for them. Stay safe, and be careful, you hear?"

"Yes, mom. I love you."

"I love you, too, honey. Oh! I almost forgot. Daniel does have a cousin named Erica who lives in Greenwich, so I think that's the same one you and Lindsay were asking about."

"Wow, what a small world. That's crazy. Does Tanya know anything about the girl? Apparently, she goes to Princeton, according to Lindsay."

"Of course she does," Alyssa says with sarcasm. "I don't know anything about her, but Tanya just confirmed that she's the daughter of Daniel's uncle."

They say goodbye once more and hang up, and Taylor heads back into her dorm room. She still feels shaken, but her mother's voice has provided a calming effect. Taylor knows, finally, what will get her out of this funk: retail therapy. She grabs her purse and walks down to El Corte Inglés, the massive department store where she bought her cell phone, this time with the sole purpose of looking at clothes and makeup and losing herself in the process. This is beneficial for clearing her head, but it also clears a portion of her bank account. She buys some sexy lingerie that she's looking forward to showing off to Manuel soon, along with some cheap sundresses, a new eyeliner, and bronzer.

The late afternoon and early evening drag on once she leaves the store. She's grappling with whether to tell Manuel what happened to her last night while leaving the metro. On the one hand, he may provide some comfort; on the other, he may be possessive and pissed off that she was irresponsible and out late without him. She decides, for now, to keep it to herself.

While Taylor takes a walk around the dorm, her phone dings. It's Manuel. He gives her the name of a restaurant in the Eixample neighborhood near his (and her future!) apartment. "21:30?" he asks. She responds affirmatively after calculating what time that actually is and then wonders what to do with herself for the next few hours. She grabs some groceries and restocks her alcohol and cigarette supply. By now it's just after 7 p.m., so she decides to start getting ready and do some more exploring of her new neighborhood (and its bars) before meeting Manuel. After touching up her hair and makeup and dressing for a night out, Taylor heads back to the metro station, willing away any apprehension she has about being back there.

Thirty minutes later she's wandering the Eixample neighborhood. She spots the bar where she first met Manuel, how serendipitous! Taylor feels a magnetic pull and heads inside. She takes a seat, the same seat as that fateful night, at the bar. The same old man is behind the bar, although he shows no signs of recognition. She sips a glass of wine and flips through her guidebook, but not with much focus, she's too busy reliving that first night when she and Manuel crossed paths, finding herself giddy with excitement at seeing him again. At 9:15 p.m., she pays the bill and heads back outside to find the restaurant.

Taylor spots Manuel about a quarter of a block away, walking leisurely and looking content on this beautiful evening. Once Taylor sees him looking at her, her eyes self-consciously tilt downwards before making contact with Manuel's. They both break into wide grins and quicken their pace, and suddenly they're embracing and kissing in the middle of the sidewalk. Fleetingly, Taylor feels like she's a leading lady in a romantic film and finds herself wishing she had someone there to snap their photo.

The chemistry between them is, much to Taylor's relief, even stronger than she remembered. Absence makes the heart grow fonder, so they say. They walk, hands intertwined, to a casual restaurant and take their seats outside. The night is perfect, seventy degrees and clear.

After an hour of drinking wine and catching up about what the past few weeks entailed for each of them (Manuel describes a low-key, quasi-boring yet relaxing vacation with his family; Taylor gives a glossy overview of her time in Ibiza and St. Tropez, obviously leaving out the parts she assumes will piss him off), they finally order dinner. Just after the waiter takes their orders, Taylor's phone dings with a message. It's an unfamiliar number; the country code is 44. She decides to ignore it, but when Manuel gets up to go to the restroom a minute later, she checks.

D: Hi Taylor, this is Daniel Collins. Hope you love Barcelona! I'm in London. Your mom gave my mom your number, hope that's ok. Anyways, some friends and I are coming to Barcelona next weekend. Would love to hang out, maybe you can show me around a bit? We get in on Thursday. It would be great to see you, so let me know.

What the fuck, mom?! Taylor thinks to herself. She skims the message a second time, deciding to wait until tomorrow to respond. Bad idea, bad idea, she keeps repeating in her head. She drops her phone into her bag just as Manuel returns to the table. She composes herself and pushes Daniel out of her mind by the time Manuel sits down.

They spend a lovely evening together; it is apparent as soon as they enter his apartment that Manuel had been missing Taylor, physically, as much as she had been missing him. They finally fall asleep around 1:30 a.m. Manuel has to go back to work tomorrow morning but has told Taylor to sleep in and spend as much time there as she'd like. He leaves around 9 a.m., kissing her lightly on the cheek. She dozes off and on for another hour, then decides to get up and get moving. She does some light snooping around the apartment, just opening a few drawers here, checking out some papers there, but there's nothing much of interest, which is a good thing, she reminds herself.

Taylor feels herself falling hard for Manuel; spending last night with him has solidified her feelings after their time apart. She wonders where he imagines this going. She knows if she brings it up with any of her friends, they'll just tell her to ask him directly, which she knows, rationally. She's just not quite ready to have that conversation yet, not quite ready to completely freak the guy out. And, she reasons, maybe going full steam ahead with Manuel will allow her feelings for Daniel to simmer down a bit. Lord knows she's spent far more time obsessing over him than she thought possible.

She sighs to herself and decides to tidy up the bedroom. She makes the bed and gathers her things, locking the door behind her with the spare key Manuel gave her. That key must mean something, she thinks. Guys don't just give spare keys to any random hookup. Taylor descends the stairs and goes out into the sunlight. Another gorgeous day here in Barcelona. As the warm sun hits her face, she decides right then to return to her dorm, do an hour or two of writing and catch up on emails, and then spend the rest of the day at the beach. Classes are starting soon, so her wide-open days are coming to an end. She has to make the most of every free moment.

Returning to the dorm, Taylor takes a quick shower and then hunkers down to get down to business. She checks her emails, responds to a few, and marks potential travel dates to meet up with friends. She's avoiding responding to Daniel, but she knows that she needs to. She finally re-reads his text and responds:

T: Hi! Hope you are enjoying London. Would be great to meet up. Maybe we can hang out Thursday night when you get in? I'm around; school doesn't start until the week after. Let me know!

Taylor breathes a sigh of relief after pressing send, now the ball is back in his court. The problem is, as much as she's digging Manuel, she's worried if Daniel makes any moves, she may be unable to resist. She thinks back to the night they spent together regularly, often wishing they could do it all over again. She regroups and gets ready for the beach, opting to wait and worry about Daniel once he arrives.

The rest of the weekend is a blur of beach-going, window shopping, packing, and hanging out with Manuel. She has already enlisted him to help her move; he doesn't have a car, but one of his friends does. So, Monday morning he picks her up at 8, they load up the car, Taylor checks out of her dorm (fortunately she got her security deposit back in full, in cash), and they make the fifteen-minute drive to her new apartment on Carrer Roselló.

Manuel helps her drag her suitcases and miscellaneous stuff up to the apartment. Once everything is in, he kisses her and has to run to work for a meeting. He promises to check in later in the day to see how she's doing with moving in.

Once he's left, Taylor sits on the small bed in her room. She is happy, and a bit shell-shocked, that this little place will be her home for the next nine months (at least). She starts by unpacking her picture frames, placing them around the room to remind her of her friends and family. Next, she unloads her toiletries and makeup. Clothes and shoes are the last to be unpacked, she's lacking in hangers but manages to unload everything, happily stashing her suitcases as deep into the tiny closet as she can. Once the unpacking is complete, she wanders around the empty apartment. There's an itty-bitty balcony, which seems to house a marijuana plant. Interesting, Taylor thinks to herself. Carla, the landlord, didn't strike her as a pothead, but who knows?

Taylor wipes a bead of sweat from her brow; all of the unpacking has made her sweaty and ravenous. She decides to run out to explore the neighborhood. There's a small supermercado a block away, so she stops in there first. She gets some fruit, cereal, snacks, and wine, and heads back home (another new home!) and unloads her loot in the kitchen. There's a stack of sheets and towels folded neatly on her bed, so she puts the sheets on the bed and checks out the bathroom. It is alarmingly small; it appears to have shrunk by about half since Taylor originally viewed the apartment.

"Jesus," she mutters to herself. Fortunately, it's relatively empty, save for a hand towel, soap, and hair care products in the shower. Nicholas must still be on holiday with his family.

Taylor showers in the tiny shower, struggling to shave her legs given the lack of space. It has hot water, she reminds herself, something her home often lacked growing up. Five people sharing one shower was rough, and being the youngest, she usually had last pick for shower time. She can make do with this.

The week proceeds uneventfully; Taylor feels more like a local every day. She finds little places in her new neighborhood, orients herself to the nearby metro stations, and finally meets her roommate, Nicholas. He shows up Wednesday afternoon while Taylor is sitting in the living room typing up a review of the Gaudí houses, which she visited on Tuesday, and smoking a cigarette. Nicholas bursts into the apartment, adorably disheveled and so obviously British. Taylor quickly stubs her cigarette out in the ashtray and pops out of her seat.

"Hi there, love," he exclaims enthusiastically, proceeding to kiss Taylor on both cheeks. He's in his mid-twenties, from the looks of it, and waifish in his appearance; his jeans, which would be skintight on anyone else, hang loosely below his waist, revealing a Calvin Klein label on his underwear. He has tattoos running along most of both arms and three studs in his right ear. His blonde hair is rumpled, and it is apparent that he's spent the past few hours traveling.

"Hi," Taylor responds, noticing she is a good two inches taller than him, even without shoes on. "It's so nice to meet you. I just moved in on Monday," she says nervously.

"You're even prettier than Carla described," he says with an easy laugh. "She told me a 'really cute American girl' was moving in. I can tell," he says, his eyes narrowing while giving her a once-over. "We're going to have a lot of fun going out, yeah?"

Taylor laughs and feels herself blushing, par for the course anytime she receives a compliment. Her outfit definitely screams "Fun American Exchange Student," and she's just bumming around the apartment. "Thanks, and I also imagine we're going to have a lot of fun. I'm a party girl at heart, and Carla told me you know all the hotspots all over the city."

"One of the perks that comes along with my gay card . . . we're the first to know about the good clubs. Usually, they start as gay clubs and then go mainstream once you heteros get a listen to how good the music is," Nicholas responds with a smirk. "Sorry, I'm just assuming you're straight. How rude of me . . . it's been a long day. A long month, really, been with my family nonstop, so I'm totally exhausted."

Taylor laughs at his bluntness and confirms, "Yes, I am straight. But I love a good gay bar as much as the next girl. Sounds like you need a good night out to recover from family time, eh? I'm free tonight; the guy I'm seeing has a work thing, so if you need a partner in crime, I'm all yours."

"Done. I'll take you up on that. We mustn't miss these opportunities to go out this week before classes resume. Carla told me you're an exchange student. I'm working on my doctorate in education; my classes start up next week."

"Same here," Taylor interjects.

Nicholas holds up his pointer finger. "Hold on," he says, eyes narrowing. "You've only been here a handful of weeks, and you're seeing someone? Is he a local, or a fellow exchange student? Please don't tell me your college boyfriend came along with you here," Nicholas says, exasperation in his voice.

"No, no. He's from Barcelona. He actually lives in this neighborhood. We met at the little tapas bar around the corner and just hit it off."

Nicholas looks at her, vaguely skeptical, and nods. "Alright then. Look, I need a nap, but let's get dinner around here tonight and we can go out afterward, yeah?"

"Sounds perfect. Hey, I'm running out to el supermercado. You need anything?"

"Thanks, I definitely need stuff, but I'm so brain-dead right now I can't even think of what it is that I need. I'll go tomorrow. Let's plan on dinner around 10 p.m. We can have cocktails here before dinner," Nicholas says, gesturing toward a liquor cabinet Taylor hadn't yet noticed. "I don't have many domestic skills, but I am one hell of a mixologist and can make you the best martini you'll ever have."

"Perfect! I accept. Go get some rest, I'll see you later," Taylor tells him, excited by the promise of a great martini.

Nicholas gives Taylor a little salute and heads off to his room. Taylor sits back down at her computer and spends a few more minutes writing before heading out to the store. She goes to the tobacco shop, then back to the supermarket, where she picks up breakfast foods, some cheap red wine, and more snacks. She assumes she'll be eating lunch on campus most days. She also grabs some toilet paper and toiletries she's running low on.

Nicholas emerges from his room around 8:30 p.m., showers, and they start drinking shortly thereafter. Over martinis and a lot of cigarettes, they get to know each other while blasting Christina Aguilera's *Mi Reflejo* album, which Taylor is immediately enamored with. They become instant friends, and Taylor feels relief at having a normal roommate whom she genuinely likes.

The wild night out Nicholas promised her exceeds her expectations. They have a quick and cheap dinner at Pans, which is basically Spain's version of McDonald's, since they didn't make it out of the apartment until close to 11 p.m. After some insanely good patatas bravas and cheap sandwiches, they get in a cab and go to a club called Danzatoria. Even though it's a Wednesday, a crowd is waiting in line to get in, everyone looking gorgeous and immaculately dressed. They meet some of Nicholas's friends from school, dance, drink, and the next thing Taylor knows it's 2:30 a.m., and she's drenched in sweat and dancing with a hot Spanish guy. Whatever decision-making abilities she has are telling her this is a bad idea, so she makes a slick exit from the dance floor and heads to the bathroom, where she texts Nicholas to find out his whereabouts.

Eventually, Taylor finds Nicholas; he has paired up with a very cute American guy, James, who is apparently heading home with them. Taylor is happy Nicholas found a cute hookup, and she and James catch up on where they grew up, what they miss about the U.S. (not much at this moment), and how great Barcelona is. As soon as they get to the apartment, Taylor bids them good night and gives them their privacy.

Thursday morning, Taylor wakes up late and decides that today, in her mildly hungover state, her time will be best spent preparing for classes next week. She can't possibly do any writing or sightseeing, so after a late breakfast, she packs up her school supplies, ensuring she has all the materials for each class. She feels a sense of relief once she's gotten her school bag organized and her schedule written down. The small sense of achievement compels her to venture outside for coffee. She makes the walk to Starbucks, it's a ten-minute walk but feels longer in the heat and with a hangover, and once she's there with a venti Frappuccino seated in the shade, she's finally beginning to feel normal again. She replays last night in her head and recalls talking to Nicholas and James about Daniel's visit this weekend.

"Bad idea," Nicholas had told her. "Not to generalize, but I'm going to anyway: There's one thing about Spanish men, and that's that they get jealous. Your novio, or whatever he is, will be pissed off and possessive, even if you and this Daniel fellow are just hanging out as friends. Trust me."

Taylor hadn't argued with him; after all, he wasn't wrong. But she was already planning on ignoring his well-intended advice. She is a grown woman, for Christ's sake; she can have a male friend while dating someone else. She is more worried about Daniel's expectations. In any case, she is excited and a bit anxious about seeing Daniel this evening.

She nurses her Frappuccino and smokes, reminding herself to enjoy these last carefree days with no responsibility before school begins. Taylor doesn't expect the classes to be too challenging based on feedback from older students at UNC, but she'll still have work to do. As she takes a long exhale and sinks back in her seat, her phone dings with a new text message. She recognizes the country code and realizes it's Daniel. She opens the message.

D: At Heathrow, damn flight delayed by two hours. Not landing 'til 11 p.m. Can we meet up tomorrow instead?

Taylor feels a stab of disappointment juxtaposed with relief upon reading the message. She responds casually.

T: Sure, no problem. Text me tomorrow once you have a plan for the day. Safe travels!

Now with an open evening in front of her, Taylor decides to ask Manuel out for dinner tonight, her treat, since he's always paying for her. Knowing he's still at work, she risks it and calls him. He sounds genuinely happy about the dinner invitation, and they agree to meet again at the bar where they first met around 9 p.m. for drinks and dinner.

Taylor and Manuel have another great evening together, which ends with him coming over to her apartment and meeting Nicholas before they retire for the night. Manuel and Nicholas seem to hit it off, having far more to talk about than Taylor expected. This is a weight off her shoulders; knowing that her boyfriend and male roommate can coexist in the same room without some sort of pissing war or other bizarre male conduct is a major relief. She supposes that Nicholas being gay alleviates such behavior, but is relieved nonetheless. Over dinner, she even ventures to tell Manuel that she'll be busy the following night, as she will be going out with a friend visiting from London. She omits the fact that it is a male friend whom she's actually had sex with, but he doesn't ask.

Manuel sets Taylor's old-fashioned alarm clock for 8 a.m. the following morning so he'll have time to go home for a shower and change before work. They cram into Taylor's minuscule bed, half of Manuel's body hanging off the side. After spending ten minutes trying to contort their bodies into a quasi-comfortable arrangement, they make a mutual agreement that nights together should, going forward, be spent at Manuel's place.

Taylor stirs when Manuel wakes up, but after he kisses her on the cheek and quietly leaves her room, she falls back into a deep sleep. She wakes again around ten, feeling energetic and well-rested. The sun is shining through her curtains, and she decides immediately to make today a beach day.

An hour later, Taylor is on the beach, which is markedly less crowded than her previous visit with Manuel. She spends hours alternating between reading, napping, and dipping in the water. She can feel her tan darkening, thank God! She feels so pasty compared to the Spanish women. After a few hours in the sun, she gets a text from Daniel.

D: Hey, finally here, staying in a hostel off Las Ramblas. Meet tonight? Dinner and then go out?

Taylor can't help but smile. She texts him back a few minutes later.

T: Sure, sounds good. I know a good tapas place on Passeig de Gràcia, not far from you. Then a dance club by the water? Let me know what time, no one eats here until after 9.

He responds immediately.

D: 9:30 then? Tapas place sounds great. Can you text me the address later? Looking forward to seeing you.

Taylor pulls out the matchbook she took from Tapa Tapa on her first night in Barcelona. She texts Daniel back.

T: Same, here's the address, Passeig de Gràcia 44. See you at 9:30!

Now that she has a plan, Taylor has to figure out what to wear. She knows she's treating this too much like a date, but she can't help herself. There's a possibility that Daniel will show up with, like, five of his friends, and she'll be a total third wheel. Or he'll come alone, thinking this is in fact a date, which would be even more awkward.

Turns out it's just Daniel and his "flatmate," Ethan, one of his pals from Duke. (Taylor thinks to herself, *Christ, he's been in London a week and he's already being a pretentious ass... couldn't he just say roommate like a normal person?*) In any case, Ethan seems relatively normal and nice, and the three of them spend the next two hours drinking sangria and ordering various tapas, swapping their experiences living abroad thus far. Both Daniel and Ethan are wowed by Taylor's travels, knowledge of Barcelona, and the fact that she independently scored an apartment in such a cool neighborhood. Taylor learns that Daniel, Ethan, and a third friend, Will, are sharing an apartment in London. All in all, they have a great time exchanging stories, and any awkwardness Taylor had been expecting isn't there.

After paying the bill (split by Daniel and Ethan, as a thank-you to Taylor for showing them around the city and helping them order the least frightening food off the menu), they hop in a taxi and take a quick ride to Maremagnum. Taylor's hip Spanish boyfriend may be unwilling to come here, but these two American guys, lured by stiff drinks and familiar music, are easy to convince.

The club Maremagnum is housed in a massive shopping center near the port; there are restaurants and a mini-golf course among the shops, making the whole scene a random configuration of destinations and their respective clientele. The music from the club is audible from the street, and the trio, fueled by strong sangria at dinner, is pumped to get inside. The club isn't terribly crowded; Taylor, Daniel, and Ethan get in without a line and head straight to the bar. After ordering rum and cokes, they watch wide-eyed as the bartender fills their glasses 2/3 of the way up with rum and only the remaining 1/3 with coke. Taylor had warned them about this over dinner, but seeing it with their own eyes, the guys are taken aback.

"You weren't kidding about the drink ratios," Ethan exclaims enthusiastically above Christina Aguilera belting out *Come On Over*, the Spanish version. "We're gonna get fucked up." He high-fives Daniel.

Taylor stifles an eye roll. Of the things she's been missing from home, wasted frat-boy behavior isn't high on the list. But she can't help but join in their enthusiasm, so she clinks glasses and says, "Salud! To a great night in a great city."

"With great people," Daniel adds, giving her a wink. *Oh boy,* Taylor thinks to herself. Over dinner earlier in the evening she had mentioned Manuel but can't recall whether she'd actually used the word boyfriend, so she readies herself for the possibility that Daniel will try to hook up and she'll have to push him away. Ethan decides at that moment to go to the bathroom and "do a lap" of the dance floor to see if there's anyone interesting, which Taylor interprets as him looking for someone he considers hookup-worthy.

Taylor and Daniel hop onto bar stools, and Taylor lights a cigarette, blowing the smoke away from Daniel, as he's a non-smoker.

"So! Our moms would be super proud to see this," Taylor laughs. "Their little February babies, all grown up and exploring bars in foreign lands."

"My mom will never forgive me for not studying in Spain or South America," Daniel responds with a shake of his head. "She spent months trying to persuade me, but I've had my eye on London forever. Plus, for a business degree, London makes the most sense. But she won't get over it," Daniel laments.

"Hey, you don't have to justify your decision to me," Taylor says. "Although, between you and me, you're missing out on living in the world's greatest city, but whatever." She gives him a playful elbow and continues, "Come on, she's a Spanish teacher! Of course Tanya wanted you to be somewhere you can practice your skills. As a consolation, let her know that until tonight, I've spoken almost entirely in Spanish since I arrived here. That ought to make her proud."

"You know they're coming to visit, right? Our moms, like, together?" Daniel asks Taylor.

"I know, my mom is super excited. Good for them! They deserve to explore Europe together and spy on their kids. You know that's what they're really doing, right? Checking on us?" Taylor asks.

"I figured as much. It's fine. I mean, you know we'll at least get some free meals for a few days, so there's that."

Taylor and Daniel talk for a few more minutes before Ethan returns and provides them with his hilarious analysis of the club. As Taylor looks out at the dance floor, she realizes his descriptions are not only funny but spot-on. The British guys are drunk and loud, the Americans are just loud, and all the guys are trying to dance with the handful of locals. The locals are trying to ignore everyone else and just dance among themselves.

"Well, let's go and join the loud Americans," Taylor exclaims unnecessarily boisterously as Michael Jackson's "Beat It" remix transitions to Madonna's "Like a Prayer." Taylor hasn't been out once in Barcelona without hearing this song, she realizes, as the guys follow her onto the dance floor.

After dancing for a while, at some point Taylor decides to take a break. She signals to Daniel that she's heading to the bar. He whispers something to Ethan, who smiles and gives him a high five before immersing himself into a group of young women in the middle of the dance floor. Taylor has to hand it to him: Ethan may not have any actual game, but he makes up for it with unwavering, unsubstantiated confidence.

Daniel meets Taylor at the bar, where he orders another round of rum and cokes. Taylor tries to keep her cool and not let this handsome young man, whom she's known her entire life, sabotage her relationship with Manuel. As she's thinking all of this, Daniel hands her the rum and coke, and they find two empty bar stools. Then he starts talking.

"So, I've been meaning to be in touch with you, Taylor. Like, way before now. I feel like a dick about what happened between us last year, or at least the way I handled things afterward. When you called me, you know, after that night, I was so torn. Sarah and I had just gotten back together, and I wanted to give her another chance. Looking back, that was a huge mistake. The night you and I spent together... well, it was one of the best of my life; I will never forget it, and I've replayed it in my head so many times."

At this, Taylor feels her cheeks burn and her heartbeat quicken.

"You don't need to apologize, Daniel. It was a really special night for me, too, but I understand you were sort of in a rough place. What's the story with you and Sarah? Are you still together?" she asks, already knowing the answer.

"God, no. We broke up again the second semester of freshman year, not long after we got back together," Daniel says with a sigh. "It just didn't work."

"And have you been seeing anyone, like, since then?" Taylor asks cautiously.

"Here and there, nothing serious. I'm single now if that's what you're wondering." As Daniel says this, he places his hand on her knee, and Taylor freezes.

"Okay, well, there's something I should tell you," Taylor says once she regains her composure and remembers how to speak. She gently removes his hand from her knee and looks him directly in the eye. She feels like they've been sucked into a void, where only the two of them exist. The previously bumping music seems to quiet around them, and she can only focus on Daniel. *Sweet Jesus, this is painful,* she thinks to herself.

"I'm seeing someone here, in Barcelona. We met on one of my first nights here and have been dating since. I think I mentioned him at dinner; his name is Manuel."

Daniel appears crestfallen for a moment; the look on his face makes Taylor feel like a total asshole. He quickly recovers, smiles, and tells her,

"I can't be surprised, to be honest. You're too gorgeous to be single. So, who is the guy? Another exchange student?"

Daniel asks with a fake smile plastered on his face, and Taylor has to remind herself of how disappointed she was last year, when he basically rejected her to get back together with Sarah. This alleviates some of her guilt, but not all of it. God, not nearly all of it.

"Actually, no. He's a local, if you can believe it! He's twenty-six, actually. So, maybe don't tell your mom; I just don't want my parents freaking out, is all. I'll tell them soon. And thank you for the other stuff, that's very sweet of you to say. And for the record, you also look really good. Great, actually."

Taylor gives a nervous laugh. "Just so you know, I've kind of been dreading this conversation. I'm glad we can talk freely about this stuff, by the way."

"An elderly Spaniard!" Daniel laughs, though his eyes continue to project a melancholy that he's covering up. "What will your mother say?" Daniel asks mockingly. "Or better yet, your brothers!"

"Ugh, stop it. I can't even imagine telling any of them yet," Taylor says with an eye roll.

"Well, for what it's worth, I appreciate your honesty. I obviously came here with other intentions, but can we still hang out?"

"Of course," Taylor gushes, feeling relief with a pang of lingering guilt. Desperate to change the subject, she asks Daniel,

"Also, did you know I'm doing some travel and 'lifestyle' writing for your grandparents?" Taylor finds herself unable to say the word *lifestyle* without using air quotes; it sounds far too cheesy to say with any semblance of seriousness.

"My mom told me that. She actually emailed me one of your write-ups, the one about Park Güell, I think it was. Can you give me the in-person tour while I'm here? You're a talented writer, so I really hope they're paying you fairly," Daniel says, successfully changing the subject and lightening a hint of the awkwardness.

At the fair pay comment, Taylor nearly spits out her rum and coke.

"That's hilarious! It's not totally fair, but I'd say I'm the one on the winning end. They've been beyond generous. They're basically funding, like, my life here, aside from tuition."

"Well, if that changes and they get stingy, let me know. I've got a direct line to the big boss," Daniel says with a wink.

There's an amicable silence, and just as Taylor is ready to suggest that she head home and let Daniel and Ethan hunt for girls, Ethan comes over, drenched in sweat, directly off the dance floor.

"Hey mates," he says in a crappy mock London accent. "You guys ready to bounce? Check out another club?"

"You guys go," Taylor tells them, while signaling to the bartender for the check. "I'll go back home, and maybe we can meet up tomorrow? I'll give you guys the tour of Park Güell and anywhere else you want to see; my day is wide open until dinner."

They agree, and Daniel and Ethan decide to head over to La Oveja Negra, a Barcelona institution, not far from where they are now. Daniel kisses Taylor on both cheeks and gives her a warm hug, promising to text her in the morning so she can show them around.

Despite the late hour, (it's already well past midnight), and her uncomfortable shoes, Taylor decides to walk home. It's at least a thirty-minute walk, but she needs the fresh air, and all the streets are filled with people out on this Friday night. She can't help but reflect on tonight and how things played out (or not, depending on how you look at it) with Daniel. She feels, for perhaps the first time in the twenty years they've known each other, the potential for a really great friendship. They just need to get over their romantic feelings for one another.

Easier said than done, she thinks to herself while lighting a cigarette. Her phone dings with a new text message. It's from Manuel; he's checking in to confirm their dinner plans for tomorrow night. His brother's friend has an in at a super posh restaurant where it's nearly impossible to get a table any night of the week, but since Manuel has the connection, they have a reservation for Saturday night. Taylor texts back and asks if Manuel wants to come over before dinner for a cocktail. He does, it turns out, so Taylor adds going to the liquor store to her to-do list for tomorrow.

As she turns her key in the door of the apartment, Taylor finds herself willing Nicholas to be out for the night. She adores him, of course; she's just exhausted from tonight and doesn't have the energy to talk to anyone, drained from so much socialization, if she's being honest with herself. She's also too deep in her own thoughts, contemplating everything Daniel said tonight, and trying to figure out how to keep him as a friend without their feelings complicating things. As she enters, the apartment is quiet and the lights are off, so if Nicholas is here, he's asleep. Taylor does her nightly routine and is asleep almost instantly.

The next morning, Taylor checks her phone and finds a text from Daniel that arrived at 3:36 a.m. She's afraid to open it, knowing full well he was far from sober when he wrote it. She clicks to open it and laughs out loud after reading it.

D: It was sooo grAt to see you tonight. See you tmorow.

Poor Daniel, she thinks to herself, imagining how shitty he must be feeling right now. She texts him back right away.

T: Hope you're feeling okay today! Great seeing you too, let me know when you're ready for Park Güell! Xoxo, Taylor

It's only 10 a.m., so it's unlikely she'll hear back from him anytime soon, but she feels better having reached out. Before she can change her mind, she puts on running gear and takes a jog, blissfully ending her route at Starbucks, where she rewards herself with a Frappuccino and a cigarette (the irony of smoking after a workout isn't lost on her, but it's one of Taylor's greatest pleasures, that post-exercise cigarette).

The day blows by, and a little after 2:30 in the afternoon, Daniel finally texts her.

D: Oh my God, holy fucking hangover. Sorry, I know it's late in the day, but I'm just now okay. You up to meet at Park Güell in like an hour?

Taylor is already showered and ready to go, so they agree on a place and time to meet. Deep down, she knows Daniel doesn't actually give a shit about seeing Park Güell. It's a combined win for him, being able to say he saw some sights in Barcelona while also spending time with Taylor. She doesn't mind at all and is looking forward to spending a few sober hours with him.

When Daniel arrives (ten minutes late) at their designated meeting place, he looks like hell. He gives her a hug, eyes bloodshot, and apologizes for being late and for the drunk text last night.

"Oh please," Taylor tells him. "We've all been there. I'm sorry you're not feeling well. The drinks here, like I said... they'll hit you like a Mack truck." They sit down on a bench on the outskirts of the park.

Daniel laughs and says, "Sorry, but that was like the most Wisconsin thing I've heard in a long time. Most girls don't have a clue what a Mack truck is." They laugh and catch up on the rest of Daniel's night out for a few minutes before an amicable silence ensues.

Looking Taylor directly in the eyes, Daniel tells her, "You're funny and genuine, on top of everything else you've got going for you. How does it feel knowing that you could literally get any guy you want? I mean, look at you, Taylor, you're perfect."

"Daniel," Taylor says with surprise and a bit of resentment, "that's not true, first of all, and second of all, I thought you were less shallow than that! I'm not interested in just getting any guy, especially just based on my looks. I hope that's not how you see me."

Taylor looks away, her eyes landing on a group of Asian tourists blocking the entire path, cameras everywhere. One guy even has his camcorder out. Taylor focuses on him to distract herself from her current irritation. She wonders under what circumstances this guy will ever watch the videotape of his tourist group visiting this park in Barcelona.

Meanwhile, Daniel puts his head in his hands and sighs, interrupting Taylor's thoughts.

"Shit, Taylor, that obviously came out wrong. I didn't mean it the way you interpreted it. I'm sorry, I'm probably still drunk. I meant to say that I think you're incredible. You're smart and funny, on top of being stunningly gorgeous. There you have it," he says, sounding apologetic.

Taylor turns her focus back to him, the tourists now on the move. She gives Daniel a small smile and takes a deep breath.

"Sorry for overreacting. It just kind of sounded like you think I can get anyone based on my looks, which is certainly not the case. And it's not like you're hurting in any of the aforementioned departments!" she tells him with an exasperated sigh. "Maybe we should start over. Thank you for complimenting me. I think you're equally wonderful, and..." Before Taylor finishes her sentence, Daniel pulls her into him and kisses her. Without any hesitation, she's kissing him back, and loving every second of it.

After a few moments, Taylor finally comes to her senses and pulls away.

"Shit," she says, standing up suddenly and looking around. "Shit, that wasn't supposed to... I can't do this."

"Taylor, I'm sorry. I shouldn't have kissed you. I just couldn't help it. I'm sorry. Fuck." Daniel wrings his hands together and looks the other way.

"I should go. I have to go. Can we just, I don't know... not mention this?" Taylor asks while gathering her purse and smoothing out an imaginary crease on the front of her sundress.

Daniel looks right at her and nods. He puts his hands in his pockets, looking up at the sky. He looks broken, Taylor thinks. And she broke him. Her heart hurts when she turns to leave, giving him a small wave that he doesn't return.

Taylor hurries off, not sure where she's going, just feeling the desperate need to get the hell out of there and put as much distance between herself and Daniel as possible. She wants to crawl into a hole and disappear. Her guilt is twofold: she was unfaithful to Manuel, and she clearly shattered Daniel just as they were developing what she thought could become a real friendship. And, to make matters worse, she has to pull herself together in the next few hours and see Manuel for dinner. There's no benefit in telling him, she reasons immediately and concretely; it won't help anyone. She will have to live with this guilt and deal with it on her own.

In the meantime, what she really needs at this exact moment is a drink. A stiff drink. She walks toward the nearest metro station and finds a bar along the way. It's late afternoon, and the place is dark and nearly empty, save for a few older men watching a soccer game on the TV above the bar. *Perfect,* Taylor thinks. She orders a vodka with soda and lights a cigarette, exhaling forcefully. She's left alone to ruminate, asking herself how she could have fucked things up so grandly before her classes have even started.

Years later, Taylor will look back on this afternoon and analyze it to death. She will ask herself how she didn't connect the dots earlier. Why, for instance, her guilt as she sat in that dark bar was more about Daniel's hurt feelings than her infidelity to Manuel. Why her feelings about an old family friend, who, sure, she'd hooked up with but didn't really know that well, not really, trumped those of her current boyfriend, with whom she spent multiple nights a week. When she rehashes the events of today, it will all be so obvious. In the moment, however, she just feels misery and shame in every bone of her body.

Taylor eventually peels herself off the barstool and makes it back to her apartment. She goes through the motions of having dinner with Manuel and spending the night with him afterward, but her mind is elsewhere.

School starts on Monday, and after a few days of classes, Taylor is able to push the constant thoughts of Daniel aside. She has decided to wait until October to travel, allowing herself the month of September to see the sights in Barcelona, while simultaneously forcing herself to focus on schoolwork and get the semester started on the right foot.

September flies by. There are visits from friends and acquaintances from UNC who are also studying abroad in various European cities, during which Taylor is both tour guide and translator. Whatever places she takes visitors, she writes about: Sagrada Familia, the Boqueria Market, Las Ramblas, Montjuïc, Camp Nou Stadium, you name it. In September alone, she submits three writing pieces. All are excellent, according to her editor, and she suspects that Daniel will be reading each and every one, an assumption she tries to push aside while doing her writing.

It turns out her suspicion was correct. Towards the end of the month, she gets an email from Daniel. Rather long and rambling, she assumes he wrote it under the influence of alcohol or something else. He basically apologizes for his advances while he was in Barcelona but holds firm that he has feelings for her and, if she ever feels the same way, he will be there. He also commends her on her recent writing, mentioning that his hard-to-please grandparents have been extremely impressed with her skills.

Taylor bides her time for a few days before acknowledging Daniel's email. When she finally responds, she tells him that she enjoys spending time with him and hopes that they can remain friends and stay in touch, if he's open to that. She reiterates that she's currently attached but lets him know that she has spent the past eighteen months thinking of him often. She asks him if she were to visit London later this year, would he be up for hanging out? Before she can change her mind, she hits the send button and closes her computer.

Having sent the email, Taylor leaves the school campus and walks slowly back to the metro station, enjoying the late-day sun on her face. It's the first of October, though you'd never know it from the still-toasty temperatures. It's a Wednesday, and tonight she's meeting Manuel for dinner. He's been traveling for work the past week, and Taylor is heading to Salamanca tomorrow afternoon, where she'll meet up with Katie and Lindsay and see some other UNC friends.

September progressed in such a blur; Taylor feels like she barely had the opportunity to see Manuel. She is so busy with school, not necessarily the academics per se, but the social piece. She's made a nice group of core friends who she goes out with on the regular. They sing karaoke, go dancing at Danzatoria, and complain about their hangovers over coffee on the weekends. It's an eclectic group: students from the U.S., England, Sweden, and Germany. Some are gay, some are straight, some are bisexual. The lack of judgment among this group has delighted Taylor and her liberal leanings, and she's learning a lot from her non-straight friends in particular. Their one and only rule is that, when they go out, they only speak Spanish. So, by this point, Taylor, who was "proficient" in Spanish upon arriving in Barcelona, is now basically fluent. She loves showing off her new vocabulary words to Manuel. Tonight, she's going to throw her newest word into conversation: *resaca*, hangover. How it took her this long to learn, she'll never know. Apparently, that wasn't a particularly important vocabulary word in her AP Spanish classes back in high school.

As she exits the metro station near her apartment, Taylor stops dead in her tracks. About 100 feet ahead of her is Manuel, walking with a petite, gorgeous (at least from behind) woman with jet-black hair. They're walking close, too close for "just friends." It's only two hours before she's supposed to meet him for dinner. Taylor panics. She doesn't know whether to run up to them and start screaming at him, pretend she never saw it, or wait until dinner to confront him. She resumes breathing once Manuel and this mystery woman round the corner, she doesn't know how long she'd been holding her breath, and opts for the third option. Maybe it's nothing.

Taylor arrives home and is surprised to see Nicholas at home; he's usually at school, working, or out. He doesn't seem to need more than four hours of sleep.

"My long-lost roommate," she yells enthusiastically, and the two hug. "What's going on? You're never home at this hour."

"Oh, I'm burned out. Needed a night in, so I bummed off from work tonight. You want to go eat or drink something?" Nicholas asks.

"I'm having dinner with Manuel in," Taylor checks a watch that isn't on her wrist, "I don't know... two hours? But I would love to grab a drink beforehand if you're up for it."

"Indeed! Give me five minutes to get my shit organized, then we'll head to the bar." 'The bar' is their local place, around the corner. It's a dump that caters to old-school locals, but everything is extra cheap, and by now most of the staff know Taylor and Nicholas and treat them well. As such, it's become their favorite neighborhood watering hole.

Taylor nods, relieved that she has someone to talk to about the Manuel situation. She goes into her room and adds a few items to her little suitcase for her trip to Salamanca tomorrow, and putters around in the kitchen while she waits.

Nicholas emerges from his room, looking as dapper as ever in skintight jeans and a gorgeous leather jacket, despite the hot weather.

"Well, damn, I'm a lucky lady going out with this stud," Taylor exclaims. "Please promise me you'll actually come back home after drinks and get some rest? You've been burning the candle at both ends."

Nicholas gives her a naughty wink and promises, with sarcasm oozing from his mouth, that he'll be a good boy and rest up tonight.

Within minutes they're seated on barstools, and Taylor has begun telling the story of seeing Manuel on the street earlier today. Before Nicholas has a chance to opine, Taylor also blabs about her rogue kiss with Daniel, and how she's kept it from Manuel and how guilty she feels on all counts, adding that she has no real right to feel angry at Manuel for whatever she saw, since she made out with Daniel.

"The plot thickens, my lovely," Nicholas says with a wicked grin, rubbing his fingers together like some villainous professor.

"This is serious," Taylor wails. "What do I do? Confront him about fucking around and not mention that I did the same?"

"First of all, a kiss is hardly an affair. You're making too much of this kiss with Daniel. Let it go. He initiated anyways, so it doesn't really count. As for this situation with Manuel, you need to confront him. Maybe it was a coworker or an old family friend, but you'll never feel okay until you ask him." Nicholas takes a long swig from his beer and dramatically lights a cigarette. "I mean, how certain are you that it was even him that you saw? There are a lot of well-dressed, good-looking men in this neighborhood who look similar from behind, trust me. On this topic, I am officially an expert."

Taylor laughs and plucks the cigarette out of his hand, taking a long drag.

"You're right, maybe I'm overreacting. I don't know for sure that it was him, but I'd bet a lot of money on it. Fine, I'll tread lightly. You make a valid point," she sighs with resignation.

"And whatever you do," Nicholas continues, "don't mention the kiss with Daniel. You think it will eradicate your guilt, but you'll carry it with you regardless, and it'll only piss him off."

"Thank you, old wise one," Taylor says with a hint of sarcasm and a lot of gratitude.

"Who you calling old, you daft cow?" Nicholas exclaims with mock offense.

They both laugh, and Taylor gives him a kiss on the cheek.

"Oh, I love when you get all British on me! Daft cow. I only wish I could get away with saying that."

They chat for a while longer before Nicholas stands up, drains his beer, throws down a handful of euros, and tells Taylor,

"I'm off. You sit here, finish your drink, and relax before you go to dinner. It's on me. I'm going to sleep early, but if you need to talk, wake me up, promise?"

"Sure thing. And Nicholas? Thank you. I appreciate your words of wisdom."

He blows her a kiss and walks out the door, leaving Taylor alone with her thoughts, the last place she wants to be. She agrees with everything Nicholas said but is still having a hard time processing what she saw on the street earlier. She and Manuel have never actually declared that they were exclusive, but given how often they see each other (and are in bed together), Taylor assumed it was a given. She'll have to broach the subject tonight.

She smokes one last cigarette, finishes her drink, and thanks the bartender while walking out the door. Taylor decides to get to the restaurant a few minutes early. She can order a glass of wine to calm her nerves and hopefully be somewhat composed by the time Manuel arrives. They are meeting at a bougie tapas restaurant only a few blocks away, so she begins the walk over.

After arriving at the restaurant, Taylor asks the hostess for an outdoor table for two and is quickly seated, given a menu, and provided an ashtray. She orders a glass of red wine and checks her phone, which is flooded with text messages from Lindsay and Katie, making plans for their weekend in Salamanca. She starts reading through the texts and is so engrossed that she jumps in surprise when Manuel leans over her and kisses her on the cheek.

"Hola mi amor, qué pasa?" he asks as he sits down.

"Oh my God, you scared me!" She laughs. "Sorry, hi! How are you? Er, cómo estás?"

They talk for a few minutes, catching up on what's been happening in their respective lives. Before Taylor can mention what she saw earlier this evening, Manuel lets her know that his cousin, Paula, is visiting from Madrid for a long weekend. She's staying at his place, so he asks sheepishly if perhaps they can spend the night at Taylor's apartment. Also, would Taylor like to meet her after dinner?

Taylor lets out a sigh of relief that she hopes isn't too obvious and lets Manuel know that yes, he can absolutely spend the night at her place (even though, as they've previously discovered, Taylor's bed is approximately the right size for a Barbie doll), and yes, she'd love to meet Paula. Nicholas was right, after all, that brilliant bastard. She sends him a quick text letting him know as much from the bathroom of the restaurant.

After dinner, they meet Paula at a local bar where she had met up with some friends. Taylor is again relieved, this time to see her in the flesh and have confirmation that she is in fact the woman who was walking with Manuel earlier this evening. She's a little spitfire, twenty-three years old, right in between Taylor and Manuel age-wise. They get on well, so well in fact, that Paula has invited Taylor to come and visit her in Madrid anytime. By midnight, Paula is heading to another bar to meet some other friends, so Taylor and Manuel make the short walk back to Taylor's apartment after saying good night to Paula.

Later, after a spectacular performance in bed (hard to do, given the tiny bed and tiny room, but they manage to make do), Manuel hugs Taylor into his chest and asks her about her trip to Salamanca tomorrow. Who is she seeing? Where is she staying? He wants to know everything. She inhales the smell of him, his cologne mixed with alcohol and sweat, and she finds herself wanting to bottle the scent of him and keep it forever.

After breathing him in for a moment, Taylor tells Manuel the details about her trip, but he seems on edge. She asks him if everything is okay, and finally he asks if she is planning on dating anyone else. *He beat me to the talk,* she thinks to herself.

"No, solo tú. Y tú, ¿estás pasando tiempo con otras mujeres?"

"No! Sólo tú, mi amor," he says with a smile and gives her a kiss.

Taylor is almost gleeful that they've established this, even more so since Manuel was the one to bring it up. They drift off to sleep, and when Taylor wakes up the following morning, there's a note on top of her backpack from Manuel, who has to be at work early. He wishes her a good time in Salamanca and asks that she text him once in a while to let him know she's okay.

She holds the note to her chest and smiles. After a moment of basking in the glow of Manuel and having established their exclusivity, she resumes packing and getting ready for her trip to Salamanca later today. Katie did most of the planning; among the three friends, she has the lightest course load and seems to have plenty of time to meander the streets and cafés of Paris and plan trips. Taylor is happy to let her take the reins; now she just needs to show up.

An uneventful train ride out of Barcelona finds Taylor arriving at a markedly different Spanish city. Salamanca, home to Spain's oldest university, is smaller and far less glamorous and chic than Barcelona, but it feels familiar, as if everything Taylor learned in her Spanish courses thus far was derived exclusively from this city alone. She wanders around the train station for a bit before finding the hostel where she's meeting her friends. Lindsay, being used to five-star accommodations, had already told them that if the hostel was gross, she'd be finding them all a hotel room. Taylor is fine with that plan, but it turns out that the hostel isn't awful and is in a super convenient spot in town.

She checks in, gets settled, and waits for Katie and Lindsay. They arrive shortly after Taylor, and the reunion between the three of them can only be described as epic; they may have scared the German backpackers sharing the floor of the hostel with their shrieks and hugs. They have already agreed that, for the first night, the three of them will have dinner together and go out, just the three of them, and wait until the following day to meet up with their other UNC friends.

It turns out that Katie has planned an incredible weekend, filled with visits to cultural sites, which Taylor spends jotting down notes about in her notebook so she can write about the city later, along with coffee meetups, meals, and drinks with a bunch of their college pals who are studying there.

By Sunday, Taylor is hungover, exhausted, and full (literally and figuratively), stuffed with good food, good wine, and delight from seeing her friends (they went through at least three rolls of film; Taylor can't wait to get the pictures developed and hopefully put some in frames). She departs the hostel by late morning and heads back to Barcelona to face a busy week at school filled with papers due and midterm exams. As her mind wanders to Manuel and getting cozy with him in bed soon, she leans her head back on the uncomfortable train seat and promptly falls asleep. She wakes briefly to get her Eurail pass stamped and drifts back to sleep, eventually arriving back at Barcelona Sants train station with enough time to unpack and get some studying done before Monday rears its ugly head.

Chapter 8

Daniel

September 2003, London

While Taylor spends September gallivanting around sunny Barcelona, Daniel finds himself brooding in London.

"Does it ever stop fucking raining here? We should have gone to southern Europe. Or Australia," he tells his flat-mate Will one Saturday evening.

But Will is enchanted with London: the culture, the nightlife, the scenery of the countryside when they take trains to the charming little towns outside the city.

"This is the best place to be, man. You're just bitter about Taylor and that asshole guy she's dating, Marco, or whatever his name is." Will hands Daniel a beer and continues, "Look, we're going out tonight. You need to find a pretty girl and distract yourself. Okay? We've got three months left here; you need to make the most of it."

Daniel grunts in agreement and accepts the beer. "Fine. Where are we heading tonight? Somewhere in Soho, yeah?"

"Madame JoJo's. Ethan has already been there; he said it's lit. We'll take the tube there. Maybe a cab home? Dinner at the pub downstairs first, though."

Will arrived in London and it was as if he'd been studying British expressions for months: the tube, the loo, the flat, crisps. It was mildly irritating at first, but it wasn't long before Daniel was doing the same thing.

The pub "downstairs" is their local place that seems to serve beer and fish and chips exclusively. It is a moderately dingy place, but the beer is cheap, at least by London standards, and they always have the best soccer matches on TV. More often than not, it's where Daniel, Will, Ethan, and their fellow exchange students begin their evenings out, or spend their evenings, period, depending on the night.

Daniel and Will dress for the evening, spraying too much cologne and using far more hair gel than necessary. They head out around seven, evenings in London starting hours earlier than in Barcelona. After too many beers and a meager dinner, Daniel, Will, Ethan, and two other guys from their Economics program head to the Underground; en route to Soho. While standing on the tube, Daniel finds himself running an internal monologue, basically a pep talk, through his brain: *Forget about Taylor. Find someone else to hook up with. You're studying abroad, for Christ's sake!* By the time they are in the queue for Madame JoJo's, he finds he is just drunk enough to follow his own advice.

They wait for a while; a posse of five guys is a hard sell to gain entrance to a club, despite their good looks and nice clothes. Eventually, after a few pounds are exchanged with the bouncer, they are let in. Will pushes his way to the bar and gets the first round, and Daniel scopes the place out. The crowd is young, mainly mid-twenties, he suspects, with plenty of attractive women dancing and milling about.

The club music blares, and Daniel and a few of his pals make their way to the dance floor. The song is an odd remix of Madonna's "Vogue," and within a few minutes, Daniel finds himself surrounded by what appears to be a bachelorette party, or hen night, as he has learned they are called in the UK.

"What the fuck?" he mutters to himself. The girls are laughing and yelling, eventually pushing the future bride, he assumes, given she is dressed all in white and wearing a crown, toward him. Daniel obliges and dances with this beautiful woman, who, up close, appears much closer to thirty than twenty, while her friends snap pictures of them and laugh. As the song changes, he kisses her cheek and gets the hell out of there. While he's fantasized about getting with an older woman, a bride-to-be out on the town for her hen night is hardly what he has in mind.

After his dance party with the bachelorettes, Daniel realizes that he has lost his friends, so he heads to the bathroom for a respite. As he waits for his turn, he once again thinks back to Will's pep talk earlier in the evening and his self-pep talk on the tube. He needs to hook up with someone tonight, if only as a distraction from what has become a nagging, all-consuming obsession with Taylor Evans.

He's literally known Taylor his entire life. They were born on the same day in the same hospital, for Christ's sake, and Taylor's mom, Alyssa, was a sort of mentor to his own mother in the early days. Alyssa already had two kids and knew what she was doing, while Tanya, a recent widow, hadn't a clue. Daniel has always considered Taylor to be absolutely stunning, if a bit intimidating. She has always been unapologetically smart, smarter than any of the guys at their high school, which, for better or worse, he found daunting to keep up with. Daniel never had the balls to consider dating her back in high school. They said hello and made small talk occasionally, but he never managed to try for anything more. The term "out of my league" always came to his mind when thinking about Taylor. But ever since they randomly bumped into each other at that frat party back at Duke and had the best sex of his life, Taylor has been occupying a significant portion of Daniel's brain space.

It wasn't just the sex, though. Taylor is smart, funny, and someone he could imagine spending years with without running out of things to talk about. The fact that she works for his grandparents certainly doesn't help; they are constantly sending him her articles and pointing out her literary talents. And reminding him that she's white, pretty, and attending a top-notch college, as if his own attendance at Duke is meaningless?!

Finally, it's Daniel's turn to use the toilet, and he snaps out of his reverie about Taylor. As he washes his hands and checks himself in the mirror, he makes a pact with himself: get shitfaced and hook up with someone, literally anyone, tonight.

Now on a mission and with a sense of purpose, Daniel heads back toward the bar area. He spots Will conveniently ordering shots of vodka. Daniel yells to his friend to get him two, while Alice Deejay's "Better Off Alone" blasts from the speakers. *At least we're back in the 21st century with the music,* Daniel thinks to himself. Once they have their drinks, Daniel tells Will his goal for the evening, and Will points to a group of students from their exchange program who just arrived. All female, all dressed to the nines, a mix of Americans and Europeans. Daniel is immediately drawn to Sofia, a Danish girl with long blonde hair and long legs accentuated by a very short skirt.

Daniel takes the first shot, then walks over to the girls and asks them if they want drinks. He's at the point now where he has enough liquid courage to do this without much awkwardness, and the girls follow him to the bar. Pleasantries are exchanged all around, lots of "wow, what are the odds we'd all end up here tonight?" bullshit, before Daniel finally orders a round of drinks and starts talking to Sofia. Her English is precise and nearly perfect, save for a few mistakes that Daniel finds charming. They've talked a few times in their Econ class, and Daniel uses this familiarity to his advantage.

"Do you want another drink, Sofia?" he asks.

"Sure. After which I'd like to go dancing. Do you dance?" she asks him innocently.

"I dance," Daniel tells her with a wink. "Hold on, I'll go and get us another drink."

Don't wink at her, you stupid fuck, Daniel says to himself after he's turned around. He orders the drinks and looks over at Sofia, who is looking at her mobile and slowly drinking her vodka-cranberry. After what feels like an eternity, Daniel has a beer for himself and another drink for Sofia. He carefully walks back to her, intently focusing on not spilling the drinks, and delivers her cocktail.

"Thank you, Daniel," she exclaims, slamming down the remnants of her first drink with a surprising amount of gusto and placing the glass on the high-top table she has managed to score. They sit on the barstools and start the mundane process of learning about one another: siblings, sports, academic interests, etc. Daniel is impressed with Sofia, she has one younger sister, she is a talented soccer player, and her future career (in finance, she hopes, starting out as an investment banker) is well mapped out. He feels like a slacker in comparison.

After the obligatory "getting to know each other" chat, they make their way to the dance floor. There is a group of their friends already dancing, which makes all of this less awkward. Daniel sees Sofia whispering to one of her friends with a smile on her face, after which they both look over at him. At this point, he thinks to himself: it's in the bag. Don't fuck this up.

And he doesn't. After dancing for hours, Sofia and Daniel stumble out onto the street, both quite drunk by now, and flag down a taxi to bring them back to Daniel's flat. Within a minute of opening the door, they are in Daniel's bed. They don't actually have sex, but they do everything but.

"May I borrow a shirt?" Sofia asks coyly afterward. "I assume it is okay that I stay here tonight, given the time?"

"Of course you should stay here," he tells her. He puts on his boxers and digs through his drawer in search of a clean shirt. "Here you go," he says, handing her an oversized gray t-shirt that he recalls washing recently. He's not sure what time they fall asleep; it must be well after 3 a.m. Not long after they've drifted off, Daniel hears Will stumbling inside, and what he thinks is a female voice attempting, and failing miserably, to whisper. Good for Will, Daniel thinks as he falls back asleep.

In the harsh reality of morning, Sofia awakes and looks over at Daniel, who is still fast asleep. *What am I doing here?* she asks herself while looking out at the rainy street.

She scribbles a note for Daniel, telling him she's heading off to the library to study, which at least is true, and leaves him her mobile number, asking him to call her if he wants to hang out again. With that, she quietly excuses herself, uses the bathroom, and heads back to her own flat.

Daniel wakes a few hours later to the sound of rain outside his window. He immediately recognizes Sofia's absence and puts his pillow over his face. "Fucking rain," he mutters. As he gets up, he sees a scrap of paper on his desk, basically Sofia explaining her premature exodus this morning. He adds her mobile number into his contacts and goes about his day, occasionally thinking about the events of last night and whether he can convince her to do all of that again.

As September carries on, Daniel finds himself enjoying London more. The rain lets up a bit, and while he and Sofia aren't officially dating by the end of the month, they seem to have a shared agreement that being friends with benefits is a perfect situation.

By the end of September, Daniel realizes he needs to address his feelings for Taylor. So, after a boozy night out with his pals (Sofia is in the Cotswolds with some of her Danish friends, so his chances of getting any action are nil), he returns to his room and opens his laptop.

He composes an email to Taylor, basically apologizing for hitting on her while he was in Barcelona. After that, he tells her that he still has feelings for her and, if she ever feels the same way, he's around and in for it. He writes some other stuff about her writing skills and how much he enjoys reading her work. Before he can delete the email, he sends it, closes his laptop, and passes out. In the days after sending it, Daniel finds himself checking his email more often than usual. A few days pass, and finally Taylor responds.

She reminds Daniel that she's attached (that bastard Manuel, Daniel thinks to himself), but she acknowledges that she does in fact have feelings for him and asks if he would be open to being friends and hanging out should she find herself in London. Somehow, Taylor even writes eloquently in her emails, especially compared to the drunk, rambling trash that Daniel sent her. Rather than respond right away, he sits on it for a few days and tries to figure out what to say... how to say, "Yes, I'll hang out with you and be your friend!" without the air of desperation he feels internally.

The following Sunday afternoon, after a long weekend in Prague, he responds. He starts out with a quick summary of his trip to Prague (the word "epic" may have been involved, unfortunately) and then gets into the real stuff: that being, of course, he'll hang out in London (when is she coming?), and he'd love to be friends, etc., etc.

An hour later, there's a short response from Taylor: she just got back from Salamanca and hasn't figured out when she'll be in London, but is aiming for the end of October/early November... will he be around?

He shoots back a quick email, letting her know he's heading to Edinburgh for a weekend mid-October but doesn't have any other trips planned yet. Before Taylor can respond, Daniel closes his email and starts working on the schoolwork he has neglected all weekend, most of it due tomorrow, bracing himself for a long night. He pours himself a beer and gets down to work.

Chapter 9

October–November 2003, Barcelona

If there's anything better than Barcelona during the month of October, Taylor has never experienced it before. She's not sure if it's due to her current situation, hot Spanish boyfriend, loads of friends in her study-abroad program, a cool apartment in an even cooler neighborhood with a fabulous roommate, but she's happier than she's ever been.

After the trip to Salamanca, she has to buckle down and focus on schoolwork for a bit, but by the middle of the month, she's confident that the most demanding part of the semester is behind her. She can finally pay Finn a long-overdue visit down at his beach bar, where he tells her with great sadness that he has to return to Scotland in just two weeks to help care for his aging grandfather.

"I'll be back," he tells her after pouring them both a round of Jägermeister shots. "I just need to be there and help my mum out with her pop. He doesn't have much time, and my mum's all alone back there. But my heart is in Barcelona, you know that."

"I know," Taylor wails. "But you will be missed. I feel like a shit friend for not being around more lately. I had no idea. You were my first friend here, Finn! I'm so sorry."

"I know, Taylor, and you've been a great friend, too. I'll have the same mobile number, so we can stay in touch. And as soon as I know when I'm returning, you'll be one of the first to know." Finn comes out from the bar and envelops Taylor in a warm hug.

"I'm so sorry, Finn," Taylor repeats. "I wish your family the best through this, and please keep me posted and let me know if you need to talk."

They hug once more, and Taylor heads back to her apartment.

As she emerges from underground at the Hospital Clinic metro station, her phone is buzzing. It's an American number calling.

"Hello?"

"Taylor," her mom says, breathlessly, clearly excited about something. "Eric and Lauren are engaged! They're getting married," her mother elaborates, needlessly.

"Oh my god, that's fantastic!" Taylor shrieks into her phone, while trying to ignore the strange looks people on the street are giving her. "Wow, I knew they were serious, but this is huge!"

"Yes, well, I'll let him tell you all about the proposal, but they're having a small engagement party next month in Greenwich, where Lauren is from, and the wedding will be in April... in New York City, at the fucking Palace Hotel," her mother yells with such enthusiasm that Taylor has to hold the phone away from her ear.

"Wow, this is all so fast, isn't it? And the Palace Hotel? Is that actually a real place?" Taylor asks with a snort of laughter.

"That's what I said, but apparently Lauren's family basically has a staff of people who work for them, so planning a posh wedding in just a few months should be easy."

"So, how did he do it? Not some cheesy jewelry commercial proposal, I hope."

"Well, they went for dinner at Picholine, apparently Lauren's favorite restaurant in Manhattan, and he asked her then. I hear it was all very romantic, but I'll let Eric tell you all of those details."

"Wow, I can't wait to hear about this! I can't believe my dipshit brother is actually getting married," Taylor tells her mom with a laugh.

Alyssa ignores the insult directed at her eldest child and continues, "Now, one snafu. Given the date of the engagement party, I'll have to cut my trip to visit you short by a day. Unless you want to come back for the weekend for the engagement party?" Alyssa asks hopefully.

"That's a hard pass, mom, sorry," Taylor responds quickly. "I'll come home for the wedding, of course, but I can't go back for this. But I totally understand if you have to leave a day early. I can help you shop for a dress while you're in Barcelona."

"Okay honey, I know this is a lot to take in. But if you change your mind, you're obviously invited to the engagement party. Who even has engagement parties? Have you heard of that?"

"Rich people," Taylor mumbles. "What does Dad think of all this?"

"Oh, he's oblivious. He told me to tell him where to be and what to wear, and he'll oblige."

"Sounds about right," Taylor says with a laugh. "And what about Alex? How's he taking this?"

"He's as excited as he can be. You know Alex. Alex is the best man, of course, so I presume he's worried about giving a speech. Oh! And there's been talk of you being a bridesmaid."

"Oh, come on," Taylor groans. "I've never even met her. I can't be a bridesmaid, that's ridiculous."

"Taylor, Lauren just wants you to feel like you're a part of the wedding. I think she recognizes how strange it must be for you, finding out your big brother is marrying someone you've never met, that's all. Think about it, will you?"

"Fine, I'll consider it," Taylor huffs, with no real intention of considering this insane idea. "I'm going to call Eric now and get the scoop from him, okay? I love you, Mom; I'll talk to you soon."

They hang up, and Taylor finds a bench near a bus station. She sits down, lights a cigarette, and calls her eldest brother. He answers on the third ring, clearly distracted and on edge.

"I hear congratulations are in order, Mi Hermano," Taylor says casually.

"Hey! Little sis, I'm getting married. I take it Mom told you?" Eric says with a laugh.

"Yes, I just got off the phone with her. Jesus Christ, Eric, a little warning would have been nice. This almost gave me a heart attack."

He sighs into the phone. "I know, sorry. It's just that I got the ring, and I couldn't wait any longer. I'm so excited for you to meet her, T. I've told her all about you; she can't wait to have a sister. Lauren's an only child, fertility issues or something with her parents, I dunno, but she's always wanted to be a part of a big family."

Taylor resists the overwhelming urge to roll her eyes at the sister comment and instead responds, "Well, I can't wait to meet her. I can't get back for the engagement party, but I'll obviously be at the wedding. Why do you need an engagement party, anyway? A wedding isn't enough, you big snob?" She teases him in the way one can only do with a sibling.

Eric laughs. "I know, I know! It's ridiculous. It's an East Coast thing, I've been to a few, older friends from college. Ours is going to be small, just family and close friends. Her parents are throwing it at their house in Greenwich."

"So, I'm told. Is it a house, though, or an estate?" Taylor asks in her snootiest voice, enjoying the opportunity to mess with her big brother. "Just because I've never been to Greenwich doesn't mean I don't know what it's like."

"Estate would probably be the proper classification," Eric replies, stifling a laugh. "Look, they're fucking loaded, okay? But you'd never know it, that's the thing. I mean, Lauren wears certain brands, and she does work in fashion, but she's not a snob about it. Or about anything, really. She's with a Wisconsin boy, after all."

"Yeah, that's the piece I'm trying to figure out... how'd you make the cut? Eric, I'm messing with you, dumbass. I'm legit excited for you, and I can't wait to meet her. Now, am I allowed to bring a date to this soiree?"

"A date! How bold of you to ask. Um, yeah, I think that can be arranged. Something you need to tell me, Taylor? Do I need to beat anyone up at any point?" Eric asks.

Taylor laughs, exhaling the smoke from the final drag on her cigarette. "Who knows if we'll still be together, but I've got a boyfriend. Manuel. He's great. He's older, he's from Barcelona. We've been seeing each other for a while now, basically, the entire time I've been here, actually."

"How much older?" Eric asks warily.

"He's twenty-six. So, around your age."

"What the fuck, Taylor? How did that happen? He's clearly a predator. You're only twenty, must I remind you? You can't even drink legally, for Christ's sake."

Taylor hadn't expected such a visceral reaction from her older brother, but she continues. "I can drink legally here, for what it's worth. And he's not a predator, he's a smart, handsome, successful Spanish man. So there," she retorts, petulantly.

Taylor can picture Eric burying his face in his hands upon learning this new information. "Okay. Okay. Just be careful; I don't want you to get fucked over by some guy who seeks out young, naïve exchange students."

"Yeah, thanks, I'm alright, really. Jesus, Eric, Dad doesn't even care. Or maybe Mom never told him, but in any case, chill out, will ya? I'm not naïve, either, for Christ's sake." Taylor takes a deep breath in an effort to calm herself, then continues, "This conversation is supposed to be about you and Lauren. Don't worry about me. I've got to go, it's really late here, but congratulations. Mail me some pictures of you two, okay?"

"I will. And just be careful, that's all I'm saying. And get your schoolwork done and go to bed. Love you, sis."

At this, Taylor does roll her eyes and responds, "Love you too. We'll talk soon."

They hang up, and Taylor immediately calls Alex, confident that he'll be willing to dissect this new development further and give her more intel on everything.

After a brief but snarky conversation with Alex, Taylor is left missing her family but genuinely happy about Eric's wedding bombshell. Alex gave her some gossip about Lauren's family, how they're rich "beyond our comprehension," and that the wedding planning is already in the works. While he didn't use the word "bridezilla," he implied that Lauren and her mother are acting as such, so Eric is basically keeping his mouth shut and letting them plan as they wish.

Taylor goes to bed that night and dreams of puffy white gowns, cloudlike in nature, champagne flutes, and sparkly chandeliers. When she wakes up, the first thought in her brain is how to invite Manuel to a wedding in another country that is happening in six months. If she waits, she's worried he'll have plans, whether a weekend trip away with friends or a work trip. But if she asks him now, she's worried she'll appear desperate and overly enthusiastic.

She spends her day in classes and at the school library, half studying, half pondering how to solve this dilemma. The wedding isn't until April. Her spring semester ends in May, and she's traveling around Europe after that. So, the duration of this relationship is questionable, despite the fact that it is great right now. Who knows if they'll still be together in six months? After much deliberation, she decides to just mention the fact that her brother got engaged that night at dinner, as she and Manuel already have plans to go out. She'll gauge his reaction then and go from there.

Uncharacteristically, Manuel is already there when Taylor arrives at dinner, drinking what appears to be whiskey on ice, a bold choice for a weeknight, Taylor thinks to herself. But having already drunk nearly half a bottle of cheap wine with Nicholas while getting ready earlier, she's in no position to judge.

Manuel stands up when he sees Taylor and kisses her on the cheek as he pulls her chair out for her. He looks off, she thinks, puffy and red-eyed, but Taylor can't picture him crying about anything; he's cool and secure to the point of stoicism. Before she can ask what's going on, he exhales sharply, takes a swig of his drink, and tells Taylor that his mother has been diagnosed with stage-two breast cancer. He just found out this morning and has been on the phone with his family and doctors all day, trying to figure out the best path forward.

"There are so many things to consider," he tells her. "Surgery is imminent. Radiation and chemo after, I think, based on today's conversations with my mother's treating team. Or do we roll the dice and try to find a clinical trial?"

As Taylor takes all of this in, she thinks for a second about just how fortunate she is to have been so ignorant on this subject. No one close to her (to date) has had to deal with anything remotely serious, health-wise. She offers Manuel her hands over the table, and he takes them in his. She tells him that she'll be there for him in whatever way he needs, and she's taken aback by her own sincerity. She represses the sudden and overwhelming urge to get up, hug him, and tell him that she loves him.

Meanwhile, the waiter, who has been intrusively pacing near their table, clearly trying to eavesdrop on the serious conversation, finally comes over and takes their orders. Taylor is relieved when he brings her wine. Manuel is eager to change the subject, despite Taylor's questions and offers to help. She offers to ask her parents to contact everyone they know at the university's hospital to see if they have any ideas, which Manuel seems to consider before sighing and asking her how she's doing and what's new.

After filling him in on the mundane details of her week thus far, Taylor casually mentions Eric's engagement and the upcoming nuptials. He offers a hearty, "Felicidades!" and starts grilling her on the details, clearly relieved to be discussing anything besides his mother's diagnosis.

Taylor tells him everything she knows, the who, when, and where of the wedding, and then gets into the more intriguing stuff, such as the bride's family's obscene wealth, who may be on the massive guest list, and whether or not she'll get roped into being a bridesmaid. Manuel, while acting interested, is clearly upset and distracted by the recent upheaval to his world, so Taylor tries to minimize her enthusiasm as she goes through the details.

Manuel is consistent with whiskey as his drink of choice this evening. This is moderately concerning to Taylor; while he drinks regularly, it's almost never straight liquor, and rarely this much. Before their main courses arrive, he asks her whether she'll be allowed to bring a date to Eric's wedding.

She answers affirmatively: as the groom's sister, she will definitely get a "plus-one," and she'd be happy if he would be that person. He smiles, the first legitimate smile she's seen from him all night, and responds, "Sí, claro," while again taking her hands across the table. Taylor breathes a sigh of relief and tells him how nervous she was all day about asking him this. He laughs, then gets up, comes to her side of the table, and kisses her. Once their meals arrive, he seems a little less dejected, his mood a little lighter. As they eat, Taylor offers to come over and spend the night with him, assuming he'd appreciate the company after such a difficult day. He agrees, and shortly thereafter, Manuel has paid the bill (which is primarily his alcohol charges), and they walk back to his apartment.

Despite the inherent sadness of the evening, Taylor wishes she could press a pause button or snap a Polaroid of this moment. Part of this desire is pure vanity; she and Manuel look good together, there's no denying it, and they're both particularly well dressed this evening. The city is beautiful, her life is exactly where she wants it to be, and she's going home to offer moral support to her gorgeous boyfriend. The moment passes, as they all inevitably do, and soon Taylor is guiding a very inebriated Manuel into bed. She puts a glass of water on his nightstand and digs around in the closet, eventually finding Advil that may or may not be past its expiration date for when he wakes up in the morning. She sets an alarm on her phone, brushes her teeth, and lies down next to him. She's asleep quickly despite what feels like a million thoughts swirling around her brain, and it feels like only seconds pass before the shrill sound of the alarm clock wakes her.

Manuel is, shockingly, already awake and in the shower. The Advil is gone, his water glass is empty, and for perhaps the first time ever, Taylor feels like a competent adult, capable of helping someone else. Before she can get any more self-righteous, Manuel emerges from the bathroom in just a towel. She's surprised, once again, at how attractive and fit he is, and pops into the bathroom to brush her teeth and pee. She's barely dried her hands before he's opening the door and pulling her back into bed.

They both finish quickly, and Taylor is emboldened by starting her day off with incredible morning sex. *We should do this more often,* she thinks to herself as they're dressing and getting ready for the day.

Before they say their goodbyes, Manuel tells Taylor that he's going to Málaga next weekend to visit his mom and see what he can do to help navigate her treatment decisions. He'll leave next Wednesday and return Sunday. Taylor has already planned her London trip, she will be meeting Katie there on Thursday, October 23, and hopefully spending some (platonic!) time with Daniel. She's already let Daniel know the dates, and he's confirmed that he'll be around and would love to see her. Now Taylor feels a tug of guilt knowing that while she's partying in London, Manuel will be seeing his sick mother and offering moral support to his father, who is apparently a total disaster since learning of his wife's diagnosis.

"Off to class," Taylor tells Manuel. She still needs to go back to her apartment, change clothes, and get all of her stuff for school, which, given the current time, is going to be a challenge. No Starbucks stop today; she'll have to settle for the crap coffee on campus. She gives Manuel a kiss goodbye; he looks insanely handsome in his work clothes, and they make plans to get together again tomorrow night.

"If you need company before then, please let me know, okay?" She leaves his apartment, ensconced in what she'll come to think of as the official scent of her fall of 2003: the Davidoff Cool Water cologne that Manuel uses liberally, cigarette smoke, and the nebulous scent of having just had sex. Later in life, she's transported right back here to Barcelona anytime she catches a whiff of Cool Water cologne.

With that, she's off to her Thursday classes and, assuming she gets all of her work done, which she knows she will, a night out with her study abroad posse at "La Macarena," known for its killer music on Thursday nights, awaits. Taylor hasn't been yet, but apparently, it's *the* place to be for the cool kids, even the locals.

Inspired by the night ahead, Taylor manages to get home, change, grab some breakfast, and make it to her first class on time. The day drags on; after classes end, she meets some fellow students in the library to finish up a group project, and it's 6 p.m. before she's even leaving campus. She gets onto the crowded metro and rides back to her apartment, thinking about Manuel and feeling the ever-increasing sensation that she's leading a double life: one as a bubbly American exchange student, another as the girlfriend of a charismatic, incredible Barcelonian man. For better or worse, her two worlds rarely collide. Manuel isn't into the same scene as her study abroad friends, and he's at least five years older than most of them. So, between her travels, her writing gig, and spending time with Manuel, Taylor feels like she's been neglecting the "American exchange student role" and is excited for tonight.

She and Nicholas hang out, listen to music, and make dinner together; Taylor isn't meeting her friends until 10:30 p.m. She texts Manuel to check in; he's fine but working late tonight to make up for the time off he's taking next week to see his family. After dinner is cleaned up, she and Nicholas make cocktails (he's truly a master with a cocktail shaker) and smoke cigarettes until it's time for Taylor to leave. She'd invited Nicholas to join them, but he already has plans (as usual) at some hip, fabulous new club. They bid farewell, and Taylor pops down to the metro just down the block from her building.

The night progresses typically. Taylor and all of her pals finally arrive at La Macarena around 11 p.m., but, not surprisingly, they're still among the first ones in the club. By midnight, things have picked up, and the entire group is drunk, sweaty, and dancing on the crowded dance floor. At some point in the evening, someone produces a camera so they can have evidence and memories of this madness. Taylor calls it quits at 3 a.m., while most of her friends are still going strong. She slips out onto the street, finds a cab, and heads directly to her apartment and into bed. Tonight, will officially go down as one of her favorite nights in Barcelona, the simple lightheartedness of letting loose on the dance floor with no reservations whatsoever.

The next morning is more difficult, and Taylor is once again grateful for not having classes on Friday. The weekend passes in the blink of an eye, as they so often do. She spends a lot of time with Manuel, happy to provide him with a distraction from his anxiety over his mother's health. Before she knows it, Taylor is packing for London. She blasts a Sheryl Crow CD in the living room while dancing around her room, trying to figure out how to dress for the markedly different weather in London while Sheryl sings about soaking up the sun. Taylor and Katie have spent a ridiculous amount of time texting and emailing back and forth about plans, outfits, and who they need to avoid (Katie has a nasty ex who happens to be in the same exchange program as Daniel, so they'll need to be strategic and have an escape plan in case they cross paths, however unlikely that may be).

And just like that, Taylor finds herself flying out of Barcelona, off to a new destination once again. There's nothing quite like seeing a major city, or anywhere, for that matter, for the first time, and as the plane descends into London's Heathrow Airport, Taylor recognizes the butterflies in her stomach as excitement. Katie has once again managed to score them a clean hostel, with a private bathroom in their room, which is such a relief to Taylor that she's okay with paying what seems an exorbitant amount of money for a hostel.

"It's more like a hotel, really," Katie assures her. "I know neither of us wants to be sharing a room, or a toilet, with, like, eight random people."

Having been warned by Daniel about the outrageous taxi fares, Taylor already knows how to get from the airport to their hostel in Soho via public transportation, which should take just under an hour. Katie has already arrived and promised to be waiting for Taylor in the room, with a bottle of wine open.

The weather cooperates far better than Taylor had anticipated, especially given Daniel's complaints about the constant, relentless rain. It's chilly, but the sun is out the entire weekend, until Sunday afternoon, which is when she's flying back to sunny Barcelona anyway. With only three nights and two and a half days, Taylor and Katie don't waste any time. They go sightseeing, shopping, and out on the town. On Friday night, they meet up with Daniel and his friends; Katie and Taylor recognize a handful of familiar UNC faces among the crowd at the bar that Daniel chose. Fortunately, Katie's ex isn't one of them.

Daniel greets Taylor and Katie with a hug, and Taylor is genuinely happy to see him, although she finds herself having to actively squash down the romantic notions that are flooding her brain. He leads them to the bar and introduces them to his friends, a plethora of names that Taylor knows she won't remember by the end of the night. Daniel orders them each a drink, and Katie runs across the room to say hi to one of her close UNC friends. Taylor and Daniel use this time as an opportunity to catch up. The awkwardness that they'd both independently been anticipating isn't there. They talk about school, travel, and Eric's upcoming wedding.

"So, I hear you're going to have a sister-in-law," Daniel says enthusiastically.

"You heard correctly." Taylor laughs. "Can you believe it? Part of me thinks she must've gotten knocked up and that's why they're getting married so quickly. I don't know, isn't it young?"

"They're young to get married, especially for New York. But from what I've heard, from the Greenwich gossip chain, you know it must be true," Daniel says with an eye roll. "Lauren is a great girl. Smart, funny, philanthropic. And her parents are fucking loaded; did you know that part?"

"Yeah, Alex, along with everyone else, already told me how crazy rich her family is. It's hard to imagine, isn't it?" Taylor asks, having a hard time picturing a life where money was a given and she wasn't hustling all the time.

Daniel changes the subject and says, "You know I have a cousin from Greenwich, right? Erica. She's at Princeton now."

"You know what's really funny? Remember my friend Lindsay? She was with me the night we saw you at the Duke frat party."

"Ah, THAT night," Daniel says with raised eyebrows.

Taylor feels her cheeks reddening and continues, "Yeah, well, Lindsay went to camp with your cousin. She's been to her house and everything. It sounds like they were pretty close for a few years but grew apart."

"Wow. Small world," Daniel says, clearly surprised. "Between us," he continues, "Erica is a bit of a mess. She's always been super fun and smart, but she started drinking at, I don't know, twelve years old or something ridiculous, and has been doing coke since freshman year of high school. Whatever snooty private school she went to had plenty to offer."

"Jesus. Lindsay had a similar description of Erica. Eric mentioned that Lauren's from Greenwich, so I kinda wondered if she maybe knew your family. They're having an engagement party there, like, next month."

"Wow, are you going? Can you, with our moms coming here next month?" Daniel asks.

"No, no engagement party for me. I'll obviously be at the wedding, but I can't justify the flight and time away from school for a party, you know? Christ, I had kind of forgotten the old ladies were coming. I just talked to my mom last week and somehow blocked the fact that she's actually visiting."

Daniel laughs and responds, "Well, I'm their first victim. They're coming to London first, then down to you."

"Good luck to you. Don't let my mom corrupt you or try to score weed. She probably thinks it's legal here."

"I'll do my best," Daniel says with a hearty laugh. "So, you'll fly back for the wedding? That's good, so I'll see you there. I wasn't sure, since you'll still be in Barcelona in April."

Taylor hadn't thought about the obvious fact that Daniel and his mom would be invited to the wedding. *Wow, another layer to unpeel,* she thinks.

"Can't miss my brother's wedding! Do you really think Alyssa would allow that?" Taylor laughs.

Katie returns then from her other friends and orders a round of drinks for the three of them, completely ignoring Daniel's roommate, Will, who is attempting, poorly, to flirt with her.

"I like her," Daniel says with a laugh as he watches Katie completely disregard Will and push her way to the bar.

"Yeah, she's one of a kind, that's for sure. Doesn't take no shit from no one, our Katie here," Taylor puts her arm around Katie after she's delivered their drinks.

"Thanks, Katie," Daniel says. "Don't mind Will over there," he continues, nodding in Will's direction. "He thinks you're hot."

"Well, that's very flattering, but I'm off guys, for now. I'm sick of the bullshit. I'm celibate, in fact," Katie says with a straight face, subtly winking at Taylor. "I'm looking into becoming a nun, if you must know."

"I think that ship has sailed, my love," Taylor tells Katie with a smirk.

As the evening proceeds, Katie allows Will to, if not outright flirt with her, at least engage in conversation, and they end up exchanging email addresses at the end of the night. After Will's relentless pursuit, they eventually start dating, travel the world together, and years later end up getting married in France. Taylor and Daniel, both of whom will be at the wedding, recall this night, October 24th, 2003, the fateful night when the pair first met, as one of their fondest memories.

But for the moment, Katie primarily ignores Will, and she and Taylor have a nearly perfect weekend in London. There's a bit of awkwardness when Taylor and Daniel have coffee Sunday morning; as they hug goodbye over their café Americanos and scones, she can sense his desire to kiss her, and she stifles her own similar feelings. Instead, he wishes her a safe flight, and they promise to keep in touch.

Upon returning to Barcelona on Sunday, Taylor is relieved to hear from Manuel; a family friend connected his mother with a top cancer specialist in Madrid, where she will undergo surgery and begin treatment in the coming weeks. Manuel, his siblings, and his father will take turns staying with her. Although this will inevitably mean Taylor will have less time with Manuel, she can sense the relief in his voice when he tells her about the treatment plan, and she feels her own anxiety about the whole situation decrease.

Taylor gives Manuel the cliff notes version of her weekend in London, and they make plans to get together later in the week. She also gives him a heads-up that her mom is visiting in November, and she'd love if he could accompany them to dinner one night while she's in town. He's surprisingly comfortable with the idea, and Taylor feels a conflicting sense of relief that he's into it, along with terror that her mother will embarrass the hell out of her. Before panic sets in, she remembers that Tanya will be there as well, Tanya, Daniel's mom, the Spanish teacher, who can converse with Manuel in Spanish, no problem. Having her there will make everything less painful, Taylor thinks.

As October comes to an end, Taylor submits her write-up of London, gets ahead on her schoolwork, and celebrates the bizarre event that is Halloween, Spanish style, which isn't Halloween at all, but rather *Día de Todos Santos*, followed by *Día de los Muertos*. While it's a cultural awakening, to be sure, Taylor prefers Halloween American-style (candy, alcohol, inappropriate costumes) but learns what she can about these Spanish holidays and manages to write a compare/contrast article, which her editor deems "dazzling."

Lindsay comes for a visit the first weekend of November and stays with Taylor at her apartment. Taylor cleared this not only with Nicholas, who couldn't have cared less about having an extra body in the apartment, but also with Carla, her landlady. Carla let Taylor know via text message that this was fine, so long as no messes were made. Taylor assured her there wouldn't be a mess, referring only to the apartment, not to their general well-being. Time with Lindsay was always messy, but in the best possible way.

Sure enough, the first night Lindsay spends in Barcelona, she manages to find Mark at a club. Mark, who had been in their freshman dorm at UNC, was known among most of the female student body as a total player and, more often than not, kind of a dick. Taylor has a class with him here in Barcelona, and they've chatted a handful of times, but other than that, she hasn't seen much of him.

But Friday night, standing in line to get into Danzatoria, Lindsay looks behind her and says, "Oh my God, Taylor, it's hot Mark!"

It was true. Hot Mark is standing a few people behind them in the line, accompanied by several of Taylor's study abroad crew. She waves to them, and they agree to meet up at the bar once everyone gets inside.

"Well, tonight just got more interesting," Lindsay says with her eyebrows raised. Taylor rolls her eyes and laughs, saying only, "Behave, think about Walter."

Long story short, Lindsay gets rip-roaring drunk, makes out with Mark on the dance floor most of the night, and ends up going back to his place. Lindsay texts Taylor the following morning, essentially asking Taylor to come and rescue her. Over a long brunch near Mark's apartment, Lindsay confesses that she and Mark slept together.

"Eek, Linds. Are you going to tell Walter or let this go under the radar?"

"I'm not telling him! Oh my God, what a shitstorm that would create. It's not like Mark is some random dude from Barcelona; he goes to school with us. This is between you and me, promise? Besides, Walter and I are on a break," Lindsay says hesitantly.

"I promise. I know you guys are on a break, but still. Whatever, no judgment from me, you know that. Now, you and I have sightseeing to do today, so you need to eat some greasy food, have a Bloody Mary, or whatever they serve here to cure a hangover, and pull yourself together, ok?"

And so, they order glasses of cava, along with patatas bravas and fried calamari to ease their hangovers. Just like that, the day is salvaged.

"Cheers," Taylor says while clinking her glass to Lindsay's, "to good friends and hair of the dog!"

They stroll around the city center, so Taylor can show Lindsay all of her favorite spots. Tonight, they're having dinner with Manuel at a trendy bar off of Las Ramblas, and Taylor has a vague sense of apprehension about whether Lindsay and Manuel will get along. Lindsay has a strong personality, which Taylor loves, but which some may find off-putting or overly intense.

As they walk past La Sagrada Familia and the throngs of tourists waiting in line to enter, Lindsay nudges Taylor and says, "So tonight's the night I meet the famous novio, sí?"

"That's correct! I hope you guys hit it off. I really, really like him," Taylor tells Lindsay.

"Don't worry, T, I promise I'll behave," Lindsay says with a wicked grin. "Now, remember that siesta you promised me earlier? I need it, or I'm going to fall asleep at dinner."

"Sounds good. We'll head back to the apartment and rest. That cava at lunch and all this walking tired me out."

A few hours and a nap later, they're showered, made up, and dressed to the point where no heterosexual male will be able to take his eyes off them. As they stroll along Las Ramblas, Taylor pulls Lindsay into a bar so they can have a pre-dinner cocktail. They smoke cigarettes and gossip, eventually starting to discuss Eric's upcoming wedding.

"I wonder if my camp friend's family will be there, you remember, Erica, Daniel's cousin?" Lindsay asks.

"Christ, I hadn't even thought about that! As you always say, it's a small world of super-rich people, so maybe. I mean, Daniel and his mom are going, so it's definitely possible."

Lindsay narrows her eyes. "Wait, back up. Didn't you tell me earlier that you're bringing Manuel to the wedding? Now you're telling me Daniel will be there? How the fuck are you planning on managing that?"

"Ugh, please. I can't even begin to process how awkward this is all going to be," Taylor groans. "I have months to go, so let me remain in my little bubble where I don't have to worry about this, will you?"

"Fine. Fine, but when you're ready to face reality, you just let me know," Lindsay responds with a wink. "Now, let's pay and go meet this boyfriend of yours, shall we?"

The rest of the night is, Taylor thinks later, remarkably unremarkable. Lindsay and Manuel get along surprisingly well, and the three of them talk for hours at dinner, alternating between English and Spanish. After polishing off an obscene amount of alcohol, they split a cab back to the Eixample neighborhood, and Manuel kisses Taylor good night after walking her and Lindsay to Taylor's apartment building.

The next day, Sunday, November 9th, Lindsay leaves to return to Rome. Taylor offers to bring her to the train station for a more economical trip to the airport, but she insists on taking a cab. They hug and make promises of calling and texting, and Taylor feels a surge of love for her dear friend for making the trip to Barcelona. Now it's back to the grind; she needs to tidy up the apartment and get ready for the week.

The rest of Taylor's Sunday, after cleaning up the apartment, is spent in the library, where she frantically tries to get ahead on schoolwork so she can spend as much time as possible playing tour guide when her mom and Tanya visit.

Chapter 10

Daniel

November 2003, London

Meanwhile, back up in London, Daniel does his best to prepare for his mom's visit. He cleans up the apartment as best he can; Will is a bit of a slob, so Daniel and Ethan end up picking up the slack. He makes some dinner reservations and thinks of some cool places to bring her. But he keeps wondering whether Taylor's mom will be along for everything. He can't help but question if Tanya and Alyssa have some secret plot to get him and Taylor together. "It's fate," they'd say. He can't deny that the same thought has crossed his mind dozens of times. They were born on the same day, at the same place, for God's sake. There's more sexual attraction between him and Taylor than he's ever felt with anyone else, by a long shot, and on top of that they genuinely like each other. So, maybe, if he can get rid of this Manuel bastard, it could work.

His reverie is disrupted by a ding on his mobile; Sofia is wondering if he wants to hang out later. Thinking it would be a good distraction, and because he's horny, he agrees to meet her for dinner and maybe a club afterward, it is Friday night, after all. He and Sofia have been "hanging out," as she calls it (more like hooking up, he thinks). He's beginning to understand how women feel when they're used for sex, as Sofia seems to consider Daniel her personal sex god, with no intention of anything more serious. Not that he minds, quite the opposite, really, in this situation.

An hour later, Daniel is showered and ready to go. He and Will are meeting Sofia and her friend for dinner, then going to a pub not far from where they live, and afterward meeting up with some of their fellow exchange students. Daniel foots the hefty bill for dinner. He's generous to a fault, having inherited a substantial sum from his father's side of the family. Most of it is still wrapped up in a trust fund that he can't access, not yet, at least, but his mom was able to withdraw a decent amount for him to attend college and study abroad.

There's a guilt associated with this money that Daniel can't shake. Sure, he's beyond grateful for it, but the money comes from the parents of his dead father, who passed away before Daniel was born. Plus, there's the awful way his grandparents treated his father when he broke family tradition by attending a "hippie" school rather than the Ivy League universities they approved of. Plus, although it's never been declared outright, he imagines his father's side of the family have some issue with the fact that his mother is Black, not some WASP-y East Coast snob. Tanya let all of these secrets slip after too much wine one night, after managing to keep them from Daniel for the first sixteen years of his life. He keeps his family's wealth to himself and is relatively modest with any spending, but by no means takes for granted the security net it provides him.

In the here and now, though, he shares what he has with his friends while trying to live humbly, as his very practical mother has taught him. After dinner, they all head to the pub, where the whole group gets pretty much obliterated. It's Friday night, most of them just submitted a massive econ project, and they're twenty years old in London, which feels like the center of the universe. Sofia, in particular, has had too much to drink, and Daniel finds himself escorting her back to his apartment, where she proceeds to change into one of his t-shirts, tells him she wants to fuck him, and passes out within thirty seconds. He tucks her into bed and pulls a blanket over her, chuckling to himself at how the night played out. She's taking up literally the entire bed, so Daniel ends up sleeping on the couch, which is more of a makeshift futon than an actual couch.

He tosses and turns all night, and at 9 a.m. gives up on getting a good night's sleep. His mom and Alyssa are coming straight from the airport, since they can't check into their hotel until the afternoon. Daniel tries to wake Sofia, but she's totally out. Fuck, he thinks to himself, it's after 10 in the morning, and his mom will be here any minute. How's he supposed to explain the beautiful Scandinavian girl passed out in his bed? Just then, Will stumbles in the front door, reeking of alcohol and dressed in last night's clothes.

"Dude, my mom will be here any minute. Can you shower or something?" Daniel asks him with annoyance.

"Yeah, okay. Where's Sofia? What the hell happened last night? I woke up in bed with Claire."

"Sofia's asleep in my bed. You guys were all bombed. Did you and Claire hook up?"

"Sort of, but I wasn't at my best, if you know what I mean," Will says sheepishly while chugging orange juice straight from the carton. "I'm hoping to give it another go tonight."

"Fair enough. But really, dude, go shower. You smell like a fucking bar," Daniel tells Will with irritation.

Will laughs and gives a salute before stumbling toward the bathroom. What a nightmare, Daniel thinks. He's got a drunk roommate and a girl in his bed. Welcome to London, mom! Ethan is nowhere to be found, so there remains the possibility that he will make as grand an entrance as Will just did.

Just then the buzzer rings, and Daniel, after a brief moment of panic, goes downstairs to help his mom and Alyssa with their luggage. After hugs on the sidewalk, they go upstairs. As they enter, Will is leaving the bathroom with wet hair, wearing only a towel.

"Hi there, ladies, a pleasure to meet you! I'm Will."

Alyssa and Tanya are trying to contain their laughter, and Daniel rolls his eyes, telling Will to "put some clothes on, for the love of God." Will smirks and proceeds to sneak into his room, and Daniel, despite being mortified by his roommate, says with forced enthusiasm, "So, this is our place. What do you think?"

"Well, it's... nice," his mom says without much conviction as her eyes move around the cluttered main living room. "Let's see your room, Daniel."

"Well, about that. A friend of mine actually stayed over last night. She's still asleep." Daniel can feel his cheeks burning and imagines his mom putting the pieces together. "Maybe we should go out for coffee and breakfast, you guys must be starving after the flight."

"That's a great idea," Alyssa says quickly, putting her arm around Tanya. "The coffee on the plane was complete crap. Let's do that." Daniel feels an immediate sense of gratitude for Alyssa in that moment, remembering that she has two sons of her own and has likely encountered similar situations over the years.

As they're gathering their belongings, Sofia emerges from Daniel's bedroom, bleary-eyed, wearing just her underwear and Daniel's old Tupac T-shirt. Her black eye makeup from the night before is smudged under her eyes, yet she still manages to look sexy. She stops dead in her tracks as soon as she sees Alyssa and Tanya, her face immediately turning the color of a ripe strawberry. She gives them a deer-in-headlights look, waves slightly, and books it back into Daniel's room.

"Uh, just a minute, guys," Daniel says without making eye contact with his mother. He goes into his room to apologize, only to find Sofia laughing uncontrollably. She's sitting on the bed, hunched over in an attempt to silence her laughter. It's contagious, and before long, Daniel is laughing his ass off too.

"Sofia, this is so ridiculous. Get dressed and come meet them, will you? I'm sorry about the timing, really."

"I look so awful; how can I meet them? This is mortifying, I think is the word," Sofia moans, burying her face in her hands while still laughing.

"It's not ideal, but you look fine. They won't judge you. And we're leaving anyways to go get breakfast, so come say a quick hi and then you can go home."

"Fine." Sofia finishes getting dressed, throws Daniel's borrowed clothes on his bed, and walks to the door.

"Mom, Alyssa, this is my friend Sofia. She's in our study abroad program. She's from Denmark."

"A pleasure to meet you, Sofia!" his mother exclaims, clearly attempting to avoid the inherent awkwardness of this situation. "We're heading out for breakfast; would you like to join us?"

A look of panic crosses Sofia's pretty face, and Daniel jumps in to rescue her. "Mom, Sofia has a meeting for a group project that she's got to get back for."

"I do. Yes, I have a group project meeting," Sofia stutters, "but thank you for the offer. I hope you have a nice time here in London! It was nice to meet you. Sorry about... all of that."

With that, Daniel walks Sofia out to the hallway, kisses her on the cheek, and says he'll text her later. They share a look and a laugh, and then she's gone. Daniel takes a deep breath before going back inside.

His mom and Alyssa share amused expressions, and Alyssa says, "Why, Daniel, we've only been here ten minutes and all of this excitement already. I can only imagine what you've been doing in your free time. Let's go eat." Daniel blushes and they head out, leaving Will behind to recover from his hangover.

The air outside is crisp, and the sun, for once, is actually shining.

"Well," his mother says, "what a lovely girl Sofia is. She's stunning, really. You said she's Danish? Are you guys dating?"

"Yeah, she's pretty and super smart. And Danish, yes. Like I said, we're friends," Daniel says, looking straight ahead, knowing that if he makes eye contact with his mother, she will know exactly what is going on, if she doesn't already.

"Mmmhmm, a 'friend' who sleeps over and happens to be a gorgeous young woman?" his mom responds, doing air quotes around the word *friend* and elbowing Daniel playfully.

"Mom, seriously, can we talk about something else? Like, literally anything else. I'm sorry your arrival was so chaotic. Will was probably still drunk, and I obviously wasn't expecting Sofia to be here when you got in," he responds, flustered and sulky. Daniel and his mom have always been close, but he isn't looking to discuss his sex life with her.

Tanya softens and says, "Hey, it's alright, honey. From what I recall, this is what studying abroad is supposed to be like, so I'm just happy to see you're enjoying yourself."

Alyssa laughs and covers her mouth with her hand. "Oh, the stories I heard through the grapevine about Eric when he was abroad. I almost had a heart attack at the time. I swore up and down I would never allow little Taylor to leave the country."

"Well, for what it's worth, I think little Taylor is doing quite well. I've read some of her writing, it's incredible. She's so talented," Daniel says sheepishly.

"Daniel, that's so nice of you. I'm sure she would appreciate hearing that, especially from someone as intelligent as you," Alyssa beams. Daniel smiles awkwardly, wondering if his mom and Alyssa are as clueless as they're letting on. They keep walking for a few more blocks, the women pointing out all the quaint little details around the neighborhood that Daniel has never noticed before.

They eventually find a place to have a late breakfast, and after they've ordered food and everyone has coffee, the conversation quickly turns back to Taylor, for which, given the events of the morning thus far, Daniel is actually grateful.

"I heard my daughter was in London recently," Alyssa says enthusiastically. "She said you guys have seen each other both here and in Barcelona. How wonderful that is. That makes your mommies very happy," she laughs.

"I'm sure it does. We hung out here in London, and I was in Barcelona back in September. Taylor was an excellent tour guide; she took me all around. I'm afraid the only places I showed her in London were dark bars."

"I should hope she was a competent tour guide. She's written enough articles about every spot in the city," Alyssa laughs. "Your grandparents are keeping her very busy, and affording her the ability to gallivant around Europe, you know."

"So, I've heard. They're beyond impressed with her writing, Alyssa," Daniel says.

"She really is talented, Alyssa. Is she going to make a career of this?" Tanya asks.

"Thank you both. Who knows? I do agree, she is a talented writer. But I think for now she's just happy to have the income. Gosh, I can't help but feel jealous of you, young ones," Alyssa tells Daniel. "Such freedom and opportunities!"

"Youth... wasted on the young," Tanya says with a smile.

After that, the conversation turns to wedding planning, and the moms gossip about the Greenwich elite and whether Alyssa likes the bride-to-be. Daniel tunes out and checks his phone, which has a recent text from Sofia apologizing for the "awful morning." She made it safely back to her apartment, where she's planning on remaining in bed for the rest of her life. Daniel laughs at this, and his mother and Alyssa look at him expectantly.

"Sorry, that was from my friend Sofia. She apologized that you guys saw her in that state this morning; I think she's really embarrassed."

"Oh please, we've all been there, right, Tanya? Daniel, not to be too nosy, but is she really just a friend? Beautiful girl, even hungover," Alyssa says, prying.

Daniel stutters for a minute before coming up with an answer. "We are friends but have been on a few dates, if you must know. Nothing serious, though, which is why I never mentioned her, Mom."

By the grace of God, their meals arrive just then, forcing them to stop discussing Daniel's love life before either of the mothers can use the term *friends with benefits,* which is what they'd been thinking all morning. The conversation quickly moves to why English food is so lousy, and Daniel is fleetingly safe from their interrogation. After they eat, the women return to Daniel's apartment to get their luggage, then head over to the hotel to rest. Daniel and his mom make dinner plans for later that evening, and Daniel, suddenly exhausted, returns home for a nap.

The rest of the weekend is nice, better than Daniel had expected. He enjoys showing his mom and Alyssa around the city, and other than a few random mentions, the subject of dear Taylor is kept to a minimum. On Monday, he leaves the women to their own devices while he returns to classes. They're hitting up some museums that Daniel has already visited. He sees Sofia around campus; she has nearly recovered from her embarrassment. He calms her down a bit, letting her know that his mother wasn't upset or judgmental in the least. They make plans to hang out later in the week once his mom has departed for Barcelona.

In the blink of an eye, it's Tuesday already, and the moms are heading for Barcelona on an afternoon flight. Daniel blows off his morning class, despite his mother's insistence that he needn't miss classes for her sake, in order to have breakfast with her before she leaves for the airport. They have a great time together, both agreeing that Tanya's time in London has been too short but pleased that Daniel will be home in just over a month to celebrate Christmas in Madison with his mother, as he has done for all of his twenty years of life.

As they finish their meal, Daniel tells his mom to say hi to Taylor for him, to which she responds, "So, is there any connection there? I mean, I know you guys have seen each other, which is just fantastic, you have no idea how special that is for Alyssa and me, given our, and your, history. But I have to ask, is it really just a friendship? Or is there more going on?"

Daniel groans. "Mom, seriously? I love you, but I can't have this conversation with you right now. Taylor and I are friends. I'd go as far as to say that it's complicated, but we're not dating or anything. In fact, last I heard, she has some older Spanish boyfriend."

"Yes, I knew about that. I was just curious," his mother says, a tiny smirk on her face.

"Besides," Daniel continues, "she's staying in Barcelona all year anyway, so it's not like we'll even see each other until next summer." He hates how he sounds, like a petulant child, but he really doesn't want to deal with this.

"I know, and I'm sorry to intrude. I just like to know what's going on with my little boy, that's all," she says, squeezing his arm. "My little boy who is well over six feet tall and looks like a full-grown man," she laughs.

"It's fine, Mom," Daniel says with an exaggerated eye roll.

They pay the bill, and Daniel sends his mom off to find Alyssa, with whom she'll share a ride to the airport. They hug, and his mom tells him she's so proud of him, for what, exactly, he's not entirely sure, but he accepts the compliment and wishes her a great time in Barcelona.

Chapter 11

November 2003, Barcelona

Later that day, while Daniel carries on with his life in London, Alyssa and Tanya arrive in sunny Barcelona. Taylor will meet them at their hotel later, where they will have drinks and head out for dinner. Despite Taylor's suggestions to stay closer to her place in Eixample, on Passeig de Gràcia, for example, Alyssa and Tanya insist on staying near the beach, at the Hotel Arts. Although it's out of the way, Taylor is thrilled to have a reason to check the place out. She's been eyeing this glam hotel since she first arrived in the city.

As she gets ready for the ladies' night out, Taylor feels a pang of nostalgia and excitement at the thought of seeing her mom tonight. It is, she realizes, the longest amount of time she's ever been away from her family. And despite the fundamental strangeness of spending a night with Daniel's mom, Daniel, the guy she grew up with, fucked, and then (sort of) cheated on her boyfriend with, Taylor has always loved Daniel's mom. She has fond memories of Tanya being around while she was growing up, helping Taylor with her Spanish classwork while sitting together at the island in her family's kitchen, and just being a warm presence in her life.

Taylor sips a glass of cheap, cold white wine while she applies bronzer and mascara, finishing up with a dab of her Lancôme Juicy Tube lip gloss before lighting a cigarette. She can't smoke in front of her mom; she would literally kill her if she found out. In the Evans family, marijuana is acceptable; nicotine is not. She drains her wine, stubs out her cigarette, and sprays herself with a healthy mist of Calvin Klein Truth.

The November evening air is cool and refreshing, and Taylor decides to splurge on a taxi rather than deal with the metro. She's wearing four-inch heels and isn't in the mood for stairs, or men looking at her, for that matter. In her three months here, in Barcelona and everywhere else in Europe she's visited, the attention from men has been almost too much to bear.

Aside from the subway fiasco, she hasn't been touched inappropriately, but the looks, the flirting, the nonstop assessment from the men here have nearly brought her to a breaking point. Even when she's with Manuel, for Christ's sake. He's noticed it, of course, but he seems to brush it off rather than get angry or possessive. Taylor isn't sure which she'd prefer: for him to keep his cool and ignore it, or get mad and claim her as his. Neither, she supposes; her actual preference would be to no longer be objectified. Another goal to add to her life plan, she thinks, though this one seems to be the most difficult to achieve. Did her brothers behave like that around women? Her father? She shudders at the thought and hails a taxi, heading to see two of her favorite women on earth.

As the taxi makes its way to the Hotel Arts, Taylor's phone pings with a new text message. Assuming it's from Manuel, arranging dinner for tomorrow evening, she sees it's actually from Daniel.

D: Good luck with those two, I hope you have fun. Hopefully your mom doesn't interrogate you like mine did! Let me know how it goes. Miss you.

Taylor feels her pulse quicken as she reads the final line. Unsure of what to say, she decides to respond later, and instead of obsessing over an acceptable reply, she focuses on paying her taxi fare. She does, in fact, find herself wishing for Daniel's company. The two of them, after sleeping together back at school and their inappropriate kiss in Barcelona, have somehow managed to find an easy discourse, an actual friendship.

Taylor enters the gorgeous hotel lobby and immediately spots her mother and Tanya hovering near the bar. Her mom runs toward her and envelops her in a hug. Taylor recognizes the subtle hints of Chanel No. 5, her mother's signature fragrance (surprisingly sophisticated for such a practical woman), which is so familiar and soothing she's nearly brought to tears.

"Taylor, my goodness, you look so grown up. I barely recognize you. Those shoes! They're stunning. How can you walk in those? Did you find us okay?" Alyssa pummels Taylor with questions while holding onto her shoulders.

"Hi, Mom. I look exactly the same; I'm just better dressed here. European women don't seem to wear sweatpants, so I've had to step up my fashion game, that's all. And yes, you guys were pretty easy to spot. Hi, Tanya!"

"Hi, honey, it's so great to see you. I agree with your mother, you look so grown up, and even more stunning than ever, if that's possible. You're truly radiant," Tanya gushes while giving Taylor's hands a squeeze. Taylor finds herself blushing from the praise and quickly thanks Tanya.

"So," Taylor says enthusiastically, "what's the plan? You guys must be tired from the travel. I can't wait to hear about London. Shall we get a drink at the bar here, or go straight to dinner?" They don't have a reservation anywhere, but it is a Tuesday night, so Taylor isn't particularly concerned about finding a place.

"We are tired, hon. We're old!" Alyssa laughs. "A drink here sounds perfect; we can take it from there. Speaking for myself, I'd be happy to have dinner here and head to bed early, but we can do whatever you guys want."

"That's fine, Mom. Save your energy for our busy day tomorrow!" Taylor only has one class tomorrow morning, so she has a full day of sightseeing and shopping planned, followed by dinner with Manuel, the dinner where he'll meet her mom for the first time, for which she's both excited and terrified.

The three of them walk through the elegant hotel lobby, taking it all in. "Wow, this place is gorgeous! I know I suggested you stay closer to me in the city center, but in retrospect you made the right call by staying on the beach. This is perfect," Taylor tells them.

"And did you know they have a casino? Right here in the hotel," her mom declares excitedly. Taylor smiles at the irony of a woman who has never once gambled being so enthused by a casino. They make their way to the bar, which is relatively quiet, given the early hour.

"Just so you both know, Barcelona is on a whole different meal schedule. People eat lunch at, like, three in the afternoon, and no one even sits down to dinner until at least 10:30 at night, except tourists. I've gotten used to it, but the first few weeks were tough. I had to embrace the beautiful art of the siesta, along with loads of espresso," Taylor explains, forgetting that both her mom and Tanya already know all of this.

"Ah, espresso," Tanya muses as she scans the cocktail menu. "Is that how you're so thin?"

"No, it's all the walking! Believe me, I've been thoroughly enjoying the local cuisine. My boyfriend is a local and knows all the best restaurants, so I'm eating very well here."

"Let's hear more about him, Taylor," Tanya says.

"Drinks first, please," her mom says with a laugh. "If I am hearing about my daughter's love life with a real adult man in a foreign country, someone who hasn't been properly vetted by her brothers, I'm going to need alcohol."

"Fair enough, Mom," Taylor says, while simultaneously waving the bartender over. The three of them sip their cocktails and take an array of pictures, which will later be framed, placed in an album, or relegated to the reject photo shoebox once Tanya and Alyssa return home.

After a few drinks and placing their food order, Tanya and Alyssa tell Taylor about their time in London. They spare no details, and

Taylor is stunned, and momentarily jealous, when they tell her about their "hysterical" encounter with Daniel's *friend* Sofia and his still-drunk roommate, Will.

To cover up her distress, brought on by imagining Daniel with another girl, she quickly jumps in. "Ah, yes, the famous Will. Or maybe *infamous* is the better descriptor. I've met him a few times; he's a funny kid. He really took to my friend Katie while she and I were in London. I thought they'd make a cute couple, but she'd temporarily sworn off men while we were there, so it probably won't go anywhere."

"I wouldn't necessarily categorize Will as a man, my dear. He's an overgrown boy, don't you think?" Tanya asks with a smirk.

"I suppose so. I'd say your son Daniel is the more mature flat-mate, as they call themselves. We never met the third one, Ethan. Apparently, he was traveling while we were in town."

"Oh, don't get me started on that. So pretentious, those boys, *flat-mate, the loo, the tube*," Tanya laughs, poking fun at her son. "They spend, what, a week in London and suddenly they're locals," she says with an eye roll.

Taylor laughs along with her but can't shake the image of Daniel's female friend emerging from his bedroom after a night of God knows what. She downs the remains of her drink, orders another, and excuses herself to the bathroom. On her way, she slips outside and smokes half a cigarette at record speed to calm herself down. She washes her hands excessively to rid them of the cigarette smell and returns to the "old ladies", *las viejas*, as Tanya and Alyssa have begun referring to themselves.

The night concludes with arguments over who should pay the bill, and Alyssa trying to coerce Taylor into staying over at the hotel tonight. She declines (politely), citing the fact that she doesn't have any of her things, not even a toothbrush. As much as she'd love the luxury of this hotel for a night (and a bed that isn't designed for a toddler), she needs space and, if she's being honest with herself, time to ruminate over the Daniel information she's learned tonight.

So, they all hug and make plans to meet at Taylor's apartment at noon tomorrow, once she's back from class.

The following day is gloomy and chilly; it feels more like London than typically sunny Barcelona. Despite the crap weather, Taylor, her mom, and Tanya have a fun, busy day checking out the must-see sights and shopping, with a traditional tapas lunch mid-day. Taylor insists that her mom and Tanya return to their hotel for a lie-down before dinner, so they don't fall asleep in their calamari at their highly anticipated dinner with Manuel. In keeping with tradition, she's taking them to La Barca de Salamanca so they can enjoy being spoiled and overfed, all while being within walking distance of their hotel. Plus, Taylor can remind her mom that this place was Eric's favorite; Alyssa will appreciate the fact that Taylor actually took some of her brother's advice.

After a positive introduction to Manuel and an hours-long dinner, Taylor considers her mom's brief visit to have been a success. She's a bit taken aback, then, when her mom, while hugging her goodbye before leaving for the airport, tells her, "Be careful with that man. He may seem shiny and mature and wonderful, but you're still twenty years old, and as much as you don't want to admit it, you're not a resident here." Rather than get into an argument and ruin their final moments together, Taylor just nods and keeps her mouth shut. Her mom just doesn't get it, she thinks.

But later, once Alyssa is heading back to the U.S. and Taylor has had time to deliberate on the comments, she's pissed off and desperate to prove her wrong. *Just wait until Manuel shows up to Eric's wedding and wins everyone over,* she thinks. Maybe then she'll understand that this is real and good. Later, Taylor will recognize that her anxiety in this moment is actually about making Daniel jealous when she and Manuel show up at the wedding, rather than about her mom's comments about her relationship.

Taylor decides to simmer down, at least until after Eric's engagement party. She could sense her mom's apprehension over this event; while Alyssa may pretend not to care about money and class, the idea of her son marrying into this level of wealth is, without a doubt, intimidating as hell. As such, Taylor gives her the benefit of the doubt and keeps her feelings to herself.

Over the next few days, Taylor chaotically tries to plan a weekend getaway with Manuel. He's suggested that they "get away" for a few days before she heads back to the States for Christmas and has asked her to pick a city to visit. They have settled on Vienna, but between her school schedule, his work schedule, and his mother's illness, finding a weekend before the holidays is proving difficult. Nicholas is obsessed with this development, informing Taylor that taking a "mini break" with someone is serious, and that this means Manuel is the real deal.

"Didn't you watch *Bridget Jones's Diary*, for the love of Christ?" he exclaims with exasperation while they sit around the dining table smoking and drinking Estrella Damm on a lazy Sunday afternoon. "It means he's not planning on going anywhere, okay? Like, he's not going to be screwing around with anyone else while you're back in the States for Christmas and the New Year," he tells Taylor matter-of-factly, as if this little weekend in Vienna indicates she should start planning their wedding and naming their future children. She truly hasn't given either much, if any, thought, and Nicholas's obsession with this "mini break" is provoking a mild panic within her.

Nevertheless, Taylor carries on and plans out some sights to see and restaurants to check out in Vienna, promising Nicholas she will rewatch *Bridget Jones's Diary* to better understand the significance of a weekend away with her beau.

Chapter 12

December 2003, Vienna

And so, on Thursday, December 11th, barely a week before she's returning home to Madison for Christmas, Taylor leaves behind her study abroad pals, who are living it up in Barcelona this weekend, knowing it's their last full one there together, to fly to Vienna with Manuel. While disappointed to miss the shenanigans with her schoolmates this weekend, Taylor is giddy with the thrill of traveling, for the first time really, with a boyfriend. Sure, she's been to some fraternity formal weekends back at college, but not with anyone she actually cared about. Just the two of them, together in the hotel room, for three days. A bit nerve-wracking, actually. How will she go to the bathroom discreetly? Use the lobby bathroom if she has to take a shit? Also, despite spending many nights together, Taylor isn't sure Manuel has seen her without any makeup on. These little things are making her nervous. For all her worries, Manuel has none, at least none that he's shown.

Manuel has mapped out some things to do and made dinner reservations, but they plan on doing a lot of wandering and exploring the city. For his part, Manuel hasn't been here since he was a young child, and the city has changed drastically since then, so for all intents and purposes he's a first-timer as well.

They arrive at the Barcelona airport late in the afternoon with plenty of time to spare, so they get through the security check and have a drink near their gate. Taylor is once again delighted by the glamour of this airport. People are dressed well, attractive, sipping cocktails and smoking cigarettes. Half of the people are wearing sunglasses indoors. It sure beats the Milwaukee airport, where she often has layovers on her way from school back home to Madison, where the smoking lounge is filled with beer-bellied old guys. No, as much as Taylor loves her home state of Wisconsin, her heart and soul are here, in cosmopolitan Barcelona. For a fleeting second, while she and Manuel toast one another and their trip with an enthusiastic "Salud!", she considers just staying here. Finishing college here, getting a job, becoming a true Barcelona resident. Surely, stranger things have happened.

For a few moments she's lost in the reverie of living the rest of her life in Barcelona, a life filled with fashionable trips all over Europe, a fabulous apartment in a trendy neighborhood, and cool, fun friends. Her fantasy is abruptly interrupted when the boarding of their flight is announced; she and Manuel finish their drinks and get in line to board the plane.

Two hours later, they step out of the Vienna airport, shivering at the markedly colder temperature, and get into a cab. It's already pitch-black, and the cold is momentarily shocking. Manuel has outdone himself, Taylor thinks, as they pull up to the swanky Grand Hotel Wien, which is clearly a five-star hotel and absolutely breathtaking. The hotel lives up to its name and is not only grand but festive with Christmas décor, which Taylor finds more appropriate here in a colder climate than in Barcelona, which is still relatively warm for December.

Their room is small but luxurious, and within five minutes they're in bed, having what Taylor will come to know as vacation sex, which is somehow better than any other kind. She's amazed at how quickly her body reacts, especially since Manuel's hands are still cold from their brief time outside. They finish quickly and are both glistening with sweat. Manuel takes a quick shower while Taylor stretches out on the bed, relishing the sensation of the crisp white sheets against her body. She notices an ice bucket with a bottle of champagne and two glasses, which they overlooked upon arriving and rushing into bed. She pops the cork open, carefully, using a towel and pointing it away from her; perhaps the best advice, her brother Alex has ever bestowed upon her, and pours the bubbly into the glasses.

"Aquí, mi amor," she says to Manuel, handing him a glass as he emerges from the bathroom in just a towel. For the second time today, they clink their glasses together in a toast. Taylor fixes her hair and makeup, which have been significantly mussed, while Manuel dresses and calls the hotel restaurant to see if he can secure a reservation. It's only 8 p.m., which is far too early to eat by Barcelona standards, but Taylor is ravenous and quickly puts on a fancy dress, tights, and high-heeled boots.

The next three days are a whirlwind of sightseeing in the chilly temperatures, enjoying the beautiful Christmas decorations all around the city, shopping, eating, drinking, and having lots of sex. Like, multiple times a day, each time better than the last. By the end of the trip, Taylor feels gluttonous: bloated, sore, and vaguely hungover. But she and Manuel have had many conversations broaching topics they've largely avoided in Barcelona, or in "real life," as Taylor considers it.

While waiting in line for the opera on Friday evening, Manuel asks her out of the blue if she would consider staying in Europe and finishing school in Barcelona. Caught off guard, though not entirely unpleasantly, Taylor tells him that while she's going to complete her senior year back at UNC as planned, she would move back to Barcelona in a heartbeat as soon as she has her diploma in hand. Her daydream from the airport yesterday of completing school in Barcelona seems too much to manage logistically. Plus, she has to admit, she wants to be back at UNC with her girlfriends for senior year. This answer seems to appease him; the brief disappointment he shows while imagining being apart for the better part of a year is replaced with a contented smile upon knowing that she wants to return.

The next day, after an afternoon of shopping and checking out the Hofburg Palace, they are drinking white wine at Griechenbeisl, which is apparently the oldest restaurant in Vienna, dating back to 1447 and a favorite of Mozart, Beethoven, and Mark Twain. In between sips of the crisp wine, the conversation somehow turns to New York City and how neither Manuel nor Taylor can imagine themselves living there permanently. While they both love the frenetic pace of Barcelona, Manhattan is a different kind of beast. In turn, they end up discussing Eric's wedding, and Manuel admits, bashfully, that he's nervous about meeting Taylor's entire family. Taylor is stunned that this smart, confident man is intimidated by anything, while simultaneously flattered that her family's opinion of him is so important.

She manages to reassure Manuel that her family will go easy on him; after all, they'll be busy and focused on the wedding details, so Taylor is hoping that she and Manuel, her "plus-one," are an afterthought at the big event. Even so, he's worried about what her brothers and father will think of their younger sister and only daughter, respectively, dating someone so much older. At this, Taylor waves her hand dismissively and tells him, "They're hippies, my parents. I don't know how to say that in Spanish, but they're very liberal and have never believed in policing my brothers and me. *Son liberales, vale?*"

Manuel laughs and nods appreciatively, responding in English (which they almost never use while together), "I got it. Liberal hippies. *Gracias, cariño.*"

"My brothers may be a little more difficult. But Eric, the one getting married, will be too busy dealing with wedding stuff to bother you. Alex may come off as tough, but he has a heart of gold. They'll love you, don't worry."

With all of these issues settled and classes wrapped up for the semester, Taylor is at peace to enjoy her remaining five days in Barcelona before heading home for Christmas. Sunday evening, after returning from the glorious trip to Vienna, she tidies the apartment, starts packing, and buys groceries for the week. She and Nicholas enjoy watching a so-bad-it's-good show on TV, *Aquí no hay quien viva*. And here Taylor thought trashy TV only existed in the United States. It's the perfect evening, and Taylor declines Nicholas's invitation to join him with some mates at a new discoteca, preferring instead to fall asleep by 11 p.m. for the first time in as long as she can remember.

Taylor spends her final days of 2003 in Barcelona writing about her jaunt to Vienna, packing, and spending time with Manuel. She packs half of her suitcase with Christmas gifts she's picked up at some local shops, chocolates, fancy stationery, a pretty scarf for her mom, along with T-shirts and soccer jerseys for her dad and brothers. Despite the warm temperatures, there is a festive Christmas feel in the air. People are running here and there to holiday parties, restaurants have lights and decorations up, and Taylor has begun to feel her usual excitement at spending the holiday and New Year back in Madison.

Friday afternoon, Taylor submits her piece on Vienna, checks that she's packed everything, and heads over to Manuel's apartment. She spends the night with Manuel at his place, where they have a passionate farewell evening before saying goodbye Saturday morning, the day of her departure. They wish one another "*Feliz Navidad y Feliz Año Nuevo*" and promise to be in touch while Taylor is away. Manuel walks her outside to get a taxi, and they share a final goodbye kiss on the sidewalk. It is so terribly romantic that Taylor feels as though they're on a movie set.

Before she can even process how much she will miss Manuel over the holiday break, Taylor is sitting on the plane, embarking on the nine-hour journey to Chicago, then on to Madison, where she will be picked up at the airport by her parents. Just in time for a weekend of debauchery with her high school friends, acquaintances, former hookups, along with the masses of her brother's friends who seem to come out of the woodwork over the holidays. It's inevitable that she will come across at least five of her brother's friends on any given night out in Madison. Taylor's parents joke that between her two brothers and her, they know everyone between eighteen and twenty-five years old in the entire city of Madison.

This year's Christmas break brings a new element, a new possibility for high-level drama: Daniel. He has already emailed Taylor the dates he'll be home, along with where people are going out on Christmas Eve once they've spent the obligatory time with their families. She knows she'll see him multiple times, and the addition of alcohol to the equation, which is basically a given, well, it complicates things, to say the least. The chances for disaster are infinite.

Chapter 13

December 2003, Madison, Wisconsin

On a snowy Saturday night just five days before Christmas, Daniel sits at the KK (Kollege Klub bar, a Madison staple for college students and locals alike), wondering if Taylor's plane has arrived yet. His mother has been going on and on about how great it was seeing Taylor in Barcelona; she's so gorgeous, and smart, and kind, and independent, blah blah blah. Tanya has managed to identify all of the traits in Taylor that Daniel is so attracted to and impressed by, and it is, frankly, driving him insane. He's been in touch with Taylor via email, figuring out dates when people are going out and where, but this Christmas break, like all of the others before it, will likely be a drunken blur, time split into distinct fragments of drinking with family members, drinking at bars with high school friends, and sleeping off hangovers. There will be regrettable hookups for many, rekindled flames for others, and for the lucky ones, they'll finally get together with that person they fancied back in high school. Daniel isn't sure yet which camp he'll fall into this year; he just knows there's only one person he really wants to be with, and she's currently on an airplane heading back here, back to the home they have both known for all of their (nearly) twenty-one years. Oh, and she happens to have a boyfriend back in Barcelona.

While Daniel drinks beer with his buddies, Taylor sits in the back of her dad's car as he drives slowly through downtown Madison, braking for drunk people running around and because of the falling snow. *Now this is what Christmas should look like,* Taylor thinks to herself. There will never be anywhere better than home for the holidays, even though most of these breaks are just spent in drunken stupors with her high school girlfriends, reliving their glory days, but now with better fake IDs. And she'll do just that. Starting tomorrow, that is. It's something like 11 p.m. in Wisconsin, meaning to her tired and confused body it feels like 8 a.m. the following day. The availability of free alcohol and decent movies on the plane made it nearly impossible to sleep, and the fatigue has hit her so hard she nearly falls asleep on the twenty-minute drive home from the airport.

Neither Alex nor Eric have arrived home yet; they are due back Monday and Tuesday, respectively. So, Taylor has one full day alone with her parents before total chaos ensues. But now, the only thought in her mind is crawling into her bed, feeling safe and loved in a way that can only happen in one's childhood home.

Taylor sleeps a solid twelve hours and is surprised that it takes her a few seconds to remember where she is. After eating breakfast (or lunch, really) in the living room with the TV on next to a blazing fire, her dad finally caves and asks for the full rundown of her semester in Barcelona. She gives him the highlights, starting with school, followed by her friends from her study abroad program, the special friendships she has formed with Nicholas and Finn, her travels, her cool apartment, and finally, just as he appears to be losing interest, Manuel. She knows her mom has told him about Manuel, but this is the first time Taylor and her dad have really broached the topic directly.

"Christ, Taylor, he's as old as Eric. Where did you find this guy?"

"Dad, calm down," Taylor tells him while suppressing an eye roll. "We met just after I arrived in Barcelona. I was having dinner by myself at a tapas place near my apartment. And he's not 'some guy,' he's super smart and, more importantly, kind. And successful, too, if you really want to know. He works in finance. Like Eric." Taylor realizes how defensive she sounds and takes a deep breath before speaking again. "And yes, I realize he's older than me, but that's not a bad thing. Twenty-year-old guys are not particularly mature; in case you've forgotten what your dear sons were like."

At this, her father snorts with laughter and just says, "Be careful, that's all. And if this Spanish playboy breaks your heart, I'll beat the shit out of him, okay?" With that, he stands and brings their plates into the kitchen to be rinsed. And that was that.

Taylor's mom is out doing her final Christmas shopping, which Taylor couldn't handle today. Shopping with her mother is the equivalent of being taken hostage for ten hours, at a crowded mall rather than a dark room. Her mom's indecision and inability to shop quickly has infuriated Taylor since she was a child, so she avoids shopping with Alyssa as much as possible while simultaneously trying desperately not to hurt her mother's feelings. She succeeded today by claiming exhaustion, which wasn't a total lie.

Now she has the day to unpack, do laundry, and get ready for a night of total depravity with her high school friends. State Street Brats, 10 p.m. Drinks at someone's house first, the details are still TBD. As she folds clothes and places them into her drawers, her mind wanders to Daniel, and she finds herself fantasizing about what would happen if she saw him out tonight. She shakes the thought from her brain and carries on with her laundry.

A few hours later, after Taylor has had dinner with her parents, four of her best friends from high school appear at her house, one of whom is inconspicuously clutching a bottle of vodka in one hand and a giant bottle of cranberry juice in the other. Hugs are exchanged all around. Taylor's mom ignores the alcohol and offers the girls a snack, which no one accepts. After a few minutes of pleasantries, Taylor and her friends bring the vodka and cranberry juice, along with some red Solo cups and ice, up to her bedroom, turn on Beyoncé, and pour themselves drinks. Although they've kept in touch by email, there is nothing like catching up in person; they are talking over each other, a million miles a minute, trying to get up to speed on the lives they've been living over the past four-plus months.

Taylor's friends are devastated to hear that Eric is getting hitched; he and Alex have always been considered hot commodities among them. Taylor groans at the idea of her dipshit brothers being objects of desire among her friends and pulls out her pictures from Barcelona as a distraction, proudly showing off Manuel and a handful of their adventures together.

"T, he's gorgeous! Holy shit," quips Heidi, who has been one of Taylor's best friends for nearly seventeen years, ever since they went to preschool together. As the girls gush over Manuel, Taylor finishes applying her makeup and calls a cab to take them to the bar. As she waits for the cab company to answer, she asks her friends, "I'm assuming no one wants to drive, right?" Four heads shake a decisive no. Despite all of their ludicrous behavior over the years, this group is responsible when it comes to drinking and driving, they just don't go there. A few minutes and a few shots of vodka later, they're crammed into a taxi that reeks of stale cigarette smoke combined with pine air freshener.

"Ah, smells like Christmas," Taylor snickers as they head off.

Their chatter about who will be there tonight, who people have hooked up with over break so far, and general Madison gossip drowns out the crappy easy-listening music the cab driver is blasting on the radio. There's talk of which guys have gotten better looking versus those who have gained weight or look worse; Daniel is solidly in the former category. Taylor keeps their history to herself, resisting the urge to spill about what has transpired between them over the past two years, but secretly noting how pissed off she'll be if any of her friends try to hook up with him while they're all home. Not that she has any claim over him, nothing like that, but she can't help the feelings that he evokes within her.

By the time they arrive, the place is packed to the gills with friends and acquaintances from high school, the ages spanning between eighteen and twenty-four. Taylor sees some of Alex's friends, whom she hugs hello as she and her friends make their way to the bar. Shots are poured and passed around, and Taylor, already buzzed from the drinks at her parents' house, quickly realizes she's going to end up wasted tonight.

"Cheers," Taylor and her friends exclaim, clinking tiny shot glasses filled with vodka.

As soon as she sets the shot glass down on the bar after draining it, Daniel's arm is around her shoulder and he's kissing her on the cheek. "Wow, what a nice surprise," Taylor exclaims while giving Daniel a big hug. "How are you, Daniel? How's your mom?"

"I'm good, she's good. You look great, Taylor. When did you get back?"

"Yesterday. I'm still fighting jet lag, but the girls dragged me out tonight," Taylor tells him, gesturing toward her pack of friends, who have, luckily, ordered another round of shots and therefore have a distraction to keep them from picking up on the obvious vibes between her and Daniel.

The rest of the night unwinds as so many of them do: a haze of shots, too many cigarettes smoked outside in the freezing cold, which is only moderately diminished by the alcohol, and conversations that will be forgotten by dawn. Taylor balances her time between Daniel, whose friends have apparently abandoned him in search of their high school crushes, and her girlfriends, who have stationed themselves at the bar and have the bartender on high alert to keep the drinks flowing. Flow they do, and before she knows it, Taylor realizes it's 1:30 a.m. and she's spent. Despite total exhaustion, she has the drunken idea that staying until closing time is the best plan. She rallies herself and her friends and orders another round of drinks, vodka cranberries, and even in her inebriated state, she can tell the bartender went heavy on the vodka and light on the cranberry juice; the drinks are practically clear.

Barcelona-style, she giggles to herself.

After toasting to Christmas break and everlasting friendships, everyone disperses into the crowd and, before long, Taylor finds herself alone. She takes her drink out to the patio for a cigarette and is surprised to see Daniel out there, sitting alone with a beer.

"Hey there," Taylor slurs, trying not to trip as she sits down next to him. "Mind if I smoke?" she asks after she's already lit her cigarette.

Laughing, Daniel says he doesn't mind, and he allows her to sidle up next to him for warmth. "You alright there, Taylor? You look a little tipsy," he tells her with a smirk. He puts his arm around her and draws her close to him. She doesn't protest.

"Understatement of the century," Taylor says loudly, with a giggle and a little hiccup. "I'm really, really drunk, Daniel. I'm sorry."

"For what? You're allowed to get drunk. It's quite cute, actually."

"Pfff, I'm sure. My makeup is a mess, and it's too fucking cold here to even wear anything cute. Where'd all your friends go? Where'd all *my* friends go?" Taylor asks, looking around and exhaling a mouthful of smoke.

"Who knows. It's that point in the night when I give up keeping track of anyone. But I knew you were here, so I was just chilling and waiting to talk to you," Daniel says sheepishly.

Taylor leans her head onto his shoulder, breathing in his familiar smell, tonight mixed with beer and smoke, and looks up at him. "Well, I'm glad you did. Let's talk! Tell me everything about the rest of your semester in London," she says. "I heard our moms had a run-in with your lady 'friend' one morning at your apartment! Excuse me, I mean your *flat*," Taylor adds with a hint of sarcasm, hoping there's no trace of the jealousy she still feels about Daniel's relationship with Sofia.

Daniel buries his head in his hands and groans. "That was literally the most awkward moment of my life. I can't believe they told you that, those traitors."

"Amateur. You should know by now that they're already two little old gossipy ladies. So, who was your friend?" Taylor asks.

"Sofia. We were seeing each other for a bit. Nothing serious, though," Daniel adds quickly. "It sort of fizzled out toward the end of the term."

"Well, look at you, Mr. London playboy," Taylor says, nuzzling closer to him. "Sofia was a lucky lady. I heard she was quite gorgeous, too."

"And what about you? Are you still with that guy?" Daniel can't bring himself to say it out loud, although he's well aware of Manuel's name (the bastard).

"Yes, we're still together. I'm surprised, actually! I mean, it's just the age difference, and the fact that he's a local, I don't know. I didn't expect it to last this long, that's all."

"But are you happy?" Daniel looks Taylor dead in the eye as he asks, and she's flustered by his gaze.

"I am happy, yes." She smiles at him and, to lighten the mood, offers him a sip of her drink before he can ask anything else. She really doesn't want to be talking about Manuel with Daniel, especially now, when she's feeling these vibes with him.

Eventually Taylor's friends stumble outside, and she subconsciously scoots away from Daniel. If he notices, he doesn't show it.

"TayTay! There you are," slurs Heidi. "We're leaving, are you ready? Wanna share a cab?" Taylor shakes her head and mouths a *no thanks* to Heidi.

Heidi continues, "Hi Daniel, you're looking dashing! You were in England, right?"

"Hey Heidi, good to see you. Yes, London. How about you?"

"Oh, I stayed right here in good old Madison. Couldn't leave the cheese, ya know," she says in an exaggerated Midwestern accent. "So, Taylor, what are you doing? It's fucking freezing," Heidi adds unnecessarily.

Taylor hesitates, knowing she should go but not wanting to leave Daniel's warmth. She looks at him, searching for an answer. Nothing.

"You guys go. I'm going to stay and catch up some more with Daniel. Talk tomorrow, okay?"

"You betcha. Get home safe, lovie." With that, the girls depart after making quasi-plans for tomorrow, which Taylor doubts will come to fruition given everyone's current state of inebriation.

"You didn't have to stay, you know," Daniel says with a smile.

"I wanted to! It's nice talking to you. When are you going back to Duke?"

"Middle of January. Classes don't start until the 20th, so I've got a nice long break. I can't believe you've got a whole extra semester in Barcelona. I have to say, as excited as I am to get back to school, I'm a little jealous."

"I'm going to miss being at school for sure, but I feel like I belong in Barcelona, does that make sense? Like, I got there and almost immediately felt like I was finally home. I'm thinking ahead and trying to formulate a plan for how I can end up there after graduation."

"Seriously? I could tell how at ease you felt there, so I get it. But would you really live there, like, long-term?" Daniel shakes his head and looks at her with quiet awe. "And for what it's worth, I've read all of your articles, and they're fantastic. You can do anything you want to do."

"Oh, stop it, Daniel," she says, playfully poking him in the arm. "You're just saying that because you're drunk."

"I'm not *that* drunk, and it's true. Anyways, I love that you have a plan and know what you want to do. I feel like I'm kind of floating aimlessly. I mean, I'll hopefully end up in New York at a bank, but I don't know if I truly want to do that yet." It's the first time Daniel has ever said this aloud, and he's surprised at how true it feels. "I want to travel and see more of the world before I'm old and settled and boring, you know?"

"Um, yeah, you're talking to the right person. Miss Wanderlust over here, so I get it. You should travel before you 'get serious.' We have our whole lives to do the grind, why not do, like, a gap year between graduation and starting your career? I'd be happy to accompany you on your adventures!" Taylor says with a smile.

"Something to think about," he says, once again totally charmed and impressed by Taylor, trying desperately to resist the urge he's had to kiss her for the past twenty minutes. Her smell, the way she keeps gazing up at him through her glassy eyes, it's fucking impossible.

"So, are we staying? If so, I'm getting us a quick refill before last call." Before Taylor can answer, he adds, "You stay put right here, I'll be right back."

No use arguing, Taylor thinks. "Okay, I'll keep our bench warm. 'Tis the damn season, after all, right?"

Daniel flashes his insanely adorable grin at her, and Taylor starts to wonder what the hell she's doing, and what, exactly, she expects to happen tonight.

Daniel gets their drinks just before last call is announced and returns to Taylor, who is smoking yet another cigarette. That's her flaw, he thinks. Perfect specimen of a person, minus the smoking. And yet, even the way she holds the cigarette is somehow sexy, and she knowingly blows the smoke away from him. It's hard for him to find fault with anything she does.

Once the bar starts emptying out and the remaining crowd begins their search for taxis, Taylor and Daniel walk down State Street, shivering and laughing. Neither of them is aware that Daniel's parents stumbled around this exact place some twenty-five years earlier, their history something of a mystery to Daniel; Tanya didn't share many details about their relationship, focusing instead on how proud Daniel's father would have been of him and the injustice of Daniel never getting to meet his wonderful, kind father. But at this moment, Daniel is thinking only about how beautiful Taylor looks right now, all bundled up in her winter jacket and scarf.

"Are we going anywhere in particular?" Taylor asks with a giggle. "It's kind of freezing, you do realize that, right?"

"Yeah, I know it's cold. It's just nice, isn't it? Walking together in arctic weather? Getting frostbite together?" At that moment, Daniel slows to a stop, grabs Taylor's hands in his, and pulls her in for a kiss.

She kisses him back, unable to deny the attraction that's been building all night, or, if she's being honest, for nearly the past two years. She's unsure how long they stand there kissing, but eventually they get into a cab and, without discussing it, decide on only one stop: Taylor's house.

They are both eager to finish what's been started, and Taylor has managed to squash any guilt she feels over being unfaithful to Manuel, overwhelmed by her feelings for Daniel. Nor does she consider the inevitable awkwardness bound to occur when Daniel walks downstairs tomorrow morning and sees her parents.

They're up until sunrise. They have sex quickly and spend the rest of the night kissing and talking, eventually dozing off as the first light of dawn appears. They talk about everything, from Daniel's uncertainty about his future, to Taylor's wanderlust, to finishing school and their families. The one topic that goes undiscussed is either of their love lives. Daniel doesn't ask about Manuel, and Taylor doesn't dare go there. This night, spent tangled up in Taylor's childhood bed, will forever remain one of the best nights of their lives, though neither has the wherewithal to acknowledge it at the time.

Taylor wakes up with a headache and the sense that she *should* feel an overarching guilt, but doesn't. Which somehow makes all of this worse. She tries to ignore this lack of morality but can't help feeling like total shit about what she's done to Manuel. *Traitorous,* she thinks. But then she looks over at Daniel, still sleeping peacefully beside her, and out the window, pleased to see that snow has blanketed the trees and grass and is still falling. She can smell a fire burning downstairs and feels so safe and protected in this moment that she begins to question whether returning to Barcelona is the right move after all.

Before she can pursue the thought any further, she climbs over Daniel, desperate to pee. She brushes her teeth and puts on mascara before heading back to her room. Just as she places her hand on the doorknob, she hears her dad's voice.

"Late night, huh, kiddo? What time did you get home, anyway?"

Taylor freezes and turns around slowly. "Hey, Dad. Yeah, it was a late one, sorry. It sure is pretty outside. How much are we supposed to get?" she asks, desperate to escape the conversation.

"Three to six inches. Hopefully no more; otherwise, I don't see your brother making it home today. There's breakfast in the kitchen when you're ready," he says, heading down the stairs.

"Thanks, Dad. I'll be down in a bit."

Taylor opens the door to her room to see a rumpled, disheveled Daniel sitting on the edge of her bed, looking both amused and terrified.

"Fuck," she whispers theatrically as she sits beside him. "What do we do? How do we explain this?"

"I can sneak out the back door and beeline home," Daniel suggests.

"No way. This house is too old and creaky, they'll hear you. Plus, it's snowing, and you're at least a mile from home. Fuck!" Taylor exclaims again before bursting into laughter.

Daniel starts laughing too, and they're both doubled over on her bed, fighting back tears. "Taylor, just think how happy this will make our moms," he says sarcastically.

Taylor rolls her eyes.

"Okay," Daniel continues, "let's just say I was in bad shape last night and you were watching out for me, brought me back here to make sure I was okay. Will they buy that?"

"No, but that's probably our best option. Unless I hide you in here until my parents leave the house. They have to leave eventually, right? Oh my God, this is too much."

"Or we can just waltz into the kitchen and pretend like nothing happened," Daniel says with a laugh. "Your brothers aren't here to kill me, so I'll just need to worry about your dad."

Taylor looks at him for a minute and decides that this plan is just crazy enough to work. "You know what, let's do that. What are they gonna do, ground me for having a boy in my room? I'm twenty years old, for Christ's sake," Taylor says defiantly.

"You sure?" Daniel asks warily, unsure how this will play out and secretly terrified of Taylor's brothers, who will surely hear about this whenever they get back to Madison.

"Yeah. The bathroom is down the hall if you need it. I'll wait here?"

Daniel nods, pulls on his jeans and shirt from last night, and tiptoes off to the bathroom. Taylor tries to compose herself, but the urge to laugh is overwhelming. She puts on an old T-shirt, a UNC hoodie, and a pair of sweatpants, and pulls her hair into a messy bun. Checking the mirror, she's pleased to see she looks better than expected given last night's shenanigans. She meets Daniel in the hallway.

"You ready? Let me do the talking, okay?"

"My pleasure," he responds sarcastically. He takes a deep breath and follows Taylor down the stairs and into the kitchen, where her mom is pouring coffee. Upon laying eyes on Daniel, she does a double take; her jaw drops briefly before an amused look crosses her face. She raises an eyebrow and greets them good morning.

"Why, hello there, Daniel. What a nice surprise. Er, would you two like any coffee?" Alyssa asks.

"Sure, Mom, thanks," Taylor says with a smile. "The fire smells amazing."

"Yes, once the snow started coming down your father insisted. There are bagels from Bagels Forever on the counter; cream cheese is in the fridge," Alyssa tells them.

At that moment, Taylor's dad walks into the kitchen, clearly keen on investigating the male voice he heard from the living room.

"Well, Taylor, you didn't mention that you had company," he says stoically, though with a twinkle of amusement in his eyes. "Nice to see you, Daniel. How was London? How's Tanya doing?" he asks, trying to stay calm.

"Uh, hi Mr. Evans," Daniel stammers. "My mom is great, thanks for asking," he says with excessive enthusiasm. "The house looks great. London was great, too." *Stop saying great, you jackass,* he thinks. "When do Alex and Eric get into town?" he asks, anxious to keep the conversation from turning to the inevitable, why in the hell is he sitting in Taylor's kitchen, totally hungover, with her parents on a Monday morning?

By this point, Taylor's father has poured himself another cup of coffee and is doing his best to ignore his daughter's flushed cheeks and, really, the entire scenario. "Alex gets home tonight, hopefully, and Eric tomorrow. Although with this snow piling up, who knows? Speaking of which, does your mother know where you are, Daniel? I'd hate for her to be worrying about you."

The comment is delivered with a mildly warning tone and a raised eyebrow. Daniel takes the hint and asks if he can use their phone. At the very least, it gives him an excuse to get the hell out of the room.

While Daniel escapes to the living room to make the call, Taylor putzes around the kitchen to avoid making eye contact with either of her parents. On any normal Monday morning they'd be at work, but they took time off this week to spend extra time with Taylor and her brothers and prepare for Christmas. Taylor rinses dishes that don't need rinsing and spends an uncomfortable amount of time staring out the window at the snow. Her mom seems to be doing the same, clearly equally unnerved.

The silence becomes so dreadful that Taylor feels a palpable sense of relief when Daniel reenters the room, announcing that his mom will be there in twenty minutes to pick him up and say hello, an ordeal that may last anywhere from five minutes to three hours, depending on how much Tanya and Alyssa feel like torturing them.

"That's great, Daniel. Let me just go make myself presentable," Alyssa chirps excitedly.

Taylor's dad uses this as an excuse to leave the room, and Taylor and Daniel are left alone in the kitchen, surrounded by bagels and sexual tension so thick it could be sliced with a knife.

"Well, this is turning out well," Daniel says cynically. "They're going to talk for so long that I'll end up sleeping here again tonight! What have we gotten ourselves into?" He dramatically buries his face in his hands.

Taylor hands him a Gatorade and turns on the TV, hoping the sound of the weatherman droning on about snowfall will ease the tension. They sit in companionable silence, cursing their hangovers and doing their best to keep embarrassment at bay.

A few minutes later, the doorbell rings. Tanya rushes in, snow dusting her hair and jacket, greeting Alyssa with a big hug. Their loud reunion quickly dissolves into hushed voices and giggles. Taylor and Daniel exchange an eye roll and laugh.

"In here, Mom," Daniel calls.

"Hello, beautiful darlings," Tanya gushes, hugging Taylor warmly. "Daniel, next time you're going to stay out all night, at least give me a heads-up. I woke up this morning and found your room empty and was so worried something went wrong. You know how I am with the snow, after your father's accident," she says solemnly, immediately regretting the guilt trip.

"Sorry, Mom. Really. It wasn't planned, we were just out late, and, you know... ended up here. I didn't mean to worry you."

"It's fine, honey. And of all the places to end up, you picked the right one. Taylor, you look fabulous as always. How was the rest of your semester in Barcelona? When are you going back?"

"Thanks, Tanya. It was really good. I'm heading back January 11th. I want to do some travel within Spain and get some writing done before classes start again."

Tanya smiles and shakes her head. "So ambitious. I love it. And of course, we're all loving your pieces. My former in-laws are beyond impressed with you, and they're rarely impressed by anyone who isn't a billionaire or socialite."

Taylor blushes and quickly changes the subject. After a few minutes of small talk, panic sets in, *what if Tanya brings up Manuel?* Sensing the danger, Taylor looks at Daniel and blurts, "Come upstairs with me, I forgot to show you my pictures from last semester!"

They escape upstairs, and once inside Taylor's room with the door closed, Daniel exhales audibly.

"Good move," he says. "Do you actually have pictures, or did you just want me back in your bedroom? Or was that purely an escape tactic?"

"My answer is D, all of the above," Taylor says with a smirk, pulling him in for a kiss.

He's instantly hard, but before his hands can wander, she stops him. "We can't do this now. Not with all of them around."

"I know," Daniel moans into her neck. "I just really want you. Like, right now."

"Me too," she admits, locking the door and pushing him back onto the bed, finger to his lips. Ten minutes later they're both spent, tangled together. At one point he murmurs, "If I could stay like this forever, I would."

Eventually he dresses, again, in last night's clothes while Taylor lingers in bed. Daniel pokes around her room, examining old photos, before sitting beside her.

"Look," he says quietly, "I know you're leaving soon. I don't want to know what's going on with Manuel. But I need you to know, I'm crazy about you. Ever since that night freshman year, I haven't stopped thinking about you. Just thinking about you turns me on. I had to say it, sober."

Taylor takes a deep breath. "A day hasn't passed since that night when I haven't thought about you. Can we make a pact? To stay connected, whatever that looks like?"

He hooks his pinky with hers. "You're not getting rid of me. Promise me I'll see you again before Christmas?"

"Of course. I'll let you know where we end up. Now go, before this gets weirder."

He kisses her once more and heads downstairs.

Later, as Taylor showers, reality creeps back in. *What am I doing?* Being home makes Barcelona feel unreal. Manuel feels distant. Daniel feels inevitable. She knows she'll see him again, and sleep with him again, before she leaves. The guilt will come later.

For now, she decides, she'll enjoy Christmas break.

Chapter 14

January 2004, Barcelona

Christmas break comes to an end faster than seems possible, and Taylor returns to a colder, less glittery Barcelona than she remembered. The holiday decorations have been put away, and the energy of the city, while still vibrant, is toned down significantly on this uncharacteristically cloudy Monday morning. Adding to the circumstances is the internal battle she's currently fighting: Daniel versus Manuel.

Does she tell Manuel about Daniel and what went down over Christmas, which was basically a passionate three-week love affair? Taylor spent so much time with Daniel over the break that she eventually had to break down and tell her friends what was going on, after they interrogated her about all the sneaking around, she'd been doing. She was actually worried she'd end up with a UTI given the amount of sex they had.

Her dilemma is exacerbated by the fact that Daniel basically told her he was in love with her and wanted to be with her, apparently undeterred by the Atlantic Ocean that would separate them for the next five-plus months. They discussed the Manuel situation only briefly, when Taylor came clean to Daniel that she was really happy with Manuel when they were together in Barcelona, but that she had no idea what the future held. Hadn't she been mapping out her entire life in Barcelona just a few weeks ago? And wasn't Manuel a huge part of those plans? What had come over her?

She never thought she'd be the type to cheat, yet here she was, seeing two very different guys on two different continents.

She and Manuel had spoken only a few times while she was home; the time difference made it tricky to connect, and they were both busy with family obligations. So, as she sits on the train heading into Barcelona from the airport, jet-lagged and bloated from too much holiday cheer, she shakily sends Manuel a text to see when he's free this week. Taylor has two full weeks before classes start, and she's planning to take the train to Madrid later this week and possibly sneak in another quick trip somewhere else in Spain next week.

He responds immediately, asking if she's free tomorrow night, he's dying to see her but has a work dinner tonight. They make plans to meet at his place at eight the following evening, and while she's excited to see him, Taylor feels a lingering sense of dread about how she's going to handle this. The more she thinks about it, the more appealing keeping her mouth shut seems, and for the moment she decides to go with that.

After settling back into her apartment and getting some groceries, her phone pings with a text from Finn just as she's lying down for a nap. He's back in Barcelona and wants to know if she's around later to hang out. Thrilled to have a distraction, and to have him back in town, she invites him over for drinks later, after getting the okay from Nicholas, who says he may be working late in the library anyway.

She nods off to sleep and is shocked when she wakes to see it's already 6 p.m. "Jesus," she mutters, stumbling into the bathroom to shower. An hour later Finn knocks on the door, a bottle of rum and some Coca-Cola Light tucked under his arm.

"Hola, mi amiga," he bellows while enveloping Taylor in a hug. "How are you? How was your holiday?"

"Finn, it's so good to see you. I'm fine, but I have a lot going on at the moment. You're just the person I need to talk to about everything, but we'll get to that later. That requires alcohol. More importantly, how's your grandpa?" she asks, leading him into the living room.

He looks down at the floor, and Taylor knows immediately. "He passed away, just a week before Christmas. It was inevitable, I realized once I got home. He was in much worse shape than my family was letting on. But I had some solid time with him before he passed, so I know going home was the right move."

"Oh, Finn, I'm so, so sorry. And right around the holidays, that makes it even harder. How's your family taking it?"

"You know, good days and bad. But all in all, we're doing fine."

Taylor hugs him and pours a stiff rum and Coke. They take a seat at the dining room table.

"Well, I'm glad you were able to get home and spend time with him. You're a good grandson."

"Thanks, Taylor. I appreciate that. Cheers to my grandfather," Finn says as they clink their glasses. "So, what's going on with you that you need to talk about? Is everything okay?"

"Yes, sorry. Just some drama. A lot of drama. But it seems so irrelevant compared to what you've been dealing with."

"Taylor, like I said, it was his time. I'm okay. Nothing would give me more pleasure than hearing the intricacies of your love life," Finn says with a laugh.

"Okay, well... do you remember my friend Daniel? The guy I grew up with? Our moms are best friends, and we hooked up back in freshman year?" Taylor asks.

"Course I remember. Why? Oh no. Did something happen back in the States?" Finn asks, eyebrows raised.

"That's one way of putting it," Taylor says glumly. "We spent most of Christmas break together... together in bed, that is." She buries her face in her hands. "Please don't judge me. I already feel like such an asshole. What do I do about Manuel?"

"Yikes. That's a lot. Although, I will say, I'm not surprised."

"What's that supposed to mean?" Taylor asks, surprised and mildly offended.

"No, no, not in a bad way," Finn says quickly, blushing. "More like... when you talked about Daniel a few months ago, something in you lit up. Sorry, that's probably not helpful."

"No, not really," Taylor laughs. "I mean, I care deeply about Manuel. He's a great guy, and we have so much fun together. And there's chemistry..."

"But?" Finn prompts. "I can hear it coming."

"There isn't one. Not really. A month ago, I was trying to plan my life so I could live permanently in Barcelona, and Manuel was, *is*, a major factor in that. Plus, I've been trying to be supportive while his mother is dealing with cancer. Then I go home for a few weeks, have this thing with Daniel, and suddenly I can't imagine my life without either of them. I'm totally fucked."

She leans back, takes a long swig of her drink, and lights two cigarettes, handing one to Finn.

"Am I a terrible person?" she asks.

"Of course not," he says. "But Manuel's mom's cancer definitely complicates things. Whatever you do, you have to keep that in mind."

"I know," Taylor groans. "Whenever I feel guilty, which is often, the worst part is thinking about Manuel and his family. God, I feel like trash."

"Hey, don't say that," Finn says more lightly. "You're amazing. That's why you've got two great guys essentially fighting over you, whether they know it or not. But you *do* have to choose eventually, or you'll drive yourself mad. Follow your heart."

"I know. You're right. My brother said the same thing. The problem is my heart is pulling in two different directions. I guess I have a lot of thinking to do. I'm heading to Madrid later this week, alone, so I'll have time to figure shit out. Thanks for listening. Let's change the subject."

"Sure. Like, what are we doing for dinner?" Finn asks with a smile.

Taylor laughs and refills their drinks. "I'm up for anything, but nothing heavy. I spent three weeks eating cheese and drinking beer, mandatory in Wisconsin. Let's do tapas."

"Perfect. And we're making it an early night. You took an overnight flight and are probably jet-lagged as hell. The last thing I want is to send you into your return to Barcelona with a hangover."

They head to a hole-in-the-wall tapas bar in Eixample and end up drinking sangria and talking until nearly midnight, when Taylor's eyes start to droop.

"Finn," she says as they part on the sidewalk, "thanks for being such a good friend."

"Anytime. You'll figure this out," he says with a wink.

The next morning, Taylor spends a few hours at the neighborhood internet café planning her Madrid itinerary. After being surrounded by Daniel, her family, and friends for three straight weeks, she finds herself craving solo travel, the independence, the escape from reality. Right now, escape is exactly what she needs.

As the day unfolds, she starts to feel a little better about the Daniel-Manuel situation. *Just don't say anything,* she tells herself. *Act normal.*

Before she knows it, it's past 1 p.m. and she's starving. She grabs patatas bravas from Pans, changes into workout gear, double-checks her Eurail pass, and goes for a jog. An hour later she's sweaty, exhausted, and feels a hundred times better.

That evening, Taylor spends an inordinate amount of time getting ready. She blow-dries her hair and applies more makeup than usual. Despite her anxiety, she still wants to look good for Manuel. She sips a glass of wine while blasting a mix CD filled with Semisonic, Britney Spears, NSYNC, and Ricky Martin, songs from a simpler time, before relationship drama.

By 7:45 p.m. she's antsy and heads to Manuel's apartment. The walk is crisp and refreshing; fifty degrees in Barcelona feels balmy compared to Wisconsin. Manuel buzzes her in, and he's waiting at the door when she reaches the top of the stairs. His grin hits her like a punch to the gut.

She feels a sharp pang of guilt, then tells herself to forget about Daniel. For now.

They embrace in a hug, then a kiss, before even making it into the apartment. In a matter of minutes, they're in Manuel's bed, and Taylor no longer has to convince herself to forget about Daniel. She'd forgotten how quickly her body responds to Manuel, and as they're tangled up in his sheets, there is nowhere else she'd rather be.

"Dios mío," Manuel mumbles as they finish. He pulls Taylor tightly into him and kisses her neck as she pants for air.

"Oh my God, Manuel," she exclaims. "Esto fue increíble."

"Tú eres increíble, mi amor," he whispers into her ear as he gets up and heads to the bathroom.

Taylor stretches out in his bed and allows herself to enjoy the post-coital bliss. A few moments pass, and Manuel returns to the bedroom, pulling on his jeans. They decide to go out for dinner; Manuel had planned on cooking but hadn't had time after work to make it to the store. Taylor stretches out again, still naked, and Manuel admires her as he finishes getting dressed.

"Eres magnífica," he says, and Taylor blushes as she starts getting dressed.

She knows she has what men, and other women, consider a "great body," but she's never been able to appreciate it. Instead, like every other young woman she knows, she fixates on what she'd rather have: bigger boobs, better abs, smaller thighs. She resists the urge to cover herself up as she dresses, instead allowing Manuel to keep admiring her. Self-conscious or not, it's nice to see how much he appreciates her.

They head out to a new chic restaurant Manuel heard about from a colleague at work. The food is amazing, and the portions are just small enough that Taylor's guilt over the patatas bravas she ate for lunch, and all of her holiday bingeing, vanishes. The restaurant is packed and loud, making conversation difficult, but over the incessant loop of Avril Lavigne and Kylie Minogue songs, Taylor manages to piece together that Manuel's mother is responding well to treatment and was able to enjoy Christmas with the family.

By the time they get the check, Taylor's ears are buzzing from the noise. It's an easy decision to stay at Manuel's place tonight; they're closer to his apartment, and Taylor is grateful to be back in his company. She falls asleep almost instantly, and when she wakes the next morning at 8:15 a.m., Manuel has already left for work.

Taylor lingers in Manuel's apartment and showers; his bathroom is infinitely nicer than hers. Around 10 a.m., she finally makes her way outside. The cool air is invigorating, and she feels a renewed sense of energy. With her trip to Madrid only a few days away, she decides she needs to talk to Lindsay ASAP. Lindsay's family has spent a lot of time traveling the world, so she likely has advice on restaurants, museums, and off-the-beaten-path spots.

As Taylor pulls out her mobile phone, she remembers the time difference, it's only 5 a.m. back in Massachusetts. She makes a mental note to call Lindsay later today. Plus, she can spill the dirt about her torrid affair with Daniel to Lindsay, who will listen and offer advice, judgment-free.

In the meantime, she uses her surge of energy to clean the apartment and do some shopping with her Christmas money. By late afternoon, she has a spotless apartment, three new sweaters, and a few cheap bottles of wine for nights when she and Nicholas want a glass.

When the time feels right, she calls Lindsay, who answers on the second ring, clearly thrilled.

"I miss you **soooo** much, T," Lindsay exclaims. "Tell me everything. What's going on with your hot Spanish man? Are you bringing him to Madrid with you?"

"Oh, Linds, I miss you too. Part of me really wishes I was heading back to UNC with you and Katie next week. But no, Manuel isn't coming to Madrid, he's got work and other boring adult responsibilities. Things are complicated, actually."

Taylor explains the entire Daniel-Manuel situation, knowing Lindsay won't judge her.

After she finishes, Lindsay is quiet for a moment. "Hmm. With Manuel, you're a woman, independent, mature, and let's be honest, you two look super glamorous together. He's your picture-perfect European catch. But with Daniel, you're safe. You're still a girl. He takes you back to your childhood. I mean, your moms are best friends, for Christ's sake. Remember in St. Tropez when I joked that you were literally born for each other? Maybe that wasn't so far off. Does that about sum it up?"

Taylor is momentarily speechless. "Um... yes. Wow. You should totally be a psych major," she jokes, fully aware that Lindsay actually *is* one. "Is it really that easy for an outsider to see?"

"I'm not an outsider, Taylor, I'm one of your best friends. And a psych major. But seriously, I can't tell you who to choose. First, it's your decision. Second, they're both good for you in totally different ways. Neither is a bad choice. Or you ditch them both and live your badass life. But you can't keep seeing both. It's not fair, to them or to you. I can hear the stress in your voice."

Taylor sighs and digs around for her cigarettes. "You're right," she says, lighting one. "With Manuel, everything feels perfect. He makes me happy. And then there's his mom's cancer, that's another layer of guilt. I can't break up with him now. And I definitely can't tell him about Daniel. But with Daniel, everything feels easy. Like all the bullshit has eroded away. And the sex is amazing."

Saying it out loud makes the reality sink in: she's going to break Daniel's heart in the coming days. She can't leave someone wonderful while he's in the middle of a family crisis. She'd never forgive herself.

Daniel can happen later; she tells herself after hanging up. She half-listens as Lindsay rattles off Madrid recommendations, already planning what she'll say to Daniel.

Rip it off like a Band-Aid.

That night, fortified by a glass of wine, Taylor heads to the neighborhood internet café and writes Daniel an email, apologetic, firm, decisive. Before she can reconsider, she clicks send and exhales sharply, realizing she's been holding her breath.

"Oh God, I am such a bitch," she mutters, eyes stinging. She doesn't reread the email or wait for a response. She leaves immediately.

She notes the date: January 14th, 2004, the day she breaks Daniel Collins's heart for the second time. Distance makes it easier.

It's only 7 p.m. Manuel is working late but tells her to come over; he'll be home by 11. She can't stand the idea of being alone tonight, so she opts for dinner with Nicholas, then heading to Manuel's later. She leaves for Madrid tomorrow afternoon and wants tonight with him.

Nicholas arrives just after 9 p.m. to find Taylor mixing cocktails, blasting Christina Aguilera's *Mi Reflejo* and belting out "Ven Conmigo."

"You started the fiesta without me, you cheeky cow!" he laughs.

They clink glasses. "Only sandwiches for dinner," Taylor says. "But homemade, so I'm calling it cooking."

They eat, chat, and laugh. By 10:15 p.m., Taylor is slightly buzzed and aware she needs to head to Manuel's soon. After cleaning up, she grabs her coat and heads out into the night.

Taylor and Manuel talk and catch up for a few minutes, then quickly collapse into bed, Taylor from the emotional weight of having crushed someone she cares about so deeply, Manuel from sheer exhaustion, around midnight. They wake at 7:30 the following morning, and Manuel gives Taylor an extra-tight hug as he leaves for work.

"Cuídate en Madrid, cariño," he tells her as he kisses her one last time. "Nos vemos el domingo, verdad?"

"Sí, te llamaré cuando regrese el domingo, vale?"

"Está bien, mi amor." And he closes the door and is off to work.

Taylor showers and makes Manuel's bed before heading home to finish packing. She can't help stopping at the internet café on her way home to see if Daniel has replied. As she logs into her email, she sees his response, which appears to have been sent only a few hours ago, very late at night back in the States. Reluctantly, Taylor clicks on the email and forces her eyes to focus on the grimy computer screen.

D: Taylor. I have to say, I think you're making a huge mistake. Why, after everything?? But I respect you and your decisions, so I won't be in touch again. I thought this meant so much more. Enjoy Barcelona.

Taylor buries her face in her hands, realizing that she has lost not only any romantic connection she and Daniel shared, but also his friendship. And that hurts infinitely more than she ever could have expected. She doesn't respond; instead, she flees the café for the second time in the past twenty-four hours, in tears.

Madrid is far more different from Barcelona than Taylor imagined. Barcelona's charm and allure are more in-your-face, apparent in the architecture and in the people walking around the city. Madrid, while no doubt gorgeous, lacks the luster and gleam

Taylor has grown accustomed to. Historically and culturally, Madrid has the upper hand, she thinks. The museums are stunning and world-renowned. Madrid also allows her to day-trip to Seville, which she manages to write about despite only spending five hours in the city.

The trip was fine, Taylor thinks in retrospect. It served the purpose she needed it to: she got much-needed alone time to think, and she got some writing done. Being in a new environment allowed her mind a break from obsessing over Daniel.

Upon returning to Barcelona, Taylor feels reenergized and invigorated, excited to start a new semester, meet the new students arriving in the study abroad program, and, above all, happy to have Manuel by her side through all of it. If nothing else, her brief voyage to Madrid made her miss and appreciate Manuel, and she returns almost giddy with excitement at seeing him.

Where, she wonders, was this feeling over Christmas break? What was it about being with Daniel in her hometown that led her to essentially forget about Manuel, with barely a hint of guilt? She thinks about it ad nauseam and cannot, for the life of her, come up with a reasonable answer.

Despite her guilty conscience, Taylor has very little time to dwell on her questionable choices. The spring semester proves far more difficult than the fall. She took mostly filler classes in the fall, assuming she'd need time to get grounded and familiarize herself with Barcelona, as well as allow for near-weekly excursions around Europe. Now, she feels the strain, spending far more time in the library and far less time in bars. Her eighteenth-century Spanish literature course is particularly brutal, with weekly papers on the most obscure topics she's ever encountered.

January, February, and March fly by in a whirlwind of school and time spent with Manuel and his friends, whom she genuinely enjoys despite the age difference.

Before she realizes it, the countdown to Eric's wedding has begun. Taylor's days off are approved by her professors, and Manuel is using desperately needed vacation days; he's been burning the candle at both ends, juggling his mother's treatment schedule with his demanding work and social calendar. They're flying into JFK on Wednesday, April 21st, returning Monday, April 26th, enough time to see New York and attend the seemingly endless wedding-related events: welcome cocktails, rehearsal dinner, the wedding itself, the day-after brunch, blah, blah, blah.

Through conversations with her brothers, Taylor begins to understand the level of wealth her future sister-in-law comes from. She hopes it won't change Eric. He's humble, down-to-earth, and kind, and she worries this new world could alter that.

Lauren, to her credit, seems relatively normal; Taylor has spoken to her a few times on the phone. She successfully weasels out of being a bridesmaid, citing her inability to participate in bachelorette festivities. Fortunately, Lauren caves without much of a fight.

Now all Taylor has to do is show up and somehow avoid Daniel and his mother for the entire weekend. Given the size of the wedding, she reasons, this shouldn't be too difficult, especially since Daniel and Tanya won't attend the welcome cocktails or rehearsal dinner. Still, Taylor practically breaks out in hives whenever she imagines running into Daniel on the dance floor while with Manuel.

"That's what alcohol is for," Finn tells her one night over drinks. Touché.

Once April arrives, Taylor decides she needs a dress. Manuel already has a tux from his older brother's wedding, so he's set. On the first Saturday in April, Taylor finds herself walking along Passeig de Gràcia, which, despite now knowing it's a major tourist area, remains one of her favorite parts of the city. She wanders in and out of five different stores before finding the perfect little black dress.

The wedding is black-tie (of course), so she needs something formal. She settles on a lacy spaghetti-strap dress that is short and oh-so-tight. She may need to lose a pound or two just to breathe, but the dress, she decides, is absolutely perfect.

Now she just needs to find shoes to match; once that task is checked off, she can tell her mother to stop harassing her about finding an outfit for the wedding. Exhausted and sweaty from trying on so many dresses, Taylor decides to save shoe shopping for another day.

After calling her mom to let her know the dress situation has been solved, she returns to her apartment to rest, tonight is a big night. All the spring study abroad students in her program have arranged a night out, and this is a raucous crowd. They've decided on meeting at Josh and Mark's apartment, two great guys who share a place in the El Raval neighborhood, not too far from Taylor's apartment. El Raval was formerly Barcelona's version of a red-light district but is now hip and considered one of the city's ideal places to see and be seen.

Josh is from New York City and goes to college at Columbia; Taylor has wondered on more than one occasion if he'd ever left the island of Manhattan before coming to Barcelona. He has already given Taylor the scoop on what to do and where to go while she was in "the city," as he so annoyingly insists on calling New York. Mark (a different Mark than "Hot Mark," who Lindsay hooked up with last semester) goes to the University of Colorado in Boulder and is a huge stoner and an even bigger drinker. Between Josh and Mark, the pre-party is sure to be a success; alcohol and various drugs will be free-flowing, for sure. Manuel is spending the weekend in Madrid with family, so the timing for Taylor to act like a belligerent twenty-one-year-old is perfect.

After a post-shopping shower and a quick siesta, Taylor starts getting ready. She puts on her favorite low-rise jeans, a red halter top, and her highest heels, which means tonight will be miserable for walking, but she figures she'll be drinking enough to overcome whatever pain her feet are going to feel. On that note, she pours herself a small glass of wine, the dregs of a bottle that has been open for God knows how long, and blasts some music to get into the mood. She puts her hair up in a messy bun, does her makeup, and is out the door by 9:00 p.m.

The closest metro stop to Josh and Mark's place is Drassanes, so Taylor takes the blue line to Diagonal station and transfers to the green line. After four stops, she's there, her feet already in agony. She manages to find their apartment despite the totally convoluted directions they'd provided and is shocked to find she's the first guest to arrive.

"Taylor," Mark says, ushering her inside. "You're the first one here. Everyone else has adapted to Barcelona time, it appears. Can I get you a drink?" Taylor adjusts to the dark apartment, the smell of young men not quite masked by smoke and excessive amounts of body spray and cologne.

"Hey! Wow, I guess so. I'm never the first one to arrive. Yes, please on the drink. Rum and Coke? Light, if possible?" Taylor asks.

Mark rolls his eyes, presumably because she asked for it light, and pokes his head into the fridge in the tiny galley kitchen. "It's funny, Josh made me get the Coca-Cola Light today. He said that's what girls drink. I think he's secretly worried about his waistline." As Mark pours Taylor's drink, Josh emerges from what Taylor assumes is his bedroom, shirtless, overly cologned, and smoking a cigarette.

"Hey-o, Taylor! What's going on?"

"Hey, Josh. Thanks for having us." Taylor gives Josh a hug and a peck on the cheek. "Where is everyone?" she asks, accepting her drink from Mark and lighting a cigarette of her own.

"You know, taking their sweet-ass time. Primping? Pre-gaming for the pre-game? I like that you're punctual. Did you eat? We've got snacks."

"I ate already, thanks," Taylor lies. She'd had a bowl of cereal and a banana, hardly enough sustenance for a night of drinking, but she has a dress to fit into in just three weeks.

Out of nowhere, Usher, Lil Jon, and Ludacris yelling "Yeah!" start blasting, and Taylor can't help but sing along. Within minutes, more schoolmates straggle in and people start pouring drinks and dancing; now it's Outkast on the stereo.

By 10:30 p.m., it's a full-fledged party, and one of Josh and Mark's elderly neighbors has already knocked on the door and politely asked them to turn down the music. They oblige, but everyone realizes they need to take the party elsewhere soon. The apartment is smoky despite the open windows, and drinks are scattered everywhere. Taylor takes a break from dancing and helps the guys tidy up. Shortly thereafter, cameras begin to emerge, and after taking approximately five million photos, the crew of fifteen drunk study abroad students stumbles out of the apartment. By this point it's just after 11 p.m., an acceptable, albeit early, time to arrive at the club.

There's already a line when they finally locate the club, but it's early enough that the whole entourage gets inside after only a ten-minute wait. Alice Deejay blasts from the speakers, and Taylor is temporarily transported back to her junior year of high school when "Better Off Alone" was *the* song. She smiles to herself and joins her friends on the dance floor. She's already forgotten the name of the place; it's one of many new, cool, hard-to-get-into clubs popping up around the city, this neighborhood in particular.

Out of nowhere, Josh sidles up to her and hands her a drink.

"Hey, thanks, you didn't have to do that," Taylor shouts over the music. He clinks her glass, toasts "Salud," and gently ushers her to the bar, where two stools have just become available. They sit down, and before Taylor can fill the uncomfortable silence, Josh starts talking.

"Taylor, Taylor, Taylor," Josh says, blowing a perfect ring of smoke into the air. "You know you're, like, this enigma to everyone, right?" he says with a smirk. "Beautiful girl, older Spanish boyfriend, savviest person I've ever met." He looks straight into her eyes and continues; she's momentarily speechless and totally unsure where he's going. "So, what's the story? Inquiring minds want to know."

Taylor is taken aback, not only by what he says, but by how direct he is. She stammers, "Um, Josh, I'm really not all that interesting. I met Manuel, my boyfriend, right when I got here back in August. And

I'm only savvy because I've been living here, like, three times longer than the rest of you."

"So, you and this Manuel guy, it isn't really serious, then, is it?" Josh asks.

"Yes, I'd say it's serious. I mean, he's coming to New York for my brother's wedding later this month, so I think that makes it serious, right? I love him, if that's what you're getting at," Taylor responds, defensively.

Josh smirks again and mock-groans. "Well, that'll depress the hell out of all the guys in our program, myself included."

"What are you talking about? There are plenty of other eligible, single ladies here," Taylor says indignantly, vaguely gesturing toward the dance floor.

"Not like you, Taylor. You, my dear, are one of a kind." Josh stands and kisses the top of her head. "And your hair smells fucking amazing." With that, he orders another drink for her, tells the bartender to put it on his tab, and disappears into the crowd.

"What the actual fuck?" Taylor mutters once he's gone.

Maybe she's been naïve to think all these guys are enchanted with her *just* as a friend. Another reason, she tells herself, that being with an older, more mature guy is the better option. Once she regains her composure, she rejoins everyone on the dance floor. Despite dancing and lip-syncing with the group, something feels off, and suddenly all Taylor wants is to be in bed with Manuel. After a few songs, she tells her friends she's not feeling well and needs to go home.

As she heads toward the door, Josh grabs her elbow. "Hey, I didn't mean to freak you out back there. I just wanted to tell you, you're incredible." His hand grazes her waist, and she pushes it away.

"Well, you kind of made everything awkward. I mean, Josh, we're all friends here, right? So why, knowing I'm in a committed relationship, would you even go there?"

"Because we're twenty-one and in Barcelona? And we *are* friends. I just wanted the full story. Now I have it, let's forget this happened, yeah? No need for you to leave. I'll keep my hands to myself," he says, backing away.

Taylor gives him a tight smile. "Okay. Thanks. But I'm calling it a night. Thanks to you and Mark for having us. And promise me no awkwardness at school?"

"I promise. Get home safe," Josh says, already heading back to the bar.

Taylor inhales sharply and leaves the club, walking quickly. She needs to clear her head. She wants to talk to Manuel, but it's late and he's with his family, and the last thing she wants is to deal with him worrying or getting possessive. Instead, she calls her brother Alex. Luckily, he picks up.

"Buenas noches, hermanita," he bellows. "¿Qué pasa?"

"Hi. Hi! How are you?" Before he can answer, Taylor launches into a rant. "Am I totally naïve to think I can have platonic male friends?"

"Well, yes. Probably," Alex replies.

Taylor ignores him and continues. "A guy from my study abroad program basically told me tonight that he, and other guys, are into me. And they *know* I have a boyfriend. Why would he do that? Now things are going to be uncomfortable."

Alex sighs. "Taylor, you're twenty-one. Haven't you figured out yet that men are basically shit and want to fuck any pretty girl they come across? Hate to break it to you, but any guy you're friends with probably wants to sleep with you. Unless he's gay."

Taylor blinks. "Well, that's disappointing."

"Hey," Alex says, softer now, "they probably like you as a person too. But yeah, they also want to sleep with you. Sorry I'm the one breaking this to you. If it helps, I'd happily fly over and kick some ass."

Taylor laughs. "Thanks. I'll keep that in mind."

They talk a while longer as she walks home, and when she hangs up, she realizes she's only a few blocks away. She resolves to put the strangeness of the night behind her, despite the disappointment of realizing the guys she thought were 'friends' weren't necessarily so. She can hear her girlfriends' voices in her head: *Episode five million of being disappointed by men.*

She smiles to herself, annoyed, unsettled, but, if she's being fully honest, the tiniest bit flattered, too.

Chapter 15

April 2004, New York, NY

Early to mid-April is basically a whirlwind of school projects and papers; Taylor has to submit things early since she'll be missing classes for the wedding. Before she even has time to process it, she and Manuel are on a plane to New York.

"Wednesday, April 21st, 2004... my first trip to *los Estados Unidos*," Manuel says excitedly just as the plane is taking off.

"And your Spanglish is, quite frankly, *perfecto*," Taylor teases with a smile. "I'm taking a nap, enjoy your flight."

Despite her resolve to speak exclusively in Spanish while living in Barcelona, Taylor and Manuel have settled into a mutually agreeable combination. He wants to practice his English, and occasionally Taylor finds the effort to find the right words to properly express herself in Spanish too taxing. So they alternate between the two languages, teaching each other new words and inflections along the way.

The preceding weeks have left Taylor exhausted. Between schoolwork, listening to her family's wedding drama, going out, and writing, she's barely had time to think, much less sleep. She has also been spending an unhealthy amount of time thinking about Daniel and how she's going to manage seeing him at the wedding. Taylor would very much like to be cordial and talk to him, but she doubts he's of the same mindset. He probably wants to either completely ignore her presence or shout obscenities at her. Given that she basically broke his heart, it would be a reasonable, if disappointing, response.

Taylor spends the first four hours of the nine-hour flight to New York in what feels like a coma. She wakes with a start when the flight attendant comes by with refills and lunch.

"Vino rojo, por favor. Y la comida vegetariana. Gracias."

Manuel is equally enthralled by the free drinks on international flights; he'd mentioned this to her multiple times in the days leading up to their trip. Funny, Taylor thinks, how free alcohol, even shitty airplane wine, makes actual adults practically gleeful. They press their cups of wine together for the first of many times in the upcoming days. By the time the plane begins its descent into JFK, Taylor and Manuel are well-rested and relaxed from the wine.

Standing in line at immigration, Taylor thinks about how her mother once described how women forget the pain of childbirth, thereby allowing them to want, and eventually have, more children. She idly wonders which is worse: standing in line with thousands of international travelers who, from the smell of it, haven't showered in days, or having a baby. Nearly an hour later, an hour that feels like an eternity, they make it out of the hell that was the airport, bags and all.

In the taxi from Queens to Manhattan, both Taylor and Manuel are enchanted by the city's skyline. "Welcome to New York," Taylor says to Manuel with a smile. They both immediately notice the absence downtown, where the Twin Towers stood just several years before. Amazing how a city that has suffered such a tragedy remains alive and buzzing. *No wonder Eric and Alex live here,* Taylor thinks.

The taxi zooms up Third Avenue before they hit traffic at 44th Street. Taylor looks over at Manuel, who has been so mesmerized by the hustle and bustle of the city that he's barely spoken the entire ride. She smiles at him, and he grabs her hand, finally admitting that he's nervous about meeting her family.

"Don't be nervous! You've already met my mom. My dad is chill, Eric will be too busy with wedding shit to try and intimidate you, and Alex is... well, Alex may give you a tough time at first. But I can guarantee you'll be drinking with him, and you'll be buddies by the end of tonight," Taylor reassures him.

Manuel laughs and shakes his head just as the cab lurches forward and takes a sharp left onto 51st Street, screeching to a halt on the corner of Madison and 51st, they've arrived at the Palace Hotel. The hotel's façade lives up to its name. It's a stunning building, and they can see St. Patrick's Cathedral, where the wedding ceremony will take place, only a block away. Saks Fifth Avenue is also just a block over; Taylor's mom has already promised her a trip there to get shoes to match her dress.

Manuel pays the cabbie, they stopped at an ATM at the airport to take out cash in dollars, and takes all the luggage from the trunk. Bags in hand, they walk into the lobby, both looking up in awe at the magnificent chandeliers.

"Jesucristo," Manuel mutters. "De verdad es un palacio."

Taylor giggles and tries to act as though she belongs there. They check into their room, which, though small, is poshly furnished and has an incredible view of St. Patrick's. Taylor flops onto the king-size bed and closes her eyes. Manuel putters around the room before getting into the shower, so Taylor takes the opportunity to unpack their bags, which were just delivered by the bellboy. She pulls out the new racy lingerie she brought and quickly changes into it, excited to surprise Manuel as he gets out of the shower. She realizes these few moments before meeting her family are likely the only time they'll have alone over the next five days, and she intends to make the most of it.

Not five minutes after they've finished having sex, the hotel room phone rings.

"So it begins," Taylor mumbles. "Hello?"

"Taylor, honey, you made it!" her mother gushes. "We're meeting in the lobby for cocktails at six p.m., does that work? Just me, Dad, Alex, you, and Manuel. Eric is off with Lauren for some silly co-ed bachelor/bachelorette party."

"Hi, Mom! Yes, we made it. Cocktails sound perfect. We'll start getting ready, are we going straight to dinner?"

"Yes. Dinner is at seven p.m., at Picholine. Some swanky French restaurant Lauren is sending us to."

"Dinner at seven, how very American," Taylor laughs.

"We assumed you kids would be exhausted with the time difference, so we figured tonight should be early."

"Thanks. We'll be down soon. Can't wait to see you."

As Taylor hangs up, butterflies flood her stomach. Manuel is meeting her whole family, it's actually happening.

She leaves Manuel in bed, where he's trying to figure out the TV, takes a quick shower, and redoes her makeup. Manuel is ready by the time she comes out.

"Okay, are you ready? Let's sneak down and have a cigarette before they get there."

Manuel checks his watch, notes they have fifteen minutes, and nods. He's visibly nervous, and Taylor knows a quick smoke will help. They sneak around the corner, smoke half a cigarette each, and head into the hotel bar. Taylor had already given Manuel the rundown on drinks in the U.S., they're weak as hell compared to Spain, so they opt for wine and head to a round table in the center of the bar.

Five minutes past six, Taylor's parents rush in, looking frazzled and excited all at once.

"Taylor! Manuel! So great to see you both." Alyssa pulls them into a warm hug while Taylor's dad, John, hangs back, looking amused. Taylor disentangles herself and hugs her dad.

"Dad, it's so great to see you. This is Manuel. Manuel, this is my dad, John."

"Pleased to meet you, sir," Manuel says in his best English.

"Likewise," John booms. "But please, call me John. Thanks for making the trip across the pond."

"Thank you for having me. This is a very special occasion. I'm pleased to be here to celebrate," Manuel replies.

Just as they sit down, Alex arrives. He looks great, healthy and happy, and Taylor runs over to hug him. He and Manuel are introduced, and soon everyone is settled with a drink in hand. The fireplace roars, the bar smells incredible, and Taylor feels overwhelmed with happiness, surrounded by her family (most of them, at least), Manuel, and such a beautiful setting.

At that moment, Eric jogs in from the lobby.

"Eric!" Taylor squeals. "I didn't think you were coming tonight!" She jumps up and hugs her eldest brother.

"Hey, baby sis. I've got fifteen minutes, then I've got to bounce. I'm on a strict schedule this week. But I had to say hi. Mom, can you order me a gin and tonic?"

Taylor brings Eric over to Manuel, who's already standing and extending his hand.

"Hey man, nice to meet you. Thanks for making the trip," Eric says, flashing his contagious smile.

"Thank you for inviting me, and congratulations to you," Manuel replies enthusiastically. "It is nice to finally meet you, I have heard only great things about all of you from Taylor."

Eric pulls up a barstool and starts telling them about what he has going on tonight. Taylor glances over at Manuel and smiles; he looks relieved and much calmer than he did twenty minutes ago. Eric downs his gin and tonic and says his goodbyes, promising that he'll hang out with them tomorrow and that he hopes they enjoy dinner.

"This restaurant you're going to tonight, it's phenomenal. It's where we went the night I proposed to Lauren, so it's a special place. I wish we could join you. Have fun, guys."

As soon as he's out of sight, Alex pokes Taylor. "He's a 'we' person now. No more solo Eric."

"Alex, that's normal," their mother sighs, exasperated. "At least we like Lauren. I'd be more concerned with him being a 'we' person if she was awful. Taylor, I can't wait for you to meet her, I think you guys will really hit it off."

As if by magic, everyone's drinks have been refilled, even though it's twenty minutes before seven and they should be on their way to the restaurant. As if reading her mind, Alyssa says, "Drink up, kids. We need to head to Picholine in a minute."

Everyone finishes their drinks, and they make their way to the taxi line outside. Within seconds, a minivan cab speeds up Madison Avenue heading toward the restaurant. Alex points out places of interest to Manuel, who listens intently, while Alyssa bombards Taylor with the nuances of wedding planning. John sits quietly, looking out the window of the cab, seemingly content to have most of his family together.

Just as Alyssa is boring Taylor with some wedding dress debacle Lauren had to deal with, the taxi squeals to a stop on West 64th Street. The five of them pile out and head into the elegant restaurant.

Dinner is a long, drawn-out affair; halfway through the entrées, both Taylor and Manuel are ready for bed, the combination of jet lag and too much wine finally hitting them. Aside from the fatigue, and having to make a valiant effort not to face-plant into her dinner plate from exhaustion, it is officially one of the best meals Taylor has ever had.

They manage to power through, and Taylor is confident that both Manuel and her family have made good impressions on one another. As they are wrapping up the meal, Alex casually tosses his napkin on the table, turns to Taylor and Manuel, and says, "Well, let the games begin. Shit's about to get real tomorrow, guys."

"What do you mean?" Taylor asks.

"Listen, Lauren is great. She's a bit nuts about the whole wedding, but otherwise I think you'll like her. Her family, though?" Alex snorts. "Entitled snobs. Just prepare yourself. They're not our type of people, if you know what I mean."

"Well, Eric gave me fair warning. I go to school with plenty of rich trust-fund kids who will never have to work a day in their lives. Bring it on," Taylor says with a smirk.

"This is a different stratosphere, T. Just don't say I didn't warn you."

"Enough, Alex," Alyssa says with an eye roll. "Lauren's family has been nothing but generous."

"I should hope so," Alex mutters under his breath.

Taylor laughs, appreciating her brother's honesty (and cynicism), and they make their way out of the restaurant. Alex says his goodbyes and heads toward the subway to go back to his apartment; the rest of them flag a taxi heading down Fifth Avenue. The remainder of the evening is a blur of fatigue, and Taylor only vaguely remembers crawling into bed when she wakes up on Thursday.

The rest of the weekend is jam-packed with activities. Taylor and Manuel are having lunch with Lauren and Eric today at 1 p.m., after which Taylor and her mom are going shopping. Tonight is the welcome cocktail party for all the out-of-town guests and close friends (the guest list is over one hundred, apparently). Tomorrow, Friday, is sightseeing during the day and the rehearsal dinner at night.

Taylor wakes up at 9 a.m. on the dot and heads down to the hotel gym; Manuel is still sleeping, even though it is late afternoon in Barcelona. Apparently, jet lag has gotten the best of him. Or he's exhausted from the stress of meeting Taylor's entire family, likely a combination of the two, she thinks.

Happy to have the alone time, Taylor goes all out on the elliptical machine and stretches for ten minutes after her thirty minutes of cardio. Around 10 a.m., just as she is finishing up her workout, Manuel saunters into the gym, looking rumpled and insanely handsome, as he so often does in the mornings. There is only one other person in the gym, so Taylor doesn't hesitate to kiss Manuel full-on the lips when he comes in.

"Hola, guapo," she says, raising her eyebrows.

He laughs and hits her on the butt with his gym towel.

"I'm going to shower, have a good workout, babe."

"Gracias, mi amor," he replies with a smile.

Taylor returns to the room, takes a long shower, and gets dressed in a short denim skirt (with tights and boots, it's far colder here than she was hoping) and a black sweater. By the time she's started her makeup, Manuel is back from the gym and making his way into the shower.

By noon, they are walking in the blustery sunshine down Fifth Avenue toward Rockefeller Plaza. Tourists clog the sidewalks, even though it's a Thursday in the middle of the day. They're meeting Lauren and Eric at the Sea Grill, right in Rockefeller Center. Taylor can't help the butterflies in her stomach at the prospect of meeting her future sister-in-law, despite everyone's claims that she's lovely and kind. There's an uncertainty about welcoming a new family member, and it's crept up on her all at once.

Lauren and Eric beat them to the restaurant and are already seated when Taylor and Manuel arrive. The hostess brings them to the table, and Lauren pops up, a petite bundle of energy. Taylor is taken aback by how tiny she is, even though she's wearing at least three-inch heels. Lauren has long brown hair with caramel-colored highlights and beautiful features. Her eyebrows are perfectly waxed, and her makeup is subtle enough to complement her beauty rather than overwhelm it.

She can't be more than five foot three, and she appears to weigh about ninety pounds. She is adorable and bubblier than Taylor had expected.

"Taylor! It's so nice to meet you," Lauren gushes, giving Taylor a tight hug. "And you must be Manuel, thank you both so much for coming this weekend. It really means the world to us!"

Lauren talks so fast and with so much gusto that Taylor realizes she's equally nervous. Manuel and Eric shake hands, exchange pleasantries about last night's dinner at Picholine, and they all sit down.

Bloody Marys are ordered, except for Lauren, who claims she's on a pre-wedding diet and orders only seltzer. How she could possibly get any smaller is a mystery to Taylor; she's as thin as she is short. Taylor breaks the ice by asking about last night's wedding festivities. Lauren tells them everything, who was there, the games they played, the drinks they had.

Taylor notices that Lauren has the annoying habit of talking about her friends as though Taylor and Manuel already know who they are, a trait she's come to associate primarily with East Coasters. But overall, Lauren is charming, polite, and eager to get to know Taylor. The waiter eventually intervenes to deliver their drinks and take their orders.

Taylor tells them about her time in Barcelona thus far, how she and Manuel met, and what they enjoy doing in the city. Lauren asks, without hesitation, what they're going to do once Taylor returns to UNC for her senior year: long-distance? Take a break?

"We haven't really discussed it," Taylor replies nervously, eyeing Manuel. "But I'm hoping we can make it work. I've saved a lot of money writing, so I can visit periodically." Lauren smiles, the naïve smile of someone who has never had to worry, let alone think, about money.

"We will make it work, of course," Manuel says with a smile. "Taylor is incredible, so I will figure things out." He leans over and kisses Taylor on the cheek, and she blushes and smiles. She grabs his hand under the table, a sense of relief flooding over her that they finally broached this topic she's been avoiding for months.

"So, where are you guys going on your honeymoon?" Taylor asks.

"Eric, how have you not told your sister where we're honeymooning?" Lauren asks, aghast. She doesn't wait for an answer, adding, "New Zealand and Fiji. I've been researching it since the day Eric proposed," she says with a laugh.

"Oh wow," Manuel says, clearly impressed. "I've dreamt of going to both places. Please tell us everything about your trip. I hope to take Taylor to Fiji one day."

Eric kicks Taylor under the table and raises an eyebrow. She has to stifle a laugh, appreciating her older brother's protectiveness, and the fact that he can still act like a child. Lauren delves into their itinerary, which is nearly two weeks long and sounds incredible (and prohibitively expensive).

After the food arrives, Lauren asks Taylor about Eric as a kid and what growing up in Madison was like. Taylor gushes about Madison: how it's a totally down-to-earth, no-nonsense place, and how much she loves going home for visits. She tells Lauren how Eric was generally a good brother growing up, but once, along with Alex, locked her and her friend in a closet while blasting Milli Vanilli for over an hour.

"Eric, how could you torture your sweet sister like that?"

"She was spying on us," he replies sheepishly. "But it was a brilliant punishment, am I right?"

Lauren laughs and looks at Eric adoringly. "I suppose so. God, I've heard so many great things about your childhood and having each other, I'm quite jealous. I'm an only child, so I feel so lucky to be gaining you and Alex as siblings," Lauren says, placing her hand over Taylor's.

"We're happy to have you join our crazy crew," Taylor responds, surprised by how much she actually means it.

"I certainly hope you two can come back another time when things aren't so nuts. You always have a place to stay with Eric and me."

"Says who?" Eric retorts.

"Fuck off, Eric. It's clear who wears the pants here, and it isn't you," Taylor says with a smirk.

Eric makes puppy-dog eyes and looks down, laughing. The rest of lunch is pleasant, and after her Bloody Mary, Taylor is feeling nostalgic and so pleased to be here. Manuel is clearly at ease, despite not saying much. It must be strange for him, Taylor thinks, remembering the first time she went out with his friends and how terrified she was that they wouldn't like her.

It's after three o'clock by the time they pay the bill, and Lauren is in a rush to get her pre-wedding manicure and pedicure done before tonight's reception, so they part ways outside the restaurant. Taylor, Eric, and Manuel meet Alyssa at Saks Fifth Avenue to buy Taylor shoes for the wedding, and some last-minute honeymoon attire for Eric. If Manuel can survive an hour in a swanky department store with her mother, Taylor thinks, he's definitely a keeper.

Alyssa is already browsing in the women's shoe department when they arrive. "There you are! Hola, Manuel. How was your lunch with Lauren? Taylor, do you like her?"

"Yes, Mom, she is great. Really sweet. What have you been up to all day?"

"I met Tanya for lunch; we went to this adorable Italian place near Union Square." As soon as Taylor hears the name Tanya, she can feel the color drain from her face.

"Oh, wow, she's here already? I thought she and Daniel were only coming for the wedding on Saturday."

"Well, technically they are, but she wanted some time in the city to explore a bit and hang out with Daniel. Speaking of Daniel, have you two been in touch? I'm sure he'd love to see you more than just at the wedding." Her mother blabs on, completely oblivious.

How can she be so dense? Taylor wonders. Fortunately, Manuel and Eric are out of earshot, ogling the prices of the women's shoes and laughing among themselves.

"Mom, let's lay off the topic of Daniel for now, yeah?" Taylor whispers.

"Ah. Okay, you got it. There's clearly a story here, but you can tell me another time. I imagine this has something to do with all the time you spent together over winter break?" her mother asks, raising an eyebrow.

Taylor rolls her eyes and chooses to start looking at shoes rather than respond. Ten minutes later, she's got a pair of four-inch heels that will look fabulous with her dress and are almost certainly going to give her blisters and leave her feet in agony after ten minutes.

"Manuel, it's a good thing you're so tall," Alyssa says as they're leaving the shoe area and heading to the men's department. "Otherwise, our Taylor here wouldn't be able to wear all these super-high heels that she loves so much."

"Thank you. Taylor does look very nice in her heels," Manuel responds, red in the face from the attention.

"Manuel, if you see anything you like, I'm happy to buy you something here. Why let Taylor and Eric have all the fun?"

"Oh, Mrs. Evans, I could not accept that generosity, but thank you for offering."

"Of course. And please, I beg you, call me Alyssa. Mrs. Evans is my mother-in-law. Hell, my own children call me Alyssa instead of Mom half the time. But I do appreciate your manners."

Taylor rolls her eyes but is grateful for Manuel's response; he knows her family has a modest financial situation and that nearly all of the wedding extravagance is being fronted by Lauren's family.

After a few minutes of roaming around, Eric concludes that all he actually needs is a new pair of sunglasses, so they're out of the store in less than thirty minutes. A record, Taylor thinks.

Three hours, and a lot of makeup and primping, later, Taylor is standing with Manuel and Alex at The Water Club, a posh venue on the East River where tonight's party is being held. It's clear who is associated with who: Lauren's parents are as WASPy as can be; her mother is dressed in a classic Chanel look, and her dad is wearing navy pants and a shirt that must be made by the male equivalent of Lilly Pulitzer. All of their friends look exactly the same.

Alyssa and John's friends and some family members are here as well, and although they're all dressed nicely, there's something about them that screams, "I'm not from New York, or anywhere near the East Coast!" and they stand out in a big way. But everyone is mingling and making polite small talk, while the bartenders stay busy with nonstop gin-and-tonic orders.

Eric and Lauren's friends, on the other hand, are loud, drunk, and generally a very attractive crowd. Taylor and Manuel are introduced to most of them, Lauren gushing over Taylor and how she's so happy "to finally have a sister" to everyone they see.

At one point, Lauren is whisked away by her mother to chat with some ancient relative, and Taylor escapes to the bathroom, leaving Manuel with Alex. She decides to take a chance and run outside for a cigarette, craving both nicotine and alone time in equal measures. All of this socializing is exhausting. The night air is crisp, with a hint of spring coming, but not any time soon. Taylor shivers and heads back inside, not wanting to leave Manuel to fend for himself for too long.

Once she's back inside, hors d'oeuvres are being passed around. Taylor has a hard time envisioning any of these "society women" (as her brother Alex refers to them) actually eating anything. As she takes in the scene, Manuel appears behind her and hands her a new drink, a glass of champagne, now being passed around on trays.

"Gracias, mi amor," she says, pecking him on the cheek.

Before they've had a chance to flag down any of the circulating waiters, Lauren is speaking into a mic and asking everyone to quiet down for the welcome speeches.

Welcome speeches? Taylor wonders, realizing how uninformed she is about all things wedding-related.

Eric speaks first; his remarks are short and sweet, at first. He thanks everyone for traveling, welcomes them to New York, and thanks Lauren's parents for their generosity. He calls Lauren up and proceeds to tell the story of how they met, fell in love, and are now here today, ready to be married. It's cute, but more scripted than Taylor would have expected... Perhaps Lauren had a hand in writing it? Or, more likely, wrote the entire thing herself.

Once Eric is done, he passes the mic to Lauren. She thanks everyone and tells what feels like a million inside jokes, one for every friend or family member present (and some for those missing). After ten minutes, and the crowd losing interest, she wraps up, encouraging everyone to enjoy the food and the open bar.

"Finally," Alex mutters. He appears out of nowhere midway through Lauren's speech, desperate to escape from their parents.

"What about your speech?" Taylor asks. "You're the best man, for Christ's sake."

"Yes, and since I'm so important to this blissful union, my speech is given at the actual wedding, not at one of these bullshit pre-wedding things," he responds with a smirk.

"Have you even written it yet?" Taylor mocks.

Alex rolls his eyes. "Yeah. I had to promise Lauren a week ago that it was done and ready to be delivered. It's good. Just you wait. Prepare to be blown away. Now I'm going to the bar for a real drink. You guys want to join me?"

Taylor nods, and she, Alex, and Manuel make their way to the bar, which is packed with twenty-somethings asking for shots, the champagne apparently insufficient for getting them hammered. Lauren's friends order shots for the three of them, and the rest of the evening becomes an alcohol-infused blur.

Later, Taylor remembers dancing with her parents and Manuel, a photographer roaming around capturing every moment for the holy wedding album. All in all, everyone has a great time, despite their raging hangovers on Friday morning.

As if anticipating this, Lauren has booked Taylor and Manuel massages at Bliss Spa on Friday, just a few blocks away from the hotel. She advises them to sweat out their hangovers in the spa's steam room, have their massages, and enjoy the showers and sauna. It is fucking magical, and Taylor emerges refreshed and ready for the rehearsal dinner later that evening. Manuel has the same reaction, looking bright-eyed and relaxed as they walk back to the hotel.

The wedding rehearsal and rehearsal dinner proceed as if scheduled by a drill sergeant. Taylor isn't surprised to learn that the wedding coordinator has been tasked with making sure everyone in the wedding party shows up on time and in the correct place. Everyone takes it a little easier on the booze tonight; between last night's shenanigans and the wedding tomorrow, no one wants to be the person who shows up hungover to the nuptials, or, rather, the hair-and-makeup suite, where all the ladies are meeting in the morning.

Once they're back in their hotel room getting ready for bed, Taylor tells Manuel, "Thank God I'm not a bridesmaid. They have to be there at 9 a.m. I'm less important, so my arrival time isn't until 11. I can sleep in a bit."

Manuel kisses her. "Or perhaps you don't need so much time with makeup, because you're perfect as you are."

Extremely flattered but exhausted, Taylor feels his hardness against her and succumbs. They have quiet, lazy, incredibly satisfying sex. She falls asleep immediately afterward but wakes drenched in a cold sweat just after 2 a.m.

She slips quietly into the bathroom, careful not to wake Manuel. As she uses the toilet, she realizes she was dreaming of Daniel just before she woke up. In the dream, she was wearing a wedding gown and holding a bouquet but had no recollection of a groom, or anyone else, for that matter, aside from Daniel. His face was blurred, but she knew it was him. He stood on the landing of a staircase, looking disconsolate and broken.

Taylor sighs and washes her hands, splashing cold water on her face to combat the sweat. Butterflies churn in the pit of her stomach, now truly terrified at the thought of seeing Daniel at the wedding. After a few deep breaths and an internal pep talk, she returns to bed, into Manuel's loving arms. Still, she tosses and turns all night, finally giving up on sleep at 7 a.m. and deciding the gym is the best place to burn off her nervous energy.

After forty-five minutes on the elliptical, a venti iced coffee from the Starbucks on the corner, and two cigarettes smoked back-to-back, Taylor has calmed down enough to shower.

Once her hair is dry, Taylor puts on a loose T-shirt (as instructed, so as not to disturb her professionally done hair later), leaves a note for Manuel, and heads up to the "beauty suite," as it's being called. She feels self-conscious arriving barefaced, not even a hint of mascara. Lauren had promised that the makeup artist was "a genius" and could have Taylor ready in five minutes.

From the hallway, she hears giggles and chatter, Lauren and her bridesmaids have been getting ready for hours. Taylor knocks lightly and is relieved when her mom opens the door, looking utterly ridiculous with curlers in her hair. Her relief quickly turns to embarrassment.

"Mom, what the hell?" Taylor laughs. "Curlers? Are we back in the 1950s?"

"Shhhh. I know, but the hairstylist insisted this would give me soft waves, and I wasn't about to argue," Alyssa whispers, ushering Taylor inside.

Lauren and her bridesmaids are wearing matching light-pink silk robes, sipping mimosas and looking so elegant that Taylor briefly considers fleeing, feeling utterly out of place.

"Taylor, welcome!" Lauren gushes, standing to hug her. "Here, have a mimosa and get settled. It's your turn. Hair first, then makeup. God, your skin is perfect."

Feeling uneasy, Taylor instinctively turns toward the hairstylist after accepting the mimosa. "Thank you for including me, Lauren. This is so nice."

"Of course. I'm just so happy you're here. Jacquie is amazing, she can do anything with your hair. And Chloe? Total makeup genius."

Taylor sits as Jacquie oohs and aahs over her hair. They decide to keep it simple: straight and worn down. Taylor secretly hates updos, ever since senior prom, when so much hairspray was used that her hair stayed frozen for twenty-four hours. She went to breakfast the next morning in sweatpants and an incongruous rhinestone-studded updo with approximately four hundred bobby pins.

After thirty minutes of hair and ten minutes of makeup, Taylor finally looks in the mirror. She's a far better-looking version of herself. Lauren was right, these women work magic.

By then, Lauren and her bridesmaids have left for "pre-getting-dressed" photos. The only ones left are Taylor, her mom, Lauren's mother, and a random aunt who appears to have overindulged in mimosas.

"Taylor, you look, wow. Absolutely stunning," her mother says.

"Thanks, Mom. You look damn good yourself. Prettiest mother of the groom I've ever seen."

Alyssa tears up immediately.

"No crying," Taylor laughs. "You'll ruin your makeup."

"I know, I'm sorry. It's just... Baby Eric getting married. How did this happen?"

"It's okay, Mom. Hopefully you won't be a grandma for at least a few more years."

"Jesus Christ, Taylor. Don't say that."

Taylor quickly changes the subject and heads back to Manuel. When he sees her, his face lights up.

"Dios mío," he murmurs.

"Is that good?" she asks.

"It's very good. You look incredible, mi amor."

"No funny business," she warns. "You'll ruin my makeup. Let's eat."

"Okay," he says with a grin. "But you're breaking my heart."

After Caesar salads from the hotel restaurant, Taylor and Manuel head back to the room to get ready. Midway through lunch, the male contingent of the wedding party, along with some stragglers (friends and random relatives who tagged along for lunch and drinks), rolls into the hotel. Eric, Alex, and John stop by their table to say hi and deliver instructions that Taylor and Manuel need to be in the courtyard at **4 p.m. sharp** for pictures.

"And actually *4 p.m.*, Taylor, otherwise the wedding planner lady will come hunt you down," Eric says, laughing but, Taylor suspects, not exaggerating whatsoever.

"Okay, fine, we'll be there," she says, rolling her eyes. "I wouldn't do anything to mess up your wedding day, Eric. At least not intentionally."

"So sentimental, little sis," Eric says, pretending to put Taylor in a headlock.

"Hey, watch it. Don't mess with the hair. It took the ladies upstairs forever to do this. Good luck explaining to your wife that you're the cause of my ruined hair," Taylor tells him, shaking him off.

"Fiancée, at least for a few more hours," Eric corrects her, glancing at his watch sheepishly. "All right, I'm needed somewhere. Four p.m., courtyard. Be there," he yells over his shoulder as he trots away.

John and Alex head upstairs to "rest" (aka watch hockey playoffs on TV) before the chaos of the wedding ensues. Just as Manuel is signing for the bill, Taylor spots Daniel walking through the lobby with his mother. He doesn't see Taylor, but for a moment she's transported back to her dream from the night before, and her knees go weak with nerves. She realizes in that moment what a complete disaster tonight could be if she's left to her own devices with Daniel.

She sips her water, forcing Manuel to linger a moment longer; the last thing she needs is to share an elevator with Manuel, Daniel, and Tanya.

Maybe it's the nerves, but Taylor can't keep her hands off Manuel once they're upstairs. They have sex, quick and rough, standing up in the bathroom, Manuel taking her from behind. Taylor claims it's to keep her hair and makeup intact, but part of her just feels the need to be punished. The guilt she feels over the Manuel–Daniel saga returns almost instantly.

Once they finish, Manuel hops straight into the shower and Taylor starts getting dressed. She checks her face in the mirror, she's definitely going to need a makeup refresh after that. Her hair still looks fine, and her dress somehow looks even better now than it did in the store. She slips on her shoes, adds some lipstick, and is ready by the time Manuel emerges from the bathroom.

"Wow," he says, giving a long whistle. "Bellísima."

"Gracias," she says, giving a small curtsy. "Now get dressed. I can't wait to see you in your tux. And we need to be downstairs in a few minutes."

"Tan guapo," Taylor tells Manuel as he fastens his tie.

He flashes a sly smile. "We're going to be the best-looking couple at this wedding," he says with a laugh. "Let's go down for these photographs, okay?"

The courtyard is, for the moment, limited to family members and the wedding party. After everyone oohs and aahs over one another, a seemingly infinite number of pictures are taken, every variation of friends, family members, and couples, to the point that Taylor has a flashback to the permutations and combinations she learned in last year's statistics class. They're maxing this out, she thinks, idly wondering how the photographer will ever narrow the selection; at this rate, the wedding album will contain upwards of ten thousand photos.

After what feels like an eternity, the pre-wedding cocktail hour begins, and the coordinated chaos becomes a total shitshow. When Taylor first heard the guest count, she had a hard time imagining what 300-plus people in a confined space would look like. Most of the weddings she attended growing up were small, family affairs with fewer than a hundred guests. Lauren and her bridesmaids have already ducked out to ensure guests don't see her dress before she walks down the aisle. They're presumably back in the bridal suite getting hair and makeup retouched and sipping champagne.

Taylor and Manuel stand near the bar, nursing their drinks and taking it all in. "This is something else," Taylor mutters.

She spots Daniel and Tanya across the courtyard, deep in conversation with a couple from Greenwich, friends of Lauren's parents and acquaintances of Daniel's grandparents.

Taylor feels her pulse quicken and her cheeks flush. She knew this moment was coming; she'd even dreamt about it. But she isn't prepared to see, much less speak to, Daniel or his mother.

Before she can spiral, Alyssa trots over, telling them it's time to head to the church for the ceremony. It's a quarter to six, and the wedding planner has timed the evening down to the second; starting late is not an option.

Taylor obeys, grabbing Manuel's hand and leading him toward the doors. They finish their drinks quickly and make their way to the magnificent St. Patrick's Cathedral, where the wedding of the century is about to begin. Taylor wonders aloud how difficult it must have been to book the venue, it's not as though they allow just anyone to stroll in and exchange vows. One needs connections, and presumably an enormous bank account.

The wedding party is already there, and the remaining guests are en route, causing passersby to stare, mouths agape, at the parade of beautifully dressed people heading into the cathedral.

Taylor and Manuel take their designated seats in the front row. A string quartet plays traditional pre-*Pachelbel's Canon* wedding music, and the entire scene is breathtaking. Taylor finds herself gazing up at the vaulted ceilings throughout the ceremony. Tears are shed all around; Lauren is an even more stunning bride than Taylor imagined. And yet, despite the beauty and love surrounding her, Taylor feels an aching sense of dread, one she can only attribute to her fear of seeing Daniel at the reception.

Manuel squeezes her hand as Lauren and Eric exchange vows. Alex and the other groomsmen do their best not to look bored, while the bridesmaids attempt (with varying degrees of success) to hold back tears. Taylor's parents beam throughout the ceremony. And in less than forty-five minutes, her brother Eric is a married man.

As Eric and Lauren run back down the aisle, beaming, Eric calls out, "Now it's party time."

And party they do.

The reception is as raucous as the ceremony was beautiful. Everything dazzles, the bride, the groom, the food, the drinks. Around 10 p.m., after dinner, speeches, and cake, the dance floor erupts. Alex, fresh off what may go down as the most epic best man speech of all time, is in full party mode. Everyone is smiling, buzzing, euphoric.

Manuel sits at a table, deep in conversation with one of Eric's groomsmen who spent years living in Spain and hopes to return. Taylor takes the opportunity to step outside for some air and a quick cigarette.

She has just lit it when a familiar voice says softly,

"Hey, Taylor."

Taylor swivels around to see Daniel facing her, looking gorgeous in his suit, his tie in his hand and the top buttons of his shirt undone. *He must have followed me out here,* she thinks.

"Hey, Daniel. It's good to see you. Listen..." Taylor takes a drag on her cigarette, blowing the smoke in the opposite direction. "I'm really sorry about what happened and how I handled it. I didn't mean to hurt you."

Daniel smirks, and Taylor isn't sure what to make of the gesture.

"Well, you hurt me," he slurs, and Taylor realizes he's drunker than he's letting on. "But I get it. Rich, older Spanish guy? Hard to say no to that."

"Daniel, you know it's not like that. Come on, let's not do this. Should we go back inside?" Taylor asks, both hurt and exasperated.

"Why? So I can watch you canoodling with Manuel for another three hours? No, thanks."

"Well," Taylor huffs, "this is my brother's wedding, and I'm going back in. No matter what you think, I care about you. Very much. Please remember that, even if you're angry with me, okay? And you have every right to be angry with me... I know I didn't handle any of this well, and you deserve so much better." Tears sting her eyes as she says it.

Daniel looks up at the sky and doesn't respond. Taylor hesitates, giving him the opportunity to accept her apology, or at least say something, but he turns his back on her, staring in the opposite direction. Taylor spins on her heels and returns inside, shaking slightly.

Another drink is what she needs. Immediately.

She hightails it to the bar, where Eric and his friends are taking shots.

"Lionel! Add another for my little sister," Eric shouts to the bartender over the music. "How ya doing, kid? Having fun?"

Taylor forces a smile. "The best time. Everything is perfect, Eric. I'm so happy for you and Lauren," she says, hugging him. "You really did it. She's a catch, so don't fuck this up, yeah?"

"I'll drink to that!" Eric laughs as Lionel, the slightly annoyed bartender, slides shots across the bar with an eye roll. Taylor swears she hears him mutter *kill me now* under his breath and has to stifle a laugh. She can't blame him, the crowd is rowdy and drunk, and the poor man must be miserable trying to keep up.

"Cheers, everyone," Eric says. "We're drinking to me not fucking up my marriage!"

A collective "Cheers!" rings out, and everyone knocks back their shots. *Jägermeister,* Taylor realizes a moment too late as it burns her throat on the way down. She orders glasses of wine for herself and Manuel and heads back to their table.

She spots her parents getting down on the dance floor and feels equally mortified and happy for them. They've kept their love alive all these years, raising three rambunctious children and managing careers. Later, while flipping through the thousands of photos from the weekend, a shared favorite will be one the photographer captured at this moment: Taylor pausing with two drinks in her hands, admiration written across her face as she watches her parents embarrass themselves on the dance floor. Years later, she'll smile seeing it framed in the homes of her parents and both brothers.

When the moment passes and reality sets back in, Taylor's urge to get shitfaced and forget her interaction with Daniel takes over. She hands Manuel his drink, takes a generous gulp of her own, and drags him onto the dance floor. From there, the night becomes a haze, and for that, she's grateful.

Fortunately, Manuel is somehow sober enough to set an alarm for Sunday morning, the farewell brunch begins at 10 a.m. sharp. When the alarm beeps at nine, Taylor groans and pulls a pillow over her head. Her feet throb from dancing in heels, her head aches from too much alcohol, and she's dying of thirst. Manuel, seemingly telepathic, hands her a bottle of water and kisses her shoulder before heading into the shower.

Taylor pieces together the blurry fragments of last night. After her encounter with Daniel, she remembers seeing him on the dance floor, pressed close to one of the bridesmaids. Based on how they were dancing, she assumes they probably went home together. *Well, good for him,* she thinks spitefully. *Hopefully that means he'll be too hungover to wander around the hotel today, and I can avoid him.*

She forces herself out of bed and into the bathroom to brush her teeth, surveying the damage in the mirror. She fell asleep without removing her makeup and now has mascara smeared across her face.

"Christ," she mutters, just as Manuel steps out of the shower.

"How are you feeling, my darling?" he asks with a smirk.

"I feel as good as I look, which is fucking awful. How are you so awake? Did you have fun last night? I really hope you did."

"I drank extra water, and I actually ate, unlike you. But yes, *anoche fue increíble. La mejor boda de toda mi vida.*"

"*Me alegro.* Now I need to shower and pull myself together." Manuel is right, Taylor barely ate, sticking mostly to alcohol so she wouldn't feel bloated in her skintight dress. A huge mistake.

After showering, she feels marginally better, and she and Manuel manage to get dressed and make it to brunch by 10:30. Eric and Lauren look as though they never went to bed, Lauren's hair is delightfully disheveled, and Eric reeks of booze. They appear elated, exhausted, and possibly still drunk.

Unsurprisingly, none of the other young guests have arrived. Some had early flights, but Taylor assumes most of them just crawled into bed and have a fifty percent chance of showing up at all. After grabbing food and chatting with her parents, it becomes clear the brunch is meant for the older crowd. Taylor tells Manuel they can stay briefly, then head out to see the city.

"Central Park and the Met?" Manuel whispers.

"Perfect," she replies, kissing his cheek. "We just need to say goodbye to Lauren and Eric, they're leaving for their honeymoon tonight. We can meet my parents and Alex later for dinner, if that's okay."

Manuel nods, and Taylor goes in search of the bride and groom. She finds Eric first.

"Hey! We're heading out in a minute. I can't drag Manuel all the way to New York and not let him see the sights."

"Right on, sis," Eric slurs.

"Eric, are you still drunk?"

"In fact, I believe I am. Jesus, what gave it away? Fun wedding, though, am I right?"

"You reek of booze, your eyes are bloodshot, and you're slurring your words," Taylor says, punching his arm. "But yes, it was amazing. Especially last night. The whole weekend was perfect."

Lauren hugs Taylor next. "Congratulations! I was just telling Eric how wonderful everything has been. The wedding was spectacular."

"Oh, I'm sooo happy to hear that! We hope you had fun," Lauren says, leaning in and whispering with a giggle, "Can you tell we're still drunk?"

Taylor nearly spits out her coffee laughing. "Yes, a little, but if it helps, you're in much better shape than Eric."

"Well, that's something. And between us, I was so nervous about meeting you. But you're lovely. And normal!"

Taylor blushes as Lauren rushes to clarify. "No, no, that came out wrong. I was just worried you wouldn't like me. Sorry, I'm rambling."

"It's fine. I was nervous, too. Honestly, I think you're far too good for my smelly older brother, but I'm thrilled you two got married. I warned him not to fuck this up."

Lauren laughs, hugs them both again, and finally lets them escape. Taylor makes plans to meet her parents later, and she and Manuel step out into a gloomy, cold New York afternoon. Yesterday's sunshine is gone, replaced by biting wind and dark clouds. They opt for a taxi instead of navigating the subway, which, compared to Barcelona's clean, efficient metro, feels confusing and filthy.

Taylor and Manuel roam the Met for a few hours, far longer than Taylor could have tolerated on her own, but she has no interest in Central Park in this weather, and Manuel is into it, so she wanders from exhibit to exhibit without complaint. Once Manuel has seen the Greek and Roman Art exhibit, he is finally ready to go. *Thank God,* Taylor thinks to herself.

They do end up wandering over to the Great Lawn in Central Park, which is underwhelming given the weather, and eventually make their way down Fifth Avenue, taking in the sights, dodging tourists, and making a game of distinguishing locals from visitors. By the time they're back at the hotel, it's already 5:30 p.m., and all Taylor wants is a warm drink.

Her parents and Alex are seated at a table in the hotel bar and summon them over.

"What have you two been up to all day? Where the hell were you at the brunch?" Alex asks.

"Um, we were at the brunch on time. Or almost on time. Where the hell were *you?*" Taylor snaps back.

"You guys just missed each other, relax," their mother chimes in. "It was a lovely morning, but unnecessary, really, given the rest of the weekend. But what have you two been up to all day? Taylor, you look freezing."

"I *am* freezing. What happened to the sun? We went to the Met and walked around Central Park for a bit."

"How nice," Taylor's father says. "How'd you like the museum?"

Manuel finally weighs in. "It was wonderful, just as good as I'd heard. And the Greek art section, how incredible."

Taylor smiles and lets her dad and Manuel discuss their favorite sections of the Met while flagging down the waiter and ordering two glasses of a deep, heavy Cabernet. *This ought to warm me up,* she thinks.

An hour later, the five of them decide on dinner nearby at Avra Estiatorio, over on 48th Street between Lexington and Third Avenues. It's a perfect end to an absolutely fabulous weekend in New York, they all agree. Alex skips out before dessert, claiming urgent studying he neglected all weekend, but gives Manuel a warm handshake and hug before leaving.

"Hey man, thanks for coming all the way here. It means a lot to our family, especially to Taylor. You're a stand-up guy, and I'm glad I got the chance to meet you."

"Likewise," Manuel says. "It has been truly special meeting you and Taylor's family. Thank you for welcoming me."

Alex nods and turns to Taylor. "Safe travels, kiddo. See you this summer? You pick the place. New York? Madison? Barcelona? Antarctica?"

Taylor laughs and hugs him. "Antarctica. And you're paying."

Alex says his goodbyes to their parents, who are also leaving tomorrow, and heads downtown to return to his real life, which, he claims, the wedding prevented him from dealing with all week. Once the bill is paid, Manuel, Taylor, and her parents walk back to the hotel.

"Manuel, do you mind if I steal Taylor for a quick glass of wine before we say our final goodbyes?" Alyssa asks suddenly.

"Of course not. Taylor, I'll get a bottle of wine and bring it to the room. Stay here with your mom," Manuel says diplomatically. He retrieves a bottle of wine and two glasses from the bar and heads upstairs.

John says goodnight to his daughter and goes to his room, not wanting to intrude on whatever female business is unfolding between his wife and daughter, though he privately suspects it has something to do with Daniel Collins, that rascal who'd been sneaking around his house with Taylor over Christmas break.

Taylor settles into a plush banquette while her mom orders two glasses of the cheapest red wine on the menu. They clink glasses.

"So, what's up, Mom? Why the mystery meeting? No one's dying or getting divorced, right?"

Alyssa laughs. "No, nothing like that. I just wanted a few minutes alone with you. We've been so busy all weekend, it doesn't feel like we really caught up." She takes a sip of wine. Taylor waits. "But it's late, so I'll cut to the chase. Daniel is in love with you."

"Pffft, Mom, that's ridiculous. What are you talking about?" Taylor gasps, louder than she intends.

"It's obvious to anyone. And I talked to Tanya for hours the other day over lunch. She said he's been bereft since you went back to Barcelona. Apparently Christmas break, when you two were spending all that time together, was the happiest she's ever seen him. Now?" Alyssa shakes her head. "He's a mess."

Taylor takes a moment to absorb this. Deep down, she already knew, but hearing it aloud, especially from her mother, brings an uncomfortable intensity.

"So what am I supposed to do?" Taylor wails. "I live in Spain now. For three more months. I'm with Manuel. Why are you telling me this?"

"I'm not trying to intrude or make you feel guilty," Alyssa says gently. "Quite the opposite. I just want you to know you have options."

"Maybe I don't *want* options," Taylor says petulantly, crossing her arms and taking a larger-than-necessary gulp of wine.

"Then enjoy what you have," Alyssa replies. "But what happens when you go back to UNC? Is Manuel prepared to do long-distance? Is that what *you* want? And after graduation, are you really prepared to move to Spain? I just want you to think it through."

"We *are* thinking it through. Can we drop this, please? I don't want to fight. Let's just pretend this conversation didn't happen."

"Okay. I'm sorry, Taylor. I just love you and want to protect you."

"Whatever, Mom. I don't need protecting. Tell Eric and Alex the same."

An uncomfortable silence settles in, then Alyssa abruptly shifts gears and launches into gossip from the wedding. Within minutes, the tension dissolves. Apparently, gossip is all they need to reset.

"All right, Mom, I'm sending you to bed. You've got an early flight," Taylor says, grabbing her purse.

Alyssa sighs. "You're right. I'm missing you already. This was wonderful. I wish we had more time, but it's been such a treat seeing you and Manuel."

They hug and head to the elevator, promising phone calls once they're home.

As soon as her mom gets off, Taylor presses the *down* button and hustles back to the lobby, then outside for a cigarette, something she's been craving since dinner. Five minutes in the cold air later, she's calmer.

Back upstairs, she glosses over the conversation, telling Manuel her mom was just emotional about the wedding and needed reassurance. Manuel doesn't question it. Taylor feels a flicker of guilt, then he hands her a glass of wine and kisses her, and the guilt evaporates.

Taylor pushes him back onto the bed, and they make the most of their last night in New York.

Chapter 16

April–May 2004, Barcelona

On the flight back from New York, Manuel tells Taylor how much he liked meeting her family and traveling with her. He again broaches the topic of next year and the future beyond that. Taylor is, once again, thrilled that he is looking ahead, but apprehensive about what the future may hold for them. Her plans remain vague; she can't help but wonder how Daniel plays into all of this. Taylor and Manuel could do long-distance next year while she is a senior at UNC. Between school breaks and Manuel's vacation days, they could figure it out.

It's after graduation where things get complicated. Manuel seems to assume that Taylor will return to Barcelona and get a job, and that they can carry on without missing a beat and live happily ever after. While she isn't ruling that out, she can't wrap her head around committing to it one hundred percent. There is still so much she wants to see and do. And after spending the long weekend in New York, knowing that her brothers would be there, she finds herself considering that option as well, even though she never in her wildest dreams thought living in Manhattan would have such appeal. So she takes the easy way out and agrees that they'll carry on long-distance next year and take it from there.

***

All of a sudden, it is May, and the weather in Barcelona reaches a new level of perfection, warm, but not hot. School will wrap up in the coming weeks, and Taylor still hasn't booked a flight home. Rather than get a typical job for the summer, as her friends are doing, she has a tentative travel itinerary and plans to write her ass off in order to pay for her travels. Her writing for the school paper and for Daniel's grandparents' magazine has been highly regarded and widely shared; she's made thousands of dollars doing what she loves, essentially getting paid to visit amazing places and do cool stuff, and then put it down on paper afterward, which she'd be doing for free, if she's being honest.

She has decided to keep renting her apartment through the end of July and then spend most of August back home in Wisconsin. And Manuel has made it abundantly clear that she can stay with him as needed.

While on the flight back from the wedding, Taylor uses a cocktail napkin to map out her hot spots to visit once school ends. The trip to New York has inspired her to travel more; sitting on the plane returning to Barcelona, she feels giddy with the excitement of visiting places for the first time. Paris will be at the end of May. Italy sometime in early June, she's hoping to see Florence, Milan, and Rome, possibly more if time and money allow. Greece and its islands will be at the end of June or in July; she wants to be there during high season. She mentions all of this to Manuel, and while he doesn't say as much, Taylor can sense his unease about her traveling alone.

A few weeks later, the topic of Taylor's independent travel comes up again, innocently enough. She and Manuel are at a dinner to celebrate the end of her academic year (along with good grades). School had just ended the day before, Friday, May 21st. Manuel surprises her Saturday evening when he picks her up at her apartment with a bouquet of roses to congratulate her on a job well done. Nicholas, who happens to be home for once, whistles when he sees the flowers.

"Well done, my man," Nicholas says.

Manuel blushes and shakes his hand. "Gracias, amigo. I have to celebrate this beautiful, intelligent young lady."

"Claro, ella es magnífica," Nicholas responds with a smirk, elbowing Taylor in the ribs.

"Shut up, Nicholas. You're worse than my brothers," she replies. She pours drinks for the three of them, happy to catch Nicholas for a few minutes before they all part ways for the night. An hour, two cocktails, and half a pack of cigarettes later, Nicholas heads out to some uber-fashionable gay bar, while Taylor and Manuel venture out for dinner at their favorite tapas bar in the neighborhood.

After their second round of tapas, Manuel leans back in the banquette they're sharing and asks Taylor about her plans for the upcoming months. He knows she'll be traveling, but hasn't been able to pinpoint where, exactly, she'll be. Taylor gives him locations and vague dates, not to be evasive, but because she still hasn't booked any of her train or plane tickets yet.

"So, Taylor," Manuel begins, "you have finished school for the year. *Felicidades.* Where are you going first? Paris, correct?"

"Yes, I need to book everything, but that's the plan," Taylor replies. "I think I'll leave next week, maybe Wednesday or Thursday, and spend five days there. There's so much to see, I should be able to crank out at least three articles while I'm there, don't you think?"

"Of course you can. But Paris is *la ciudad de todas las cosas románticas... y del amor.*" He pauses. "Do you really want to be there by yourself?"

"I know, I'd obviously prefer to be there with you," Taylor responds, somewhat defensively. Then she softens her tone. "But stupid work gets in the way. I promise I'll take lots of pictures and send you updates about everything I do, okay?"

"Thanks. I just worry about you, that's all. Make sure you are careful, yes?" Manuel says, a touch testily.

Taylor nods. "Trust me, I've done plenty of traveling alone. I'll be fine, Manuel. And if you have any suggestions on where to go in Paris, I'd love them. I've done some research and know the main spots, of course, but if you or your friends have any hot tips, I'm all ears."

Manuel nods. "And after Paris?"

"Italy, I think. I'm planning to spend a week there, Milan, Florence, Rome, and possibly Sicily. I was hoping you could join me for part of it. Maybe take a long weekend and meet me somewhere?" Taylor knows the offer will help assuage his unease about her traveling alone.

Manuel smiles. "Of course. I'll check my schedule. I need to spend some time with my family this summer, but I'd love to go to Italy with you, especially now that my mom is doing so well."

"Great," Taylor says, smiling. "You pick the city and dates, and I'll plan around you."

They finish dinner and move on to other topics, but Taylor can still sense Manuel's lingering disapproval about her travel plans.

Despite his hesitation, Taylor forges ahead. Before she knows it, she's just one day away from boarding the overnight train to Paris. The past week she's spent holed up in the neighborhood internet café, despite the discomfort it gives her, as it triggers memories of that painful January night when she sent Daniel the email that ended everything. Still, the café is relatively clean, cheap, and allows smoking.

On one unusually gloomy afternoon, Taylor spends four hours there researching hotels, neighborhoods, and restaurants in Paris. With her trusty travel journal open beside her, she notes must-see spots, makes phone calls to restaurants, and, most importantly, secures a great deal at the Hôtel d'Orsay. Located across from the famed Musée d'Orsay, the hotel would normally be well beyond her budget. After explaining to the manager that she's visiting to write about Paris hot spots and promising him a write-up in one of her articles, he agrees to give her two free nights on top of the three she's paying for.

Five nights for the price of three, she thinks, not a bad start to my time in the City of Love.

Chapter 17

May 2004, Paris

Somehow, it's nearly the end of May, and Taylor has nothing left on her calendar other than traveling and writing, having already wrapped up the academic year. On Wednesday, May 26th, after a long overnight train ride, Taylor arrives at Gare du Nord in Paris, bleary-eyed and absolutely famished. It's still early, and she can't check into her hotel until the afternoon, so she finds a small café inside the station and orders coffee and a croissant. She spends an hour eating, smoking, sipping her coffee, and watching the morning rush of the train station. Everyone is in a hurry; the pace reminds her more of Manhattan than Barcelona.

The women are as glamorous as she expected, generally thin, polished, and impeccably dressed. Taylor feels frumpy in her jeans and sweater, but she dressed for comfort on the train ride rather than for strolling the streets of Paris.

After finishing her coffee and studying the Paris guidebook she bought last week at her favorite Barcelonian bookstore, Taylor navigates the metro and takes it to the Les Halles station, not far from the Louvre. She roams the museum, impressed not only by the collections but by the sheer scale of the place. Eventually, like everyone else, she ends up at the Mona Lisa, Da Vinci's tour de force, which to her surprise has been housed in the Louvre since 1797. Over two hundred years.

She stares at the painting for a full ten minutes, mesmerized not only by the work itself but by its value and fame.

When she finally pulls herself away, Taylor visits a few more exhibits before realizing it's already 2:30 p.m. She can now check into her hotel, and it's also a perfectly acceptable time to stop for lunch. She gathers her bag and crosses the Seine via the Pont du Carrousel, heading toward the Left Bank and her hotel.

Consumed with hunger, Taylor walks a block past the Quai Voltaire to Rue de Lille in search of food. She immediately spots Le Bistrot de Paris and beelines for it. There are only a handful of open tables, but she's seated right away and given bread with butter along with her menu.

No longer caring about appearing "too American," she scarfs down a piece of bread instantly before the waiter returns to take her drink order. She orders a glass of Bordeaux, assuming any wine in Paris is bound to be good. The prices, however, are astonishing compared to Barcelona, it feels more like New York. She settles on just an appetizer and the wine, deciding to save her euros for dinners and nights out.

After paying the bill, Taylor walks the remaining few blocks to her hotel and checks in. By sheer luck, the manager she spoke to on the phone is working the front desk and confirms the discounted rate. He hands her the key and directs her to the elevator.

The room is small but nicely furnished, with an adorable balcony and an impeccable view. Taylor drops her bags, uses the restroom, and is asleep within minutes on the double bed. As she drifts off, the phrase *overcome with exhaustion* has never felt more accurate.

When she wakes, it's already getting dark. She checks her phone, it's nearly 7 p.m. Clearly, she should have splurged on a sleeper berth on the train; the economy seat was far from conducive to rest. Still, after sleeping for over two hours, she feels refreshed and ready for the evening.

After a quick shower and blow-dry, she changes clothes and does her makeup. Despite aiming for "Parisian chic," she still looks like a tourist. Probably for the best, she thinks, her French is limited at best, and this way people might assume she's American and default to English.

Taylor hadn't reached out to any of her college friends who spent the semester in Paris; she assumed they'd already gone home. The next few days in the City of Light are for Taylor, and Taylor alone. She needs the solitude. She isn't feeling stifled by Manuel exactly, but she's beginning to question the long-term viability of their relationship. His occasional jealousy doesn't help. Still, the sex is incredible. Consistently satisfying. And he's affectionate and genuinely fun to be around.

No, Taylor thinks as she rides the elevator down, these days will give her space to think clearly, to reassess the future and appreciate what she has with Manuel.

With her guidebook and map tucked into her bag, Taylor does what any American tourist would do and walks to the Eiffel Tower. After the obligatory photos, she sits down for dinner at 9:30 at a nearby café, Le Beaujolais. After house wine, escargot, and a salad, she pulls out her notebook and begins jotting observations while sipping the rest of her carafe.

Between the food and the charming waitstaff, Taylor is completely enchanted. She decides immediately to include the restaurant in one of her Paris write-ups. It's cozy, the food is outstanding, and it feels so thoroughly French it's almost surreal.

As she pauses her note-taking and glances around, she notices two attractive waiters speaking quietly and glancing her way, smiling. She smiles back, blushing. A few minutes later, a fresh glass of wine, one she didn't order, appears on her table.

"This is on the house," the younger of the two waiters says, in a thick French accent.

"Merci," Taylor replies awkwardly. "I'm sorry, my French is terrible. I write for a travel magazine, and I've decided to feature your restaurant. It's lovely, and the food is incredible."

The waiter looks at her, clearly surprised, but in a good way.

Taylor continues, "Do you have any information about the restaurant you can share with me so I can include it in the article? You know, the history, the owners, that sort of thing. Also, what's your name? I'm Taylor."

"Wow, that is so kind of you. I am Hugo. My aunt and uncle own this restaurant, and I've been working here for a few years. Their son is over there," he says, nodding toward the older waiter. "His name is Claude. He knows more than I do. I will send him over to you, yes?"

With that, Hugo tops off her wine glass and sends Claude her way. Twenty minutes later, Taylor has the full story of the restaurant and its proprietors, along with Claude's phone number, email address, and work schedule. She tells him she's spoken for, but he just winks and replies, "That's okay. I am happy to show you around the city."

Mildly baffled by his response, Taylor eventually finishes her wine and pays the greatly reduced bill. She kisses Hugo and Claude on the cheeks as she leaves, promising to stop by again over the next few days.

It's nearing midnight by the time she departs, and despite her earlier nap, Taylor still hasn't recovered from the overnight train ride. She takes a taxi back to the hotel and calls it a night. After drinking an excessive amount of water in an attempt to offset the wine, she wakes Thursday morning surprisingly clear-headed.

She goes for a quick jog along the Seine, making her way down to Notre-Dame, where she pauses to marvel at the magnificent French Gothic details of the thirteenth-century cathedral, the spire, the gargoyles, the stained glass. Taylor now understands why Marcel

Aubert described it as "a masterpiece of composition and execution." It is exquisite.

On her way back to the hotel, she passes chic Parisians heading to their offices, well dressed, wearing sunglasses she knows she could never pull off. Most are either shouting into mobile phones or smoking cigarettes as they rush toward their destinations. It's hard to tell whether the men or women in this city are more beautiful.

After a post-run shower and an unexpectedly elaborate breakfast buffet, Taylor sets off for Versailles. About an hour away by train, she spends the ride writing in her notebook, pausing frequently to watch the countryside blur past the window. She's read plenty about Versailles, Louis XIV's self-indulgent palace, but nothing prepares her for the sheer decadence. The interior is breathtaking, but it's the grounds that impress her most.

Taylor spends hours wandering the palace and gardens, snapping photos and taking meticulous notes. The day passes in the blink of an eye, and suddenly she realizes she needs to sprint to catch the train back to Paris, the next one isn't for another hour. She arrives at the station breathless, with barely a minute to spare.

As she sinks into her seat, her phone buzzes.

Hola mi amor, cómo estás? Estás disfrutando París? Espero que todo vaya bien y que estés segura. Un beso, Manuel.

She smiles and replies that she's safe, having an amazing time, and tells him about Versailles. They exchange a few messages before Manuel has to return to work, and Taylor promises to check in tomorrow.

She arrives back in Paris late in the afternoon, well after the lunch rush, and stops at a small café overlooking the Jardin des Tuileries. Ravenous from the day, she orders a glass of champagne and a tomato-and-mozzarella salad. The people-watching is sublime, as is the champagne, and the cigarette she smokes alongside it.

She isn't sure if it's hunger, the champagne buzz, or simply being in Paris on a perfect afternoon, but this might be the best meal she's ever eaten. She lingers, savoring every bite. Years later, many details of this trip will blur together, remembered mostly through photographs, but this single hour, champagne in hand, sunshine on her face, will stand out as the purest memory of Paris.

The next few days are cliché in the best possible way. Taylor checks off guidebook sights, explores museums, drinks wine, and eats with gusto. On Saturday night, she finds herself back at Le Beaujolais, confident that Claude and Hugo will be working.

The restaurant is packed, it's Saturday night, after all, and she briefly wonders if coming was a mistake. She waits at the hostess stand, growing increasingly self-conscious, until she spots Claude flirting shamelessly with a table of forty-something women. She laughs to herself and catches his eye. His face lights up instantly; he nearly trips over himself getting to her.

"Bonsoir, mademoiselle! You have returned," Claude says enthusiastically.

"Bonsoir," Taylor replies. "I was hoping to have dinner, but it looks like there's no room."

"For you, Taylor, we will find a table. One moment, yes?"

"Of course," she says. "Take your time."

Less than a minute later, she's seated at a cozy corner table for two. Before she's fully settled, a carafe of the same wine from her previous visit appears.

"Well, thank you, what a welcome. You'll be happy to know I've already written about your family's restaurant," she tells Claude, smiling. "I sent the piece to my editor just before coming here tonight."

"Thank you, Taylor. Your meal this evening is, as they say, on the house."

Taylor smiles as he leaves her with a menu and returns to the bustling dining room.

Her time in Paris has been incredibly productive, museums, parks, churches, shopping, all checked off. Tomorrow, her final full day, she's heading to Giverny to see Monet's garden. It's an easy day trip, and she's always loved Monet's work. Another story, another roll of film, there's no better way to spend it.

After ordering dinner, Taylor pulls out her small Paris guidebook and maps out her itinerary for visiting the gardens tomorrow. After a few minutes, she sets the book down and starts people-watching, making up scenarios about the other patrons. Just as she's concocting a complicated story about the table to her left, two young men and one young woman deep in an intense, hushed conversation, her appetizer arrives.

Claude wishes her *bon appétit* and returns to work.

She feels a pang of disappointment that he didn't sit down and have a drink with her. *Don't be ridiculous,* she tells herself. *He's in the middle of his shift, and you have a boyfriend, for God's sake.* Once again, Taylor is disappointed in herself and her apparent lack of loyalty when it comes to Manuel. She ignores her food for the moment and lights a cigarette, which seems like the appropriately dramatic thing to do when these thoughts surface. It's what they do in films, after all.

Eventually, after she gets over her self-inflicted crisis regarding Manuel, Taylor eats her food, and the restaurant begins to clear out. As she's on her second glass of wine, Claude sits down across from her.

"Hello there," Taylor says, more flirtatiously than she intends. "Wine?"

"Yes, thank you," Claude replies in accented English. "I'm not bothering you, am I? I've been on my feet all evening, and the opportunity to sit across from a beautiful woman and share wine is too much for me to resist." His eyes twinkle dangerously.

"No, of course you're not bothering me. Cheers, or should I say *à votre santé.*" Taylor giggles at her atrocious French and focuses on pouring him wine. They clink glasses, their eyes meeting in the candlelight. They talk, laugh, smoke, and drink until the restaurant prepares to close, Claude occasionally getting up to tend to his duties, most of which his cousin Hugo has taken over by now.

As they drink more of the delicious wine, Taylor realizes two things with startling clarity. First, she's drunk. Second, Claude is going to make a move on her, and she's going to let him.

A fleeting thought flashes through her mind: *I'm twenty-one years old, living in Barcelona, visiting Paris for a long weekend.* If there were ever a time to make out with a Frenchman, this is it. She wouldn't go further than a kiss, though. Even in her drunken state, she knows she has to draw a line. Or so she tells herself.

As Taylor gathers her sweater and purse, Claude wraps things up, whispers something to Hugo, who smiles, and they shake hands. He helps Taylor to her feet, and they step out into the clear night, the air crisp but refreshing.

"May I walk with you?" Claude asks politely.

"Of course, I'm this way," Taylor says, gesturing in the general direction of her hotel. She'd considered taking a cab, but the air feels good, and she enjoys having Claude to talk to. Besides, the walk might sober her up.

They stroll along the Seine, and as they near her hotel, Claude takes her hand and abruptly turns onto a side street, gently pressing her against a building. Their eyes lock, and he leans in to kiss her. Her knees nearly buckle, it's perfect, dizzying. She isn't sure how long they stay like that, only that it feels heavenly.

When Claude's hands begin to slip into her underwear, Taylor stops him. It's not that she doesn't want this, quite the opposite, but she doesn't want it to happen on a street corner. She guides his hand away and tells him her hotel is just a few blocks away. They disentangle themselves and practically run, giddy with the excitement that only a first-time hookup can bring.

Inside the room, Taylor ducks into the bathroom, she's needed to pee since they left the restaurant, and she needs a moment to collect herself. Instead of talking herself out of what's about to happen, she surprises herself by letting go entirely.

"Just go with it," she whispers to her reflection.

When she emerges, Claude is standing by the window. She takes him in and inhales deeply. He turns, the top buttons of his shirt undone, smiling.

"Taylor, come here," he says gently.

They resume kissing; soon their clothes are kicked aside and they're on the bed, naked. He kisses her slowly, deliberately, everywhere. When she's on the brink, he shifts her onto her stomach and enters her from behind. At some point, he pulls a condom from his jeans and puts it on.

They both groan as he moves inside her, slow, controlled, impossibly intense. Not long after, Taylor comes, burying her face in the pillow. Claude flips her onto her back, lifts her legs, and continues with more urgency now. As his hands move over her breasts, she comes again; he follows soon after.

They lie there, sweaty and breathless. *Carnal* is the only word Taylor can think of. Claude returns from the bathroom with two glasses of water, handing one to her before lying beside her.

"Wow," he says softly. "That was incredible. You have the most perfect body I have ever seen."

He traces a finger along her inner thigh, sending shivers through her. After a few minutes, Taylor slips into the bathroom, she read somewhere, probably *Cosmo*, that peeing after sex helps prevent UTIs.

When she returns, she's surprised to find Claude already hard again.

"Again?" he asks sheepishly.

Taylor laughs and climbs on top of him, kissing him from his neck downward before taking him into her mouth. After a few moments, he pulls her up and guides himself inside her. They both come quickly.

The rest of the night blurs together, sex, half-sleep, sex again, until the sky lightens and morning creeps in through the curtains. Taylor is sore and utterly spent; she's probably had five orgasms in a few short hours. Eventually, they pass out for real and don't wake again until 10 a.m.

Claude is already awake when Taylor opens her eyes. He's moving around the room, purposeful. Before either of them speaks, she feels the shift. He's dressed, he isn't touching her, isn't looking at her the way he has all night. The hunger is gone.

Taylor rolls toward the nightstand and drains the remaining water from her glass.

"Bonjour," she says, her voice rough, sitting up and pulling the sheets tight around her naked body.

"Bonjour," Claude replies, softer than before. "Taylor, listen." He drops into the desk chair and turns to face her. She braces herself. "You are wonderful. Beautiful. But I have made a mistake. I am not single."

She keeps her face still. Neutral. She has no moral high ground here. Before she can fire back with *well, neither am I*, Claude inhales deeply.

"I'm engaged," he says. "I'm getting married in August."

Her jaw drops. The words hang in the air, heavy and irreversible. She can't speak.

Claude covers his face with his hands.

"Wow," Taylor finally manages. "I really wish you'd told me that, before now. I don't want to be the person who ruins your engagement. I don't even know what to say." Tears sting her eyes; her heart pounds violently in her chest.

"This is my fault," Claude says. "Not yours. I've never cheated on Julia. Something overtook me last night, I found you *irrésistible*. But now I must go." He hesitates. "I hope you aren't angry. You're beautiful. Inside and out."

Still naked, still stunned, Taylor watches as he stands, kisses her cheek, and walks out of the room.

"Oh my God," she whispers to herself once the door clicks shut. "What the fuck am I doing?"

She turns onto her side and breaks apart, sobbing so hard it steals her breath. She cries for everyone she's hurt, Manuel, mostly, but also Daniel, and Claude's fiancée, a woman with a face she'll never know. And in that wreckage, clarity hits her hard and fast: she has to end things with Manuel.

The evidence is overwhelming. One betrayal is a mistake; this is a pattern. He deserves better, someone who can make it through a weekend without destroying everything. There's no version of this where he forgives her, and no universe in which she keeps these secrets without rotting from the inside out.

She lies there for a long while, cycling between disgust and despair, until she forces herself into the shower. She cranks the water as hot as it will go, welcoming the sting. Penance. When she's finished scrubbing herself raw, she dresses quickly and heads for Paris–Saint-Lazare. She can't stay here. She needs movement. Noise. Anything.

Giverny will have to do.

The train ride is agony. She rehearses endings that don't exist, ways to let Manuel down gently without detonating his heart. She decides, again, to spare him the truth. There are enough clean reasons to walk away: distance, age, futures that don't align. Daniel, too, lingers like a bruise she can't stop touching. Claude was simply the final proof.

The day is gray and heavy, perfectly aligned with her mood. And yet, the gardens are breathtaking. Monet's house, the Clos Normand, the Water Garden, she drifts through them all, taking photos, taking notes. The lily ponds stun her into temporary silence. For brief, merciful moments, she forgets herself entirely.

She stands on the Japanese bridge, wisteria drooping overhead, willows bowing toward the water. She tells herself she'll write about this later, when she's capable of focus again, when she's less disgusted with herself.

By the time the gardens begin to close, it's nearly six. She asks a nearby tourist to take her picture. Years later, she'll look back and recognize the girl in that photo: the forced smile, the quiet devastation. But for now, she thanks the serious German woman and walks away, pretending that everything is fine.

Her final night in Paris is unremarkable; Taylor opts for a touristy bistro near the Jardin des Tuileries. She feels gritty from the day spent wandering outside and her feet are in agony from all the walking. She snags a tiny table outside and immediately orders white wine and lights a cigarette. The wine is cold and delicious, she feels her body relaxing with each sip. She orders light, just a tomato and mozzarella salad. It's exactly what she wants, to be an inconspicuous patron at a restaurant where she knows no one and can barely communicate with anyone else. She can revel in self-pity, smoke too many cigarettes, and drink too much wine. Eventually her feet have recovered and are ready for the remainder of the walk back to the hotel, so she pays the bill and heads back to the cozy hotel room that she escaped so hastily just this morning.

After washing up, she lies down in bed and is asleep almost immediately. The lack of sleep last night coupled with her emotions and the physical activity today work harmoniously together, allowing her a good ten hours of uninterrupted sleep before her alarm blares cruelly the next morning. And just like that, Taylor's springtime jaunt to Paris has come to an end. As has her longest, most wonderful relationship with a guy, all because she can't manage to be faithful. She tries to tell herself that when one door closes a new one opens and all of that positive thinking bullshit, but she can't deny the heartbreak and misery she feels in her final hours in Paris, as she contemplates how disastrous her behavior has been.

<h1 style="text-align:center">Chapter 18</h1>

May–June 2004, Barcelona

The breakup with Manuel is ugly, far uglier and more painful than Taylor ever imagined. She returns from Paris on a Monday night and asks him to meet for coffee after work the following day. She's sworn off booze for the moment; nothing good ever seems to come from it.

After a brief hug and the ritual ordering of cappuccinos, Taylor launches into her speech. She tells him she doesn't see their relationship working long-term. She leaves out the cheating and blames logistics instead, distance, uncertainty, the future. She rambles, saying she doesn't want him weighed down by a long-distance relationship with someone who may or may not return to Barcelona next year. They both know he will stay. His family, his work, his life are all here. She admits that as much as she wishes otherwise, she can't promise she'll come back after graduation.

Manuel explodes exactly as she expects. He slams his cup onto the table, unbuttons the top of his dress shirt, buries his face in his hands. He offers solutions, he'll wait, they'll make long distance work, whatever it takes. People at nearby tables start watching, openly curious about what could possibly be tearing this beautiful couple apart.

Taylor cries. She feels monstrous. Even though his mother is responding well to treatment, the timing feels unforgivable. She keeps repeating it to herself like a mantra: *He deserves better. Someone who doesn't crumble at the first temptation.* Clearly, that isn't her.

After nearly an hour, him yelling, her sobbing, they arrive at a fragile truce: they'll stay civil, try to keep in touch. Taylor apologizes for what feels like the hundredth time. Manuel reaches across the table and gently wipes mascara from her cheek.

"Gracias, Manuel. Lo siento muchísimo, pero esto es la única solución en este momento. Siempre te amaré."

"Te amo, Taylor. Tú eres una persona magnífica," he says with a heavy sigh before switching to English. "I will always treasure the time we had together."

"Well, you're certainly not making this any easier," Taylor says with a weak laugh, squeezing his hands.

They walk out of the café together, smiling the saddest smiles. On the sidewalk, unsure how to end things, Manuel pulls her in for one last hug. One last kiss. They repeat their promises to stay in touch, to wish each other well.

Then he leaves, heading west toward his apartment.

Taylor stands there for a moment, hollowed out. She lights a cigarette and starts walking home alone, calling her mom as she goes. She reaches both of her brothers. Lindsay too. By the time she curls into bed that night, she's exhausted but held together by other people's voices.

Everyone is kind and supportive, but all are baffled by her choice. She tells only Lindsay the full truth, because Lindsay, blessedly, is incapable of judgment. Lindsay makes her laugh, reminds her that this is not the end of the world. Within six hours, Taylor goes from feeling like the worst person alive to someone who is still loved despite her catastrophic decision-making.

The next few weeks, her first real stretch of singledom since arriving in Barcelona, feel strangely liberating. Nicholas and his gaggle of gay friends adopt her immediately, treating her like a wounded stray kitten once Nicholas spills the sordid details. She goes out dancing, wild and unselfconscious, in clubs where no one looks at her twice because she's a woman and therefore irrelevant. She mostly avoids alcohol and feels better than she has in months.

During the days, she wanders into lesser-known corners of the city, writes about them, and submits something every week. Her bank account grows steadily, buoyed by discipline, productivity, and the generous salary provided by Daniel's grandparents.

Instead of going to Italy as planned, Taylor decides to stay put and take day trips, Girona, Montserrat, Tarragona, Sitges. She reasons that skipping Italy gives her the perfect excuse to return to Europe someday. Eric and Lauren reinforce the decision: Italy in June would be sweltering and overrun with tourists. Barcelona, at least, comes with a beach. *First-world problems*, she reminds herself.

And Greece is coming soon.

Italy had excited her, but Greece makes her giddy. The itinerary changes daily: Athens for two days, then island hopping. She longs for Santorini but recoils at the prices. Every island she researches looks impossible to eliminate. She briefly considers asking Manuel, they've managed to maintain polite, platonic texts, but decides that soliciting advice about a solo Greek island adventure might be unnecessarily cruel.

So instead, most evenings find her at the Internet café, scrolling obsessively through the brand-new travel site TripAdvisor, trying, and failing, to narrow her choices.

Finally, on June 15th, Taylor finalizes her itinerary and books her trip to Greece. She'll fly into Athens on Wednesday, June 30th, returning on July 14th. The schedule gives her two days in Athens up front and roughly twelve days of island-hopping before heading back to Barcelona, and eventually the U.S., where her senior year of college awaits.

After booking the flights, she texts Manuel to see if he'd like to grab a drink and say hello. He responds immediately, and they decide to meet at the neighborhood bar where they first met. Nostalgia, apparently.

Taylor arrives early and orders a rum and Coke from the ancient bartender, the same man who was there on the night she and Manuel first locked eyes. It's her first drink in weeks, she realizes, and the alcohol hits fast. A few minutes later, Manuel walks in fresh from work, looking as unfairly handsome as ever. They hug warmly and settle in to catch up.

Manuel tells her his mother is doing very well, he's visiting her this weekend, actually, and that he's in line for a promotion. Taylor feels an immediate sense of relief. His life hasn't unraveled since the breakup; if anything, he's thriving. The knowledge loosens some of the guilt she's been carrying. She gives him vague details about Greece and makes sure to mention that they'll have time to see each other again before she leaves for the States. He agrees, and they part ways amicably after two drinks each.

Later that evening, soothed by the fact that Manuel seems okay, and doesn't hate her, Taylor's thoughts drift, inevitably, to Daniel.

They haven't spoken since Eric's wedding. Not even an email. Still, she's picked up occasional updates through her mom. Alyssa is careful, never volunteering information about Daniel's love life. Taylor only knows that he's spending the summer interning at a big bank in Manhattan and hoping for a full-time offer after graduation. The path mirrors her brother Eric's so closely that she wonders if Daniel ever reached out to him for advice, and whether Eric would have told her if he had.

She makes a mental note to ask.

The next day, once it's late enough in New York for Eric to be at the office, Taylor calls him.

"Hola, hermanita," Eric booms. "What's up?"

"Hey. How are you guys?"

"We're great. Boring, married people," he laughs. "Settling into domestic bliss. Also trying to survive the post-honeymoon depression. But we're good. What's going on? Everything okay?"

"Yeah, just checking in. Actually, I need Greece tips. I vaguely remember you telling me about all the islands you partied on."

Taylor can practically picture him leaning back in his chair. "Oh man. I have stories. I'm at work, though, and HR would escort me out immediately if anyone overhears this. I'll email you. Which islands are you thinking about?"

"I haven't booked ferries yet, so I'm flexible. Athens first, then about twelve days of island-hopping. Maybe Rhodes, Paros, then Mykonos. Save the party island for last, right?"

"That sounds incredible. I did Corfu, Santorini, and Mykonos. I don't know much about the others, but I can absolutely vouch for Mykonos. You'll love it. And Rhodes sounds familiar, Lauren might've been there. I'll ask."

"Thanks. I'm excited about everything, even the ferry rides. The sea, the buildings, it all looks unreal."

"It is. I just wish I remembered more of it," Eric says, laughing.

They chat a few more minutes, and just before hanging up, Taylor casually asks if Daniel Collins ever reached out to him about work.

"Daniel, as in Tanya's son?"

"Yes. That one," Taylor says, rolling her eyes.

"He did, actually. Earlier this year. He ended up interning at a rival bank, but I looked over his résumé and helped with his cover letter. Why?"

"Just curious. I figured you'd be a good resource."

"That's it?" Eric presses. "Nothing to do with the fact that you're newly single?"

"Yep. That's it. Now wipe that smirk off your face, asshole," she jokes.

"Whatever. I'll send you the Greece rundown later. Love you."

"Love you too."

After hanging up, Taylor feels a small, irrational satisfaction knowing Daniel and Eric were in touch. One thin thread still connects them, even after she's severed so many others with her own disastrous behavior. She pushes the thought aside and focuses on enjoying Barcelona and preparing for Greece.

But one afternoon, about a week before her flight to Athens, she stops by the Internet café to check her email after a lazy day at the beach. Slightly dazed from the sun, and the beer she drank while lounging beside the Mediterranean, it takes her a moment to register the unfamiliar email address staring back at her.

Someone from Lehman Brothers? she mutters, clicking the email open.

It's from Daniel.

Hey Taylor,

I hear you're still in Barcelona for a bit, I hope you're having a great time. I'm in Manhattan for the summer, working at Lehman and staying in the NYU dorms. Living the dream, haha. It's fun when I'm not at work, which isn't actually that often. But it's good experience.

Eric helped me get the internship, so please thank him again for me. I mostly just wanted to say hey and hope we can still be cool. I know things ended kind of weird, and I'm sorry about that, especially how I acted at the wedding. That wasn't cool.

I think about you a lot and hope we can at least be friendly when we see each other. I'll be back in Madison for a few weeks in August. I heard through the grapevine (our moms, obviously) that you'll be back too. Maybe we could grab coffee or a drink?

Cheers,
Daniel

Taylor exhales, realizing she's been holding her breath the entire time.

It's a kind email. Unexpected, but kind. After everything, especially the disaster at Eric's wedding, it feels like a small gift. Relief washes over her, followed quickly by something else. Hope.

Before she can overthink it, she replies.

Hey Daniel,

It's really good to hear from you, thanks for reaching out. And congrats on the internship! I know that's a tough one to land. I hope New York is treating you well. Feel free to call either of my brothers if you ever need a friendly face or a drinking buddy.

I'm still in BCN. School ended last month, so I've just been bumming around and doing lots of writing for your grandparents. I'm heading to Greece next week (I literally cannot wait), then back to Madison toward the end of the summer. I'd love to meet up when we're both back.

Keep in touch.

Taylor

She hits send and heads back to her apartment, buoyed by the exchange. It's remarkable how quickly her mood lifts, how easily the weight in her chest loosens, at the simple reminder that broken things aren't always broken forever. That forgiveness, even after serious damage, is still possible.

Chapter 19

June 2004, Greece and Barcelona

Athens at the end of June is dusty and unbearably hot. Hellish, really. Despite her intention to cram as much sightseeing as possible into two days, Taylor spends most of her time there submerged in the hotel pool. She does see the Acropolis and the Parthenon and wanders through Plaka, ducking in and out of shops, but by midday the heat is oppressive. She's in Athens for two days but only one night; given the length of the ferry ride to Rhodes, she's opted for the overnight crossing.

So after sweating her way through the city, on Thursday, July 1st, she heads to the port and boards the correct ferry, the one that will, after roughly thirteen hours, deliver her to Rhodes.

By 6 a.m., she gives up on sleep entirely and heads to the deck to watch the sunrise, and more urgently, to drink coffee and smoke a cigarette. The deck is quiet, most passengers still asleep. Taylor is awestruck by the view. The water is an otherworldly shade of aqua, broken by distant landmasses she assumes are smaller, uninhabited islands. It's the most beautiful sight she's ever seen. She runs back to her seat to grab her camera and snaps photos as the sun continues to rise.

Her brother told her the islands were beautiful, of course, but she was utterly unprepared for the Aegean's magnificence.

After an hour, and a full roll of film, Taylor retreats to the main cabin for more coffee and a mediocre breakfast sandwich. With no school and no boyfriend, she's spent the past two weeks obsessively researching the Greek Isles and now has a solid grasp of their geography. Still, she pulls out her guidebook and studies the map, trying to identify the islands they're passing.

Later, back on deck, which is now packed with other passengers, she watches as the ferry slips past Tilos and Simi before finally arriving in Rhodes. There's a shared hush among the tourists as they take in the view, their languages and backgrounds momentarily irrelevant. Rhodes, often cited as the most beautiful of the Dodecanese islands, lives up to its reputation.

The water is an even deeper blue against the island's white buildings. As the ferry docks, the calm dissolves into a mad scramble for luggage.

Though she's eager to explore the medieval city immediately, Taylor knows she needs a place to stay first. Eric warned her: once you disembark, locals hover, offering rooms, apartments, even entire houses. The idea feels foreign but oddly appealing. She's set on Rhodes town for its proximity to archaeological sites, nightlife, and transportation. Eric also assured her taxis are cheap enough to make even the remotest beaches accessible.

The port is chaotic, taxis honking, locals holding handwritten signs in multiple languages, families reuniting, noise everywhere. Taylor takes it in before beginning her search. A few men approach her with lodging offers. Too sketchy. Hard no.

Then she spots a grumpy-looking woman in her fifties who appears deeply annoyed just to be standing there. *Perfect,* Taylor thinks.

She approaches with a smile, bracing herself for a language barrier.

"Hello, dear," the woman says in a thick Greek accent. "You need a room?"

"Yes," Taylor replies, relieved. "In Rhodes town, preferably."

"Yes. One bed, private bath, small kitchen, big terrace. Sea view. Very beautiful. Five minutes from here."

"How much?" Taylor asks.

"Seventy-five American dollars per night. Minimum four nights."

"That's perfect," Taylor says. "I'll take it."

"Good. Follow me."

They walk toward Hippocrates Square, making awkward, halting conversation. Twenty minutes later, they reach an apartment building. Winded, the woman unlocks the door and leads Taylor up to the third floor. The studio is airy and bright, sparsely furnished, with a spectacular terrace overlooking the sea. It's clean, simple, unmistakably Greek, and exactly what Taylor hoped for.

The woman gives her the keys, collects the money, and mentions she lives on the first floor if Taylor needs anything.

Once alone, Taylor showers off the ferry grime and city dust. She considers a nap but can't resist exploring. She heads out, visiting the Archaeological Museum, the Palace of the Grand Master, and the Church of Agios Fanourios before realizing it's already 3 p.m. and she's starving.

She stops at the first taverna she sees. The official lunch rush has ended, so it's quiet. Soon she has a massive Greek salad and a crisp glass of assyrtiko in front of her. Stray cats weave around her table, and she can't help thinking how perfectly, stereotypically Greek it all feels.

As she eats, she mentally drafts her write-ups, jotting notes so she won't forget anything. Afterward, she attempts to head back to the apartment, and promptly gets lost. Barcelona had been easy; Rhodes is not. After thirty minutes of wandering, she miraculously ends up back at the building.

Rather than fall into bed, which is what she really wants to do, Taylor types up her notes on her laptop. The piece nearly writes itself. An hour later, she collapses onto the bed and falls into a deep sleep.

She wakes just after 8 p.m., still exhausted from the overnight ferry, throws on makeup and going-out clothes, and heads back out, careful to trace her steps this time.

Her first stop is a packed, trendy bar, tourists spilling into the street. A crowded bar is usually a good sign. Inside, she notices plenty of attractive men, many with British accents. She reminds herself that this trip is about writing, exploring, and self-care, not random hookups. Still, there's no harm in looking.

She elbows her way to the bar just as an Italian couple vacates their stools mid-argument. She claims a seat and waits while the bartender, unfazed by the chaos, moves at a glacial pace.

Eventually, she's rewarded with a rum and Coke. It tastes inexplicably different here, as it has everywhere she's traveled. She noticed it first in Spain and now considers it a universal truth.

She doesn't bother opening her guidebook; there's too much happening around her. Her thoughts drift to Daniel. She imagines him beside her, traveling Greece together, sharing a drink. She lets herself linger in the fantasy and decides she'll email him tomorrow.

Naïve? Absolutely. But she can't stop herself.

After her drink, she wanders until she lands at Restaurant Wonder, near the edge of Rhodes town. Rather than sit alone at a table, she takes a seat at the bar and orders grilled squid and cheap Greek wine. For two hours, she eats and people-watches.

She chats briefly with another solo traveler, a thirty-year-old, recently divorced woman from Los Angeles, deep into yoga and self-discovery. A bit odd, very earnest. After enough talk of spirituality and reinvention, Taylor says goodbye, pays the bill, and is back in her apartment and asleep before midnight.

She wakes with sunlight pouring through the windows, startled by how deeply she slept. When she checks the clock and sees it's already 11 a.m., she laughs aloud. "Fuck me."

Feeling unusually refreshed, she heads down to the local market for fruit and an iced coffee, easily one of the best she's ever had. She makes a halfhearted attempt not to think about how much sugar and milk must be packed into the cup and quickly abandons the effort. With her plan to be on the beach by ten completely shot, Taylor revises her day: internet café first, submit her writing, email Daniel, then the beach.

Choosing a beach is nearly impossible; they all sound incredible. Today she settles on Kallithea Beach, close to Rhodes town and highly recommended by Lauren, her well-traveled sister-in-law, who had indeed been to Rhodes and offered plenty of advice. Most of Lauren's recommendations, nightclubs, upscale restaurants, are well outside Taylor's budget, but the beach tips are solid.

After some wandering and finally asking a local for directions, Taylor finds herself at the internet café about an hour after waking. She sends off her Athens and Rhodes pieces with ease. The email to Daniel is harder. She can't exactly say *I miss you, I'm newly single, and I wish you were here with me in Greece.* But she also doesn't want to sound distant. After a long internal debate, she lands on something breezy, hinting at solo travel, lingering affection, and the hope of seeing him in Madison later that summer.

She hits send, pays her fee, and heads back to the apartment to change into her swimsuit and cover-up. With her beach bag and camera packed, she hails a taxi.

The ride is harrowing. The driver barrels along winding roads, overtaking buses and motorbikes with terrifying confidence. Taylor grips her thigh, bracing for impact, until the aquamarine water comes into view and her fear dissolves into awe. The driver drops her off and disappears just as quickly.

She walks the shoreline looking for the cheapest sunbed, snapping photos of the clear water and rocky sand. A small taverna offers a sunbed, towel, and bathroom access for ten euros. Perfect. She orders a beer and runs straight into the sea, already overheated.

The water is blissfully cool, not cold, not warm, and for a moment Taylor is convinced she's stumbled into paradise.

She floats, swims, returns to her beer, orders a snack, and spends the afternoon alternating between napping and plunging back into the water. By six, she's spent and sandy. She catches the bus back to Rhodes town and endures the crowded, bumpy ride.

Normally she'd write immediately, afraid of losing details, but she's too relaxed to care. She showers, opens a bottle of white wine, adds ice, and sits naked but for a towel on the balcony, smoking and drinking slowly. Life, she thinks, not for the first time, is pretty fucking great.

And yet.

She's here alone. Not sharing the view, the feeling, especially not with Daniel. An ocean separates them, despite all the invisible threads tying them together. She wonders if he's read her email, and, more importantly, if he's replied. She resists the urge to sprint back to the internet café and instead distracts herself by getting ready for another night out.

The next few days fall into a pleasant rhythm: sleeping late, writing in the mornings, beaches in the afternoons. She eats well, drinks good wine, and sleeps deeply.

On the final night in Rhodes, leaving feels unbearable. Taylor briefly considers scrapping the rest of the trip and staying put, but reminds herself there's only so much she can write about one island. Paros will be different, a perfect combination of history and nightlife. Mykonos, well, that will certainly be lively and chaotic. She forces herself to zoom out, this is a life she never imagined for herself. Gratitude steadies her.

On July 6th, Taylor rises early, says a quiet goodbye to the apartment, and heads to the port for the eleven-hour journey. Since she'll arrive late, she's booked a modest hotel in Parikia, Paros's main port. The ferry ride drags. She reads, photographs passing islands, watches the sea change colors. When they dock around 6:30 p.m., that familiar thrill returns, the excitement of someplace new.

The hotel is a short walk from the port. It's simple but well-located, close to restaurants and small shops. Taylor drops her bags and settles in.

Paros mirrors Rhodes in rhythm: sightseeing first, writing second, a different beach every day. The nightlife is livelier; she has one especially late night, but overall it's calm and productive. Mykonos is the opposite. She skips the historical stuff entirely in favor of beach clubs, all-night parties, and too much booze. But damn, is it ever fun.

Taylor returns to Barcelona on July 15th, still deeply in love with the city, though Rhodes now comes in at a close second. She promises herself she'll return to Greece as soon as she can and see as many islands as possible in her lifetime.

Taylor's final two weeks in Barcelona are a whirlwind of packing, shipping stuff back to the States, partying with Nicholas, hanging out with Finn, and spending some quality time with herself while visiting off the beaten path restaurants and chilling out at the beach. On her final night before returning to the States, Taylor and Nicholas have a teary, laughter-filled happy hour together before he sets off to another fabulous party. They say their goodbyes at the bar, knowing that Nicholas may very well still be out partying when Taylor leaves for her flight the next morning.

"Taylor, you're a fucking rock star," Nicholas says in his ridiculous British accent. "Don't let anyone tell you otherwise. And, I've extended my lease another year. You'll have a place to stay when you visit. We might have to share a bed, but I'm fine with that."

"There's no other gay man I'd rather share a bed with," Taylor laughs. "You've been my partner in crime, and a real friend. Thank you for always having my back."

"Well, don't go getting all soft on me again," he teases.

"Sorry," she says, wiping a tear from her cheek. "I'm just going to miss you."

"We have email. Phones. The internet. I can still harass you constantly," he says, kissing both her cheeks. "You can't get rid of me that easily. I love you."

Nicholas slips out, having already paid the bill. Taylor follows, returning, one last time, to her apartment on Carrer Roselló. Tomorrow she'll leave Barcelona, at least for now. And on this warm July night, a piece of her heart quietly breaks in what might be the most intoxicating city in the world.

Interlude

August 2004, Madison, Wisconsin

Taylor returns home from Barcelona with a melancholy that takes several weeks to shake. She spends the better part of August 2004 holed up in her parents' house, not wanting to go out with the high school friends who were in town. Languishing, that's the word. Languishing, wondering if coming back to the States was a huge mistake, whether ending things with Manuel was a huge mistake; essentially, questioning every decision she'd made in the past year. Despite the fact that, the past year has been, hands down, the most wonderful year of her life, for so many reasons. She has matured what feels like five years in just one and suddenly feels older and more experienced than her friends. She isn't sure if this is from living abroad for a year, dating an older guy, or what, but it makes her feel more adult and less inclined to gossip and hang out with her high school crew. And it was just plain fun. Ridiculously fun. She didn't always appreciate it in the moment, but as soon as she stepped onto the plane leaving Barcelona, it hit her; just what a damn good time she had over her year abroad.

After weeks of emails with Daniel, and persistent nudging from her mother, Taylor finally leaves the house and agrees to meet him for happy hour, a week before they're due back in North Carolina for their senior year. She arrives sun-bronzed from Greece and Spain. Daniel, by contrast, looks pale and worn down, the kind of tired that comes from fluorescent lights and too many hours at a desk.

They meet at the Boathouse at the Edgewater Hotel, where mutual friends work behind the bar and pour generously. Daniel is already seated when Taylor arrives. There's a half-empty beer in front of him, and a rum and Coke waiting for her.

The fact that he remembered makes her chest tighten.

He jumps up when he sees her, nearly knocking the drinks over in his haste. They hug, longer than expected, a little stiff. Neither is quite sure whether to go for a cheek kiss, so they end up standing there, staring awkwardly, until they both laugh and blurt out some version of *Oh my God, it's so good to see you,* before sliding back onto their stools.

Two hours and a few drinks later, they seem to have reached a mutual understanding on several topics. A tentative peace agreement, if you will. First, Taylor accepts responsibility for being an asshole by leading Daniel on and treating him so poorly earlier in the year. She accepts full blame and attributes their winter break fling to a temporary loss of morality and sanity, she was just overwhelmed with Manuel and didn't know how to handle her feelings, which were real, and strong, for Daniel. Second, Daniel admits that he had been overzealous and clingy on multiple occasions and that this wasn't fair for Taylor. Third, after a handful of drinks apiece, they agree that they want to stay friends, and plan to see each other when time and schedules allow during their final year in college.

And they do manage to see one another their Senior year, not as frequently as either would have liked, but a fair amount. And they exchange lots of long-winded emails about their social lives and plans for next year; these emails never fail to make Taylor smile and laugh more than she cares to admit, and she spends far more time composing her responses to Daniel than she would ever let on.

And whether she admits it yet or not, Daniel has quietly reinserted himself into the story of her life, unfinished business, unresolved feeling, waiting patiently for the right moment to matter again.

Chapter 20

May 2005, Madison, Wisconsin

By the end of May 2005, Taylor, now twenty-two and a college graduate, finds herself back in Madison for a few quiet weeks before launching into the next phase of her life. First comes Greece again, a two-week graduation gift from her parents. Then comes adulthood.

Somehow, impossibly, she already has a real job.

Daniel's grandparents and their team are thrilled with her work and have offered her a full-time position as a travel writer for their upscale company, Immersion Travel. A salaried job. Health insurance. Direct deposit. A retirement plan. She'll be paid to travel the world, eat extraordinary food, stay in beautiful hotels, explore far-flung places, and write about it. The idea still feels unreal.

She knows it won't all be glamorous. There will be economy flights, remote hikes, questionable plumbing. She doesn't care. It's everything she wanted, and more.

Daniel, meanwhile, accepted a full-time offer after excelling at his internship the previous summer. The hours are brutal, but he's good at the work and finds satisfaction in finance. The result is that both of them will be based in New York.

Daniel has secured an apartment in the Financial District with a college friend, close to his office. Taylor will sublet Eric and Lauren's place near Columbus Circle, essentially for free. They've moved to Greenwich, as predicted, but Lauren insists on keeping a foothold in the city. Taylor will live there when she's not traveling, and Eric and Lauren will stay occasionally on weekends.

With her future neatly mapped out, Taylor spends late May dismantling her childhood bedroom. Most of it goes into boxes for the attic, time capsules to be opened years later when nostalgia hits. A few boxes are shipped to Manhattan, mostly clothes and personal things: framed photos, collages, her freshly minted diploma, favorite books. The apartment is already furnished, tastefully, as Lauren would demand, so packing is mercifully easy.

The ease leaves time for everything else. Reconnecting with friends she'd neglected. Going out nearly every night. Enjoying the strange, electric freedom of being twenty-two, freshly graduated, and already employed.

Some evenings, she meets Daniel for drinks before splitting off to see their respective friends. On one of those nights, over early cocktails, they talk about New York.

"I'm worried I'll be chained to my desk and never meet anyone," Daniel says, half-serious.

"You'll meet someone," Taylor replies, smiling. "You always do."

Their banter has stayed like this for months, light, teasing, charged but contained. They haven't slept together since that winter break nearly a year and a half earlier, but the tension hasn't vanished. It's simply been... managed.

"Maybe you'll meet someone at work," Taylor adds. "Then you'll be together, what, eighteen hours a day?"

Daniel laughs. "Painfully accurate. And meanwhile you'll be off globe-trotting, attending glamorous dinners and parties with Immersion Travel. Seems unfair."

"That's finance for you," she says. "Big money, big misery. Just don't get all snooty on me. I'll knock you down a peg if I have to, farm boy."

"Farm boy?" Daniel scoffs. "We're from the second-largest city in Wisconsin."

They both laugh, fully aware of how absurd that sounds.

"Just watch out for those East Coast girls," Taylor says lightly. "I don't want anyone breaking your Midwestern heart."

Daniel smiles, thinking, *you're the only one who ever could.* He pushes the thought away before it can take hold.

After a while, Taylor checks the time and signals for the check. "I've got dinner with the girls. And I leave for Greece tomorrow."

Daniel stands and pulls her into a warm hug. "Have the best time. I expect full reports once you're in New York. I'll even pretend to care about all your photos."

"You'd better care," she says, lightly punching his arm. "Good luck with the move. We'll meet up as soon as I'm in the city."

"Listen to you, 'the city.' You already sound like a local."

"Never," Taylor says. "I'll always be a Wisconsin girl."

They part easily this time, buoyed by the knowledge that this goodbye isn't an ending. They're on parallel tracks now, both heading east, toward the same city.

And this time, New York is waiting for both of them.

Chapter 21

June 2005, Greece

The next day, Taylor sets off on her post-graduation rendezvous back to the Greek Isles. Somehow, over a drunken phone call a month before her departure, she'd managed to convince Nicholas, her roommate from Barcelona, to meet her in Athens for a few days before getting on the ferry for more island hopping. When she leaves for Santorini, Nicholas will be heading to Mykonos. Taylor will meet up with Lindsay and her family on Santorini. They are, apparently, chartering a yacht, and the timing of their stop in Santorini happens to be perfectly aligned with Taylor's trip.

"A rough life you lead," Taylor's dad mutters as she walks him through her itinerary. And she can't argue with him. Athens with her former roommate, Santorini with her best friend, followed by Ios and Folegandros on her own. It's almost too good to be true.

And so, nearly a year to the day since she was in Athens for the first time, Taylor finds herself right back in the hot, dusty old city. After spending what feels like hours in the immigration line, collecting her bags, and guzzling an iced coffee, she emerges from the airport and lights a cigarette, stunned that it's already noon. She's disoriented and jet-lagged, and relieved that she's got the day to rest and regroup before Nicholas arrives later that evening.

Nicholas arranged the accommodations: a room with two double beds at a modest hotel near the Acropolis. Taylor couldn't argue; the place is cheap, central, and clean.

By the grace of God, the hotel allows Taylor to check in early, so she dumps her luggage in the corner of the minimalist hotel room, takes a shower, and claims the bed closest to the window. When she wakes up, it's past 3 p.m.; Nicholas is due to land around 5 that afternoon, so Taylor throws on her summer uniform of cutoff jean shorts and a tank top and heads out in search of something to eat.

She's missed the lunch rush; many restaurants are shuttered for the quiet hours between lunch and dinner, so she eventually lands at a bar with outdoor seating and a gorgeous view of the Acropolis.

She orders a white wine along with a cup of ice, a white-trash trick her mom taught her years ago, watering the wine down and theoretically making it last longer. She opens her well-read copy of *Bridget Jones's Diary* and picks up where she left off, feeling something of a parallel plot to her own life as she reads about Bridget and her two distinctly different love interests.

She smiles to herself, thinking of the Manuel–Daniel predicament from last year, while snacking on the complimentary bowl of bar nuts the bartender plopped on her table. The sun is hot on her face, but there is a tiny breeze that prevents the heat from being unbearable. She looks up at the Acropolis, sips her wine, and feels at peace, savoring the moment, knowing full well that the next week will be filled with debauchery, with both Nicholas and Lindsay being major partiers and night owls.

And true to form, after Taylor's cathartic afternoon, Nicholas bursts into the hotel, abuzz with energy and plans. They decide to take a quick swim in the hotel's small but gorgeous outdoor pool, both anxious to wash the dust of the city off their bodies.

An hour or so later, Nicholas orders four shots of ouzo at the lobby bar, which they bring back to their room post-swim. They start getting ready to head out for dinner, with Nicholas trying on three different ensembles, all nearly interchangeable.

"Jesus, Nicholas, you look fine! You take longer than me to get ready," Taylor remarks.

"Well, Taylor, my love, we can't all be as naturally gorgeous as you, can we? So drink your ouzo and let me primp." Taylor rolls her eyes but smiles affectionately, watching as he musses his hair in the mirror, applying far more gel than necessary.

Finally, they finish their ouzos and pass Nicholas's fashion test, and they head out into the warm night. The streets are packed with tourists and locals alike; having hosted the Summer Olympics the previous summer, Athens is booming. As such, they have to wait thirty minutes for an outdoor table at the restaurant Nicholas has been raving about. By the time they sit down, it's already 9:30 p.m.

"Where are we, Barcelona?" Taylor says with a laugh. "I'm not used to eating this late anymore."

"You're definitely more American than I remember you," Nicholas says. "I guess we were speaking so much Spanish back in Barcelona, I never noticed your accent. It's funny."

Taylor mock-gasps and throws her napkin across the table at him. "Jerk," she says jokingly. They split a bottle of wine and have the best grilled octopus, hummus, and babaganoush either has ever eaten.

"Wow," Taylor says, patting her stomach. "Are we really going out now? I'm too full," she moans.

"Well, pull it together, girlfriend. This club is supposed to be insane," Nicholas tells her as he motions to the waiter for the check. They both light cigarettes and drain what's left of their wine. "And it's 11:30 now, which is perfect. It really picks up around midnight, so we can get a cab and head over."

With no real knowledge of Athenian nightlife, Taylor has given Nicholas free rein to plan out their nights, a role he has accepted with glee.

"Before we head out," Taylor says, "a few things. Ground rules, if you will."

"I'm listening," Nicholas says, giving her a schoolboy expression.

"Mainly, I don't think either of us should bring anyone back to the hotel room. I mean, I don't want to spend a night listening to you and some pretty boy you hit it off with. Fair?"

"No shit, Taylor. I figured that would go without saying. However, if you or I meet someone, I think it's fair game to split up at the end of the night and go home with said person. We're both hot, single young things, after all. And it's summer." As if the season has anything to do with Nicholas's hookup mentality.

"Agreed," Taylor says with a smirk. "Okay then. That was it. Oh, and no illicit drugs from strangers. Shall we?"

Nicholas rolls his eyes, and then they're off to the club, taking a quick cab ride into a dingy neighborhood. The line to get in is significant but not too awful, at least not yet, so they quickly pay the cabbie and join the queue.

Twenty minutes later, they're inside, and house music is pumping, causing Taylor's pulse to seemingly beat all over her body. Without having to discuss the matter, they both head straight to the bar, and Nicholas orders drinks. Knowing full well that Nicholas will probably go home with someone, Taylor decides then and there that she needs to keep her wits about her, so she nurses her drink at the bar while Nicholas slams his down and heads out onto the dance floor.

She snags a seat and watches Nicholas with amusement. Barely five minutes go by before he's making out with some cute guy. Still jet-lagged and uncomfortably full after their decadent dinner, Taylor politely declines an offer to dance with a drunk Dutch tourist, finishes her drink, and decides to call it a night. She makes her way to Nicholas, lets him know she's taking off, and wishes him luck for the rest of the evening. He winks at her and kisses her on the cheek.

"See you tomorrow, love." He turns back to his new pal, graciously allowing Taylor to get the hell out of there.

The next morning, Taylor wakes up to an empty bed beside her. She checks her mobile, expecting a missed call or text from Nicholas, but there's nothing. It's only nine a.m.; she decides to give him until noon. If she hasn't heard from him by then, she'll start calling.

In the meantime, Taylor plasters sunscreen all over her fair skin and heads to the hotel pool. It's blissfully empty, with the exception of an elderly woman swimming laps. Taylor jumps in, momentarily shocked by the cold water. Although the dip feels amazing and refreshing, after only a few minutes she's bored and restless. She gets out, checks her phone, and sees two missed calls from Nicholas. Panicked, she calls him back immediately.

"Heeeyyy," he slurs, clearly fucked up.

"Hey. Where are you? You sound funny."

"I'm just leaving Jorge's apartment. Been up all night. Too much coke. Or booze. But I'm on my way back to the hotel!"

"Jesus, Nicholas, I thought we agreed no drugs." Taylor shouts into the phone before realizing she's in public. She lowers her voice. "You can't trust drugs from random strangers. I'm at the pool; meet me down here when you get back, yeah?"

"Got it, see you soon," Nicholas says, suddenly sounding more sober.

Taylor snaps her phone closed in annoyance. Although she knew going into it that these few days in Athens with Nicholas would play out exactly like this, she's frustrated nonetheless. He'll need to sleep all day to come down from whatever drugs he did and will likely repeat last night all over again. She huffs and leans back on her lounge chair.

About an hour later, Nicholas arrives, looking sheepish and carrying two iced coffees and a bag of what appears to be breakfast pastries. Taylor feels like sulking but can't help but laugh as he approaches, trying to carry all of it while holding his swimsuit up; it's too baggy and perilously close to falling down. She gets up and retrieves one of the iced coffees and the bag of pastries.

She peers inside and nods approvingly. "Am I forgiven?" Nicholas asks, batting his eyelashes.

"Not yet," she sighs, taking a long gulp of iced coffee. Nicholas sits next to her and pulls out a pack of cigarettes, lighting one for Taylor and offering it to her.

"Now you're forgiven," she says, plucking the cigarette from his hand. "So, what the hell happened last night? When I left the club, you were dancing with a very cute guy, but he definitely did not look like a Jorge."

Nicholas laughs. "I met Jorge later on, way after you left. By the way, your departure time from the club was ridiculously early. You didn't even make it until 1 a.m.? Are you kidding me? Don't think I didn't notice."

Taylor ignores the dig and continues, "How do you come to Greece, directly from Barcelona, and end up with a Jorge? I'm assuming he's Spanish?"

"Sí, claro. I guess I have a type. He's from Madrid but has been living here for years. He offered to take us out tonight, but I told him I'd need to ask you. I've got his number. No pressure, and I'm sorry I fucked up last night."

Taylor leans over and gives him a hug. "It's just the drugs I worry about. When you don't know where or who they're from, that makes me nervous."

"Fair. No more hard drugs. MOM." Nicholas smiles at her, finishes his cigarette, and is asleep within seconds.

Taylor opens the umbrella above his chair, assuming, correctly, that in his intoxicated state he did not apply sunscreen. And the next two days in Athens follow this pattern: Taylor spending her days wandering the city alone while Nicholas sleeps off the night before, coherent again just in time for happy hour, dinner, and the club.

Taylor doesn't mind; in fact, after the first day, she's started relishing the solitary time, and she and Nicholas have plenty to talk about over their evening drinks and dinners. She describes the sights she sees during the day; he describes his nights with Jorge (PG versions, thank God).

Before they know it, they check out of the hotel and head to the port. They say their teary goodbyes and promise to visit soon. Nicholas mumbles about coming to New York, and Taylor promises to make a return to Barcelona within the year; a proposal she's not sure she can keep (real-life adulthood awaits her, after all), but one that sounds wonderful nonetheless. Nicholas heads off to Mykonos; Taylor locates the ferry to Santorini and climbs aboard.

After the ferry ride to Rhodes last year, the journey to Santorini feels relatively painless. Taylor is pleasantly startled, once again, by the colors of the Aegean Sea. Nicholas and Taylor's last night in Athens was fantastic, and she is paying the price today. They barely slept, staying out until 3 a.m., at which point Taylor finally convinced Nicholas to head back. But the fresh sea air proves curative, helping with her hangover and fatigue.

The ferry arrives in Santorini at 5:30 p.m., only thirty minutes behind schedule, which, for Greece, is basically early. Taylor has pre-arranged lodging, thank God; she's not sure she could handle the scramble at the port trying to find a place. It's just a cheap hostel (relatively speaking; Santorini is shockingly expensive compared to the other islands she's visited), but it has private rooms and, more importantly, private bathrooms. Besides, Lindsay promised that she could spend the vast majority of her time on the yacht.

Jesus, Taylor thinks to herself as she disembarks, I'm actually going on a yacht. How did this happen?

Lindsay and her family are due to arrive tomorrow in the late morning, so Taylor has the first night to explore the island a bit by herself. The hostel is within walking distance of the port, so by 6 p.m., Taylor is checked into her tiny room. What it lacks in size and character, it makes up for with the view.

After a shower, Taylor sets out to explore and grab some necessities (wine and cigarettes, specifically). She has a pre-dinner glass of wine in her room and heads out to Oia for dinner and to view the sunset. After doing some quick research on Santorini before her trip, she knows that capturing the sunset from Oia is an obligatory task. Camera in hand, she joins the masses of tourists, all vying for the best pictures. It is just as stunning as the guidebooks made it out to be, and Taylor is thrilled to have captured it on camera. She hopes it looks as good once the film is developed as it does on all the postcards she's seen at the souvenir shops dotting the town.

She wanders the cobblestone streets and decides on dinner at a taverna. The views are nothing special compared to some of the other nearby restaurants, but the prices are far less egregious. Taylor has barely opened her menu when the waiter brings over a glass of red wine. Before she can argue and tell him she didn't order this, he tells her, in heavily accented English, that it is complimentary, from one of the other patrons.

"Um, okay? Who?" Taylor asks, while wondering how everyone knows to speak to her in English. It's as if she's wearing an American flag over her sundress.

"He will introduce himself to you shortly," the waiter tells her.

"Okay, well, please tell him thanks!" Taylor looks around awkwardly toward the bar, where she assumes this mystery man is sitting. But the bar is so crowded, she can't even begin to imagine which of the many men hanging around could have sent this over.

She takes a sip, ignoring the adage about never accepting a drink from a stranger. This may be the best red wine she's ever had; it certainly isn't the crappy house wine she would have ordered if left to her own devices. She savors it and picks up the menu, staring at it but unable to concentrate, trying to figure out who the hell sent her this drink.

She'd told herself that nothing would happen on this trip, in terms of hooking up, but now that seems like an unnecessary and arbitrary rule. Certainly one that could be bent, depending on who sent her the drink.

A few minutes later, the waiter returns, takes her food order, and asks if she's enjoying the wine.

"Yes," she responds. "I was just thinking this may be the best wine I've ever tasted!" she says loudly, a feeling of clumsiness and ineptitude immediately engulfing her. Calm down, she thinks to herself.

The waiter bows his head knowingly and returns to the kitchen. Taylor lights a cigarette and again looks around the busy restaurant. As she stubs the cigarette out in the ashtray, she sees a man stand up at the bar, two glasses of red wine in hand. As he approaches, Taylor puts the pieces together and realizes that this tall, tan, stunningly handsome man is the one who sent her the wine. He looks like a taller version of Jude Law from *The Talented Mr. Ripley*. He walks, no, saunters over, flashing his perfectly white teeth at Taylor on the way.

"May I?" he asks, motioning to the chair across from her.

Taylor is momentarily rendered speechless, so she just nods and smiles. He looks famous, she thinks to herself. Normal people aren't supposed to be so stupidly good-looking. As he sits down, he places one of the wine glasses in front of Taylor, putting the other on his side of the table. He looks at Taylor with piercing blue eyes and says, "I'm Jake. Pleased to meet you."

"Likewise," Taylor responds, her composure now restored, somewhat. "I'm Taylor. I assume I have you to thank for this wine. It's incredible."

"Glad you like it. I saw you when you walked in, and I realized that I really wanted to have some good wine with a gorgeous woman tonight. So here we are." Jake smiles while Taylor takes a sip of her wine, embarrassed by the flattery. He continues, "What brings you to Santorini, Taylor? Are you here all by yourself? That seems impossible."

Cocky and arrogant, Taylor thinks, suddenly annoyed. But she responds with a smile. "Thank you. Being here is my graduation present from my parents. I spent the past few days in Athens with my roommate from my year abroad in Barcelona. Tomorrow my best friend from college arrives here in Santorini, then I'm heading to Ios and Folegandros. Then it's off to begin my time in the real world." God, stop rambling on, she thinks to herself. She smiles, then asks, "And you, Jake? What brings you here?"

Dodging the question, he responds, "Wow, Barcelona! A girl after my own heart. That is, hands down, my favorite place on the planet. Best food and nightlife you can get."

Taylor softens a bit at this. "Mine too. I seriously considered moving there permanently after graduation."

"So where did you go to school? You said this was a graduation trip?"

"UNC. But I'm from Wisconsin originally," Taylor tells him. "And what about you? What are you doing here?" she asks, a hint of flirtation in her voice now, the wine kicking in.

"UNC, very nice. So, you're beautiful and smart," Jake says with a grin. "I'm here with my older brother. Long story, but he's going through a shit divorce and needed to get away for a bit. I'm playing the part of supportive brother, which I'm learning just means watching him get wasted every night and moan about what a bitch his wife is."

"Jesus, sorry. That's rough. Nice of you to be his wingman, though. And where are you from?"

"All over the world. Army brat. But we finally settled in Laguna Beach, California, when I was in seventh grade. I went to USC, and I've been in L.A. the past five years, working in the industry."

He says this with such authority that Taylor begins cursing herself for not knowing what "industry" he's talking about. She puts her dignity aside and flat-out asks him, "And what industry is that? There are a lot of them."

At this, Jake laughs heartily, throwing his head back. He quickly recovers. "Sorry, I'm so used to talking to L.A. people. Forgive me. I mean the film industry."

"Ahhh, okay. Thanks. Forgive my ignorance," Taylor says, taking a sip of her wine. "So, are you an actor or what?"

Again, he laughs. "No, I wish. Just behind the scenes, I'm afraid. I took a film class in high school and fell in love with it. Studied film at USC and went straight to work."

Taylor finds him less and less obnoxious the more he talks; she makes the executive decision that she will definitely allow Jake to kiss her tonight, if that's where things lead.

Fast forward two hours and a few more glasses of wine: Taylor and Jake find themselves stumbling drunkenly along the cobblestone streets of Oia. They've gotten to know one another over dinner, and Taylor genuinely likes him. He's far less obnoxious than he originally appeared. And he was thoroughly impressed with Taylor's upcoming employment at Immersion Travel; he'd actually heard of it and used it to plan some of his outings here on Santorini.

"Come back to my room, will you?" Jake asks, placing his hands on her hips and leaning in to kiss her. They kiss for a moment, and Taylor decides that spending the night in what she imagines will be a posh hotel room will beat her hostel room any day. She squeezes his hands and nods.

"Okay. Let's go." And just like that, her plan of not hooking up with anyone on this trip goes out the window.

Taylor wakes up the next morning in the chic hotel room, expecting to see Jake asleep next to her. She can see the sea from the window, and the room smells like gardenia. They enjoyed a long, pleasurable time in bed last night before falling asleep. No sex, but a lot of kissing and talking. It was a great evening. To her surprise, Jake's side of the bed is empty, but there's a note on the desk.

Taylor, went on an early boat tour with my brother...will be out most of the day. I had a great time last night. If you want to hang out again, my number is 310-555-1294. , Jake

Taylor smiles, pleasantly surprised by the fact that he bothered leaving a note. Her initial impression of Jake lingers a bit, he comes off as pretentious and overly confident, but he's proven himself to be a nice guy, not quite as L.A.-snobby as she originally thought.

She writes a note back: Jake, thanks for the hospitality. I had a great time as well. I'm here in Santorini for a few days; my cell is (608) 555-2649. Feel free to call or text. , Taylor

With that taken care of, Taylor takes a quick shower in the luxurious bathroom, splurging on the decadent bath products that smell like a bouquet of roses, and then heads back to her hostel to prepare for the day. In the cab ride back, she thinks about last night. Jake and his annoyingly handsome self. What a damn good kisser he was. Just as she closes her eyes and remembers the really good parts, her phone rings.

"Hello?"

"Tay! It's Lindsay." Lindsay screams into the phone, so loudly that Taylor has to move it six inches from her head. "Little snafu, we won't be in until like 5 p.m. I'm so sorry."

"Oh no, is everything okay?" Taylor asks, concern in her voice.

"Yes, yes, nothing serious. Something with the engine. We had to make a pit stop at some other random island. But everything is fine. I'll call you later when we're close and let you know where to go, okay?"

"Sounds good. I can't wait to see you!" Taylor can hear the sounds of the sea and wind from Lindsay's side of the call, and she's suddenly overcome with excitement to see her best friend.

"Me too! Okay, see you soon, love." And the phone goes silent.

This is actually better, Taylor thinks to herself, happy to have a little time to do some more exploring of this glorious island.

Taylor spends a few minutes back at the hostel to get beach-ready and grab her camera, then sets off to the Akrotiri Lighthouse. She has heard that this is another spectacular place to catch the sunset, but it's lovely even in the late morning, and there is hardly anyone else there.

After wandering around the lighthouse and snapping some pictures, Taylor heads to Mesa Pigadia Beach. The beach is stunning, rocks and caves, black-pebble sand, and crystal-clear waters. She finds an open sunbed among the rows between a taverna and the sea and rents it for the day. She takes almost an entire roll of film and takes notes on what she's seen in Santorini thus far before succumbing to hunger. Having skipped breakfast, she's ravenous.

Ready for a break from the potent sun, Taylor heads to the shade of the taverna's terraced dining area. She orders a giant bottle of water, an enormous Greek salad, and a glass of white wine. Everything is delicious; Taylor forgot how amazing authentic Greek food is, and she savors her lunch and wine while people-watching. The majority of visitors appear to be honeymooners or families; the honeymooners look elated and wonderstruck, while the families range from glamorous French couples with young kids to stressed-out American families. Taylor laughs to herself and wonders how Europeans manage to be so chic in everything they do.

She spends the rest of the afternoon alternating between swimming and reading. By 4 o'clock, she decides to call it a day and get back to the hostel. Lindsay's family is big into cocktail hour, which, Taylor has learned, for them can really be any hour of the day. So she needs to be dressed and ready within an hour if she's going to be able to imbibe with the best of them.

By 5:30 p.m., Taylor is in a cab heading back to Oia, where Lindsay's family and their yacht will be for the night. *Is parking the right word?* Taylor wonders idly. Probably anchoring, though she has no idea and suspects she'll never really need to know the answer. She's excited to see Lindsay but also a little nervous about spending the night with her family. They're not dissimilar to Eric's in-laws, East Coast elite. Though the way Lindsay acts, with her wild ways, you would never guess she comes from such a pedigreed family.

Taylor walks down to the harbor and spots Lindsay from afar, looking chic in a flowing sundress and drinking some fancy-looking pink cocktail on the deck of the boat. Her cocktail, not surprisingly, matches her dress perfectly, and Taylor can't help but laugh. Only

Lindsay. She smiles and picks up her pace just as Lindsay sees her and waves frantically, spilling some of her drink on her dress. Taylor laughs again and is assisted aboard the boat by two beautiful, tanned men. Members of the crew, she supposes, they look like they came straight from Norway with their blond hair and sturdy physiques. *This is so cliché,* she thinks, and at once she is enveloped in a hug from Lindsay, who seems to have gotten even thinner somehow, her parents hovering in the background.

"Taylor, welcome aboard!" Lindsay's mom says, kissing Taylor on each cheek. Her husband echoes the sentiment, and within thirty seconds of climbing aboard, Taylor is holding a cocktail.

"Thank you! I remember, you guys do cocktail hour right," Taylor says with a laugh. "It's great to see you all again."

Before anyone can respond, Lindsay grabs Taylor by the elbow. "Let me show you around!" And they're off, Lindsay giving Taylor the detailed tour. The boat is immaculate; the chef (a chef!) has set up a spread of appetizers on the deck.

"Okay, so... I *have* to tell you something. I wanted to wait until we were together." Before Taylor can say anything, Lindsay continues. "I saw Daniel in the city, like, the night before I flew over here."

"Daniel? My Daniel?" Taylor asks, shocked. She will soon learn that the world of twenty-somethings in Manhattan is surprisingly small and incestuous.

Lindsay laughs. "Yes, your Daniel. I saw him at Bar None, some shitty NYU bar. I don't even know how or why I ended up there. Anyway, we recognized each other and started talking. It took like ten seconds before he was gushing about you, all 'Isn't Taylor just the most amazing person,' blah, blah, blah. Taylor, he is totally in love with you!"

Taylor smiles and takes a second to process this. "What else did he say?" she asks, intrigued. She shakes her head and sighs. "Wait, there's no way he's in love with me now. I was so awful to him; I will never get over the guilt! He can't possibly ever forgive me. We're solidly in the 'friends' category."

"Trust me, you're forgiven. Taylor, he is perfect for you. Seriously. I believe I told you once, and I'll say it again, you guys were born for each other." Lindsay bats her eyelashes seductively at Taylor, and they both laugh. "But seriously. Don't even try to tell me you no longer have feelings for him. I saw the sparks at that frat party freshman year. That was the real deal. Plus," Lindsay continues, "he was talking to some girl when I got there, they were standing pretty close together at the bar, actually, but when we made eye contact, he practically ran over to me and immediately started talking about you. Mystery girl was barely an afterthought."

Taylor feels a pang of jealousy at the idea of Daniel chatting up random girls at a bar but quickly pushes the thought out of her mind. "Ugh, I don't even know what to say. I thought we'd decided to just be friends. Maybe I misread everything. I was so overwhelmed after breaking up with Manuel, and that disaster in Paris with that guy, Claude," Taylor wails. "Daniel and I have hung out like a million times; how has he not made a move if that's how he feels? And I was such a bitch to him, like, more than once."

"I have no idea, but if I were you, I'd call that gorgeous boy the second your plane touches the ground in New York. Anyway, come on, let's get another drink, then my parents will take us to dinner, and we can go out afterward, okay?"

"Perfect," Taylor says, sucking down the dregs of her cocktail. But her mind remains fixated on Daniel for the rest of the evening. She manages to ooh and aah over the sunset and pay attention during dinner, answering Lindsay's parents' questions about her year abroad, her travel writing, and where she'll be living and working in Manhattan. Her brain, though, keeps circling back to Daniel, and she feels an overwhelming urge to talk to him.

But, as usual, alcohol proves miraculous in its ability to make one forget, and by the end of the night, Taylor and Lindsay are dancing together at a club, sharing drinks and cigarettes, living in the moment.

She sees a call come in from an unknown U.S. number and assumes it's Jake. While she would love to spend another night with him, this new information about Daniel makes her think twice before answering. She ignores the call, deciding to avoid unnecessary drama and complications tonight and choosing instead to enjoy this time with Lindsay.

The remaining two days in Santorini are similar; Lindsay's parents spoil Taylor rotten, and by the time she's checking out of the hostel (where she spent only one night, surrendering instead to the comfort of the yacht), she is full of food, drink, and memories. The goodbye to Lindsay is relatively easy, given that they'll be seeing each other again in just a few weeks in New York.

Lindsay landed a job (through nepotism, but whatever) doing merchandising for Ralph Lauren. The pay sucks, and it has nothing to do with her psych degree, but she'll be well dressed thanks to the generous employee discount, and she doesn't really need the money anyway. Taylor is just happy to have her as a partner in crime as they begin their adult lives in Manhattan.

To her surprise, Taylor does end up seeing Jake again. He calls her two days after their night together, and he and his brother meet Taylor and Lindsay for drinks at a bar that night. There is chemistry between them for sure, but ever since Lindsay told Taylor about her conversation with Daniel, Taylor's brain has become too muddled for romance, even one that, by definition, would be fleeting. Jake promises to get in touch the next time he's in New York and makes Taylor promise she'll make it to Los Angeles one day so he can show her around. She agrees, confident in the knowledge that she will never see him again. But that's okay, she is twenty-two years old, after all, and these random hookups are a rite of passage. Besides, they only kissed. No sense dwelling on what *could have been.*

After living it up in Santorini, Taylor expects Ios to be a welcome respite of calm and serenity. She originally considered booking a hotel near the nightlife of Chora, but at the last minute changed her mind and opted for a calmer vibe right on Mylopotas Beach. The Ios Palace Hotel... it's more expensive than she would have liked, but her parents insisted she treat herself. It was a line of reasoning she couldn't argue with, so here she is, in actual paradise. She can see the beach from her room; there are multiple pools, and Chora is only a twenty-minute walk away, so if she finds herself craving nightlife, it will be easy to find.

When she arrives at the hotel, she is exhausted and sweaty from yet another ferry ride, so she dumps her things in the chic, minimalist room and heads straight out to the pool, which happens to have a gorgeous view of the beach. Sun loungers and umbrellas line the pool deck, and the waves from the sea are audible all the way up here. There are only a handful of people, the crowds have thinned now that it's already six in the evening. Taylor is also a few weeks ahead of the busiest time of year, so the hotel, while busy, isn't nearly as packed as it will be in July and August.

Without even testing the water, Taylor dives right in, her white bikini accentuating her tan skin, perfectly bronzed from the past few days on Santorini. The water is cool and refreshing, and after swimming for a few minutes, she decides that now is as good a time as any for a cocktail. The bartender at the pool bar, young and bored, is overly eager to serve her and chat. She indulges him, having a drink and a handful of cigarettes over the next hour.

His name is Achilles, which Taylor can barely believe, how genuinely Greek is that? He knows all the hot spots on the island, so Taylor turns their casual chat into an informal interview, which will later be written up and published.

Achilles nonchalantly invites her out with him and his buddies that evening; his shift ends at 9 p.m., and they're hitting up the best club on the island, apparently. Taylor politely declines, claiming utter exhaustion, which isn't much of a stretch, as she's truly planning on having dinner at the hotel and being in bed well before midnight. Unfazed, Achilles gives her another drink on the house "for your room," and she heads upstairs, buzzed and happy.

True to her word, she has a pleasant, peaceful dinner at the hotel restaurant poolside, overlooking the beach, and is cozy in bed by 11 p.m.

After exploring the island the following day, Taylor finds herself back at the pool in the late afternoon. She has visited the four whitewashed churches on the hillside near Chora, which involved a rather strenuous hike, so she rewarded herself by returning to Mylopotas Beach, where she swam in the sea and had a long, delicious Greek lunch at one of the trendy restaurants dotting the beach, where chilled-out house music seems to pump from the speakers twenty-four hours a day.

Now back at the hotel, as the sun begins its descent for the evening, Taylor is secretly pleased to see Achilles again serving drinks behind the bar. She spends some time reading and swimming before approaching the bar.

Clad once again in her white bikini, Achilles watches her as she walks toward him, focusing on keeping his jaw from dropping. He can make out her nipples through the thin fabric and can barely contain himself. Taylor, meanwhile, avoids making eye contact, focusing instead on not tripping as she approaches.

"Good evening, mademoiselle," Achilles says while resuming his lime cutting, a task he is using as a diversion to prevent him from staring directly at Taylor's breasts.

"Good evening. How was your night out last night?" Taylor asks with a smile.

"Oh, it was fine, nothing too special. We plan on going out again tonight, if you're interested." As he says this, he pours Taylor a glass of champagne. "On the house," he tells her with a mischievous smile.

Taylor settles herself on a barstool and thanks him. She sips the cold champagne, which is delicious, and lights a cigarette. As she exhales smoke, she responds, "I have no plans tonight. And I'm well rested after an early night last night. So, sure, if you don't mind me coming along, I'd love to."

Achilles smiles, a wide smile revealing unusually white and adorably crooked teeth, and plans are made. He will drive her to Chora on his moped. They can have dinner there and meet his friends at the club afterward. As they make arrangements, it occurs to Taylor that she has no idea how old he is.

"Achilles," she asks, drinking the remnants of her champagne, "how old are you, anyway?"

"I am twenty-five. Why?"

"I was just wondering. I'm twenty-two, in case you wanted to know."

"Taylor, you could be eighteen or thirty or even forty and that would be fine for me," he says, straight-faced, as Taylor bursts into laughter.

"Well, I'm glad we have that worked out," Taylor says, as Achilles points toward the sky.

"Look, the sun is beginning to set. No matter how many times I see this view, it is always like the first time."

Taylor concurs and takes a few pictures for good measure. Achilles refills her champagne, and she excuses herself to her room to get ready for tonight. She agrees to meet him in front of the hotel at 9:05 p.m. Somehow, it's already 8:30, time is certainly flying here, so she has only about thirty minutes to shower and make herself presentable.

At 9:07 p.m., Taylor arrives out front, breathless. She decided on a short, tight red dress and heels, her hair still damp from the shower. It is far too hot for a blow-dryer, so she's hoping the ride doesn't completely butcher her wet hair. Achilles is already on the moped, and he smiles as she walks toward him, taking in every inch of her body. He hands her a helmet and goes over basic safety information as she struggles to put it on. Once Achilles has confirmed that her helmet is on properly, she sits down behind him and grips him tightly.

"I really wore the wrong outfit," Taylor mutters to herself as she awkwardly straddles Achilles, feeling as though the entire world is getting a free view of her underwear. The next ten minutes may be the most petrifying of Taylor's life thus far; the hills and winding roads they drive on are, in a word, terrifying. At one point, she grips Achilles so tightly she worries she will suffocate him.

Somehow, they arrive in Chora unscathed, and as they get off the moped, Achilles has a look of amusement on his face.

Taylor, shaking, adjusts her dress so it once again covers her ass and tells him, "That was my first time on a moped. How did you do that?"

Achilles throws his head back, laughing. "I was wondering why you were gripping me so tightly. That ride was nothing! I ride all over the island on this."

"Well, I'm hoping to never do that again. That was fucking scary."

Achilles smiles and takes her hand, leading her to the most crowded restaurant in Chora. He greets the hostess with kisses on each cheek, and they chat in Greek for a moment while Taylor takes in the scene. There are plenty of tourists here, but also a decent number of locals, which is usually a sign that the food will be good. Achilles seems to know the entire restaurant staff, and within a minute of sitting down, they have cocktails in front of them, courtesy of the bartender, who gives Achilles a friendly wave.

Taylor takes a sip and asks, "So, do you know everyone on this island? Or just everyone in this restaurant?"

"We are a small community," he responds. "Most people know one another here in Chora. The hostess, we went to school together, and our parents are friends. The bartender is one of my best friends; he will be joining us later tonight once he has finished here."

Taylor and Achilles fall into an easy conversation after they order their food. The drinks are delicious and mask any awkwardness Taylor would normally feel while dining with a practical stranger, and she finds herself enjoying the night even more than she expected. Achilles is a smooth talker, but also kind and funny, and he seems genuinely interested in getting to know her, even though she will only be on the island for several more days.

A little after 11 p.m., Achilles pays the bill, and they step back out onto the crowded street. Taylor, a little tipsy from the drinks at dinner, allows him to hold her hand as they walk. A block before they reach the club, he slows down and leads Taylor to a small square with a fountain and some benches overlooking one of the churches she visited earlier in the day. It's even more beautiful at night. Silently, they sit down on one of the benches and he kisses her. Taylor is at once surprised and disappointed when he stops after a few minutes; he is a fantastic kisser.

"We should go," he says, but doesn't get up. Instead, he lights two cigarettes and hands one to Taylor.

"Thanks. Are your friends waiting for you?" she asks him.

"Probably. They were planning to arrive a few minutes ago. Let's smoke these and then go, okay? Plenty of time for more of that later," he says with a sly smile.

Taylor smiles back but feels apprehensive all of a sudden. Does she really need to hook up with another random guy tonight? Someone she will, in all likelihood, never see again? She finishes her cigarette in silence and starts to feel a sense of dread at going to a club, meeting new people, and the effort of it all. What's the point? she wonders. *I can just claim exhaustion or a headache and go back to the hotel.*

However, her manners win out, and she guilts herself into joining Achilles at the club. He bought her dinner, after all, and drove her here on his moped; the least she can do is put in an appearance and meet some of his friends. He is also incredibly easy on the eyes and super easy to talk to, which helps boost her enthusiasm. With a new resolve, she takes his hand, and they resume walking.

It turns out the "club" is really just a loud, smoky bar. Taylor was envisioning house music, people dancing on stages, the works. This place is more like an English pub, which Taylor is secretly relieved by; she doesn't have the stamina for dancing all night. She and Achilles settle onto barstools among Achilles' friends. Introductions are made, drinks are ordered, all the while The Cure's (of all the bands in the world to be playing at a dive bar in Ios!) "Friday I'm in Love" blasts from the speakers.

Several rounds later, Taylor decides she is actually having a good time. His friends are funny, albeit in a loud, drunken way, but she's been laughing all night. She gets up to use the bathroom, and when she comes out, Achilles is waiting for her.

"Are you doing okay?" he asks.

"Yes, I'm having a great time, thanks. Your friends are great! You okay?" Taylor asks.

"I'm fine, but I'm here with my friends in my town. I just want to make sure you are feeling comfortable." Taylor smiles and kisses him.

"I'm very comfortable."

Taken aback by the kiss, Achilles smiles. "Should we go back to my apartment?" he asks with no hesitation. "It's not far, we can walk from here. And I can drive you back to the hotel in the morning."

Despite her better judgment and her earlier reservations, Taylor agrees that this is an excellent idea, so they pay the bill, bid adieu to his friends, and wander back to Achilles' apartment.

The next morning, Taylor wakes to the sound of cooking. The sun is pouring through the windows, and the specifics from last night slowly unfold in her mind. She buries her head in the pillow, remembering the vivid, intimate details. She bolts upright when she recalls that they didn't bother with a condom.

"Fuck, fuck, fuck," she mumbles. She tiptoes to the bathroom without being noticed and uses some of the mouthwash Achilles has on the sink. Looking in the mirror, she takes a deep breath, washes her hands, and does her best to remain calm.

"Good morning," Achilles booms as she emerges. He's holding two plates piled high with eggs, and there are two mugs of steaming coffee on the table. "I hope you slept well," he says, putting the plates down and pulling out her chair, motioning for her to sit.

Taylor forces a smile. "I did. Bit of a blur, last night."

"Yeah, I think we were overserved, as they say," Achilles says with a laugh. "In any case, this should help." Achilles motions toward the food. "I hope you like eggs."

"I do, thank you. And this coffee smells amazing." Taylor takes a sip of the steaming coffee, has a few bites of eggs, and feels a little better. She decides not to broach the condom situation, although her mind is reeling over it. She has the pregnancy thing to worry about, along with having no idea if Achilles has any STDs. He seems like a good enough guy, but he works in tourism, in the Greek Isles, no less, and was able to get Taylor into bed without much effort. Who knows how many other women he's bedded?

As if reading her mind, he sets his fork down and looks Taylor in the eyes. "Listen, I'm sorry about not having a condom last night. That was stupid. I'm safe, though. I had the tests done recently, and everything is okay."

"Me too," Taylor says, relieved. "But I'm not on the pill at the moment, which is the other issue."

Achilles says something in Greek, which Taylor can only assume is whatever word corresponds to *fuck* in English. He looks at the ceiling and then back at her.

"There's a pharmacy nearby. We can go there, ask if they have that pill?"

"You mean the morning-after pill? Will they have that here?" Taylor asks, skeptical.

"I think so." Achilles gets up quickly and fires off a text message to a friend. A few seconds later, his phone dings. He translates the message to Taylor. "The pharmacy here in town should have it. My friend's girlfriend got it there about a month ago. As soon as you finish breakfast, I can take you there."

Taylor eats the rest of her eggs, brings the plate to the sink and cleans it, then downs what remains of her coffee. "Let's go now, if that's okay with you?"

"Sure. They should be open."

They walk quickly down the cobblestone streets, which, while still quaint and beautiful, are less magical now than they were last night, when everything was fueled by alcohol and the potential for romance. Reality has set in, along with a mild level of panic for both Taylor and Achilles. Plus, Taylor feels utterly ridiculous in her short dress and heels at this hour; anyone with eyes would recognize that she's doing the dreaded walk of shame.

Taylor spots the flashing green pharmacy sign from nearly a block away. Their pace quickens, and they enter the store, flushed and out of breath. Achilles speaks in Greek to the pharmacy tech, and she gives Taylor a sympathetic look. Taylor's cheeks burn at the notion of a complete stranger knowing such intimate details about her. The tech walks behind the counter, and Achilles smiles. "They have it," he whispers to her. Relief washes over Taylor, and she feels some emotional combination of love and great appreciation for both Achilles and this woman working in the pharmacy.

Taylor hands over her credit card to pay, her hands still shaking with nerves, and the woman gives her the instructions in accented English. She may feel sick for a few days, she may have spotting, the rest is a blur. She thanks the woman profusely and wastes no time taking the first pill right on the sidewalk outside the pharmacy.

"Well, that is a relief," Achilles says with a smile.

"You're telling me. Thank you so much for helping me. I was really freaking out."

"Of course." He puts his arm around Taylor's shoulders. "I'm glad it worked out." He checks his watch and does a double take. "Listen, I have to be at the hotel in, like, oh shit, twenty minutes. I'm working an extra shift, covering for a friend today. Can we head back there now?"

And just like that, they're back on the moped. Achilles careens through the hilly landscape while Taylor grips him tightly and once again fears for her life. No more funny business, she thinks to herself. She makes a vow, again, not to hook up with anyone for the rest of the trip. For real this time. And while she's making promises to herself: no more moped rides.

Achilles walks Taylor to her room before heading to the bar for his shift. Taylor promises to stop by later for a sunset cocktail, and he kisses her lightly on both cheeks. Between the panic, the lingering hangover, and the overall sensation of feeling somewhat unhinged, Taylor feels exhaustion creep over her.

She decides today will be a day for relaxing and reading on Mylopotas Beach, just steps from her hotel. She hits the beach at 1 p.m., falls asleep on the sunbed almost instantly, and wakes at 3 p.m., just in time to eat a late lunch at one of the tavernas along the beach. She sits in the shade, attempting to read while waiting for the food, but finds herself unable to focus. She's replaying the events of last night over and over in her head, silently chastising herself for being so irresponsible. She shudders and tries to convince herself that everything will be fine. It has to be, she thinks.

After lunch, she swims in the sea and reads for a while before heading back to the hotel. By now, it's 7 in the evening, so she goes directly to the bar to say hi to Achilles and have a final sunset drink in Ios. She leaves for Folegandros in the morning, so she will have to say her goodbyes tonight.

Achilles watches Taylor as she drops her towel and beach bag on one of the empty lounge chairs before walking over to the bar. He has already begun making her one of the day's specialty cocktails, a concoction of rum and pineapple juice, as she sits down on a barstool.

"Hello there," she says as he slides the drink toward her with a smile.

"Hello, beautiful. How has your day been?" Achilles asks her.

"It was nice, thank you. Relaxing. I just went to the beach. What is this?" Taylor asks, motioning to the drink, trying to act casual, as though this man wasn't actually inside of her less than twenty-four hours ago.

"Rum, pineapple juice, and some other ingredients we like to play around with in the cocktails. It's delicious, and I didn't make yours too strong. You know, because of last night."

Taylor smiles and takes a sip. "Mmmm, that is incredibly good! Thank you, Achilles. For everything today, really."

"My pleasure. I'm glad things worked out. It's too bad you are leaving tomorrow; I've had a nice time with you."

"Same. A really nice time." Taylor is surprised to feel a pang of sadness at leaving Ios and this charming, kind man. At the very least, he managed to keep her mind off Daniel for a few days, which is quite a feat these days. "Thanks for showing me around. You have an incredible little island here."

"Yes, thank you. What are you doing tonight? I should be done here a little after 9 p.m."

"I'm taking it very easy tonight. I have an early ferry tomorrow, and to be honest, I'm still tired from last night."

Achilles nods and smiles. He lights a cigarette and hands it to Taylor, then lights one for himself. They sit in a comfortable silence until Achilles has to serve another guest. Taylor stays for the sunset, then says goodbye to Achilles and heads up to her room. It's a bittersweet goodbye, they have only known each other for forty-eight hours, yet they have been through a lot in that short time. They exchange email addresses and make vague plans to keep in touch, which Taylor knows is unlikely.

Upon returning to her room, Taylor takes a long, cool shower, puts on a little makeup, gets dressed, and heads down to the hotel restaurant again for a low-key dinner. She just wants to have a nice meal on the terrace, have a drink, and crawl into bed. And that's exactly what she does. When her alarm goes off at the crack of dawn the next morning, she actually feels rested again and ready for her next adventure.

She packs up, checks out of the hotel, and takes the hotel shuttle with a handful of other tourists to the port to catch the ferry to Folegandros, her third and final stop on this tour of the Southern Cyclades.

The ferry ride is short, less than ninety minutes, which will give Taylor three full days on this tiny, sleepy island. This is the island Taylor is most excited about; there is very little written about it, so she has the potential to make a real impact with her writing. In stark contrast to Santorini and Ios, which are much more popular and well covered by the travel industry, particularly the former. She wants to really wow her bosses at Immersion Travel, and she thinks doing a banger on Folegandros will be a good start.

Taylor has a big first day planned out on Folegandros. She gets off the ferry and takes an ancient-looking bus the short distance from the port to her family-run hotel, Polikandia Hotel, which is in the heart of Chora, the old town. She drops her luggage with the hotel's proprietor, as it's too early to check in, and then heads back to the port for a six-hour boat tour that promises to visit some of the most beautiful beaches on the island, most of which are only accessible by boat.

As she walks out of the hotel, the magnificence of this island hits her. Every building and every street looks like a postcard. Donkeys wander in the fields, the sunlight seems to reflect off the whitewashed buildings, and tiny chapels dot the countryside. It is the most authentically Greek-looking place Taylor has ever seen, and she absolutely loves it.

Taylor's camera is loaded with a new roll of film, and she has her journal and pen in tow, fully prepared to document Folegandros's hidden treasures. With just five minutes to spare, she boards the boat at 11:55 a.m., along with the other passengers, mainly British and French, she thinks, based on their accents and the languages being spoken.

After a brief safety tutorial, they set sail. Stopping in tiny, hidden bays, visiting caves, and diving into turquoise waters at beaches that are impossible to reach unless by boat, Taylor uses an entire roll of film before the halfway point of the tour. She has pages of notes filled with details and the minutiae people will want to know when reading about this magical place.

Her favorite stop along the tour is Katergos Beach, set between high cliffs forming dramatic drops down into the sea. There are no accommodations on this beach, so aside from a handful of nude sunbathers, they have the place to themselves. As Taylor explores the clear waters and giant rock formations, she strikes up a conversation with a couple from the tour who appear to be in a similar state of awe that such magnificence exists on earth.

Once it's time to leave Katergos Beach and get back onboard the boat, the crew serves up a delicious gourmet lunch, chock-full of fresh seafood, fruit, and Greek cheeses, and all of the passengers, eighteen in total, decide on popping some bottles of champagne to give this experience a real sense of occasion.

It's an eclectic group, to be sure: three sullen teenagers, clearly hungover from a late night out, who appear to have been dragged aboard by their parents; a few twenty-something tourists; and some older people whose ages Taylor can't quite gauge. Despite the diversity and a few language barriers, they've formed a rare camaraderie, and Taylor finds herself making plans for the night with the thirty-something couple she chatted with on the beach. Before long, it's decided that the entire group will meet for dinner tonight at 9 p.m. at a lively restaurant in Chora. The teenagers roll their eyes, but their parents insist they join, at least for appetizers, before they hit the bars in the village.

When the boat finally docks just after 6 that evening, Taylor feels a sense of peace, along with an appreciation for her newfound travel companions, and is more than a little grateful that she has built-in dinner plans. She bids her boat group farewell for now and immediately heads to the hotel to check in and start writing. After ninety minutes of clacking away on her laptop, she has fully documented her time on the island thus far and has the photos to back it up. She takes a deep breath, hits save, and runs to the hotel pool for a quick dip before dinner.

After a three-hour dinner, Taylor exchanges email addresses and mobile numbers with a handful of her new friends from the boat tour. She falls asleep as soon as her head hits the pillow, her worries surrounding the unprotected sex with Achilles just a few days earlier now a distant memory.

Over the next two days, Taylor takes in as much of the old-world charm Folegandros has to offer as possible. She visits Kastro, the medieval-era district within Chora, the main village on the island, reveling in its aged, magical atmosphere. When the midday heat becomes more than she can bear, she finds an ancient-looking tree in one of Chora's squares and rests in the shade.

As she watches people move lazily around the square, Taylor loses herself in thought, already beginning to envision how she will describe this peaceful, beautiful island for her Immersion Travel article. Her train of thought is interrupted as a stray cat saunters by, giving Taylor a look that implies, "Hey lady, this is my turf," as it lets out a disgruntled meow. Taylor laughs to herself and makes her way back to her hotel to have lunch and relax by the pool.

In the chaos of yesterday's boat tour, she didn't have time to appreciate the simple beauty of the hotel. The pool area and her room's terrace are filled with pink bougainvillea, and aside from the occasional waft of cigarette smoke, the smell reminds her of paradise.

After a brief swim in the hotel pool, Taylor has enough energy to make the trek up to the Panagia church, arguably the most famous landmark in all of Folegandros. The walk up is brutal: incredibly steep, and she finds herself stopping to catch her breath more than once. However, the discomfort is well worth it. She has a few minutes to poke around the church and snap pictures of the view, she can see a number of other islands from this altitude, before the other tourists start to ooh and aah as the sunset nears. Taylor watches in awe as the sun makes its descent, and once it's over, she can definitively say that it is the most magnificent sunset she's ever seen.

Taylor returns to Chora in the evening for dinner and is delighted to meet a fellow solo female traveler as she's poking around a souvenir shop. Margo from Maine is how she introduces herself, and she and Taylor hit it off immediately, deciding to spend the following day together after sharing a wonderful Greek feast in Pounta Square. It turns out Margo is taking a much-needed respite after her first year of medical school and a brutal breakup with her boyfriend of three years. After plates of tzatziki and fried calamari and a few too many shots of ouzo, the two young women swap relationship horror stories, and after just a few hours together they feel like they've been friends for years. As they woozily bid one another farewell for the night, they agree to meet at the bus stop tomorrow at 11 a.m. to catch the bus to Agali Beach.

When Taylor wakes up the following morning, she feels like total hell from all of the ouzo. If it weren't for her plans to meet Margo, she would consider staying in bed and making today a pool-and-nap day. But she can't help but feel how serendipitous it was to meet someone so fun and wonderful here on this tiny, unknown Greek island, so she pulls herself together, grabs breakfast and coffee from the hotel, and trudges over to the bus stop. She is happy to see Margo sitting on a bench, trying to decipher a map. The same ancient bus that Taylor took to and from the port a few days earlier huffs and puffs its way up and down the hills of the island, depositing them at Agali Beach after a twenty-minute ride.

After an hour in the sun at Agali, Taylor and Margo make their way over to Agios Nikolas Beach, which is no easy feat. The hike up a steep cliff is not for the fainthearted, but once they see the beach it is obvious why people torture themselves to get here. The water is crystal clear, and there are trees providing a bit of much-needed shade. Taylor swims out to the rugged rock formations and wonders, not for the first time, how she got so lucky to be here. And yet, while she's enjoying Margo's company, she can't help but wish it was Daniel waiting for her back at the beach. Daniel, with all of their shared history and messiness. She sighs and swims back to shore, feeling refreshed and, most importantly, no longer hungover. Not surprisingly, a dip in the Aegean Sea has proven to be miraculously curative.

Once back on land, Taylor and Margo agree to head up to Papalagi Seafood, an island institution since 1992 with stunning views of the beach and sea.

They linger over lunch for two hours, both needing some time out of the sun. Margo regales Taylor with stories about her ex-boyfriend's crazy behavior, while Taylor dives into the Manuel–Daniel drama from the previous year.

"Yikes," Margo says once Taylor gives her the entire story. She takes a sip of her assyrtiko and continues, "It sounds like you had quite the conundrum last year. But from everything you've told me thus far, it sounds like you have Daniel waiting for you back in New York, if you want him."

Taylor considers this, staring out at the sea and wondering if this is true. "I don't know. I was so fucked up to him. I basically broke his heart, and I'm not sure he would ever trust me again. Plus, we've somehow, after all of this, managed to forge a really good friendship, so I'm wary of screwing that up too."

"Maybe," Margo says. "But from my experience, men forgive more easily than women. Think about it, he may need time, but I wouldn't run away from this one."

"You're right. Thanks for listening to me drone on. How is it that I already have to leave tomorrow and we just crossed paths?" Taylor wails. "I've had the best time with you in the past, I don't know, sixteen hours."

"Me too, Taylor. But we'll exchange info and be in touch. You absolutely must keep me informed of your love life, and if you ever find yourself on assignment for work up in Maine, you'll know where to find me."

With that, Margo signals for the check, and once they split the bill, they wander back down to Agios Nikolas Beach for a few final hours of Folegandros sun.

Taylor and Margo say their goodbyes at the bus stop back in Chora. Taylor has decided to run back to her hotel and write, and Margo needs a nap before meeting a local guy she met earlier in the week for drinks later. They exchange phone numbers and email addresses and go their separate ways.

Well, that was certainly fun, Taylor thinks to herself as she plops down with her laptop at her outdoor table back at the hotel. She has made a deal with herself: get an hour of writing done before heading out for her final dinner on this sensational island. After writing three pages about the past two days, on top of the six pages she'd already written from the boat tour, Taylor closes her laptop and enjoys a glass of white wine while she gets dressed for dinner and does her makeup.

With no actual destination in mind, she wanders into the main squares of Chora to find somewhere to eat. But first, she stops at the only internet café on the island (fortunately just steps from her hotel) and sends her write-ups to her editor. She knows what she sent is good and secretly hopes that her visit to this tiny Greek island may be a catalyst of sorts for her career.

Taylor spends her final evening here getting drunk as a reward for being so productive. She stays within walking distance of the hotel so she can stagger back without issue. She treats herself to grilled octopus and Greek salad and enjoys more wine than is really necessary. As she falls asleep that night, she feels both a sense of trepidation and a strange feeling of hope regarding the beginning of her adult life, which, technically, will begin in just a few weeks when she reports to the Immersion Travel office for the first time.

More than anything, however, she realizes how nice it was to have just a few days to herself here in Folegandros: no men, no drama, just exploring a new place, enjoying her own company, and writing. It has been a remarkable trip, one of a lifetime.

Chapter 22

July 2005 to February 2006, New York

Taylor arrives in Manhattan feeling refreshed and ready to throw herself into work, save for the minor anxiety she's experiencing about starting her real adult job and life. Although she's already done plenty of writing for Immersion Travel over the past few years, the idea of spending days in an office with actual coworkers and grown-ups is somewhat alarming. And the fact that she's on her own, without parental funds, for the first time ever. She reminds herself that everyone has a "first day at the office," and that she's lucky to have snagged a job doing what she loves.

She spends the two humid, stifling weeks in July before she officially reports for duty shopping, putting some personal touches on the apartment, and going out. A lot of going out. She meets Daniel for happy hour one night, Lindsay for dinner and drinks multiple times, and the Saturday before she starts work, Taylor meets her brother Eric and his wife, Lauren, for dinner. They meet at Asia de Cuba, a trendy Asian fusion restaurant on Madison Avenue in the Thirties.

Taylor takes the subway to Grand Central and walks the remaining handful of blocks to the restaurant, enjoying a cigarette as she goes.

She stubs it out, reapplies her lipstick, and walks in at 8:03 p.m., only three minutes late. Lauren and Eric are already seated, the snooty hostess informs her, while giving her the typical judgmental up-and-down look; a greeting that Taylor has quickly become accustomed to. "The Manhattan once-over," she calls it.

Taylor stifles an eye roll and tells the hostess she'll seat herself; she sees Lauren waving frantically and already getting up from the table.

"Taylor, oh my god, it's so great to see you! How was Greece? Did you love it? You look amazing, so tan and healthy," Lauren gushes, hugging Taylor so tightly she can barely breathe. Eric, less enthusiastically, stands and gives Taylor a hug once Lauren has finished.

"Hey, little sis. What's shaking?"

"It's so great to see you both," Taylor says as they all sit down. Before she can tell them anything, the waiter delivers two cosmos "for the ladies" and a whiskey for Eric. They clink glasses and start catching up, Taylor indulging them with her travel stories (the PG version, of course), while they tell her about life in Greenwich and their plans to start trying for a baby soon.

"A baby?! Christ, that means I'll get to be an aunt," Taylor exclaims. "I'll be the coolest aunt ever; I'll spoil the shit out of that child. Good for you two. That is so exciting."

And maybe it's the cosmo on an empty stomach, or maybe she just needs someone to listen, but before she realizes what she's saying, she finds herself spilling the non-PG details about Achilles in Ios and her morning-after pill situation. And then, as if that weren't bad enough, she blabs about Jake in Santorini. Eric, clearly uncomfortable hearing about his younger sister's sexual adventures, excuses himself to the bathroom. Lauren looks at Taylor with a mixture of disappointment and something else that Taylor can't quite identify—disgust, perhaps?

"Taylor," Lauren says firmly. "I don't want to speak out of line here, but you really need to be more careful. You can't just go out and have sex or hook up with every guy you take a liking to."

"And why is that?" Taylor snaps back, having never been judged (to her face, at least) about her sex life. "As a woman, it's I don't know; promiscuous. But if I were a guy, you wouldn't think twice about it. How is that fair?"

"But you're not a guy! And life isn't fair, especially for women!" Lauren snaps back.

Taylor's jaw drops a little, and she forces herself to remain calm. Before she can speak, Lauren softens.

"Listen, I'm not judging you. I'm glad you're having fun. I just want you to be careful, that's all. I apologize if this all came out wrong, but the reality is that society judges women very differently than men. In particular, young, gorgeous women like you. I'm not saying it's fair or that I agree, but that's how people think, even in this day and age." Lauren puts her hand over Taylor's. "I don't want to argue with you. I'm sorry."

"It's fine," Taylor says with a sigh. "You're not wrong; it's just really fucked up. Like, if we were two dudes sitting here, you'd be buying me drinks and congratulating me right now. Do you know what I mean?" Taylor sees Eric approaching wearily back to the table. "Lauren, it's fine. Let's just forget about it, okay?"

"Okay. I get it, you want equality. I agree with you, but unfortunately not everyone is quite so, I don't know, evolved or progressive. I'm just looking out for you, okay?" Taylor nods and squeezes Lauren's hand from across the table.

"Thanks, Lauren. Sorry if I was overly defensive; it's just frustrating. On a separate note, are you ready for another round?" Taylor asks, chastising herself for thinking this conversation could have possibly had any other outcome.

After that uncomfortable discussion, the rest of the evening is somehow saved and goes smoothly. They have a great meal and then head out to a nearby bar after dinner for karaoke, and make it back to the apartment around 1 a.m. Lauren and Eric are spending the night, so Taylor agrees to sleep on the couch.

But despite the fact that the evening was salvaged, Lauren's comments stick with Taylor for a long time. She hates that she cares so much; after all, as she insinuated to Lauren, if she were a guy this would be a very different situation, but she also finds herself worrying about being labeled a slut, or an easy lay, or whatever derogatory slur men use to describe women with uninhibited sexuality. As such, she makes a decision: no more one-night stands for a bit. She will focus on work, her friendships, and exploring Manhattan when she has the time. Her resolve, shockingly, holds firm for a good five months.

As Taylor had hoped, her writing about Folegandros is highly appreciated at work, and it leads to many more assignments: some exotic locations (Bali and Prague), but also some less glamorous locales (Kansas City and Dallas, to name a few). The travel; and the jet lag that accompanies it; are exhausting and not quite as thrilling as most people assume, but Taylor finds herself loving it. She enjoys the camaraderie of working in an office (when she's not on assignment) and getting to know the endless nightlife that Manhattan has to offer.

On a weekend in the city in early December, she and Lindsay meet up for Friday night dinner, as they often do when Taylor isn't roaming the world on assignment for Immersion Travel. Taylor arrives at the restaurant ten minutes early, and as soon as she steps inside, she gets a text from Lindsay: she got held up at work and will be there within an hour. Taylor rolls her eyes in annoyance and ducks back outside for a cigarette.

Light snowflakes have begun to fall, and this, combined with the Christmas decorations all over the city, makes Taylor nostalgic and happy all at once. It's just before 8 p.m. as Taylor stubs out her cigarette and begins making her way back inside. That's when she sees him. A guy rushing toward the restaurant. Tall, with blond hair, and impeccably dressed. Probably late twenties or early thirties, she thinks. No sign of a wedding ring. His suit looks custom-tailored and very expensive. As she reaches to open the door, he rushes to do it for her.

"Thank you," she says with a smile.

"Of course." He winks at her and walks to the sleek, crowded bar while she stands by the hostess stand, unsure what to do with herself. He turns around and smiles at her; Taylor smiles back, feels her face turn beet red, and finds a spot at the opposite end of the bar from this mystery guy and the group of friends he's with. She spends the next five minutes trying to get the attention of the bartender while simultaneously trying her best not to get caught staring at her new crush. When she finally manages to get a drink, she checks her phone. Nothing, aside from a text from her mom asking her, once again, to confirm her Christmas plans. As she's typing a response, the guy taps her on the shoulder. Startled, she looks up from her phone. He's even better looking close-up, she thinks, while trying to maintain some semblance of composure.

"Hey there," he says, sidling up next to her and placing an arm on the bar. "I'm John." He extends his hand, and Taylor shakes it.

"I'm Taylor. Nice to meet you."

"Taylor... a beautiful name for a beautiful girl." Taylor feels her face flush again, and he continues. "Listen, my table is ready, so I'm heading into the dining area with my buddies, and I have to assume you're waiting for someone. I have to ask though Can I get your number? Assuming you're not waiting for your boyfriend, that is. I would love to take you out sometime."

John says all of this with such confidence and swagger that Taylor can't help but swoon.

Taylor smiles. "That would be great, John." She dictates her phone number, watching as he enters it into his contacts. "And no, I'm just waiting for a friend."

"Great. Thanks. I'll call you soon, okay, Taylor? Maybe tomorrow?"

"I'd like that. Enjoy your dinner."

John turns and walks to the table where his friends are seated. *Well, this will be awkward,* Taylor thinks, trying (unsuccessfully) to imagine herself and Lindsay having a normal dinner with John sitting in the same room. *Fuck it,* Taylor thinks. Better have some alcohol to make this easier. She's halfway done with her glass of pinot grigio when Lindsay walks in, beautifully dusted with fresh snowflakes. After they hug and Lindsay gulps down the remains of Taylor's wine, Taylor looks outside and sees snow falling quickly, starting to actually stick to the sidewalks.

"Jesus, it's really snowing," she says, unnecessarily.

"No shit, Taylor. Look at me! I'm a mess," Lindsay snaps back. "Sorry. It's been a week; my boss is being a total bitch. But yes, you're correct, it's really snowing now. How will we ever get a cab later?" Lindsay groans.

"You might actually have to... take the subway!" Taylor says in mock horror.

"I'd rather walk and freeze to death, thanks." In most regards, Lindsay is down-to-earth and reasonable; you would never know her family is insanely well-off. But she is a total snob about the subways. Not that Taylor can blame her; she recently saw a rat the size of a beagle down there.

Lindsay has flagged down the bartender and ordered another round of drinks by the time Taylor returns from checking in with the hostess. "Ten minutes until the table is ready."

"Great. Here you go." Lindsay hands Taylor a cocktail of indeterminate ingredients.

"Thanks. What the hell is this?"

"A Long Island iced tea. Be careful; remember the last time we had these?" Lindsay laughs maliciously. "I think that was the night we almost got arrested freshman year."

"Oh Jesus," Taylor moans. "Only one of these, okay? I do intend to get wasted tonight, but not 'almost get arrested' wasted. Can we agree on that?"

"Of course. So, what's your occasion?" Lindsay asks.

Taylor gives Lindsay the scoop on John: he asked for her number, he's gorgeous, and he happens to be sitting at a table with his friends in the dining room, so this dinner has the potential to be extremely awkward.

Lindsay laughs wickedly. "Oh, Taylor, I thought you were off men. What happened to your celibacy?"

"It's not celibacy, just a break. It's been over five months with no guy drama, no pregnancy scares, and I've still had fun. Do I really want to get involved with anyone right now?" Taylor moans dramatically.

"He hasn't called you yet, my friend," Lindsay says, eyebrows raised. "But if he's half as cute as you described, yes, you do want to get involved. You're twenty-two years old, for Christ's sake! You're practically a virgin again by this point. Have some fun." Lindsay plunks down a wad of cash for the bartender just as the hostess arrives to bring them to their table, which is, thank God, at the opposite end of the dining room from where John and his friends are seated. He gives Taylor a little wave as they pass, and she waves back with a smile.

Taylor and Lindsay spend the next two hours catching up on work, gossiping about their friends and former classmates from UNC, and their holiday plans. They split a handful of appetizers before heading to a nearby bar to finish off the night. It's a perfect evening, Taylor thinks as she washes up before bed. She met a cute guy, saw her best friend, and there is snow coming down just in time for the holidays. She's asleep by 1 a.m. and wakes up around 10 the following morning, only mildly hungover. Cursing the Long Island iced tea, she takes some Advil and chugs a bottle of water.

She contemplates going for a run, then remembers the snow last night. She looks out the window and is stunned to see at least six inches of snow. In Manhattan! Delighted, she bundles up and heads outside to walk through her snow-covered neighborhood. After watching the white snow turn increasingly gray and sloppy the farther she gets into her walk, Taylor decides to grab a Starbucks and head home to the warmth of her apartment. As she's leaving the store with a venti chai tea latte, her phone rings. Encumbered by her giant mittens and therefore unable to get it in time, all she sees is a 917 area code.

"Fuck," she mumbles to herself. She rushes home and checks her phone again, relieved to see a new voicemail.

"Taylor, hey, it's John from last night. I know it's still pretty early, but I've been thinking about you since we met. Can I take you out? Maybe dinner tonight? Or whenever you're free. This is my number, 917-555-2998. Give me a call when you get this, okay? Bye."

Taylor lets out an exhale after realizing she's been holding her breath. Not wanting to appear overeager, she waits until after she's showered to call him back.

He answers on the third ring, and there is street noise in the background. "Hey there, Taylor. Thanks for calling back."

"Sure. What are you up to?"

"Just running around, doing errands, going to the gym. Saturday stuff," John says with an easy laugh. "Sorry for all the traffic noise. How about you? Anything fun going on today?"

"Well, I took a walk in the snow earlier, but that got old after about twenty minutes, so I'm just catching up on some work and Christmas shopping this afternoon. But I am free tonight if your dinner offer still stands." Taylor can't help but feel nervous; what if he already made other plans, or changed his mind?

"Absolutely. That's great. Have you been to Blue Water Grill? Down in Union Square? It's fantastic."

"I haven't, but I've heard great things," Taylor replies, trying to remain calm and not sound overly excited.

"Okay, cool. Let me make a reservation and call you back with the time. Should we shoot for eight? Get there a little early for a pre-dinner drink?" John asks.

"That sounds perfect. I'm looking forward to it!" Taylor says, then slaps her forehead in agony. *Who says that?* she thinks to herself. "Okay, talk to you later then. Bye."

"Bye, Taylor."

John calls back fifteen minutes later; he got them a reservation for 8:15. They agree to meet at the restaurant's bar at 7:45 for a cocktail. Taylor is giddy; it's been so long since she went on a proper date. She plays Christmas music all afternoon while writing up some loose ends from her recent work trips, runs out to some nearby stores to begin Christmas shopping for her family, and then spends an hour doing her hair and makeup, just for fun.

Taylor's long blond hair has been perfectly straightened, her bronzer, eye makeup, and lip gloss expertly applied, and she's decided to wear her most recent splurge: a pair of "Seven for All Mankind" jeans that she bought from Bloomingdale's with her first real paycheck. With a tight black sweater and black heels, she knows she looks good.

However, after spending an unnecessary amount of time primping and trying on five outfits (only to end up wearing her first choice), Taylor makes the mistake of taking the subway to Union Square and is, inevitably, late. Cursing the MTA and the tourists clogging the subway, she rushes into Blue Water Grill at 7:52. She tries to ignore the fact that her feet are now soaking wet and freezing; opting for heels after last night's snowstorm was a big mistake. She shrugs off her jacket and gives it to the coat-check guy, then scans the bar for John. She sees him, beer in hand, and rushes over.

"Hey!" She taps John on the shoulder, and he stands, giving her an awkward hug. "I'm so sorry I'm late. The subway on a Saturday night, I should have left more time to get here," Taylor says apologetically.

"No problem at all. I know how that goes. What's your poison, Taylor?" John asks, simultaneously flagging down the bartender and pulling out the barstool next to him, motioning for Taylor to sit.

"I'll start with a cosmo, thanks. But I like pretty much everything. I learned to love wine while studying abroad in Spain, so I may switch to that while we have dinner." *Stop rambling,* she thinks. *This guy knows nothing about you.*

"No shit! Where in Spain? I went abroad to Madrid for a semester."

"Really? That's awesome. I visited Madrid and loved it there too. I was in Barcelona for a year. It is probably my favorite place on Earth, actually."

"Barcelona is the best. I loved Madrid, but the nightlife and food scene in Barcelona is lit. What year were you abroad?" he asks, handing her the cosmo that has just been delivered by the bartender.

"Fall of 2003 through spring of 2004. So all of my junior year. I'm a huge travel freak, so I convinced my school to let me stay the whole year over there. How about you?"

"Wait," he laughs, "did you just graduate, like, earlier this year?" John puts his hand to his face, shaking his head. "God, I pinned you as more mature."

Unsure how to take this, Taylor nods. "Yes, I graduated May of this year. From UNC. What about you?"

"You're so young. Wow. Okay. Sorry, you're just, like, really young. I feel like an old man. I graduated back in 1997. Princeton. So, what are you, twenty-two, twenty-three?" He looks a bit shaken, and Taylor tries to stifle a laugh. She can't help but think about how Lindsay will get a kick out of this story later.

"I'll be twenty-three in February. Princeton, that's amazing. No one gets into Princeton." She starts doing the math, pinning John at twenty-nine or thirty. She should have known. No guy her age dresses this well.

"Man, I feel old," he says, slapping his forehead. "I just turned thirty last month. I'm surprised, the way you carry yourself, you seem more mature than most girls your age. That's all. Maybe it's the height; you've definitely got an extra six inches on the average girl."

Taylor smiles and thanks him but is secretly irked that he used the word "girl" instead of woman. This is a major pet peeve of hers: guys who refer to adult women as girls. She decides to let it slide. They chat a bit more about their time in Spain, and eventually, as her drink is running low, Taylor says enthusiastically, "So! Should we check to see if our table is ready?"

"Sounds good. I'll just settle up here." John drains the last of his beer and pays the bar bill, then the two of them make their way to their table. Taylor catches a glimpse of their reflection in the windows as they walk through the restaurant; they look really good together. She knows it's vain, but they look like they belong in an Abercrombie ad.

Over dinner, they get to know each other and really hit it off. Taylor learns that John is from Westport, Connecticut, and works for a hedge fund. He lives here in Manhattan, in Chelsea, and absolutely loves the city. He has a twin brother who lives in Boston. He's had a few serious relationships but "hasn't found the right person yet." Despite the age difference, they have a great dinner together. After arguing over the bill (Taylor tries to split it; John refuses and pays the whole thing), they step out into the chilly night.

"Well, that was great!" John says. "It's only 10:30. Do you want to go somewhere for another drink? There are some great bars around here."

"Sure. I love this neighborhood. Where do you want to go?" Taylor asks, offering John her hand as they start walking.

"You ever heard of the Headless Horseman? It's on 15th Street." John points northeast, across Union Square. They agree to go there, and John gives Taylor the CliffsNotes history lesson on Washington Irving as they stroll along the now slushy Union Square. Taylor nods and fishes in her purse for a cigarette.

Once John has finished explaining the history of the bar, Taylor pauses on the sidewalk. "You want a smoke?" she asks him.

He wavers for a second, then responds, "What the hell, why not? I haven't had one in years."

And so they stand near the entrance of the bar, exhaling smoke into the dark, cold, cloudless night sky. John smokes half his cigarette and stubs it out. "Even better than I remember."

"Yeah, they're too good, really. I need to quit; I just haven't found the motivation yet. Everyone makes it sound so easy."

"God, it's impossible, from what I've heard. I was never an actual smoker, just here and there at parties," John explains. "But my brother smoked for years, pretty heavily in fact, and finally kicked it, like, two years ago. I think some combination of hypnosis and the nicotine patch. But it was hell, apparently. Shall we?" John motions to the door and holds it open for Taylor, and they make their way into the crowded bar.

They spend the next few hours learning more about one another, and Taylor finds herself liking John in a safe, big-brotherly sort of way. She can't quite put her finger on it, but the spark she's had in the past (with Manuel, and even more so with Daniel) isn't there. At least not yet.

Somehow, the next time Taylor checks her phone, it's already one a.m. "God, it's late already!"

"Time flies... you know the rest," John says with a smile. "Do you want to get out of here?"

"Sure." Taylor decides then and there that five months of not hooking up with anyone is enough and agrees to go back to John's apartment.

After a successful first date, the next two months are a flurry of activity. Taylor and John make things "official" almost immediately and begin dating exclusively just before the holidays. After returning to New York from spending Christmas with her family in Madison,

Taylor meets John's parents and twin brother at a swanky dinner at Gramercy Tavern just before they ring in the new year. John is introduced to Eric and Lauren, who approve (Lauren in particular; she tells Taylor he's a catch and will want to get married and start a family soon, given his age). This statement does little other than freak Taylor out, but she lets it go. Even Alex seems to like him, and he tends to be the toughest critic. And while she doesn't feel the passion and excitement she did with Daniel or Manuel, John is nothing but compassionate and caring.

"And rich," Lindsay tells her drunkenly during one of their happy-hour catch-ups in January.

"Well yes, that too. But that has nothing to do with why I like him. You know that. I feel secure with him," Taylor quips back, quickly asking herself if feeling secure and being in a serious relationship is what she should want at just shy of twenty-three years old.

Lindsay concedes. "I know, I know, no judgment. It's a good thing. Just an added bonus to everything else. Plus, he dresses really well, I've noticed."

"Right? He really does. Sometimes I feel like I'm dating an Abercrombie model," Taylor swoons, recalling their first proper date when she had the same thought.

Lindsay laughs. "Let's not get carried away, missy. So, most importantly, what are we doing for your birthday next month?"

The mention of her birthday makes Taylor think immediately of Daniel, her birthday twin, and she smiles to herself, making a mental note to meet up with him soon.

"Stay tuned. It is conveniently on a Friday this year, so maybe we can go out that night? Keep it open, okay?"

"Obviously. You'll be stuck with me all night whether you like it or not. Listen, I gotta run. I'm meeting Pierre tonight for a late dinner."

Pierre is Lindsay's latest beau. Taylor has met him a handful of times; he's charming, funny, and very, very French. But knowing Lindsay, Taylor doesn't get too attached to any of her flings.

Ever since she and Walter ended things back in college, she's been going through guys like Leonardo DiCaprio goes through young supermodels.

"Have fun, and I'll for sure keep you posted on the birthday plans. Once I'm back from Vermont, I'll figure it out." Taylor and Lindsay hug and say goodbye; Taylor returns home to pack for her upcoming four-day work trip to Vermont. John, who happens to be an avid skier, will be joining her. While she's scoping out the cute shops in even cuter little towns, he'll be on the slopes. In the evenings, they will go to the best spots for après-ski cocktails and dinner.

On her way home from drinks with Lindsay, Taylor texts Daniel:

T: Hey old pal, I hope they aren't working you too hard. Our birthday is in less than a month, want to plan a joint thing? Or just have all our friends meet at a bar late night? Let me know. In any case I'd love to see you soon.

She hits send and immediately her phone rings. It's Daniel, calling from his work phone.

"Hi!" Taylor says, happy to hear from him. "It's almost 8:30, why are you still at work?"

"Hi, Taylor. Thanks for the text. You know how it is. The new guys get shit on; we're here all the time. How are you? Any glamorous trips coming up?"

"I go to Vermont tomorrow through Sunday. So, an easy trip, especially since I don't ski." She decides to omit the detail that John is coming with her; over drinks back in Madison at Christmastime, Daniel had grilled Taylor about John and concluded he wasn't right for her. Despite the fact that Daniel has a new girlfriend, Michelle, who, from what Taylor can tell, is a total bitch, but she's kept that character analysis to herself. Best not to discuss romance with Daniel, given their history. Still, it pains her seeing Daniel with Michelle.

"Nice. Well, have fun. And yes, I'd love to coordinate something for our birthday. I have to finish something here, so I need to go, but let's talk next week, okay? We can figure it out then," Daniel says, clearly in a rush.

"Sounds good. Thanks. Don't work too hard, okay?"

"Ha. I'll try. Bye, Taylor." And he hangs up.

Taylor sighs and drops her phone back into her purse.

He sounds exhausted. Everyone knows the newbies in finance get the short end of the stick, but still. She has some sort of protective feeling over Daniel. When her brother went through the same thing when he was starting his career, she couldn't have cared less.

As soon as she's cozy in her pajamas back at her apartment, Taylor pours herself a glass of red wine and blasts Counting Crows while she packs her bag for the long weekend in Vermont. As Adam Duritz croons "A Long December," Taylor's mind drifts back to that strange December of 2003, when she and Daniel spent most of their Christmas break in bed together. And while it was over two years ago, she can still smell Daniel's cologne on his neck, can still feel his hands caressing her hair. She can't deny that the memory still turns her on.

Her reverie is interrupted by a ding on her phone, signaling a new text message. It's John, confirming that he will pick her up at 9 a.m. tomorrow. He keeps his car in the city and has kindly offered to drive up to Vermont. Taylor sighs, feeling guilty that she'd been thinking about Daniel when John, perfectly kind and smart, and so clearly head over heels for her, is sitting at home thinking about her.

She shakes it off and responds, confirming the time and thanking him, adding an xoxo as she signs off. She finishes packing and is in bed before 11 p.m., but is plagued with restlessness. She tosses and turns for hours before finally succumbing to sleep sometime in the middle of the night.

She wakes up to her alarm at 7 a.m., totally exhausted. Still, she forces herself to go for a quick run in the freezing January morning. It helps clear her head, and she's waiting downstairs when John pulls up outside her building at 8:55 a.m. He double-parks and hops out, grabbing her suitcase and hoisting it into the trunk. Taylor settles comfortably in the passenger seat; within minutes, they are on the West Side Highway heading north, and Taylor, exhausted from her lack of sleep the night before, promptly falls asleep.

Disoriented, Taylor opens her eyes and remembers where she is. She checks the clock on the dashboard and is mortified to find that it's after 11 a.m.

"Oh my God. I am so sorry, John. I can't believe I've been asleep this entire time. So much for being a good navigator." She grabs his hand and squeezes it, and he laughs.

"Late night last night, little lady?" John asks with a raised eyebrow. "Don't worry about it. At least this way you weren't subjected to my music. I'm glad you got some rest."

"Thanks. I should have warned you... I have a tendency to fall asleep as soon as I'm in a moving vehicle."

"Well, I suppose it's a good thing I'm driving."

They pass the time by sharing stories about their families, childhoods, and funny college memories. They stop once to fill up with gas, use the bathroom, and stretch their legs.

The farther north they get, the greater the snow accumulation along the sides of the roads. Finally, they exit the highway and arrive at their destination: the Equinox Resort in Manchester, Vermont. They will spend the afternoon exploring the town, spend their nights here, and tomorrow head to the ski mountains. Rather, Taylor will deposit John at the mountains to ski, and she will explore the surrounding towns.

The Equinox screams WASPy old money to Taylor; it is classic and beautiful, despite being in need of some upgrades. A huge wraparound porch serves drinks in the summer; on this cold January day, though, there is a fire roaring in the fireplace at the Falcon Bar within the hotel. But the hotel room itself, it is apparent, hasn't been updated in quite some time. John makes note of this immediately as they enter, seemingly annoyed that the room is quaint rather than modern and updated with all the bells and whistles. Taylor, however, finds it charming and loves everything about the place.

By the time they have their luggage and are settled into the room, it's already 3:30 in the afternoon. Taylor is anxious to get out and check out the town, so she rebuffs John's efforts at getting her into bed, promising him they can do that later; there is only about an hour of daylight remaining for them to explore the town.

John sulks a bit at her reluctance to have sex, and to hide her annoyance, Taylor goes into the bathroom. *I'm here for work, for Christ's sake,* she thinks to herself while washing her hands and staring at her reflection in the mirror as a diversion. *What doesn't he understand about that?*

She gets the sense, and she can't pinpoint exactly why, that John doesn't take her job at Immersion Travel very seriously. It's almost like he sees her job as a cute hobby rather than her career and her means of income. Given his family structure (his dad makes a ton of money, so his mom was always at home looking after the kids and the house), she can sort of see why he's like this. But that doesn't make it okay, and she finds herself growing resentful of the way he regards her work. Rather than address it now, she takes a few deep breaths as she emerges from the bathroom, a smile plastered on her face.

"Ready?" she asks John.

"Yes, ma'am. Where are we off to first?" John responds, apparently done brooding for now.

"Let's head to Hildene, the Lincoln family home. It's supposed to be stunning. Then I thought we could walk around town, get a drink, and have dinner at the restaurant here at the hotel?"

"Perfect." John kisses her on the cheek, and they bundle up in their winter coats. The drive to Hildene is only five minutes, and they arrive at the grand estate just before 4 p.m. Taylor scribbles notes and takes pictures as they walk through the Georgian Revival mansion, which was built in 1905.

"Did you know it's called Hildene because it's formed from two Old English words: *hil*, meaning hill, and *dene*, meaning valley with stream? We're up on a hill, and the Battenkill River flows through the valley below!" Taylor says enthusiastically while reading inscriptions along the walls of the mansion.

John is a good sport, nodding as Taylor delves into history and carrying her purse while she takes notes.

"I hope you're giving me a cut of your paycheck for this," John says with a laugh. "Your purse weighs more than you do. What the hell do you keep in this thing?"

Taylor laughs and squeezes his hand, responding, "The perils of being a woman whose mother always insisted she have a bag with all necessities at all times. I know, it weighs a ton. Sorry."

Given that it is January, they don't bother with the majority of the outdoor areas, although Taylor vows to return in the summer to see the property in all of its glory.

They drive back into town and go to the legendary Northshire bookstore, a local institution. Taylor chats with the owners while John gathers some books to buy. Thirty minutes later, Taylor has enough history on the store to write about it coherently, and John has three new books.

They decide to stop for a drink before heading back to the hotel; the proprietor of the bookstore directs them to Ye Olde Tavern, a colonial-era bar and restaurant dating back to 1790. John orders an Old Fashioned; Taylor decides to try the locally influenced cocktail, a Vermont Mapletini. Where else can one have vodka and maple syrup in the same glass?

They linger over their drinks, chatting with the bartender while Taylor jots down a few notes on the history of the tavern. By the time they're back at the hotel, it's nearly 7 p.m., and John can hardly keep his hands off her. They have sex; it is satisfying, if a bit perfunctory.

As they lie together afterward, John grabs Taylor's hand and leans over to her.

"I love you, Taylor."

He says it with such confidence and certainty that Taylor is taken aback. She panics for what feels like hours but is really only a few seconds. She doesn't feel ready to say it back to him, but how can she not? He looks so vulnerable here in bed, with his bare chest and soulful eyes, that she has no choice but to reciprocate.

She takes a moment and responds, "I love you too," and kisses him.

I do love him, she thinks to herself. Maybe it's not the passionate, all-consuming love she's dreamed of, or the lust she's felt before with Manuel or Daniel, but she loves him.

I'm just not in love with him, some nagging voice deep within her subconscious taunts.

She squashes the thought and gives John another kiss before saying, "Well, that certainly made me hungry. Should we get ready for dinner now?"

"Yes, that's perfect. I'll hop in the shower." He kisses her again and heads to the bathroom.

Taylor gets dressed quickly and refreshes her makeup at the old-fashioned vanity. She feels the sudden urge for a cigarette and tells John she'll meet him at the restaurant downstairs.

She grabs her purse and orders a glass of merlot from the hotel bar, charges it to the room, and hurries into the cold night air. She sits on a bench conveniently located next to an ashtray and smokes while reflecting on the past hour.

Is knowing someone for just over six weeks long enough to actually love them? Taylor wonders.

She takes a big swig of wine and a long drag on her cigarette. She should feel flattered, but in all honesty she's a bit freaked out by John's revelation, along with the fact that she responded so casually, without really thinking it through. Trying not to dwell on it, she gives herself a mental pep talk: there are worse things than a kind, handsome man loving you; give it time and maybe you'll feel the same way; and so on. She smokes one more cigarette and goes to meet John for dinner.

The rest of their Vermont journey goes by quickly and without incident. Taylor gets all of her writing done for work, John skis, and they have a great time scoping out the best places for drinks and dinner together every night. And yet... despite having a ton of fun together, Taylor feels doubts creeping in. John has a controlling side that is beginning to become apparent, and Taylor can tell he is used to getting whatever he wants in life. She's not sure this is the type of man she wants to get serious with, but on paper, he is perfect. And everyone tells them how wonderful a couple they are, so Taylor goes with it.

January is over, and now February is officially making demands.

Two dates loom large in Taylor's mind this month: Valentine's Day and her birthday. One is loaded with expectation; the other is personal, nostalgic, and, if she's honest, dangerous territory. Several brief work trips keep her busy in early February, and by the time she returns from a long weekend in Austin, Texas on February 13th, she feels wrecked. The apartment is dark and cold when she lets herself in, and she's bloated and irritable after sampling far more beer and ribs than anyone should in a single weekend. Alas, it's all part of the job.

She drops her bag, kicks off her shoes, and immediately texts John. Too much travel in too short a time has left her craving something familiar, someone familiar.

J: Of course, just finishing up at work. Be there in an hour.

Taylor smiles despite herself and opens a bottle of wine. They've already begun leaving belongings at each other's apartments, his toothbrush in her bathroom cup, her pajamas folded in one of his drawers, spare deodorant and phone chargers scattered between both places. It feels intimate. Domestic, even.

She turns on the TV for background noise and lands on *Prison Break*. She watches for five minutes before realizing she has no idea what's happening and doesn't care enough to find out. Instead, she picks up her phone and opens a new text thread, Daniel.

She tells herself it's practical. Their birthday is coming up. Logistics matter.

Still, she rereads the text three times before sending it.

T: Hey Daniel, just checking on what's happening for our big twenty-third birthday later this week! I'm up for whatever, just let me know where we should go. Maybe Michelle knows somewhere good for a group? And I'm assuming your mom will be sending her legendary angel food cake like always, right?

She sets the phone down and takes a long sip of wine.

Michelle grew up in Manhattan, a fact she manages to bring up in nearly every conversation, as if the city were a private club she somehow owns. Taylor keeps that opinion firmly to herself, but the irritation is real. Worse than that, though, is the quiet, undeniable truth humming beneath the annoyance: despite having a boyfriend she sees several times a week, Taylor is still deeply unsettled by Daniel's relationship with Michelle.

In some stubborn, irrational corner of her brain, Daniel still belongs to her.

When they were kids, Tanya had insisted on one shared birthday cake every year, homemade, angel food, frosted just so. It became a tradition, something that survived middle school awkwardness and teenage distance. Now that they're adults, supposedly past all that, Taylor wants it back. Or maybe she just wants proof that some things haven't changed.

Her phone buzzes.

D: Hey. Glad you texted; I was just planning stuff. Having dinner around 7:30 with Michelle and her parents. Good to meet up after 10. That work? Bungalow 8 good? Michelle knows a guy who can hook us up with a table. And haha on the cake, I'll let my mom know we're expecting it!

"Christ. Bungalow 8?" Taylor mutters to herself.

That place is impossible to get into. And outrageously expensive. And of course Michelle "knows a guy."

She exhales sharply, annoyed with herself for feeling annoyed at all, and responds with practiced politeness.

T: That sounds great, I'll let my friends know. Let me know if there's a limit on numbers. And thank your mom for the cake, those were legendary when we were kids!

She barely has time to set her phone down before there's a knock at the door.

John enters holding a bouquet of a dozen perfect red roses.

"Happy early Valentine's Day," he says, leaning in to kiss her. "I thought it would be nice for you to have these all day tomorrow, not just tomorrow night."

"Thank you," Taylor says, genuinely touched. "They're gorgeous. I missed you. Wine?"

"I missed you more. And yes, definitely wine. It's been a shit day. My boss was in a mood and made sure everyone else suffered too. Tell me about Texas so I can live vicariously for a minute."

"Come here," she says, patting the couch.

She rubs his shoulders while giving him the Austin highlights, live music, too much barbecue, long nights, early mornings.

"So," John says, "lots of beer, ribs, and guitars?"

"That about covers it," she says with a grin. "I'll dress it up a bit more for the article."

They finalize Valentine's Day plans: drinks at Wolfgang's Steakhouse at 7:30, dinner at 8. John admits he made the reservation weeks ago but waited to mention it, just in case she came home exhausted and wanted a quiet night in.

"You're sweet," Taylor says. "Even if I were falling down tired, I'd power through for Valentine's Day with you."

She pours the last of the wine into his glass. "But tonight, I'm officially done. I'm heading to bed."

"No problem," John says. "The Rangers are on, so I'll watch for a bit and join you soon. Love you."

"Love you too," Taylor replies automatically.

The words feel practiced now, easy to say, harder to fully inhabit.

The next morning, she wakes to find the roses arranged neatly in a vase on her nightstand. John is already back from Starbucks, handing her a venti coffee the moment she steps into the kitchen.

"You're unreal," she laughs. "Thank you."

"Happy Valentine's Day," he says. "I've got an early meeting, but tonight, Wolfgang's at 7:30."

"Perfect."

The day passes in a blur of emails and edits. By lunchtime, her Austin piece is done and sent off, but she still has no idea what to wear. She messages Lindsay.

T: What do I wear to Wolfgang's tonight? He brought me roses.

L: Short dress. Tights. Heels. A warm fucking coat.

L: Do you think he's proposing???

Taylor nearly spits out her water.

The rest of the afternoon is uneventful. At 5:30, Taylor logs off, goes to the gym, showers, and takes her time getting ready. Wine glass in hand, *Friends* playing in the background, she applies makeup with care. By 7:15, she's ready; sleek, polished, and more nervous than she'd like to admit.

John is already at the bar when she arrives. Tie loosened, two glasses of wine waiting.

Dinner is indulgent; three courses, a bottle of wine, and when John reaches into his jacket pocket, Taylor's heart lurches. Relief floods her when the box he produces is clearly not a ring.

Inside is a diamond tennis bracelet. Elegant. Excessive. Stunning.

"Oh my God," she breathes. "John... this is incredible."

"I saw it and thought of you."

She gives him his gift; his favorite cologne, and he laughs, teasing her gently. Still, as they leave the restaurant and head back to her apartment, Taylor can't stop staring at the bracelet catching the city lights in the taxi window.

She does the math in her head and immediately regrets it.

At least a month of her salary. Probably more.

The imbalance sits heavy in her chest, even as John squeezes her hand and smiles at her like she's the best decision he's ever made.

Although Taylor is full from dinner and doesn't feel much like having sex, she does it anyway; it is Valentine's Day, after all. And her wrist is covered in diamonds now.

Afterward, John falls asleep right away, but Taylor is restless. She wanders into the kitchen, pours herself a glass of water, and sits on the couch. She resists the urge to call her mother or Lindsay, unsure whether either is still awake. Why, she thinks to herself, is the perfect man asleep in my bed while I sit here questioning everything? She sits in the darkened room for what feels like hours and eventually heads back to bed. Despite the apparent perfection and joy of the evening, melancholy has taken over her, and she just can't seem to get rid of it.

The next morning, Taylor wakes up and hears the sound of John humming in the shower. At first, she found this habit endearing; today, it annoys the hell out of her. Once he's done in the bathroom, she goes in to pee. Not surprisingly, based on her mood, her period has arrived. She moans and thinks of the injustice of having to celebrate her birthday in the middle of her cycle. At least, she thinks to herself, this explains my annoyance with John this morning and my weird mood last night. John bids farewell on his way out the door while she finishes getting ready for work, and he promises to call later once he's done at the office.

"And don't forget about Friday," she says as he opens the door.

"Taylor, do you actually think I could forget your birthday? Come on." He blows her a kiss and closes the door behind him. Taylor looks at the clock on the microwave; it's only 7:20 a.m., so she decides to hit the gym before work. The last thing she wants to do right now is exercise, but she knows that thirty minutes on the elliptical will improve her mood. She queues up Usher on her iPod and walks to the gym.

The rest of the day is inconsequential, with the exception of an errant text in the early afternoon from Daniel.

D: Can you please calm down about this? We can talk later. I'm at work.

Taylor stares at her phone, confused and, for a brief moment, alarmed. What is he talking about, she wonders to herself? She types back.

T: Hey, hope you're having a good week. I'm assuming this wasn't meant for me???

And, she thinks, if it wasn't intended for me, who was it for? Perhaps there is trouble with Michelle? Taylor feels mildly guilty that this idea fills her with a bit of glee and relief; Daniel is far too nice for Michelle. Another minute passes and Taylor's phone dings again.

D: Shit, I'm sorry, not meant for you. Can't wait for Friday. Any chance you want to get drinks tonight? I should, miraculously, be out of here by 7.

T: Sure! And no problem about the text. It happens. Just let me know where to meet and I will meet you. 7:30 works for me. Where?

D: Perfect, how's Rio Grande at 7:30? Desperately in need of margaritas. If you get there before me, please order a pitcher.

Taylor chuckles to herself and then wonders what the hell is going on with Daniel. When John calls her later in the afternoon, she just tells him she is having drinks and dinner with an old friend, and she will talk to him tomorrow. John has not expressed that he finds Taylor and Daniel's friendship problematic; not exactly. If anything, he seems perplexed by the whole thing and occasionally mentions that it is impossible for a guy to be friends with a woman without harboring some deep sexual desire. He has gone so far as to ask Taylor if Daniel is gay, to which she laughed so hard that she nearly peed herself. If he only knew. In any case, it's just easier not to mention who she's meeting tonight, so she omits that piece.

Taylor leaves work at 5:30 in the afternoon and wanders around midtown, poking into a few stores before succumbing to the cold. She pops into The Ginger Man, a bar just a few blocks from Rio Grande. A glass of wine warms her from the inside; by 7:25 p.m. she is back out in the cold on her way to meet Daniel, languidly smoking a cigarette while she walks up Lexington Avenue to 38th Street.

She spots Daniel before he sees her. He's at the bar, his tie loosened around his neck, and he's placing an order with the bartender. Taylor can't help but smile when she sees him. She slowly removes her jacket and watches as Daniel makes small talk and laughs while he orders. Taylor makes her way over to him.

"Hey you," she says, giving him a hug.

"Hi! Thank you for meeting up," Daniel says, getting up and giving Taylor a proper hug. "I have literally never needed a drink so badly in my life." Taylor hears Daniel's Midwestern accent, standing out so distinctly from everyone surrounding them, and it makes her feel a little safer, a little more at home in this crazy world of Manhattan that she is now inhabiting.

They sit and order quesadillas. Daniel pours them each a glass of Rio Grande's famous frozen margaritas, which are notorious for knocking people on their asses. They go down too smoothly, Taylor thinks.

"So, why are we drowning our sorrows in tequila on this freezing February night?" Taylor asks. "Everything alright at work? With Michelle?"

"In retrospect, I should have chosen a wine bar," Daniel says sheepishly. "But this is the place to come when you need to block everything out. To answer your questions...work is fine. Michelle? Hmmm. Not great?"

"Uh oh. Did you screw up Valentine's Day?" Taylor's right hand instinctually feels the diamond bracelet that adorns her left wrist, hoping Daniel doesn't notice it.

"I didn't think so. I mean, I had to work until past 8 yesterday, which Michelle knew. The plan was to meet for a late dinner last night and then go back to my place, which we did. I took her to Gotham Bar and Grill, for Christ's sake."

"Okay, so what's the problem? Sounds like a nice night to me."

"I'm still trying to figure that out. I think it has something to do with me not buying flowers. Or chocolate, or any gift at all, really. I mean, she has a point, but isn't that kind of stupid to get pissed off about? I mean, are we twelve years old? Did she really need heart-shaped chocolates to make it a successful day? I thought a nice dinner at an amazing restaurant with, like, four drinks apiece was a pretty decent present." Daniel puffs his cheeks out and exhales, then takes a long sip of his margarita. "So, you're a girl-er, woman," he stutters, "Tell me, what did I do wrong?"

Now it's Taylor's turn to take a swig of her margarita. "Honestly? I don't know. It sounds like you planned a nice dinner and all. Is there a chance, maybe, that she's pissed off about something else and is using this as a bullshit reason to be mad at you? I just don't see Michelle actually caring about that kind of thing."

Daniel shoves some of the complimentary chips that have appeared out of nowhere into his mouth and sighs. "Yeah, we had the living together talk recently. She wants to, I don't. Not yet, at least," he adds quickly. "We haven't been together that long, we're so young, I'm just not ready!" Desperation in his voice, Daniel looks up at the ceiling and lets out another audible sigh.

"Daniel, calm down. I agree, you can't rush a decision like that. What did you say to her? Like, maybe later, or was it a hard no?" Taylor asks, while fighting her inner voice, which is telling her to say *No! Don't move in with her, Daniel!*

"It was more of a deferral than an actual answer," Daniel says sheepishly. "Like, I think I said, 'I'm not quite ready to be having this conversation,' and then she got in a huff and asked when I would be ready to get serious, and is she wasting her time, and on and on. I mean, we're not even twenty-three years old, for fuck's sake!"

Taylor can't help herself; she starts laughing at this. Suddenly Daniel swearing and getting totally flustered, which is totally out of character, coupled with the idiocy of young men causes her to double over with laughter.

"Taylor, what are you laughing about? This isn't funny." But even as he says this, Daniel starts laughing too, as though Taylor's laugh is contagious, and he just caught it.

"Honestly, for someone so smart, you're awfully dense about this shit. You really thought her real reason for being pissed was over a Valentine's Day present, when you guys just had this bombshell of a conversation? Jesus." Taylor swats him on the arm playfully, and he laughs, burying his face in his palm.

Taylor tries to speak, but has tears in her eyes. Finally, she takes a deep breath. "I'm sorry, I know it's not funny. I just can't help it. It's all so predictable! And you," she pokes him in the chest, "I expect more from you. You should have known that she'd be pushing to move in together; I'm surprised you weren't better prepared," Taylor says, while repressing every urge she has to tell Daniel to break it off with Michelle.

The evening continues in a similar fashion, with Taylor dissecting Daniel's personal life and offering him a much-needed dose of female wisdom. They eat crappy quesadillas and drink more margaritas than they should, and while there is nothing whatsoever remarkable about this night, Taylor will later recall this as one of the happiest nights of her life. She is with someone she has known forever; they laugh constantly and are both living their dreams in Manhattan. Maybe their love lives are fucked up, but tonight it doesn't matter. After the bill is paid, they walk towards Grand Central, both a bit wobbly from the margaritas. Taylor lights a cigarette and asks Daniel, "So, do you feel a bit better after drowning yourself in tequila?"

"Much, yes. Thank you for listening."

"Always."

"I feel like a dick. I didn't even ask how things are with you and John," Daniel says.

"Don't worry, we're fine. Another night. There's only so much relationship drama I can deal with in one night."

"Oooh, sounds juicy," Daniel laughs, an unmistakable twinkle in his eyes.

"Not at all," Taylor responds quickly. "You know, just nothing new to report, that's all."

As they approach the formidable façade of Grand Central, they both pause and look up. "Can you believe we're here?" Daniel asks. "Just two kids from Wisconsin, living in the big city," he says, in a perfectly exaggerated Wisconsin accent.

Taylor laughs and puts her arm around his shoulder, and they continue walking, entering the building and heading towards the subway. "I know. Our moms must be so proud."

"Well, here we are. We're on different train lines," Daniel says needlessly as they reach the subway platforms. They hug each other and agree to check in on Friday, their birthday, before the celebrations get underway in the evening.

Chapter 23

July 2007, Paris

As the plane descends into Paris, Taylor wakes up and looks over at Daniel, who is in the window seat, sleeping peacefully. She smiles and closes her eyes, thinking about how they got here, and the week that lies before them. To say 2006 was a tumultuous year would be a vast understatement. Daniel and Michelle had a messy breakup not long after Taylor and Daniel celebrated their twenty-third birthdays together. Then there was the broken engagement between Taylor and John, which nearly killed both of them. As Taylor watched John get down on one knee last September, only nine months into their relationship, she panicked and said yes to avoid humiliating him, but she knew simultaneously that it would never work.

It was an unseasonably warm September day, and John had asked Taylor earlier in the week if she'd like to spend the weekend at his parents' house in Westport to enjoy the weather out of the hot, muggy city. John's parents, his brother and his girlfriend, and his grandparents were all there for a "family dinner." They were seated around the pool enjoying cocktail hour when John vanished inside the house for several moments. Taylor didn't think anything of it; she was enjoying getting to know his brother's girlfriend. But when John arrived back to the pool deck, he had a gleam in his eyes, and everyone got very quiet all of a sudden.

Before Taylor could process that John wasn't just bringing her another glass of wine, he was kneeling on the ground in front of her.

Her mind flashed briefly to Daniel; now single Daniel with whom she had been spending more time now that he had rid himself of Michelle. This fleeting thought was replaced with sheer panic, but John's vulnerability in that moment; *he is on his knees asking for my hand in marriage in front of his family*, she thought to herself, forced her into a knee-jerk "Yes," rather than the *hmmm, let's slow this down, shall we* that she felt in her gut. They celebrated with champagne and a fancy dinner; phone calls were made to Taylor's family and all of their friends, and John's mother started rambling about guest lists, venues, and possible dates. At that point, Taylor had to excuse herself to the bathroom, where she actually got sick to her stomach as the gravity of the evening began to sink in.

The fact that John had the balls to do it in front of his family wasn't lost on her; she could never have responded "no" in that moment. Looking back, Taylor wonders if he knew that she would feel the added pressure, but it ultimately doesn't matter.

Several weeks later, when John brought up their living arrangements and suggested that Taylor move in with him, the conversation spiraled out of control. The nail in the proverbial coffin came when he suggested that she quit her job at Immersion Travel as soon as they were married. Taylor's response; something to the tone of "This isn't 1950, for fuck's sake!" led to a massive argument about expectations and antiquated gender roles, and whatever thread that was holding their relationship together was irreparably severed. It was heartbreaking and brutal; there were many moments in the weeks that followed when she doubted herself and wondered if it wouldn't be easier to just marry John after all.

After they officially called it off, Taylor tried to remain civil, but John suggested they cut all ties, as being around her was too painful for him. Of course, this made her already overarching sense of guilt even more intense, and she felt like a grade-A bitch. She listened to a lot of Sarah McLachlan and spent a lot of time crying in the bathroom at work.

Fortunately, the engagement was called off before any of the planning proceeded too far. Still, though, Taylor had to endure months of verbal abuse from John and his family and friends, none of whom could understand how she could have broken his heart. Rumor had it that John's mother actually said, "She would've made a beautiful bride and wife. She could have lived a life of leisure and gotten everything every girl dreams of. Just a shame she's so fucked in the head to give all of that up."

Her own family didn't understand either, to be honest. Neither did her friends. "He's perfect!" they all told her. He was perfect, just not for Taylor. She knew that one day John would meet his match: a woman who wanted to put her career on hold, either for a few years or permanently, stay home and pump out babies, live in a big suburban house, and drive to soccer practice. Taylor isn't ruling any of that out, not yet, but at only twenty-three years old, she just wasn't ready, and deep down she's always had this nagging feeling that she and John were never "meant to be."

The year wasn't all bad for Taylor; the upside of 2006 was becoming an aunt. Lauren and Eric welcomed a baby boy in October, which lifted Taylor out of her post-breakup funk. The baby, whom they named Charles but nicknamed Chuck, is an absolute delight. Taylor is frequently out in Greenwich to visit and is relishing her role as auntie. After one particularly grueling week at work shortly after Thanksgiving, coupled with nasty messages on social media from some of John's friends, Taylor took the train to Greenwich for the weekend to help babysit Chuck and to have a change of scenery. Lauren and Eric went out that Friday night, leaving little six-week-old Chuck in Taylor's care for a few hours so they could have their first dinner out as a couple since Chuck was born.

As she rocked him to sleep, she whispered into his tiny ear, "You have saved my life, little one." Looking back, she realizes how accurate this statement was; this baby, her nephew provided a ray of sunshine in what was the darkest time of her life.

It was around then that she finally went to see a therapist at Lindsay's urging. There was a lot to unpack: her infidelity to Manuel, her feelings for Daniel that she had no idea how to manage, along with the failed relationship with John. She now goes to therapy religiously and has "made a lot of progress," according to the shrink. She has discussed "trust issues" ad nauseam, but so many things from her past are now crystal clear after exploring them through the lens of psychology. Her reluctance (or seeming inability) to be faithful, for one. Her assumption that she doesn't deserve the men she's with, another. She can look back now at some of her behavior in college and while abroad in Barcelona with a new perspective, and rather than feel shame, she can accept the person she was and is growing to be. It's a refreshing feeling, one that doesn't come naturally to her but is getting easier by the day. And that was Taylor's 2006, in a nutshell. Long story short, she survived.

Through all of this tumultuousness, Daniel was by her side. As a friend initially, and then things evolved. They were having dinner together several times a month, commiserating about their failed relationships and work drama. Daniel's was the friendliest face when Taylor was dealing with the aftermath of her broken engagement. They traveled back to Wisconsin together at Christmas, causing raised eyebrows amongst their mothers, but at the time it remained platonic. By February, after a long Sunday of drinking, brunch that extended to dinner, Daniel came back to Taylor's apartment. And the rest, as they say, is history. They literally fell into bed together, and neither has looked back since.

Daniel all but moved into Taylor's apartment by the end of February, preferring to be with her over his finance-bro roommates, as Taylor jokingly refers to them. She likes knowing that after a long work trip, Daniel will be there to give her a hug and a kiss; his warm body will be in her bed, and his loving nature will cheer her up no matter what she's dealing with. Their attraction to one another is even hotter than it was when they hooked up freshman year and over their Christmas break fling. Taylor is continuously amazed at how such a nice Midwestern boy can be so goddamn great in bed.

And while it's not all roses and rainbows, they have their share of minor disagreements over trivial issues, to be sure, just like any couple, Taylor is happier than she has ever been.

One cold, gray Wednesday night in March, as she's going through the mail, Taylor gets a call from her college friend, Katie. She turns down Beyoncé singing *Irreplaceable* and answers the phone.

"Hey Taylor! How are you?"

"Katie! It's so good to hear your voice," Taylor beams through the phone. Daniel had just walked into her apartment straight from the office and opened two bottles of beer, silently passing one to Taylor. She blows him a kiss and mouths *thank you.*

Taylor and Katie catch up for a few minutes, Taylor telling her about her new romance with Daniel, before Katie gets to the serious business. "Hey, do you remember Will? From London, back in 2003?"

"Um, yes, of course I remember Will. He and Daniel were roommates and best friends! Why, have you guys reconnected?"

Katie laughs. "Yes, you could say that. We've actually been in touch since then and dating off and on for a few years. I guess mostly on," Katie giggles. "We've tried to keep it low-key and under the radar, you know how it is. And actually, the reason I'm calling is, we're engaged!"

Taylor nearly falls off the barstool in the kitchen. "Oh my God! Katie, that's fabulous! Congratulations."

Daniel looks on with amusement, a twinkle in his eyes.

Taylor says "hold on a sec" to Katie and covers the phone. "Daniel, you knew about this, didn't you!"

Daniel laughs and mock-shrugs. "I helped him pick out the ring, and I was sworn to secrecy."

"You bastard," Taylor whispers with a laugh before going back to the phone call. Katie gives her the lowdown on the proposal and the wedding, which will be in France in July, only four months away.

"So, as you can imagine, it will be a small affair, just family and our closest friends, but I wanted to give you the details since I would just die if you aren't there for this."

"I wouldn't miss it for anything in the whole world," Taylor tells her. "When and where?"

"It's July 19th, a Saturday, at the Domaine de Chantilly, which is a castle about forty minutes north of Paris. Can you believe this?" Katie snorts. "I'm getting married in a fucking castle!"

"Oh my God," Taylor says again, laughing, while opening her laptop to look up the venue. "Well, wherever it is, count me in. I can't wait! And if you need me to do anything, just say the word."

"Thank you. I'm not doing bridesmaids, otherwise I'd ask you to be one. Duh. Will's family is going to help with the cost of accommodation for our friends, so I just hope you can come a few days early and hang out and enjoy Paris. And obviously, bring Daniel. He's invited too, of course. The invitations will go out in May, but we wanted to give everyone plenty of time to plan."

"Umm, yes, I think I can agree to that! I can probably make a work trip out of it anyway. To my knowledge, this castle hasn't been featured in any of our pieces yet, so I can use that angle. Count us in. And by the way, how the fuck have you kept this relationship under wraps all this time? I've talked to you a hundred times and you never even mentioned Will. I'm utterly shocked."

Katie laughs and responds, "I know, sorry to be so elusive. But we've had a good thing going on and I didn't want to jinx it. Which is so stupid, but like I said, we've been trying to keep it low-key."

Taylor and Katie spend a few more minutes gossiping and catching up before saying goodbye. Daniel, apparently looking for redemption, has started cooking dinner. He's seasoning two pieces of salmon and chopping peppers and looks up sheepishly at Taylor when she approaches him.

"I can't believe you! You knew about this and didn't say anything? How could you have kept this under wraps?" Taylor giggles and pokes him in the chest. "I didn't know they were even seeing each other! What the actual fuck?"

"I sooo wanted to tell you, believe me. It's been impossible to hold this in. I nearly slipped so many times. But Will wanted Katie to tell you herself, so I had to respect that."

"Some nerve you have. So! It looks like we're going to France in July. Has Will asked you to do anything, you know, wedding-related?" Taylor asks.

"No, he's been pretty chill about everything. They're not doing the traditional wedding-party crap. But he did ask if I could get there a few days early. It sounds like it's going to be a big to-do, even though the guest list is small. Welcome drinks on that Thursday night, rehearsal dinner Friday, wedding Saturday, and probably some sort of farewell party Sunday." Daniel puts the salmon in the oven and places his hands on Taylor's shoulders. "Sounds like a great fucking vacation for us, right?"

"Wow, yeah, that sounds like almost as much hoopla as Eric and Lauren had. It was just one party after another," Taylor says, then kisses him quickly on the lips and takes a swig from her beer. "It sure does sound like a dream of a trip; my mind is going into overdrive already. And luckily for us, I can probably expense some of the trip. The wedding is going to be in a castle. I can't believe those two. I never really pictured Katie as the marrying type, but here we are. I still remember the night when they met, in London. Remember?"

"I remember," Daniel tells her. "Although, to be honest, I was more focused on someone else at the time."

"Ah, I remember, the gorgeous Danish girl you were seeing. Sofia, was it?"

"No, Taylor, I was thinking about you. Even when I was with Sofia. It's been that way since that night back in our freshman year. It's always been you."

Taylor blushes and hugs him, at a loss for words. Without speaking, they kiss and head straight to the bedroom, leaving dinner and travel planning for later. Taylor will, for the rest of her life, always remember Daniel's words: *it's always been you.* Has a more flattering, romantic statement ever been uttered?

Back to the present, Paris in July! Taylor and Daniel land at Charles de Gaulle Airport on a sweltering Sunday morning, six days before the wedding. The overnight flight has left them foggy-brained and exhausted, but the excitement of their first proper trip together dwarfs their discomfort. The hotel, which they will be at from Sunday through Thursday before going to the "wedding hotel" where all of the guests are staying, is perfectly located near the Louvre. Taylor begged Immersion Travel to spring for the Ritz-Carlton, but given its popularity and the fact that there were multiple write-ups on it already, no one could justify the price.

Taylor tries not to dwell on what happened the last time she was in Paris, when she cheated on Manuel with Claude back in 2004. Still, certain streets and landmarks bring back uncomfortable memories, which she forces herself to nip in the bud. She thinks about what she's learned in therapy; and while it's far easier to address these demons in the safe space of a psychologist's office than in real life, she's trying her very hardest. She also forces herself to remember the beautiful moments she had in Paris, whether that was wandering the grounds of Versailles, seeing the gardens at Giverny, or having a simple, lovely meal while simultaneously people-watching.

Taylor has been assigned a handful of restaurants in Paris proper, along with a visit to the Veuve Clicquot cellar in Reims, the Champagne capital, just under two hours from Paris, to write about for Immersion Travel. She and Daniel spend Sunday and Monday exploring Paris; somehow Daniel never visited while he was studying abroad in London, so they have a lot of ground to cover. They hit up museums on Sunday (the Louvre and Musée d'Orsay), fighting through jet lag. Sunday night they visit the Eiffel Tower before dinner, and both collapse into bed at 11 p.m.

Monday morning, after catching up on some very necessary sleep, they wake up refreshed and gorge on the hotel's complimentary breakfast. The day is perfect, sunny but not too hot, not a cloud in the sky. It's ideal for exploring the many gardens of the city. They start out at the Jardin du Luxembourg, where they watch kids racing sailboats in the small lake at the center of the park and see a plethora of glam Parisians taking their lunch breaks on picnic tables and park benches. After an hour or so, they cross back over the Seine via the Pont de la Concorde, finding themselves at the Jardin des Tuileries. This expansive 17th-century garden has charming alleyways and fountains, and a surprising view of the Eiffel Tower. Taylor snaps some pictures while Daniel rests his eyes on a nearby bench, seemingly oblivious to the noisy teens lurking nearby. Taylor smiles and joins Daniel, who stirs as she sits down.

"Oh man, I think I fell asleep just now," he says sheepishly. "We must have already walked a good six miles today. Are you okay if we go eat? I'm famished."

"You read my mind," Taylor says while resting her head on Daniel's shoulder. "There are plenty of cute bistros between here and the hotel, let's start walking and we'll find somewhere along the way."

They walk slowly back toward their hotel, taking in the upscale shops lining the Place des Victoires, before deciding on Chez Georges, just a stone's throw from their hotel.

"Don't overdo it," Taylor says. "Remember, we've got, and I quote, the meal of a lifetime to look forward to tonight. Better save some room."

"Noted," Daniel says, just as the waiter appears to take their order. They settle on sharing a caprese salad and a steak, not as light as intended, but the food here in France is just so good.

After lunch, they head back to the hotel and crash, exhausted from all the walking. Around 6 p.m., Taylor wakes up and surprises Daniel by going down on him as he's waking up.

Afterward, he tells her, "That was the best fucking alarm clock of my life. Goddamn." Taylor laughs harder at this than she's ever laughed about anything, and this becomes an inside joke they repeat to one another for years to come. They sit outside on their little balcony, a glass of white wine and a cigarette for Taylor, and a beer for Daniel.

"So, how are you enjoying the City of Light?" Taylor asks him.

"I love it. I absolutely love it here. But," he continues, grabbing her hand, "I could be in Omaha or Winnipeg or literally anywhere with you, and it would still feel magical. You're the best travel companion, among other things, I could ever ask for."

Taylor blushes and gives him a peck on the cheek. "That's too kind. You're not so bad yourself. All right, I'm going to get ready," she says while stubbing out her cigarette. "You stay out here and enjoy the view, and we'll leave in about thirty minutes."

Daniel gives a little salute as Taylor goes back into the room to do her hair and makeup and get dressed for their dinner. Taylor has been assigned to dine at and review a tiny bistro that only has six tables. Apparently, it is impossible to get a reservation, even on a Monday night, but the powers that be from work managed to secure a coveted 8:30 p.m. reservation for Taylor and Daniel. When they arrive, it's clear that the restaurant knows that Taylor is, if not a VIP, then something close to one, and that she's there as a reviewer. She can't help but be amused by the pampering and freebies they get all evening; it certainly helps sway her toward a positive review. She feels, for a brief moment, like Julia Roberts at the beginning of *My Best Friend's Wedding*, when she's at a swanky Manhattan restaurant and the entire place knows she's a food critic.

Despite the amazing service and extra TLC, the food and drinks speak for themselves. Once the plates of the main course are cleared, Daniel leans back in his chair and declares it the best meal he has ever had. Relaxed and comfortable after sharing a bottle of wine, they are both anxious to get back to the hotel and into bed together, but complimentary dessert and two glasses of port are delivered just as they signal for the check.

"Fuck me, more food?" Daniel mutters, reaching for his fork and digging into the chocolate soufflé.

"I know, can you eat mine? I don't want to be rude, but I literally cannot eat another bite." Taylor passes him her plate and takes a sip of the port. Somehow, Daniel manages to house both desserts, causing Taylor to feel the usual stab of resentment that men can eat like garbage and not worry about their weight. "One of many injustices of being a woman," Taylor sighs.

"What does that mean?" Daniel asks, mouth full of chocolate.

Taylor can't help but laugh; he is so adorable and oblivious. "I mean, it's so unfair. Guys can eat whatever they want and not worry about it, and women are counting calories and driving themselves completely batshit crazy to be a size two."

Daniel rolls his eyes and sets his fork down. "Taylor. You have, and I mean this, the most perfect body anyone could ever want. Please don't tell me you obsess about your weight."

"Of course I do," she says, louder than she intended. "Sorry. All women and girls do. It's like we're hard-wired to worry about it."

"Well, you needn't worry," Daniel says. "I love you just as you are, and if you gain fifty pounds, I will still love you."

Taylor tries to stop her jaw from hitting the table; Daniel has never told her that he loves her before, not to her face, at least. Before she can say anything, he grabs her hands in his and says, "That's right, Taylor Evans, I love you. I adore you. In fact, now that I've said it, I think I've been in love with you since our toddler years, when we'd share an angel food cake on our birthday every year. I just wasn't wise enough to know it then."

With a smile and a laugh, Taylor squeezes his hands. "I love you too, Daniel. I have loved you for a long time."

Now, with those inevitable words having been spoken, their time in Paris takes on an even more romantic quality, the stuff of movies, Taylor will recount years later when she tells friends about the history of her relationship with Daniel and all of the invisible strings that brought them together over and over again. Sitting in the tiny bistro on a Monday night in July, at just twenty-four years old, they can't begin to understand or imagine what challenges and joys lie ahead of them. When people inevitably ask them the story of how they met, Taylor often says, "We were born for one another," eliciting groans and eye rolls, but always a knowing smile from Daniel.

And so, on this innocuous Monday evening in Paris, the world feels wide open to Taylor and Daniel. Their entire lives lie ahead of them, and their future is brighter because it features the many lights and shimmer of their shared past. All of those invisible strings, finally, have led them to where they belong.

<h1 style="text-align:center">Acknowledgements</h1>

Thank you to everyone who picked up this book and gave it a chance. For a debut author, that means a lot. Sincere thanks to my editor Erin Young, for the terrific feedback and support. Thank you to the entire team at Blackstone Publishers for bringing this dream to fruition.

Thank you to my parents, who always have faith in me and raised me with the delusional belief that I can accomplish anything. But seriously, thank you both for my work ethic and the ability to get shit done, I can't imagine where I'd be without you.

This book, while fictional, took real snippets of my friendships over the years, so thank you to my friends for being there for me and for being such inspiring people. There's a little bit of all of you in here. My Madison ladies, I hope you enjoy the references! Heather Sheehy, thank you for being my first test reader!

Thank you to the Brewster Ice Arena, which is where I began writing this book. Spending many hours there at Players Bar while my son practiced hockey during COVID provided ample opportunities for writing (and cheap wine). Taylor Swift, my favorite artist, was a huge inspiration for this book, so I thank her for creating beautiful music that fueled me while I was writing.

Lastly, thank you to my husband Robbie and my children, Ryan and Kirsten (and my dog, Champ, who often interferes with the writing process). Robbie, thank you for being my biggest cheerleader and for always supporting me. Ryan and Kirsten, there aren't sufficient words to describe how much joy you bring me. I love you beyond comprehension, and I hope you enjoy reading this (preferably when you're a little older.)